Spirit Fall

The Guardians: Book One

Tessa McFionn

Vi,

Keep believing in magic!

Tessa McFionn

DEDICATION

To STF, the man who keeps my feet on the solid ground as my head floats
in the clouds, and to Mom, for always believing in me.

PROLOGUE

Iasi, Moldavia, 1342

Crows screeched hungrily overhead, impatient as they waited for the last few combatants to bring the latest bloody campaign to a close. Voivode Malakai Gregori Vadim, Crown Prince of the Moldavian province of Iasi, blinked through the red veil as blood splashed across his visor, his sword biting deep into the nameless opponent. The man's armor gave little protection, peeling away to reveal hewn flesh and shattered bone. Crimson froth bubbled up between the man's lips, his eyes glazing and his soul fleeing to join those of his companions as the empty shell collapsed in a heap.

Kai knelt down to attend to the young man who had called out for aid. The boy had seen too few winters to be on this field. Vacant eyes stared back at him. He heaved a tired sigh as he regained his feet.

He took the slight reprieve to survey the field before him. Bodies littered the plains and spilled into the waters of the Dnister, posed in various states of dead or dying. The groans and wails of those yet to start their journey to the afterlife mingled in cacophonous harmony with the clang of steel and the cries of the carrion birds that circled above. His father, the king, would be watching from afar, confident in his son's ability to defeat any enemy. Long had he battled alone, the curse of being the oldest son, his younger brothers barely out of swaddling clothes.

His breath flowed effortlessly, echoing within the chamber of his helm. The invading Tatars underestimated the spirit and ferocity with which his army defended their homes, their families, and their faith.

His enemy had hoped for an easy victory. What they got was a massacre.

"You fight bravely, young one."

Kai swung his blood-stained great sword level with the source of the voice off his left shoulder. His blade whistled, passing through nothing. The words had an odd intonation, making his foe an unknown foreigner.

"But, why do you fight?"

He whipped his head around, searching frantically for his latest challenger. A quick feint to his right, and Kai slammed his left elbow back, hard and fast, hoping to connect with his vaporous foe. He was rewarded with a satisfying *crunch* and the whoosh of expelled air.

Spinning again, he found himself eye-to-eye and sword-to-sword with a warrior garbed in a coat of plates unfamiliar to him. At first glance, he saw no metal. Instead, deep red leather and intricately woven golden ropes formed large panels placed in carefully measured tiers down the length of his body. Two separate pieces attached at the shoulder, offering little protection to the arms. His gilded helmet, while bowled at the crown, flared at its base, adorned with an ornate antennae-like horseshoe of metal in the center of the forehead. Everything gleamed in the midday sun.

Beneath the short visor, oddly slanted brown eyes peered out above a hideous metal grimace. With their blades locked, Kai risked a look at the slender, strangely water-stained weapon. Its slight curve spoke of Eastern origins, but the unchanged width gave him pause.

"Well done, my brother." The words escaped through the narrow mouth slit, still shrouding the man in mystery.

"I have no brother here," Kai growled, increasing the pressure against this arrogant man's blade. Perhaps he would be fortunate and, with enough force, break the spindly weapon in twain.

The eyes before him widened in surprise. "Then why do you fight, if not for your brethren?" Smooth as smoke flowing over glass, his opponent circled to his right, his sword still locked with Kai's. The movement of his feet barely stirred the blood-soaked earth beneath them.

The question rang through Kai's mind. Why did he fight? What kind of query was that? He fought because that was what he did. It was who he was. *Voivode.* Warlord. General. Fighter. Protector.

His first battle had been at age twelve, standing alongside his father as his shield bearer. The stench of the cold winter morning, blood and entrails, vomit and shit, burned the back of his throat, and the sounds of scraping steel and strangled screams scarred his memory.

"Do you fight for conquest?" asked the demon across from him.

Kai initiated a quick disengage and renewed his attack. He swung his heavy broad sword, arcing the edge with lethal accuracy toward the oddly clad warrior's chest. The man parried the blade with only a breath of effort, gracefully sidestepping the obvious assault.

"Do you fight for power?" He continued the interrogation, launching himself at Kai in a flurry of strikes. Kai staggered under the ferocity of the barrage, backpedaling yet blocking every blow. The man was quick, his light blade blurring as it flew at his head over and over again.

If he could put the smug bastard on his ass, he would have some questions of his own to ask. Once again, Kai swung, closed distance, and the blades clashed into a lock.

"Perhaps, love?"

The mocking tone set Kai's teeth on edge. Giving in to his anger, he head-butted the man, gaining the upper hand. His mysterious opponent stumbled, landing on his back in surprise as Kai raised his blade to deliver the final blow.

And halted, the edge of his sword a scant breath away from the fallen man's neck.

Kai's muscles burned and shook as air rushed frantically in and out of his lungs, yet he held off his lethal slice. All the incessant questions has wormed into his mind. Who was he and why was he here? This was not his fight. He was not a Turk.

Never one to kill without just cause, Kai had to discover the reason for his presence on the field.

"Why are you here?" Kai turned the words back onto the speaker.

His fallen opponent reached a hand into the steel snarl of his face guard and removed it with one swift movement. The face beneath was unlike any Kai had ever seen before. Slanted almond eyes of deep brown rested in a chiseled face the color of late autumn wheat, a touch of gold still visible. Thin lips broke into a smile, revealing straight white teeth and a hint of blood.

"Why, I am here for you," he replied, extending his hand.

Kai lowered his blade and stretched his arm down to aid the man.

"Perhaps it would be best if I were to introduce myself to you," he said, rising agilely to his booted feet. He adjusted his armor before continuing, deftly sheathing his long, graceful blade on his hip with a flick of his wrist and a resounding *clack*.

"My name is Tashiharo Makamuro, Samurai in the service of Minamoto no Yoritomo and Guardian Warrior." Upon completion, he bowed deeply before looking back at Kai.

Kai sized up the man. He was not as tall as he had originally guessed, an illusion created by the massive and impressive armor. As he stood still, power rolled off him in waves, tangible and electric.

"That is quite a title," Kai quipped. "I am Voivode Malakai Gregori Vadim," lifting off his helmet and returning the gesture with a dip of his head that exposed his neck.

"I am honored to meet you. But you have yet to answer my question," he pressed. In one smooth movement, he removed his helm and placed it under his arm. Raising his gaze, he locked eyes with Kai. "Why do you fight?"

"Why is it so important to you?" Kai growled. The man's tenacity was beginning to grate on Kai's nerves.

Tashiharo's eyes showed no hint of his intentions. "Please. It is important."

Puzzled, but wishing to end the interrogation, he answered without thought. "I fight to protect."

Kai marveled as the man's stoic features appeared to soften ever so slightly. "Then I have chosen wisely," he sighed.

Kai felt as if he had somehow stepped into the middle of an ongoing conversation. "And just what is that supposed to mean?"

"It means, my friend," he said, smiling enigmatically, removing his right gauntlet. "That your life is about to change. Forever."

Tashiharo's bare hand grasped his cheek. The power behind the light touch ripped a howl from Kai the instant before he lost consciousness.□

ONE

Nice view.

Siobhan Whelan looked into the dark of the night as the gentle March breeze freed a stray strand of hair from her ever-present ponytail. The occasional sounds of traffic passed idly behind her, echoing the cars rushing along Highway 163 beneath the bridge upon which she stood. Back in the fifties, the city added ornate ironwork barriers to the center section of the Cabrillo Bridge, otherwise known as Laurel Street, hoping to discourage the despondent from continuing its infamous nickname, "Suicide Bridge." It didn't seem to help, so the city renovated the parapets again adding barbed wire to the arching metal claws. She recalled news stories from her youth, images of cars crushed by the weight of falling bodies, more twisted, mangled lives to add to the total loss.

Stupid city council. As she peered over the edge of the bridge, it was obvious a fall from her current place would still kill a person. Maybe that was why there were no more news stories about the bridge. People were still jumping; they just weren't becoming speed bumps anymore.

The streetlamps cast a golden hue to the solid concrete beneath her feet. The eucalyptus trees reached up to her from the freeway below. The night air was cool; the rich scent of night-blooming jasmine masked the engine exhaust. She pulled her threadbare olive zippered hoodie closer around her shoulders. Her black tank top and worn-out cotton yoga pants offered no small measure of warmth. Maybe she should have dressed more appropriately.

The thought alone made her let out a bitter laugh. No matter. She actually used to like this weather, clear skies, cool breeze. She could even see a couple of stars blinking against the city lights.

Nice night to die.

Time slipped away. Cars passed less frequently until there were none. She hadn't seen another late-night stroller for a while. Even the highway beneath her was starting to look deserted, which was unusual for a cool Thursday night in San Diego.

Voni tried to find the exact moment when she realized that it was all pointless. She closed her eyes as the engine sounds faded into the background. The voice of her director crept into her mind, telling her she needed to be more expressive and maybe the time away would help her put things into perspective. More expressive? Perspective? After the death of her fiancé, even the attempt to keep her eyes off the ground was painful, and pleasant expressions just didn't seem to come anymore.

The tears threatened to spill again; her hazel eyes blurred as she blinked them back. She promised herself she was done with her grieving. Twelve months of living in a fog was long enough. Three hundred and sixty-five days of listening to people telling her it was going to get easier, that the pain would go away and that the nightmares would end. Five hundred twenty-five thousand, six hundred minutes spent waiting.

A year ago, she had two passions in her life, James Danton and dancing. For two years, he had been her inspiration; his silly smile and lighthearted sense of humor could always make her put the rest of her cares behind her. Then, in one instant, everything changed forever. She could still remember the moment in crystal-clear, all-too-painful, detail. The phone rang at the same time every night, even that one, but the caller had been different. James always called before leaving work to tell her he loved her and he would be home soon. But that time, the voice was different, the message all wrong.

She vaguely heard the hasty words mention *police* and *attempted robbery* and *shot*, followed by *I'm sorry*. The rest turned to babble as the receiver slipped through her fingers and crashed to the floor as the rap of knuckles on the door echoed from down the hall. His face flashed behind her closed lids as a single tear escaped, trickling down her cheek.

No one could say she didn't try. After three months, the standard length of time for mourning the loss of a lover as determined by those around her, she tried being happy. She'd been a performer her entire life; it shouldn't have been that difficult. Yet, the more energy she put into her fake smiles, the more disingenuous she believed herself to be. She would catch her reflection in mirrors, the smile never quite reaching her eyes. The days began to tread on, unending and uninteresting.

Then the nightmares began. They started rather expectedly, her mind trying to envision the event as more than dimly recalled details burned into her subconscious. But soon after, they had changed, taking on a life far beyond her imaginings. She would see James drowning in pools of blood as if she had been near enough to watch but unable to do anything to help. Figures cloaked in evil clawed at him, shredding his flesh and bones as he cried out to her, pleading for help. She awoke each morning drenched in sweat and tears, drained of any will to go on. Grief and exhaustion had taken up residence in her eyes and would not be denied.

The darkness surrounded her, overwhelming her and threatening to consume her. She pushed herself up onto the ledge, using the ironwork as a support. With a swing of her legs, she stood on the wall as she took one final look out onto the city. It wouldn't be long now.

Boredom clung to Malakai Vadim, heavy and undeniable. He'd spent seven hundred years moving from place to place, endlessly wandering the world, and was now searching for an interesting diversion. A new way to pass eternity. A friend had suggested he try Southern California. Nice scenery, beautiful people, perfect weather. Who could ask for anything more?

He took a long drag off his cigarette and pushed himself off the building he'd spent the past two hours holding up. The ritualistic thump of the heavily amplified music seeped through the bricks at his back. Looking at the line of plastic people waiting to pass beyond the velvet rope, he sighed, smoke curling around him before disappearing into the night. A leggy platinum blonde in a whisper of a dress gave him what he could only assume was her best come-and-get-it smile, including the prerequisite lip lick.

Alright, time to go. The Gaslamp club scene had officially bored him to tears. Time to take a walk. Glancing down the block, he flicked the glowing ember to the pavement before crushing it with the heel of his boot., He replied to her blatant offer with a polite shake of his head and headed away from the bright lights and techno beat.

He wanted something more. Something, anything. At first, he thought he had found paradise, complete with bikini-clad natives. But as the years passed, he began to see the truth that lay beneath the tanned and tightened exterior of Southern California. It was empty. Nice scenery? Sure, if you didn't mind sand, water, and palm trees. It was like a desert, only with more lights. Beautiful people? If he saw one more fake-tanned, fake-toothed, fake-titted woman, he was going to scream. And as for the weather, he was partial to a bit more variety.

That was the point, wasn't it? He'd come here looking for something different, and all Kai found was so much of the same thing. The lure of the scenery, the people, and the weather had succeeded in making his chosen path feel more like a prison sentence. Hell, even prisoners were given some time in the yard to break up the monotony.

He continued to wander, his black motorcycle boots muffling his languid pace. He couldn't help but wonder why the residents chose to remain here. Had humanity truly reverted to the apathetic beings his enemies sought to make them?

During his stroll, his mind turned to the day he learned of his new task and his new enemy. *"You have been chosen to take up the mantle of the Guardian Warriors. It is an ancient honor, given to those who have sworn to protect the lives of others. You were chosen for your skills and for your valor."*

The words of his old mentor brought a sad smile to his face. He had not thought of the man for many years, but something about this night made him nostalgic in his introspection. The rest of the pledge came flooding back to him.

"The world is a dangerous place, with many mysteries veiled from the eyes of man. Creatures of evil, bent of turmoil and destruction, hide within the souls of the Rogue Warriors. You have been called to do battle with your sword, your wits, and your soul. To this arsenal we give you an extended life in your current form and the ability to move with the wind. You can hear the thoughts of any mortal and can heal with a touch.

"Many miles will you travel and many lands will you discover. No place will you call home for more than two score and ten years.

"You will be drawn to your enemy across time and space. Your enemy will hide within the heart of men and within the realm of the In-Between, the void betwixt the land

of the living and the land of the dead. They will influence dreams and move in shadows.

"You will vanquish your foes, sending them back into oblivion. You will fight until you find your spiritmate. She will bring you balance and quiet your restless soul. Once you have made her your own, you will choose another to take up the battle in your stead or to bring her into the service of the Guardians."

His moody introspections had allowed something other than his feet to dictate his impending destination. The blocks and buildings melted into the darkness until he arrived on the edge of Balboa Park. Now this place was more like it. He enjoyed the park. Its neatly trimmed grassy flats surrounded by ancient shade trees, sprinkled with historic museums and architectural landmarks, sprawled across a couple miles in the heart of the city. The park had a much friendlier feel than New York's Central Park, but it still gave any visitor the impression of being in a place other than a congested city.

The hour was late, well after one in the morning, so the grounds were pretty much empty. Except for one lone figure, partially obscured by a copse of eucalyptus trees, standing against the bridge barricade. The figure was small, perhaps a teenager looking for a lost skateboard. Kai watched for a few moments when, to his horror, the figure climbed onto the ledge.

Was this for real?

He allowed a split second to pass before he *moved* to the bridge. Trees and houses rushed by in a blurred blink as he appeared a few feet away from the person whose desperation poured out from their very skin. He could almost taste the emotion in the air, bittersweet misery tempered with the salt of unshed tears.

An unfamiliar energy began to pulsate just beneath his skin, and he paused as he experienced an unfamiliar sensation. Silence. For so many years, the hum of scattered thoughts from passing strangers had kept him mental company. Could this be real? Could she be the one?

His mind raced, trying to find a way to halt the jumper, searching for the right thing to say.

"Wait. Please."

Kai reached out to gently touch the worn-out running shoe nearest to his hand. His gaze journeyed up to find the face of a young girl, her thick, wavy hair pulled into a haphazard ponytail, and her eyes closed in preparation for an untimely demise. Her body was just beginning to show curves. Small, high breasts and shapely legs were concealed by the thin clothes. No. That couldn't be right. He'd been paired with a child?

His voice must have caught her by surprise, judging by the jolt that lanced down her body. Eyes flitted behind closed lids as her chin twitched in his direction.

"What? Why?" Her voice was weak and confused.

"Because I asked nicely?"

He kept his eyes trained on her profile, carefully watching her inner struggle play across her face. Through the light contact with her body, he was able to pick up on her troubled, swirling emotions, his appearance shaking her resolve. Still, her eyes remained shut.

"Why should you care? You don't even know me. Now just leave me alone."

The spite in her voice seemed forced and insincere. He sensed she was a kind person by nature. Kind, but very disheartened. The more he heard her speak, the more he realized his initial guess at her age was off by a few years. Early twenties, perhaps. The tone was deeper and richer than most of the women he'd encountered in the city, conjuring images of Lauren Bacall and other seductresses of film noir. He needed to keep her talking. More than that, he had to stop her from killing herself. If his instincts were right, she was the other half of his spirit, and he was not about to let her go in this manner.

"True," he sighed. "But still, I did ask nicely." He leaned casually against the concrete barrier, hoping he might get close enough to grab for her should she decide to go through with her plunge. She looked small; it would be easy enough to pull her down. But somehow, Kai suspected that wouldn't stop her from trying again on another night.

"Give me a reason."

The voice sounded thin and breathy, hollow and empty. Most likely from disuse, but he detected traces of a different person than the one perched upon this ledge. Faint whispers of faded laughter and lost smiles echoed in the distant background, dimmed by despair and gloom. Loose strands of deep chestnut hair whipped around to reveal hints of pale skin, natural and unkissed by the sun. Slender and youthful in appearance, she was petite in every way, with small curves above and below the waist.

No. The longer he studied her, the more he realized her body was strong, athletic, and still entirely feminine. His efforts seemed to be wearing her down. She would have jumped already if she were truly determined.

He thought carefully before he responded.

"I can think of about a million of them, but somehow I'm not sure I'll pick the right one for you on the first try."

Great. All the Good Samaritans out there and she got a comedian. The more she listened to him the more she detected an unfamiliar cadence to the words. He definitely wasn't from around there. His voice seemed to wrap around her body, leaving a slight tingling sensation. She wanted to hear more, wanted it to wipe away the pain.

"Well," the voice interrupted her mulling. "At least, I got a little smile."

"Please go away," she pleaded. Her resolve began to crumble. Doubt started to crawl into the back of her mind. Was she really going to do it? The wind seemed colder than earlier, sending shivers marching down her arms.

"So you can splatter yourself? No, I don't think so."

His voice was delicious, the timbre provocative and enticing. Part of her wanted to crack an eyelid to sneak a peek at the only person on the bridge who seemed to care about her life at the moment.

"But if you are so determined, go right ahead."

"What?" she squeaked. "I can't do this with you watching me!" Was he nuts?

"Hmm." Her bare skin thrummed as his tone washed over it. "For someone about to make a very public exit, you seem to have an unusually skittish streak."

"Leave me alone," she implored. Her voice wavered under the weight of indecision. The simple fact that a complete stranger had tried to stop her, and was succeeding, made her rethink what she was about to do. Also, with the weather getting noticeably chillier, her shudders grew more violent. Even with her eyes closed, she knew he watched. She could feel his presence near enough to reach out and touch.

"I'll go, as soon as you're down."

Voni released the breath she wasn't aware she was holding and slowly opened her eyes. In her mind, she pictured the landmarks of her youth, the Coronado Bay Bridge arching, its glow against the black waters, the vibrant green hexagons above the Wyndham Emerald Plaza, and the landing lights of various planes heading in and out of Lindberg International Airport. But the tree-lined streets blocked much of the familiar skyline. Only the blazing red El Cortez sign stood in the forefront of the visible towers, while the other silhouettes would be seen only from a different vantage point.

"I guess you're not going to go away and just let me jump. Are you?" Her gaze turned to the source of the voice, only to find a man of unbelievable good looks. Wind-tousled, shoulder-length, black hair framed the chiseled features, with full, kissable lips and dreamy bedroom eyes. Under the garish yellow bulbs, they appeared to be an impossibly pale green. Or perhaps it was the combination of the light, his incredibly long, lush ebony eyelashes, and his very *GQ* wardrobe.

Impeccably dressed, he sported a heather-gray sweater, black jeans, and boots, with a full-length, camel coat finishing the outfit. The hand resting near her ratty New Balance cross trainers had long, tapered fingers ending in well-manicured nails. His face was near her waist, making her savior well over six feet.

"I would not be much of a gentleman if I did."

His answer perplexed her, but his outstretched hand spoke volumes."

Kai's heart skipped a beat. Turned toward him, with her eyes open, she was exquisite. The face simple and sweet, oval with a delicate nose and naturally high, defined cheekbones. The eyes peering out at him sparkled with flecks of deep green amid seas of soft golden brown. Grief had taken up residence behind those eyes, forming dark rings, but hints of past joys lingered in the shadows. Her ivory skin gave her an elfin loveliness, so much so, he had to suppress a strange urge to brush her hair back and examine her ears for points. Instead, he extended his hand, hoping it wouldn't stay vacant for long.

As the cool night wind kicked up, it carried a faint scent of sweet jasmine and dark autumn spice, the heady fragrance churning his blood as he envisioned her away from the stark amber streetlights and in the warm glow of a hundred scattered candles.

She waited a moment longer before she tentatively placed her small hand in his. He wrapped his strong fingers lightly around hers as he guided her back down to earth. Once Kai had placed his new friend on her tiny feet—how did she walk on those things?—her petite size became more apparent. Her head barely reached his armpit, making her seem more like a youth than a woman. His gaze drifted in hungry appreciation down her body, and his slacks shrunk a size in the crotch.

There was nothing childlike about her. He would have to take things carefully. The idea of getting involved in any way with a recently talked-down jumper seemed quite crazy on his part. He wondered who needed counseling more, himself or the diminutive beauty who stood next to him.

She was the most intriguing person he had seen since he first arrived in the city nearly fifty years ago. The longer he studied her, the more he was beginning to realize how this place could be paradise.

Voni looked up into the face of her mysterious savior. And up and up. Tall, dark, and handsome had nothing on the fantastic specimen of masculinity shadowing her. Sex seemed to ooze from his entire body, spilling out in waves and battering her soul. His broad chest rose and fell in hypnotic rhythm. Her heart quickened its pace, pounding in her ears and muddling her reason. The brisk night wind did not have a cooling effect. If anything, it made her more aware of her burgeoning desire. She was incredibly turned-on by a complete unknown god of a man.

She suddenly felt like a midget, and a hideously underdressed one at that. She tugged the battered, faded green Disneyland sweatshirt around her shoulders, pulling the zippered front closed in an attempt to hide her less-than-voluptuous physique from his prying eyes. She had a sudden urge to examine her worn-out shoes or the cracks in the pavement, to look anywhere but into the penetrating gaze of those gorgeous eyes, not to mention the equally yummy other parts of him. The longer she stood next to Mr. Perfect, the more she wished she had jumped.

The silence grew, reaching the uncomfortable realm, and she began to feel like a bug under a microscope. Time to get out of here.

"Well," Voni said after clearing her throat. "You've done your good deed for the day, and I'm sure you've got other heroic endeavors on your plate." As she talked on, she sidled away from him. "So, I'll just be—"

"Hang on, now." He reached a well-toned, manicured hand out for her again, gently grasping her arm. "Where are you off to in such a rush?"

"Anywhere but here," she muttered.

The pale eyes vanished behind a slow blink, and confusion screwed up his face.

"Excuse me?"

Voni let out an exasperated breath. "Look, I don't mean to sound ungrateful or anything. It's just…well, people who, you know…well, people like you don't…" She glanced around, expecting the words to come out of thin air and finding none. "Oh, never mind." The last word was punctuated with tug as she made a feeble attempt to escape her captivating savior.

He released his hold on her arm, and she immediately felt saddened by the loss. How was that possible? She didn't even know his name, much less what a gorgeous escapee from the Island of Underwear Models was doing in this part of town in the middle of the night. She forced her feet to move away from him.

"Was that intended to make any sense?" he asked.

Against her better judgment, Voni turned back to him. He stood coolly, arms folded across his massive chest, one thick, graceful eyebrow arched in her direction. Fabu. He thought she was a moron. Frustration boiled beneath the surface, drowning her previous fantastical notions of a romantic interlude.

"Can you please leave? Before I say anything even more stupid than I already have?"

She was surprised to hear a deep rumbling sound. The source was the camel-coated knight before her, and her jaw dropped as he began to chuckle. What the hell? It started as a slight smirk, growing in volume before maturing into an honest laugh. The warm, gentle sound soothed her rattled nerves. However, she was determined to be miserable, and no dreamy, yummy, extraordinarily drop-dead-gorgeous hunk was going to stop her. Was she nuts? She turned to go, praying he would stop her one more time.

"Wait, please," Kai managed to squeeze out between breaths. "Can we try this again?"

Voni turned back cautiously.

"Try what again?"

His laughter back under control, he replied, "Our first meeting."

"On or off the ledge?" she asked, her sarcastic nature unable to remain contained any longer. If he had any plans for getting to know her, which seemed to be his goal, then he'd have to deal with her razor-sharp tongue.

"Off, please," he answered without skipping a beat.

Oh, he was good. So few of the men she encountered were able to keep up with her. Except James. Darkness and despair threatened to swallow her once again.

Before she was consumed by the sudden return of sadness, her savior moved a cautious step closer.

"Allow me to introduce myself. My name is Malakai Gregori Vadim," he announced, extended his hand one more time to her. "And you are?"

For the second time in as many moments, Voni stood before the outstretched hand with a choice. Should she take it? Did she dare?

Why not? What did she have to lose? She imagined a button-down-shirt-clad figure sliding across a wooden floor in socks, lip-syncing strains of Bob Segar's "Old Time Rock and Roll" into a candlestick, and the silly memory chased away any lingering hesitation.

Taking a deep breath, Voni thrust her hand forward.

"Siobhan Brigit Whelan, but most people just call me Voni."

He curled warm fingers around her hand. She watched in rapt fascination as he bowed down, bringing her hand to his lips. His breath tingled on the back of her hand as he lightly brushed his lips lightly against her knuckles.

"My pleasure, Voni."

His gaze never left her face, boring deep into her soul, laying it bare before him. She realized she should feel something. Invaded, maybe. But she didn't. No, her feelings were more on the physical side. His eyes held no contempt or ridicule. He was genuinely pleased to meet her. Wow. Nice change of pace. Men, particularly those who looked like a Calvin Klein underwear model, would never have given her the time of day.   Since no other emotion seemed to be interested in the spotlight, insecurity stepped up to the plate.

Get real, Von, her logical mind yelled out. *He's being polite out of some twisted sense of obligation.* The tiny glimmer of hope flickered out, lost in the shadow of an embarrassing torrent of self-doubt.

"You sure about that?" her voice dripped with sarcasm and disbelief.

Kai released her hand, yet his mind continued to hold hers, searching for answers. She had a unique inner strength. He felt it in her touch and tasted it on her skin. Her eyes guarded secrets, many of which he now yearned to uncover. She intrigued him, from her dry, quick wit to her toned, petite physique. The longer he was near her, the more his mouth watered, eager for more than just his earlier sample.

A devious smile crept across his face.

"Positive."

Her cheeks pinked as the corners of her mouth tugged upward in a crooked grin.

"All right, all right." she mumbled. "That's enough of that."

Kai continued to smile as a very becoming blush rose from the edge of her neckline to the fringe of her sable bangs. Her porcelain complexion warmed, enhancing the amber of her eyes. He could drown in those honey-hued depths, dying a happy man. All too soon, she tore her gaze away from his, choosing to seek shelter by counting the cracks in the pavement.

"Enough of what?" He did his best to feign innocence, but he knew exactly what he was doing, or at least, what he hoped he was doing. Sensing her hesitation, he decided to act before she changed her mind.

"Can I interest you in a cup of coffee?" He hoped the words carried his honest concern, yet he kept his mind open, carefully eavesdropping on the thoughts that spun and swirled around behind her eyes. He knew his intervention had altered her evening's plans, and she would need time to put things back in order. Her face remained hidden, veiled by the dark curtain of hair as seconds ticked by.

After another agonizing minute, the pixie faced him, her eyes clear and cautious. The cold was beginning to take its toll, and her small frame was shaking more forcefully. Time slowed as he waited for her response. "Please?" Tempted to add the slight push of insistence to his simple word, he opted to wait.

"I think something warm might be nice," was her tentative answer. "I guess, um, maybe anywhere inside would be great," tightly clutching at her lightweight attire as another violent shudder wracked her body.

Kai released the breath he held and quickly shrugged out of his Armani trench coat before whisking it with practiced ease around her slender shoulders. His coat engulfed her petite frame. His heather-gray turtleneck provided ample warmth. Too much, in fact; his temperature was feverish as he stood so close to her.

"I have the perfect place," he replied, He trailed his hands slowly down her arms, allowing the lingering body heat trapped in his coat to warm her skin.

"Thank you." The whispered words burned through his heart. It had been a long time since anyone had shown him some gratitude, and with such sincerity. As their eyes met, a timid smile graced her lush lips.

"For what?"

Voni deepened her smile as her eyes wavered from his unnerving stare. "For stopping me from making a big mistake, for starters."

He gently cupped her chin, gazing deep into her green-flecked, honey-colored eyes before glancing down to her slightly parted lips.

"Again," he breathed, leaning in close. "My pleasure." He practically purred the words into her ear. The skin beneath his lips trembled, and her flowery scent teased him once again. Yet, the soft perfume was jaded somehow. Her inner turmoil and sadness dampened her spirit. He sensed a deep doubt resurface as she pulled away from his impending kiss. The thought of her refusal urged him on to a swift change of subject.

"Shall we?" He gestured with the crook of his arm.

Voni did not hesitate. She took his offered arm, and they began to walk.

TWO

"So how far is this coffee shop of yours, Malakai?"

They had been walking through the park for only a few minutes, and his mind had been focused on the curious pixie on his arm. His eyes were drawn to the quizzical expression on her face, her head swiveling in all directions. The trembling under his coat had ceased but, apparently, their current destination was a mystery to her. Somehow, knowing he had her stumped pleased him; the corners of his lips lifted in a victorious smile.

"It is not much further and, please, call me Kai." He angled his head down in a slight bow, his eyes lowering to watch the color rise to a soft pink on her ivory cheek. She was a breath of fresh air in this plastic place, yet he still needed to unravel the reason he found her on that bridge.

"Oh, okay, um…Kai."

The name tripped off her tongue and set fire to his blood. He forced the cool night air into his lungs, drawing her autumn-sweet scent deep into his soul as he urged the calm back into his rebelling body. They strolled along in relative silence, his mind gently peeling back the layers of her armor. She had immense inner strength, which made his task more difficult. Subtlety would be key. He wanted to know why she had chosen to end her life. Especially since he was so attracted to her. Her spirit had called to his, drawing him to find her on the bridge. Chance had very little to do with this scenario. However, he needed to handle her with kid gloves until he discovered her buried sorrow.

He led them toward the only quiet after-hours café he knew about, the Lexicon, which doubled as La Puebla restaurant during the daylight hours.

During the day, it was a stereotypical Mexi-Cali tourist trap, complete with giant margaritas and wandering mariachis. By night, the mood shifted. It was cozy, intimate, and rather secluded: a well-guarded secret among those in the know.

He approached a pair of elaborately carved doors and rapped gently as Voni stood still beside him. The door silently swung away, ushering them into the darkness beyond. Faint jazz filtered through the room, adding to the cultured ambiance. A slight chuckle slipped from his lips as her jaw dropped and her eyes soaked in the opulent beauty that surrounded them; rich red velvet armchairs and couches upholstered in antique brocade lay scattered around the large open room. Small tables held fine china cups of various styles and colors, their steam spiraling upward in unsteady curls.

Kai smiled as wonderment and awe swept over her face. He had visited the café so many times he had forgotten the initial impact of its glamorous. He spied an open table tucked in one of the farthest corners and guided her past the other patrons, but not before giving Joel, the barista, a friendly nod. He held up two fingers and pointing to their destination.

"Whoa." Voni exhaled the word.

Kai's smile deepened as he removed his voluminous coat from her slender shoulders and graciously pulled out a luxurious fireside chair for her. Voni tucked her legs under her as she sat, a gesture he found very captivating.

"I take it you've never been here before." Her head appeared to be on a swivel as she fought to see every tiny corner of the place. Her actions had a refreshing sense of innocence, causing him to again reconsider his estimation of her age.

"I didn't even know this place existed. What's it called? How long has it been here? Is it a private club? Are you a member here? And how did you know about it? I mean, I've lived here practically my whole life and never knew about this place. Well, I can't really say that. I went to La Puebla with my sister about three years ago when she was in town visiting, but I didn't realize all this was here too."

Kai marveled at the fact she was able to voice all her questions and the final statement in one breath. Things were looking up. He had to refocus his thoughts to remember the order of her earlier inquiries.

"The club is called the Lexicon, and it's been around for about twenty-five years." He watched for her reaction and was graciously rewarded with a wide-eyed stare. "As for it being a private club and my membership in said club, it is only frequented by those who know about its existence, and the owner is a good friend of mine." He paused as a waiter delivered two frothy mugs.

"This place is amazing." The aroma wafting from the steam hinted at chocolate and cinnamon, two of her favorite flavors. As she glanced around at the other tables, the patrons seemed to be indulging in similar delicacies. Maybe it was the specialty of the house? Curiosity got the better of her and she edged forward to the cup in front of her.

"What a delightful paradox you are, Siobhan Brigit Whelan."

His words stopped her midreach. She eyed him cautiously from beneath her scattered bangs.

"I've been called many things," she said, settling back into her seat empty-handed. "But never that. Why do you say that?"

"Only moments ago, you were contemplating the end of your days. And now, you are full of the excitement like a child. It does give one pause."

Although he'd meant to brighten her mood, the truth of his message rang out loudly inside her head. Paradox? More likely, his well-bred manners stopped him from calling her fickle. Guilt crept through her mind, shredding her burgeoning joy, and sorrow followed in quick order.

The smile wilted on the insanely handsome face across from her. A furrow appeared between his bedroom eyes.

"I am sorry. I did not mean to make you sad."

Voni studied a particularly interesting swirl in the wood pattern of the table, hoping she could fall through its texture and disappear. If she met his eyes again, she would lose what little rein on her emotions she had.

"That's ok," she mumbled to the table, shoulders drooping in a half-attempted shrug.

"Would you like to talk about it?"

She traced a particularly pretty whorl in the grain with a finger, her brain locked in silence.

"Then perhaps I'll do the talking. You can listen and let me know if I am on the right track."

He seemed to wait for her to stop him, but she didn't have the heart for it. His voice was a soothing balm to her soul, and she wanted to have a night without pain, even if just for once.

"It must have been something truly devastating to send you out on that bridge. Nothing silly or simple." He paused a moment before continuing. "A great loss. A death, but not an expected passing." She remained quiet. He leaned slightly forward, closing the gap between them. "Someone more than friend, yet less than family, perhaps."

A solitary tear trickled down her cheek, with more threatening to follow. She fought to keep her composure, but his insights were too keen, too direct. Her breaths came in shorter measure. She prayed he wouldn't say the words she'd heard far too many times in the past year.

He reached across the short distance, his hand moving to caress her cheek.

"Time will heal—"

"When!" Her shout stopped his hand, but she couldn't stop herself. Her head snapped up and captured his surprised gaze. "When exactly is that going to happen? I heard the same thing from everyone, friends, family, even the cashier at the friggin' bank! 'Life goes on' and 'It will get better with time.' I heard them all!"

The floodgates had been opened, and the trickle became an unstoppable torrent of feelings that had been held inside for far too long. She was unable to slow down the catharsis; the words tumbled out in a rush and she was too wound up to push Pause now.

"What is the average amount of time one is allowed to mourn the loss of someone, huh? What, a couple of weeks? A month? Two? Five?" Her voice rose in pitch as her frustrations came rushing out, drawing her out of her seat. She felt like a distant observer, watching from afar but unable to stop the stream of pent-up feelings pouring out of her. "One year I waited. One year!" She punctuated the last two words with a resounding smack on the innocent table. The mugs danced along the surface but didn't spill. "Did things get better? No! Did things get easier? Not even close! Everything got harder, and the more 'time' that passed, the worse it got." Her voice cracked as her will finally shattered.

Tears rained down her face, spilling unchecked onto the dark wood beneath her hands. The earlier tension in her shoulders was coursing through her, her entire body shuddering.

"I kept waiting. I greeted each day wondering, is this going to be the day that will be easier? And each night, I had my answer. 'Nope, sorry, Voni. Not today. Maybe tomorrow.' Day after day, the same thing,' maybe tomorrow, maybe tomorrow.' How many more tomorrows do I have to wait? How many…?"

Voni took an unsteady breath as an unfamiliar sense of calm seeped into her spirit. She lowered herself back into the seat, embarrassed as she realized the true scope of her outburst. She had just shared more of herself with him in the past two minutes than she had with anyone in the past twelve months. She watched him for only a moment. His long, dark lashes shadowed his chiseled cheeks until his gaze rose to lock with hers. She was prepared to see the standard responses: sympathy and feigned concern. However, she was not prepared for what she did see—understanding. He had the look of someone who had been in her shoes before.

"Oh God. I'm sorry," she whispered, crawling back into herself, burying her face into her hands, eager to hide from everything. "I didn't mean to—"

"You've no need to apologize. You did nothing wrong."

From the onset of her emotional release, Kai sheltered their table in a cushion of stillness, giving the rest of the patrons the image of two normal people enjoying their drinks. Yet, with all his skills, he sat powerless, able to only watch and listen as she poured out her soul. He had caused this cascade. During her release, he ached to reach out and touch her, to hold her and kiss away the tears as they fell, to somehow convince her that everything would be all right. This time, he did not stop. WIth a tender touch, he lowered her hands to reveal her beautifully sad eyes. He brushed his fingertips along her cheek, wiping away her tears and her sorrows.

"You'll not have to wait for any more tomorrows, Siobhan. Now is your time to live."

He cradled her face in his palm as she regained control of her stuttered breathing.

"I wish it could be that easy," she hiccupped, making a futile attempt at a smile.

Her eyes shone with such deep sorrow, and Kai desired nothing more than to make those shadows disappear. His smile warmed his lips gradually until it spilled across the table. He traced his hand down her arm, stopping as he reached her fingers. Cupping her hand, he brought it to his lips for the second time.

"On my honor as a gentleman, I do hereby make you this promise." He paused to place his lips tenderly on her knuckles, his eyes never wavering from hers. "I will do all in my power to keep you safe..." another pause and another brush. "Secure..." a third kiss. "And, especially, to keep you..." He paused one final time as he turned over her hand, glancing down at her exposed palm. "Satisfied." He growled the last word, his breath hot as he pressed his lips into her open hand.

He lifted his eyes to hers, and her cheeks fired from pale to passionate in record time. Hungry for so much more, he gauged her response carefully, the green in her vibrant eyes sparkling in an inviting glow.

"Well," she said. "I guess that sort of puts things into, um..." She struggled to find the right word.

"Perspective," he volunteered, still gently holding her hand.

"Yeah. Perspective. No." Voni shook her head, her eyebrows pinched in a distressed frown. "I mean, who are you and what are you doing to me?"

"Yes, Malakai, what are you trying to do to her?"

The stillness shattered, jarring him back to an unwelcomed reality.

"You wouldn't be trying to claim your spiritmate, would you?"

His quick search brought him eye-to-eye with the source of the interruption. Enshrouded by shadows in the far corners of the room, a piece of a long-forgotten nightmare stepped into the light. Dark blond hair fell straight, hiding one black eye from the world. A mouth curled into a smirk of perpetual smugness. Kai always wondered why the fucker never grew the stupid little 'stache/goatee to go along with pouty emo look he sported.

"Konstantin. I didn't realize they just let in any riffraff. I'll have to bring this up with Brandon."

"Is everything ok?" Voni's soft voice seeped into his mind, scattering the darkness. "I mean, did you...you just seemed—"

"No, forgive me. I thought..." Thought what? That he saw Dmitrius Konstantin, his counterpart in the Rogue Warriors, those bent on fomenting chaos and destruction in the name of some twisted sense of progress, hiding in the corner?

"Yes," answered the voice for his ears only, laughing. *"Why don't you tell her?"*

23

There had been a strange buzzing sound, almost like static, in Voni's ears. It was as if a radio was not quite on the station, but no one else in the place seemed to notice. No one, of course, but her dark companion. Words became audible slowly, filtering through the background noise. They whispered tales of strange things; images of pain and conflict surrounded them.

"Tell me what?"

Kai's head snapped in her direction, his eyes blazing. "What did you say?"

Voni shook her head, making another effort to sort out the real from the imagined. She squeezed her eyes shut, hoping that might help. She clearly heard a voice, not Kai's voice, echoing in her mind. It was cold and unfeeling, calculating and deadly. She didn't like it at all, and she wanted to make it stop.

"I–I don't know. I just hear this voice inside my head and…" She squeezed her palms against her temples in an effort to hold her head together. The blackness behind her eyes filled with horrific visions, images of slashing blades and blood rain, all pushing out to escape, and she felt as if her head were going to explode. Intense pain lanced through her mind as she fought to keep from crying out, echoing the wails and moans of the dying reflected in her imagination.

"Dmitri!" Kai screamed out mentally, his response quick and decisive, blasting a psychic bolt across the room. It hit its mark, and his foe disappeared into the shadows. He would be back, but not for a while. Konstantin, too busy trying to worm his way into Voni's psyche, had left himself wide open for attack. The bolt fragmented his physical form, and it would take him a least a week to coalesce again.

Time enough, Kai hoped, to undo the damage wrought tonight. He leaped out of his seat, moving like lightning to kneel before her. She looked very small curled up in the enormous chair. He dared not hesitate. Reaching out, he cradled her head in his large hands, and placed his forehead against hers. He closed his eyes as he opened his mind to hers.

Wild and chaotic images battered him from all sides, their forms weak and unfocused. Luckily for him, Konstantin had been too busy showboating and gloating to put any real teeth into his attack. A quick flick of his wrist and the hellish specters vanished in a puff of red smoke, leaving Kai as the lone intruder in her psyche. As soon as he found her huddled form, he gathered her fragile spirit carefully into his arms, singing an old lullaby softly against her hair. A pass of his hand opened the doorway out of the darkness, and he stepped through, keeping her trembling form held safe in his embrace.

Just as quickly and as sharply as the pain began for Voni, it simply faded away. The images and cries, too, dimmed and finally disappear. Her breathing and heartbeat felt normal, and like her own again. She thought she heard singing, humming actually, for there were no words, only comforting sounds. As she pried open her eyes, she found Kai's face mere inches from hers. His eyelids fluttered before his eyes opened to meet hers.

"Better?" The sound of one single word brushed away any lingering images.

"Yes. Thank you." A long moment passed before she trusted herself enough to speak again. "Do I want to know what just happened?"

Kai faltered, but Voni did not.

"I take it that's a no."

He offered her a tentative smile. "You would be right about that. At least, for the moment."

She pulled back slightly. "Do you mean I have to wait?"

"You don't miss a thing, do you?" He reached up to caress her cheek. "I made a promise and I have no intention of breaking it. Ever. I will explain everything to you, but wouldn't you like to at least finish your drink first?"

Voni let out a short, nervous laugh. "I guess you don't miss a thing, either. Yeah, finishing our drinks might be nice."

Kai stood to reclaim his chair but a tug on his sleeve stopped him.

"Um, I seem to keep thanking you. Or apologizing. It's just…"

Her uncertainty disarmed him and only fueled his need to protect her. He could feel her inner strength. He knew of many grown men who had not fared as well after a Rogue attack. It had left them violently ill, and others were quite never right again.

However, Voni appeared to bounce back without any adverse effects. If he could only find a way to build her belief in herself. As he listened to her, truly listened to her words, he noticed how often she talked around her ideas. She never spoke directly, but often referred to guesses and thoughts. That task, he realized, might take a bit of time. He had plenty to spare, or did he?

"There is no need for you to do either," he answered, giving her one of his best smiles. "I am simply keeping my promise."

"So tell me, Kai. Is your life normally this weird, or is it just me?"

THREE

The fires of Hell had nothing on the vast emptiness that was the In-Between. A huge, nebulous void, it created only what it needed when it was needed. A large wooden bed began to materialize, followed by a small table, two high-back chairs, and finally two small rocks glasses and a crystal decanter filled with something deep blue. Konstantin coalesced into solid form, storming across the space to pour out a glass full of the thick liquid. He quickly downed the drink, his throat burning, and poured another.

Raking a hand through his shaggy, sun-bleached hair, he paced the length of his cell. His black eyes took in the setting that would be home for another week. He paused only a moment, and this time, he took only a sip, savoring the taste of it. Too long he'd spent living among the humans and he had picked up their bad habits, like chugging down their alcohol as if were only water.

He had forgotten that the true way to experience the full effect of drinking the Essence of Life was to sip it. He closed his eyes as he let it roll across his tongue. In his mind, he heard simple laughter, felt joy and yet saw no color. This was the essence of a child. Though his brethren believed children offered a taste of innocence and purity, right now, he neither needed nor wanted either.

He let it slip down his throat, cooling as it passed. Yet its numbing effect only added fuel to the fire raging in his heart. The source of his torment had a name. Malakai Vadim. He hurled the glass out into the abyss, watching as a wall appeared simply for the purpose of giving the cup something upon which to smash. The shattered pieces showered the ground like sparkling, blue-tinted, rain.

"Well, that was spectacular. Probably not very productive, but at least it looked pretty."

The playful tone emanated from the void, slowly forming a rail-thin humanoid shape. Platinum-blond hair fell in careless waves surrounding piercing red eyes, which glowed within the speaker's pale features. A long white linen robe opened to reveal a body unmarred by time, perfect and cold. White flowing slacks enveloped his long, slender legs, making him appear much more angelic than his eyes betrayed him to be.

"Not now, Cabal," growled Konstantin. He was in no mood for yet another lecture from their leader.

"Oh, but now seems like such a perfect time," Cabal remarked, lazily crossing the room to come to rest in front of a chair. As he lowered himself, the chair morphed into a regal throne adorned with gilded roses and thorns of rubies. "Did you have anything else planned for today?"

Konstantin opened his mouth to answer but was not given a chance to speak.

"Oh, yes," he continued. "That's right. This was the day you were to claim that simpering human female you've been torturing for the past year. She was to throw herself from the highest point, wasn't she?" He stopped for a moment, locking gazes with Konstantin. "How did that go?"

The flat tone in his voice told Konstantin his master knew exactly what had happened. As a foot soldier of Despair, he knew Cabal loved to hear of failure on any level.

"You know damn well what—"

A flick of Cabal's hand was all the signal he needed and his words stopped instantly.

"Of course I know, you idiot. But I want to hear it from you."

Konstantin let out an exasperated sigh.

"Vadim."

The air seemed to grow thick and heavy as a palpable silence charged the room.

"Ah. I see."

The space stretched and somehow became smaller within the confines of the In-Between. Howls and shrieks from beyond seeped into the silence, bringing Konstantin to full awareness. He dared not look away from Cabal's eyes, but the unwavering stare drilled into his psyche. He stood his ground, hoping to prove he truly deserved his rank as high lieutenant of the Rogue Warriors. After a moment that lasted an eternity, Cabal released his gaze with a leisurely blink of his eyes.

"I grow tired of this, Dmitri. I think you toyed with your prey for too long. Finish this"—he stood, returning the chair to its original size—"or find another distraction. You have one standard week." He headed away from the furnishings, out into the void.

"What about Vadim?"

Konstantin watched as his question halted his retreating guest. Cabal's head angled slightly, the hint of a sadistic grin coming into view.

"Did I specify of which distraction I spoke?" He stepped forward, then vanished.

Sometimes he wished Cabal spoke in clear orders, not riddles. Konstantin returned to the table and retrieved the remaining glass. He would have to regain his form as quickly as he could. The corners of his mouth turned upward ever so slowly. One standard week until vindication. Five days until vengeance. He filled the glass and took a deep drink. He knew of patience. He would wait.

**

The crowd at Lexicon had thinned out, leaving only two shapes in the near-dark. Even the barista had finished his nightly cleaning and had gone home. Voni was unsure if it was very late, or extremely early, but she was sure of one thing: she couldn't remember having a more enjoyable evening. Her companion was mysterious, intelligent, intriguing, and not to mention drop-dead sexy. They had spent hours talking and laughing, speaking on everything and anything. And yet somehow, she still knew little to nothing about him.

He had tactfully avoided every question of hers all night long, all the while managing to turn each of them back to her. They discussed philosophy and pop culture, ethics and the environment. He had managed to learn her pet's name, her favorite movie, even her favorite color, but she hadn't even been able to find out where he'd picked up that incredibly yummy accent. Not that she truly minded, as long as he kept talking. She was in love with the sound of his voice. It crept into the dark corners of her mind, warming and brightening as it flowed across her skin. Deep and broad, rich like wine, it spoke of long, pleasurable nights.

"Okay," she said, placing her hands firmly against the table. "Where are you from, exactly? I mean, I can tell you're not from here, and I'm guessing from your name, you're probably from Eastern Europe." She locked on to his eyes, daring him to evade her question again. "Am I close?"

A leisurely smile melted across his face. "I have this feeling that you are not going to let me sneak out of it this time."

"You got it, mister." Voni did her best to look menacing, narrowing her eyes with a crooked smirk on her lips.

"If you must know—" he started.

"Yes, I must."

The action had an endearing quality that made Kai want to confide everything to her. She had withstood a mental attack by one of the more powerful Rogue Warriors and was still willing to stay and spend the wee hours with him. He was quite impressed and more than tempted.

His light banter was designed to give him time to repair any damage she may have sustained during Konstantin's onslaught. He found no traces or lingering effects; she had repelled the attack quite easily.

As the night wore on, he could sense her return to herself. She was intelligent and armed with a razor-sharp wit. He was drawn to her natural beauty. She wore no makeup, and her skin was lovely in its paleness, her lithe form the result of years of dance training, which explained his inability to guess her age at first glance. Her exact age was still a mystery, but through some of her experiences and commentaries, he estimated her to be in her midtwenties. Perhaps both of them could have specific questions answered during this inquisitional round.

He leaned into her, resting his hands across from hers. "Tell you what, I will make you a deal. If I agree to directly answer this question, you must give me one direct answer as well. Deal?"

"Hey, now. Just hold on a sec. I'm not the one who's been dodging questions all night long." His eyebrow arched gracefully at her blatant statement.

He extended his hand. "Do we have a deal?"

"What kind of question?" she countered, a hint of hesitation in her voice.

"It is not the question you are thinking, I promise." He paused, raising his hand to his shoulder. "Scout's honor."

"How do you know what I'm thinking? Oh, never mind. Fine," she huffed. "Deal." She jutted out her hand, only to pull it back as he reached toward her. "But you have to answer first."

He gave her hand a firm shake, reluctant to release it. "Deal."

She waited patiently, staring.

"I come from a small village near the port city of Varna in Bulgaria," he said, laying on his native accent as thick as butter on toast.

Now it was Voni's turn to smile, rolling her eyes as she did. "All right, Drac. That's quite enough. But you don't really sound like that. When did you move here?"

A sad expression crossed his features for the briefest moment. "It has been a very long time since I've seen my home. But, I believe that was two questions. Are we changing our deal?"

She took a deep breath, closing her eyes, bracing herself. "So, what's your question?"

"I know it is not polite to ask, but..." She opened her eyes, knowing exactly where this was going. "How old are you?"

"How old do you think I am?" That had always been one of her favorite games. She knew she looked much younger than she was, a fact she attributed to being short, but she enjoyed the responses nevertheless. She hoped he would cater to her ego and lowball her age a few years. Looking twenty and being thirty had its perks. She did her best to make her face a blank canvas, not wanting to give him any clues.

Kai studied her face carefully. By the quickness of her response, this was not an unusual question for her. Therefore, she must be older than she appeared. He could easily find the answer in her mind, but that would be cheating.

"Well, when I first saw you on the ledge, I thought you to be a teen." He paused to see her response, receiving a wide-eyed blink. "But, after talking to you, and listening to your voice, I would guess you to be...no older than...twenty...four. No, three. Yes, twenty-three."

She tried to appear crestfallen, but failed miserably once she began giggling.

"I take it I am not close?"

"No," she replied. "But you have given me quite an ego boost." An impish smile graced her face as she paused before answering him. "I'm thirty."

Now it was his turn to look stunned. "Thirty? You can't be."

"Well, I have a driver's license and high school yearbook that says I am. Besides, I seem to pass for younger because I'm short."

The rest of her words fell unheard as Kai tried to absorb her earlier revelation. Thirty? That made her just a couple years younger than he. Well, give or take seven hundred years, but basically the same age. His body responded to this newfound information, and his heart beat faster.

His spiritmate. He had found her. Now, to find his replacement. That might take a bit more time. More than the past seven centuries? He hoped not, since time was soon to be a finite commodity. And he had no intention of wasting any more of it.

A hesitant quiet caught his attention, and he brought his gaze back to her slightly parted lips. Wide hazel eyes blinked at him, and the ivory of her cheek glowed with a blush that fired his own blood. His smile broadened as one corner of her lips crept into a crooked grin; her shy smile only added to his desire to see her draped in happiness. As the moment lingered on, moved into an intimate zone, his companion bashfully shifted her eyes. The smile remained in place as she cleared her throat.

"So, um, I guess I am breaking our deal," she started, "but there's something else I have to know."

A quizzical eyebrow raised as he waited for her to continue. "Do you always ask so many questions?"

"Can't help it. I'm insatiably curious." She caught his sharp intake of breath at her choice of words, but decided to press on. "Why did you save me?"

"What was I supposed to do? Just let you fall?" He reached across the table and wrapped his fingers around a stray lock of her hair. She stared at his face, watched as he twirled one curl between his fingers. Electricity raced from his tender touch through her entire body. His smile grew as he tucked the stray strand behind her ear. Once safely secured, he trailed his touch along the slighly curved tip. "Besides, I would not have deprived the world of such a beauty, much less myself."

And her automatic defense response kicked into overdrive. She lifted one shoulder in a self-conscious shrug as her smile wilted along the edges.

"If only I could believe that," she sighed heavily in response. His eyes seemed genuine, but she still couldn't fathom why someone like him would be interested in someone plain like her.

"That was a compliment. It appears that you need more experience with them." His voice was barely a whisper, full of warmth and promise. "I believe the correct response is, 'Thank you.'"

She smiled at his gentle teasing. She could get used to this.

"Thank you."

The air grew still, and the room seemed much smaller. She became aware of the fact that they were alone in the restaurant, but now, she truly realized the scope of their privacy. The world had slipped away, leaving just the two of them, solitary and secluded. Her mind raced, keeping pace with the quickening beat of her heart.

"I think, perhaps," he stated, slowly rising to his feet, "it is time I got you home." Stepping behind her, he slid the chair free from the table, performing the task with practiced ease. He gently placed his long coat around her shoulders as they retraced their earlier path, this time, passing through a room filled with total silence. The tables were prepped and readied to begin a new day, set to greet a group of eager tourists yearning for a slice of Latin hospitality and some decent *carne asada*.

Voni was ready to greet a new day as well. The past few hours spent in Kai's gracious company reminded her of what it felt like to live. She had spent so long in the shadows, hiding in the darkness of her grief, she had all but forgotten what it meant to laugh, to smile, and to feel anything remotely joyful. She couldn't think to call it love. Lust, definitely. Infatuation, probably a bit of that too. But it felt different.

She'd had crushes before. Hell, who didn't? But this? Him? It felt more like the empty pit inside her soul was slowly and tenderly filled with pleasant images, driving a knife into the gloom and chasing away long dug-in doubt and despair. He had been patient and pleasant all evening, making polite conversation, and allowed her to do most of the talking. He seemed most interested in learning every little detail about her. No one, not even James, had asked about her childhood much less her innermost thoughts and dreams. She had often hoped James would ask her about her secrets, but now she would never know if he would.

She must have been too tired, because that realization did not drive her to tears. Her heart ached, but the pain was muted, not piercing. A strange calm now seeped into her entire being. Her earlier tirade had released one year's worth of bottled-up frustrations and fears, leaving her open for new possibilities. Was her mystery man going to be a part of that? She hoped that the way he looked at her earlier was more than her imagination.

"What about the doors? Shouldn't we lock them or something?"

He reached for the ornate doorknob, thinking quickly for a reasonable explanation. Should he just tell her he was planning on locking the door with his mind? Yeah, like that would go over well. Instead, he found a more acceptable one as he ushered her out in front of him.

"Actually, the door is already locked from the outside. Once we leave, it will secure itself." Stepping out into the preedawn dark, he gave the lock a quick mental shove and it clicked into place, the electronic alarm set as well. Kai knew he would have to be fess up about his unique talents soon. But once he was honest with her, he might not have his powers much longer. It was turning into quite a conundrum, spinning his already reeling mind. He had discovered many things about her, her simple likes and dislikes, her childhood spent studying dance, and her dreams of studying abroad and dancing around the world. Of all the secrets she shared, the most mind-boggling was the truth about her age.

"So," her voice broke into his reverie. "I guess this is where we say good night."

Voni was standing near the large double doors, idly twisting her fingers and, again, looking everywhere but at him. The more he watched her nervous habits, the more they touched his heart. He sensed that she had convinced herself their evening must come to an end immediately. He, however, had other plans. With two steps, he slowly closed the distance between them, backing her against the now-locked doors.

"Is that what you want? Would you like me to say good night?" he purred into her ear. He lowered his head, inhaling deeply, taking in the scent of her. She smelled of jasmine and spice, a heady combination of the park's natural foliage and the lingering aroma of cinnamon. It was intoxicating, spinning his senses, and fired his blood.

"Dear Gods, but you smell good," he rasped out, brushing his lips against her hair. He snaked his arms around her, pinning her body between the solid doors behind and his equally solid frame in front. As he pulled her closer, the beat of her heart changed, became quick and erratic. Was she scared? No, it was more. Her heartbeat indicated she was terrified. He knew he should back off, but his body had a different agenda. The feel of her pressed against him heated his dormant spirit, sparking his need to touch her, to caress her skin, and to taste her lips.

Voni couldn't breathe as he wrapped his arms around her. She could feel the strength of his body, and the desire within. His arms were like steel cords, binding her to this moment. Yet, as strong as he was, she somehow knew if she struggled to escape, he would release her in an instant. Her heart sounded like a jackhammer in her ears as she fought to rein in her conflicting emotions. She had never felt so alive, not even with James. She yearned to trace his jawline first with her finger followed by her lips.

The blood pounded loudly in her ears and then abruptly skipped a beat. Her body shook with anticipation. Another second passed. Another missed beat. Her breaths started coming in gasps. Short, quick gasps. Too shallow, too fast. The breathing and beating didn't match up.

Aw, shit. Don't. Not now. She focused all her mental faculties the act on breathing. Damn, she hadn't had an episode in years. Why now? She closed her eyes and concentrated on the inhale and the exhale, forcing her heart rate to find a simple rhythm.

"Voni?"

The voice above her was close and very concerned.

"Can't...breathe." She shook her head violently. "Beat...wrong. Have...to....slow d-d-down-n...shit!" Sounds became more distant, as though she was underwater, and the world seemed to close in on her, forcing her to take solace in the firmness of the ground. Strong arms surrounded her, eased her toward down.

"J-just need t-to..." she wished her voice didn't mirror the chaos in her body. If she could force the breath in, get the breath and beat to match, it would be all right. That had always worked in the past. But her lungs, it seemed, had other plans, and her heart seemed to be in on the game. She knew if she couldn't get this situation in hand right damned quick, she would pass out. She squeezed her eyes shut as her panic level spiraled further out of control and the push of tears threatened to spill from her shut lids. Yeah. Way to go. Great first impression. So much for ever seeing Mr. Sexy again.

"Hang on, Voni. I've got you. Just relax. I've got you." His words reached into her mind as the air attempted to reach down into her lungs. Her heart fluttered in and out of tempo, refusing to set a steady course. He splayed his fingers wide against her chest, as if willing her fragile heart to beat in time.

"Shhhh," he breathed gently in her ear. "Don't speak. Just relax." Kai sensed her mind would soon lose the battle for consciousness. He channeled his own heartbeat through his open palm, coaxing the wild rhythm beneath to follow suit.

"Breathe with me." Inhaling deeply, he guided her along, his lungs expanded until hers finally mirrored the task. With each ragged breath she took, he was patient, murmuring soft words of encouragement. He held her close as she fought to regain control, inhaling her sweet fragrance as her body began to function more on its own.

He reached out, searching to find the source of the problem. He had his suspicions, and he discovered her heart was the main concern. Faint scars traced crisscrossed patterns deep within her pounding heart, evidence of a hidden condition. If he were to heal them completely, it would raise far too many questions. They would need to wait for another time. For now, he was satisfied enough as her body returned to a natural rhythm, tension melting away. Her tiny frame fit nicely in his arms. He began to wonder about how other things might fit as well.

Things begin to change, just as Voni was on the verge of the impending blackness. A bright glow, warm and yet cool, starting from the center of her body, had seeped steadily through her, touching every corner and calming her frantic pulse. Air, glorious air, flowed easily, and her heart beat to a more comfortable drummer. Curious, she opened her eyes as she palced her hand on her chest to find the source of her serenity and discovered the gentle, yet undeniably real touch. His fingers, warm and soft, radiated a soothing energy, creating a soft glow in the darkness. Or so she imagined.

Her gaze followed the line of the fingers, strong and well-formed as they met arm, encased in soft gray cashmere. Her eyes continued up the circuit, finding a broad chest and wide shoulders, brushed by the edges of long black silk. Taking an unsteady breath, she looked into the face of her constant savior. His brow, furrowed in deep concentration, relaxed, and his enigmatic eyes locked on to hers.

Inches away from him, she could now see the intense, almost unreal color of his eyes. She checked for telltale signs of contact lenses but found none. His eyes burned the palest green she had ever seen, sprinkled in with silver-gray, which only added to his mystery. Her mouth dried as the appropriate words disappeared from her thoughts.

"If you wanted to kill me, you could've just left me on the bridge."

The escaping breath from her companion sounded like a cross between a sigh and a stifled laugh. He rested his forehead against hers as she regained her wits.

"True. But where would be the fun in that?"

Voni scoffed. "Yeah, you're right. I would have missed out on the brain-exploding pain and heart palpitations. Gee, thanks."

"Siobhan, I am—"

"No," she stammered, placing her fingers against his soft, firm lips. "No, I'm sorry. I have this habit of not really thinking about what I say until after, and then, well…The truth is, if you hadn't been here, well, then neither would I." She squirmed under the weight of her own admissions. "So, I guess…I mean, um…"

Her words jumbled as she became aware of a deliciously warm pressure against her fingertips, causing her to squirm even more. One corner of his lips pulled up into a devilishly crooked smile, but he made no other movement. His eyes burned into hers, clearly waiting patiently to see what would happen next.

Voni sat stunned, unable to move. Here she was, tucked neatly into the lap of the most incredibly gorgeous man she had ever laid eyes on, and her hand was pressed against his full, very kissable lips. Oh, and they were in public view of anyone who happened to be walking by at that ungodly hour in the morning. That final thought broke her out of her wild fantasy. As much as she was wickedly praying to see this dream become reality, she had no desire to get arrested for indecent exposure.

Kai watched with interest, fascinated by the way her mind moved. She began to respond to his pull, the heat of her body radiating through the thick coat serving as a cocoon. But her rational mind saw the pitfalls of their current, rather open, setting. Expelling his held breath, he pressed a chaste kiss against her slender fingers.

"Perhaps we should continue this conversation is a more private arena," he whispered. He hesitated before moving, caution playing upon his face. "Do you feel well enough to stand?"

"Yeah, I'm okay."

Kai made the first move. Disentangling his long legs, he rose gracefully, with Voni still cradled in his arms. Begrudgingly, he lowered her to land softly on her own, keeping a precautionary hold on her shoulders. He had almost forgotten how tiny she was; the top of her head was level with his shoulders. Her eyes fixed on a point in the center of his chest, as if unwilling to make the long journey to reach his eyes. He trailed his hands down her arms, hoping to give her a moment to steady herself. After she gained her land legs, he turned his attentions to her eyes, dragging his knuckles lightly across her jawline, to tip her chin up.

Even through their small points of connection, he could feel her whole body tremble. But he still sensed doubt and uncertainty; her unknown fears bled from her skin and kept her eyes firmly planted on his sternum. Somehow he needed to assure her that what was between them was real, not simply lust for a beautiful body. But how?

Her shoulders drooped fractionally, but enough for Kai to notice. His plan was still a possibility, but the venue would definitely need changing. He ducked his head slightly to catch her gaze.

"I believe we were heading toward a different destination, before this, um, interruption." Voni smiled at his description of her episode. "Shall we, then?"

Her hazel eyes peered into his very soul, and he knew it was more than chance that brought her across his path tonight. She held his gaze and gave him a simple nod in reply.

In an attempt not to have a repeat performance of the earlier "interruption," Kai placed a gentle, chaste kiss on her forehead before pulling her close. He wrapped his arms around her shoulders and found, in this position, that his chin rested quite nicely atop her deep chestnut tresses. He could definitely get used to that.

She was warm, funny, bright, strong, and yet soft in all the right places. He was beginning to think this pairing might not be such a mistake after all.

He took another deep inhale, imprinting her unique scent into every inch of himself. Now he would be able to find her anywhere. All the elements that identified her were now part of his makeup. Should she ever be in danger again, he would know, even if he was halfway around the world.

Voni couldn't believe how...right it felt being in his arms, a man she'd known for a few short hours. A man who had saved her life definitely once, possibly two other times during their brief acquaintance. An amazing, sinfully attractive god among men. And there she stood, wrapped so close to his body with his heartbeat, strong and loud, against her ear. She closed her eyes to better imagine what his body would look like without the high-fashion packaging. He had to be spectacular; she could feel it in her gut, not to mention other places a bit farther south.

"The sun will be up very soon," he said, his voice rumbling against Voni's ears. She felt the pulse all the way down to her toes. *I could definitely get used to this.*

"Yes," he whispered. "You could."

"What?" she murmured. Her jaw quivered as a yawn struggled to break free.

"Sorry. Just thinking aloud." As he disengaged from their embrace, he caught her mid-yawn. He chuckled as she vainly attempted to hide her fatigue.

"You are exhausted. I am sorry to have kept you out so long." He offered her his hand. "Come. I will get you home."☐

FOUR

The cityscape stood in mute silhouette as the sky gradually brightened around them. They walked in silence, lost in their own thoughts.

"What time is it, anyway?" she asked as they headed back toward the bridge. Her feet felt like lead as they plodded on. She couldn't remember the last time she'd stayed up all night. It had to be during college. In those days, though, she was up either studying or at a late-night rehearsal. Always working, never partying like her roommates or other friends. She had tried to convince herself she wouldn't have enjoyed being up, just for the sake of it. However, today, she had a different perspective.

Kai glanced down at the expensive-looking watch wrapped around his wrist. "Ooh. Well, I hope you do not have a regular job." He paused as he gauged her reaction. She quizzically shook her head. "Good, because it is about quarter to six."

Voni eyes widened as her mind scrambled to do the mental math. Even though she was taking a break from the company, not by choice, she still attended class, just to have something to occupy her days. So, she had awoken at her normal early time, six a.m. In fifteen minutes, she'd have been up for twenty-four hours straight.

The realization caused a groan to escape her lips. "I think I might pass on class today," she decided, the last few words elongated and finally ending with another jaw-popping yawn.

He smiled at her nonchalant appraisal of the situation. He admired her no-nonsense attitude toward things. She seemed to take everything in easy stride, even the bizarre encounter with Konstantin.

His brow furrowed as he contemplated his next move regarding his latest opponent. He would be locked safe in the In-Between for at least a week. That was the standard amount of time needed for a Rogue Warrior to regenerate a physical form. Until then, they were relatively safe. Time enough for him to seek out his replacement.

"Um." Her voice broke through his reverie. "I don't mean to interrupt, but are we heading any place in particular?"

He stopped to take a measured look at their current surroundings. Their wanderings had brought them back across the dreaded bridge and within two blocks of her apartment. He had inadvertently picked the address out of her memories and set his feet in that direction subconsciously. Perhaps he could convince her she had told him over coffee. Anything was possible.

"Is this not near where you live?"

She pulled up short, her mind trying to put meaning to his old-world style of speech. "How could you know that?" She held his gaze, wariness narrowing her vision. A heartbeat passed. She dismissed her suspicions with a wave of her hand. "Never mind. With all that's happened tonight, I wouldn't be surprised if you found it by reading my mind."

"Truly?" he inquired.

"Aw, hell. I'm too tired for anything to make any sense right now."

He nodded, feeling her pulse rate slow as exhaustion continued to take its toll. He wondered if she would be able to finish their journey or if he would need to carry her the remainder of the distance.

He leaned toward her, but she quickly ducked under his arm.

"Oh no you don't. I know that look."

He stopped, baffled at her reaction.

"I can walk on my own two feet, thank you very much." Angry, she shrugged out of the long, heavy coat and all but threw it back at him before turning sharply on her heels.

Now it was his turn to gape at her words. Had she gleaned his thoughts? Was this one of the signs of a true pairing, the ability to hear each other's thoughts?

She stormed off, muttering. "I'm not a child. I'm not made of glass. I'm so sick of everyone treating me like some kind of…forget it."

He caught up to her with two strides, still fighting to untangle the unruly piece of cloth recently returned to him. Her ire puzzled and fascinated him. Was she upset with him? Giving up on sorting out his jacket, he slung it over his shoulder.

She quickened her pace, distancing herself even more.

"Kind of what?"

She turned to face him, yet continued in her original direction fluidly without missing a beat. "Like some sort of doll, or toy." She threw the words at him as she tossed her arms skyward to punctuate her disdain. "I'm sick of it! 'Oh, poor Voni.'" Her voice took on a mewling, condescending tone, mimicking some unknown acquaintance. "'We have to be careful not to upset her. She needs to be watched. She might go over the edge.' Well, I have gone over the edge! I've stood on that damned edge and…dammit all, I just want…" Turning with practiced and perfected natural grace, she strode closer toward the gated entrance of her tiny complex.

Kai had a good idea of her unfinished desire. If he had to guess, the answer would be "peace," but he decided to allow her the chance to finish her own thought.

Her burst of speed seemed to be waning fast, and her steps slowed to a snail's pace. She came to a halt, lacing her fingers through the time-faded ironwork, heaving a sigh as she dropped her head back, closing her eyes to drown out the impending dawn.

"Look, this day will definitely be filed in my weird-shit-doesn't-even-cut-it drawer, and I feel that somehow I'm either having a massive hallucination or the worst pizza-induced nightmare ever. Whatever it is, I'll wake up with everything back to its normal crappiness. So maybe it would be best if we just—"

"Why are you so determined to dismiss everything?"

His breath warmed her face as his voice enveloped her from above.

"Because…" She opened her eyes to find his gorgeous features hovering upside down mere inches above her, the most unnervingly seductive smile playing upon his extremely kissable lips.

The overriding urge to touch him was more than she could resist. She reached out, her palm resting against his finely sculpted jawline. As she trailed her hand down—or was it up?—his cheek, a day's growth of stubble delightfully tickled her fingertips. It was prickly and decidedly male.

"Aw, fuck it," she mumbled before threading her fingers up through his hair and drawing him down to fiercely devour his surprise-parted lips.

Their current positions made things awkward, but not impossible. He returned her intensity and enthusiasm with equal fervor, cupping her face before twisting her around and locking her in an unbreakable embrace. Never once did his lips pull away from hers, his tongue probing and exploring every corner of her mouth.

Voni groaned against the force of his kiss, her eyes rolling back as her lids drifted shut. She had never been so bold, so impulsive, before in her life, and yet never had she felt more alive. She allowed her hands to roam across the expanse of his shoulders before wending her fingers into his thick black mane. His lips were strong and demanding, stealing her breath as he pressed her back against the rusted iron gate.

Kai laced his fingers through the filigreed bars, threatening to disintegrate the ancient barrier with the force of his heightened desire. As he ground his body against hers, he slid his lips from her mouth as he nibbled his way down her jaw to bury his face into the hollow of her throat. His breathing rasped, and his cock had hardened past the point of pleasurable.

"Damn, woman. When you change your mind, you really change your mind."

Voni laughed shakily. "Well, sometimes you just have to say—"

"What the fuck?" he answered, finishing the quote from one of her all-time favorite movies, *Risky Business*.

She smiled as she held his head close to her, her half-lidded gaze finding his eyes a scant breath away from hers. A moment passed as she realized the physical impossibility of their current positions.

"Um, are my feet on the ground?" she asked curiously.

His sensual chuckle thrummed against her chest. "I was wondering when you would notice."

Blinking rapidly to clear her mind, she glanced down to find her legs wrapped suggestively around his well-formed legs and halfway up his waist.

"Oops," she responded halfheartedly. What the hell was she doing? Her inner voices, both for and against, screamed in protest.

"Is that good or bad?" His voice rumbled, rough and tight.

Voni took a ragged breath, searching for the answer herself.

"Both," she sighed. She unwound her legs before reaching her toes toward the distant concrete.

Standing once again, with the reality of solid ground beneath her feet, Voni felt heat blossom all the way up to her hairline. Did she just practically molest him right in front of God and everybody? She nervously glanced around, realizing her very public, and now very brightly lit, surroundings.

Oh crap. She had! What was wrong with her?

"Omigod. I am so sorry. I mean…" Her words tumbled out as she staggered away from him, running her trembling hands through her wild hair in a vain attempt to smooth both it and her frazzled nerves. She barely knew him. He could be some kind of psycho stalker. Or worse, married.

A throaty growl escaped Kai's lips before he could contain it. His body echoed his sentiments as he released his hold, feeling every curve of her petite form as she slithered down. Gods, but this woman was driving him to the brink of his control. He wondered how slow he would need to take this. One thing he did know for sure, judging by her heated reaction, she would be well worth the wait.

Kai slowly reached out to capture her wrists, halting her agitated movements. He gently turned her face to meet his gaze. Her apprehensive expression warmed his heart even more than her surprising passionate explosion.

"Are you?"

He moved his head to hold her gaze, her attention focused on a point of interest slightly over his right shoulder.

"Please, Siobhan," he implored. "I need to know if you regret what just happened."

As she nervously nibbled on the corner of her kiss-swollen lips, he snuck a peek into her scattered thoughts. She knew the truth. But she hesitated.

He sensed her trepidation. He was pushing too much, moving too fast. Silently swearing at himself, he eased back. He had to remember the circumstances of their initial meeting; she'd been trying to take her own life. That thought sobered him, both in body and spirit.

Kai took the first step, moving away from her, giving her the space he knew she needed. "Now it is I who must apologize. It was not my intention to pressure you."

Voni snickered, shaking her head. "I practically jump *your* bones and you're apologizing to *me*." A lingering hint of a smile remained as she leveled her eyes to meet his. "Are you for real?"

"I am as real as you want me to be."

His words both calmed and excited her. But that tiny corner of her rational mind still worked, reminding her about her ever-increasing lack of sleep and the remaining vestiges of energy seeped through the soles of her worn-out cross trainers.

"And on that note"—he reached down to retrieve his coat, dropped in the wake of his eagerness to wrap himself around her—"I believe it is time for me to bid you good night—"

"Don't you mean 'good morning,'?" she quipped.

A sinfully sexy, lopsided smile was her reward as he continued. "No, because those words would be spoken before breakfast, meaning that some sort of nighttime activity had occurred, be it sleep or…something else."

Her cheeks flashed from white to pink in record time.

"So," he resumed between escaping laughs. "You know, you are quite cute when you blush."

"All right, already. That's enough of the let's-see-how-much-embarrassment-Voni-can-take game." She fished around into her jacket pocket until successfully drawing out her keychain. Four keys and a small yellow lion jingled as she fumbled to isolate the gate key.

"First order of business for me is a shower, followed immediately by sleep for, like, the next week."

The first notion conjured very explicitly detailed images in Kai's mind. He could see her, naked and slick, water running in rivers along the creamy channel between her small breasts. His groin tightened at visions of her hands roaming over the planes of her body, lathering her shapely legs, her well-curved ass, and dipping to touch…

He shook his head violently, hoping to derail his current train of thought. Grateful she had her back to him, he tried to readjust himself but that only succeeded in compounding his dangerous fantasy.

The jarring grind of metal on metal cleared her mind. The rusted gate heaved in protest at its early awakening. Shoving the gate open, Voni turned, her Good Samaritan standing still, one hand tucked into a front pocket while his long trench hung lazily over his shoulder suspended by the other. God, but he looked like something straight out of a high-fashion magazine. What in the world was he doing spending time with her?

Her smile faltered, never quite reaching her eyes. Kai sensed the self-doubt rise once again behind her eyes. What would it take for her to believe in herself? To believe in him? He knew the answer, the only answer, was time. This was going to take time, and he was more than patient. The question was, would she?

"Until later, then? In, say, perhaps, a week?"

She laughed, leaning back against the iron entryway. It slipped out of her easily, deep and throaty. The sound set fire to his blood as he remembered the feeling of her body pressed against him; the taste of her wild, spiced sweetness still lingered on his lips.

"Sounds like a date," she responded languidly. She didn't want to get her hopes up only to have this dreamy god just forget about her.

"No," he said, capturing her fingers, bringing them to his lips. "It is a promise." He held her gaze as he turned over her hand and placed a warm, passionate kiss in the center of her palm.

She swallowed hard as his eyes latched on to the rhythmic movement of her slender throat. His gaze traveled to her lips as she opened her mouth to respond, but she was interrupted by two harmonious, high-pitched squeals emanating from a doorway behind her. Cringing at the sounds, she gave Kai a weak, apologetic half-smile.

"It might be better if you left," she sighed. "And you'd better be quick about it too, before the BR sisters find you here."

He hazarded a quick glance over her head. Blinking slowly, he spied two people, one tall with skin like pale chocolate, and the second face sporting a Roman nose and olive skin, gesturing wildly in an open doorway midway into the complex. Even from this distance, he could tell that one of the "sisters" was in serious need of a shave.

"BR?"

"Brass Rail. It's a club in Hillcrest." Hillcrest was the local hub of the LGBT community in San Diego, and not very far from their current location.

"You have drag queens for neighbors?" Kai's question was simply one of curiosity. There was no judgment in his tone. He had met an interesting variety of people during his travels, but never had he truly encountered a more fascinating group than those who lived their lives trying to escape their own gender.

"Yeah. They're really great." She struggled to stifle a yawn with no real success.

Kai bowed a final time, regal and incredibly sexy. "Then I shall see you in one week's time. Until then, sleep well and stay safe." Turning, he started to head back to the club to pick up his car.

"Hang on." She reached for his arm, her touch feather-light and as unbreakable as steel. A continuous wave of squeaks and stage whispers poured down the slate-rock pathway. She looked up at him sheepishly. "You don't have to wait a week. I mean, if you wanted to. Well, that is, you could, you know…"

"I think you are trying to tell me something, but for the life of me, I cannot figure out what." His smile stole her remaining brain cells' ability to function on any level.

"Ooh." She quickly pulled herself to the tips of her toes and placed a quick kiss on his cheek. "Thank you. For everything."

She stepped past the gateway, then paused, her focus diverted by the frantic movements of her overly dramatic friends. "See you soon?" Her voice was thick with hope and apprehension.

"Definitely." Kai suddenly stood at her back, his voice a warm whisper against her ear. He took one final breath, her scent filling his lungs and burying itself deep in his mind.

Satisfied for the moment, he stepped away and strolled back into the heart of the city. He knew better than to turn back. He would see her again. Soon.

He turned the corner, found a shadowed alcove, and flashed himself back to his car. The fob in his fingers chirped, triggering the automatic doors. He slid inside the midnight-black Aston Martin Vanquish and with a turn of the key, the powerful engine roared to life, growling like a caged beast as it took to the awakening streets.

Smiling to himself, he reviewed the events of the past evening. For having such a mediocre start, things had turned out quite intriguingly. He was interested to see what the new day would bring.

Voni remained still for an additional heartbeat until she was sure that Kai was gone. She felt his presence fade, cooling her overheated blood as the chilly morning warmed around her He wanted to see her again. Giddiness bubbled up as she dragged herself down the path to face her most beloved companions.

Daphne Campari and Roxanna Bacardi, aka Daniel Erikkson and Robert Valderrama, shrieked as they rushed down the path, fuzzy-heeled slippers click-clacking the whole way like an old-school typewriter. Voni smiled at their befeathered and chiffoned approach. She had always found it funny that, no matter the hour, they were always impeccably dressed and in something more feminine than she had ever owned.

Daphne, still fumbling with the sleeve of her slinky robe, pranced around Voni like a giant mother hen. Standing an easy five foot nine with the broad shouldered, tapered body of an Olympic swimmer, she gently grabbed Voni's shoulders, her deep-brown eyes boring deep into hers.

"Aw, sweetie, what were you thinking? Are you trying to make us crazy?" The words rang against her ears, shrill and tinny. Confusion muddled her mind as Daphne continued on the tirade. "Don't you ever think about leaving us! Who would we drag to karaoke night?" The gleam of unshed tears sparkled in both pairs of waiting eyes.

"Yes!" The word squeaked out from Roxi, her Spanish accent mixed thickly with her overdramatized grief. "And we haven't finished your new wardrobe yet, *chica*!"

Realization dawned on Voni. They'd found her note. Guilt drained her of any residual vestiges of energy, and her chin quivered as the tears trickled down her cheeks. Hiding her face in her hands, she did something neither of her friends had ever seen—she sobbed. She wished she could blame fatigue completely for her breakdown, but inside, she knew the truth. The time she had spent with her own personal angel had altered her. Forever.

Four strong arms gripped her in a breathtaking bear hug. Mumbled apologies layered one on top of another as sobs filled the quiet courtyard, marring the peace of the Friday morning.

Daphne pulled out of the huddle first, wiping away the raccoon-eyed remnants of her black eyeliner before turning her attention to Voni's own tear-streaked face. She flat-handedly patted away the offending water, careful not to poke her with her dragon-lady red nails.

"Oh, I hate getting all emotional. It plays havoc with my complexion."

Voni choked out a strangled laugh. Until that moment, she'd never realized how important these two people had been to her. During the past year, they'd barely left her side. Constantly checking in on her, dragging her out to go shopping or clubbing or anywhere, they had worked so hard to help her rejoin the world. Only now did she finally see how much she loved them and how much her intended actions would have devastated them.

"I am so sorry," she started, her voice full of remorse and exhaustion. "I didn't mean to worry you guys. I'm sorry. Argh!" Voni paused, angry with herself. "I have to stop saying that. God, I feel like that's all I've said for the past few hours."

Taking a calming breath, she met their perplexed gazes. Oh yeah. They hadn't been with her all night long.

"Are you telling me," Roxi remarked, eyes widening as she spoke, "that you were with Mr. Sex-on-a-Stick?"

"All night long?" Daphne chimed in, peering excitedly through her false eyelashes. "And all you did was say, 'I'm sorry?' Girl, we gotta talk."

"Can this wait? It's been kind of a weird day." Her eyes flickered between their brown and green gazes. She hoped to find some measure of compassion. Instead, the mere distant glimpse of Kai had apparently piqued their hunger, and now she knew there would be no living with them until they had the whole story.

Daphne caved first, waving her hands dismissively. "Oh, all right, girl. Besides," she added, apparently to convince her partner in crime, "you really look like shit."

"Daph!" Roxi chided her, swatting her shoulder.

"Well, she does," Daphne concluded, folding her arms across her broad chest. Focusing her attention back on Voni, she added, "You do, ya know."

Voni couldn't help but laugh. "I'm sure I've looked better. Do you have any huge plans later today?" She was careful to clarify 'huge plans.' The last time she asked about plans, she had been rewarded with a minute-by-minute blow-by-blow of their entire day.

"Well," Daphne began, dragging out the word while thoughtfully tapping a finger on her chin. "I have a nail appointment at two…" She glanced, lids half-lowered, at her before amending, "But I can change that!"

"Oooh, honey," Roxi cooed, patting Voni on the arm. "I'd reschedule a sex change to hear the gory details." Two voices cackled in tandem, their laughter rising in pitch and intensity.

Shaking her head at her giggling friends, Voni headed toward her unit, her feet shuffling along the familiar pathway.

"Voni?" Daphne's voice called her back. She glanced over her shoulder; her friends were nearly inside their unit. The two exchanged looks before finally speaking. "We're really glad to see you, girl." Daphne's genuine smile broke easily across her face and was echoed by a similar expression from Roxi.

"Call us later! Promise!" Daphne called out before Roxi closed their bright blue door.

Voni waved a silent good-bye and returned to her front door.

The screen opened with a creak before she slipped the key into the white washed wooden door. A flick of her wrist and the door swung open, revealing the small apartment she thought she'd never see again. She took a moment to soak in the scene: pale ash bookcases lined the eggshell walls, books crammed in at every available angle; uninteresting, generic artwork hung on the wall. Tan couch, nondescript pine coffee table, standard TV set, and the requisite CD/DVD cases stood in silent testament to her drab existence.

No wonder she was suicidal. Her place was depressing. Nothing in her living room spoke to who she was. All of it was bland, unremarkable, and just plain boring. Her mind strayed to the cozy house where she and James had planned to live out their lives. It even had a postage-stamp-size front yard, complete with grass, welcoming visitors to their cottage.

Yesterday, those stray memories would have brought on a debilitating wave of despair. Yet today, in the brightening day, her sadness was muted, the edges not as sharp. Life wasn't as bleak as she had previously decided. She had to do something about this place. A new coat of paint, some color, maybe. Or maybe a bomb going off. Something, anything. But not right then.

Her thoughts began to wander aimlessly the longer she stood just beyond the threshold. Her eyelids turned into lead, drooping of their own accord. The keys slipped from her tired fingers into the change dish as she staggered through the entryway. With a heavy groan, she turned, grumbling as she shut the door and set the deadbolt.

Realizing she was fighting a losing battle, she stripped off her jacket as she stumbled toward the bedroom that was tucked into the farthest corner of the space. Letting it slip through her fingers, she stepped toward her still-made bed. Grabbing the bottom of her tank, she stopped mid-yank, exhaustion staking its claim on her remaining energy.

"Aw, the hell with this," she murmured before collapsing in a heap onto the comforting mattress. Curling her fingers around the edge of the lightweight blanket, she cocooned her body moments before sleep came crashing down.

A perturbed mewling drew her back the instant her eyes closed. She forced her lids open and found herself nose-to-nose with a pair of bright golden eyes shining out from a sleek, deep-black leonine face.

"Jazz," she mumbled. "Not now, kiddo. Let mama rest and we'll play later, ok?"

A pink sandpaper tongue flicked out, catching the tip of Voni's nose.

"Thanks a lot, butt-breath."

Her furry son continued to vocalize, regaling her with what she had believed to be the details of his activities. She had always created dialogue for every imaginary conversations with her cats, making some of her friends, including James, question her sanity. Her own mother had told her that every creature had a voice and if you took time to listen, you could befriend anything.

"Yeah, yeah. I know, I know. I'm very late and I'm very sorry." She snuggled deeper into the blanket as little feet marched the length of her body. Taking in a big breath, she kicked off her almost-forgotten sneakers and pulled up her knees, settling into her normal position on her side, and her eyes closed.

She felt Jazz wander and fuss for another minute or two before curling up in his favorite place, tucked in behind her bent knees. Sleep crept in within the span of several heartbeats. Silently, she prayed for it to be dreamless. Unless, of course, the dreams involved a man her friend had aptly described as sex-on-a-stick.

A smile crossed her lips as she finally resigned herself to slumber.

FIVE

Kai's thoughts wandered aimlessly as he fluidly slipped between the slower cars, heading toward his home in the small community of La Jolla. As he turned up the winding Torrey Pines Drive, images of the beauty with whom he had spent the past few hours drifted across his mind. He heard her laugh, deep and sensual, saw the fire in her eyes, and felt the heat ripple off her body as passion stole her reason for a brief moment. The buzz of distant voices hummed on the edge of his consciousness. Most thoughts were geared toward starting a new day, others trying to remember what had happened the night before.

The car navigated the twists and turns as if alive, Kai's reflexes honed to a knifepoint. Moments later, he veered onto the drive leading toward the large, sprawling, white, palatial estate he had called home for the past half-century or so. The security gate swung open, beckoning him. Cobblestones crackled beneath the sleek tires as the car prowled closer to the covered carport. He eased the car into its allotted space—sandwiched between the midnight-blue 1967 Shelby Cobra and the jet-black 2008 Ducati Desmosedici RR. The engine whirred to a stop and he stepped out. Passing the gunmetal-gray Maybach 62 and the matte-black 1961 Lincoln Continental, he ascended the stairs that led to the house proper.

A rhythmic mechanical beep greeted Kai as he entered the sun-brightened living room. Damn. Dropping his keys on the tile counter, he walked over to retrieve the remote that controlled the inset louvered blinds, as well as most of the house's electronic devices. With a quick flick, the floor-to-ceiling windows darkened and the dawn-hued room melted into twilight. The waking world outside faded behind the confines of the muted glass wall.

He keyed another button as he crossed the polished wood floors. His footfalls muffled into silence as the floor melted from wood to thick white carpet. He stopped to gaze out at the landscape below as music, low and relaxing, flowed into the room. He studied the muted yet picturesque scene, the jagged cliffs, and pale sands intermingling with the frothy blue of the Pacific. The ocean and the land snaked and dipped in a battle for supremacy until they disappeared into the distant horizon.

The melodious tones of Zero 7 seeped under his skin, and fatigue began to drag his eyelids down. Sighing deeply, he leaned his forehead against the thick, cool glass, allowing himself a moment to revisit her sweet smile.

The incessant *beep* bored into his brain, interrupting his train of thought. A low guttural growl rumbled in his throat as he pushed away from the window and from his reverie. A few easy strides and he reached the offending answering machine. The number five glowed a pulsing red against the black screen. He pushed the Play button as he ambled toward the large hall closet and returned his trench to its hanger.

The robotic tone marked time and date before a cultured, British voice began the litany of messages.

"Good evening, Mr. Vadim. This is Jonathan Whitman from the law firm of Millar, Jones, and Wright. I am calling to inform you that the documents you requested have posted and are ready for you to collect."

Finally. He had donated one of his properties to Becky's House, a group created to help battered women and their families. Remembering the pain his father had inflicted on his mother and on him, he gave without hesitation. Unfortunately, the hesitation came from his property management company, which claimed first rights over any sale of the building or the land. So, off to the lawyers he went, knowing his ownership would trump any claim made by bureaucratic pencil-pushers.

"Should you have any additional needs, please do not hesitate to contact us again."

Kai wandered into the kitchen, opened the stainless-steel refrigerator, and grabbed the first bottle he could find. Luckily enough, he ended up with a beer and not salad dressing. He considered putting the brew back for a moment as the time stamp played in preparation for the next call.

Voni's philosophical advice prompted him to snap off the cap. Yeah, what the fuck. A crooked smile blossomed across his face, and he took a long draught.

"Hello, friend. My name is Eric Kingsley, and I would like to speak to you about a great opportunity in the field of—" The machine gratefully cut out, programmed to disregard telemarketers. The mechanical voice announced the time, and the litany of information continued.

The breathy female voice on the machine brought him back to the moment. Rolling his eyes, he tried to remember her name. His friend and fellow Guardian Warrior, Eamon McClearon, thought it would be entertaining to give his number out to every vacuous vixen at the bar earlier that night. Eamon, with his easy smile and charming Irish brogue, had women throwing their panties at him on a regular basis.

"...I had a great time with your friend last night and would love to have a great time with you. Call me at..."

Where these women for real? Oh, wait, he remembered, they weren't. Most of the women Eamon slobbered over gave a Barbie doll depth. A gratifying *beep* signaled the end of her unwanted and extremely overt insinuations. After listening to the unnecessary descriptive message from the nameless woman, he yearned for his petite pixie.

His groin tightened, making him painfully aware of how much he yearned for her. He vainly attempted to find a more comfortable position for his raging hard-on, but he could only think of one—buried deep inside Voni. As hecradled his swollen cock, he imagined her sweet heat wrapping around the length of his shaft, muscles convulsing as he pumped hard and fast, sweat glistening off her pale ivory skin.

Growling, he quickly removed his hand. He felt like some hormonal teen, jacking off to an impossible fantasy. The main difference was he knew this was more than a simple boyhood dream. She would be his, and hopefully soon. Hell, the drive home was hard enough, no pun intended, with his damned pocket rocket at full attention. Until he finally claimed her as his own, it appeared he would have a constant, and painful, companion.

"Great, this ought to be fun," he muttered as the second wannabe temptress left a detailed account of her plans for him. He arched an eyebrow sardonically as the pornographic wordplay continued. Lucky for him, he had a time limit on message length, and the *beep* graciously cut off the *Penthouse* submission mid-whimper.

The two previous recordings gave him a good idea of the final caller's identity.

"Wake up, boyo." Eamon's familiar lilt seeped out of the small speaker. "What happened to ya? Ya went out for a smoke and just disappeared."

Shit, that's right. He had almost forgotten how the evening had originally started out. He groaned and dropped his head back against the doorjamb with a dull *thud*. Ow. He swallowed another mouthful and turned his attentions back to hear of his friend's latest conquest.

"We waited till two for ya…" We? Faintly, in the background, Kai picked out the giggles of two feminine voices. Oddly enough, the timbre was strikingly similar to those of the women in the two previous messages. Just like Eamon to share. Arrogant prig. "…so call me when ya get in."

Moans and the tittering of mindless laughter leaked out of the device before the line went mercifully quiet, the long tone finally signifying the end of the day's messages. Shaking his head as a devious smile stole over his face, he emptied the bottle with one final swallow. In the past, he had found his friend's escapades entertaining, to say the least. Today was different. Everything was different. After almost seven hundred years, his life was turning down a path completely unfamiliar to him.

The voice of his mentor edged into his mind, bringing back memories hidden for so many years.

"Once you have found your spiritmate, you will be compelled to make her your own. Your every thought and action will yearn for nothing else.. Even your body will want for only her."

At the time, Kai believed he was exaggerating, putting things out of proper perspective. Hindsight, he realized, was a harsh teacher. Now, he wished he had paid more attention to that aspect of his training. Instead, drunk with newly acquired power, he threw himself into honing his skills as warrior, mastering moving with the wind, and harnessing the power of the mind. Not wanting to pry, he never asked about how he met her or how long he courted her.

But did it have to mean that he would be stuck with a perpetual boner?

Grinding his teeth, he slammed the empty bottle onto the granite counter. That prospect did not sound enticing, but the final payoff would be well worth a few days of discomfort.

Days?

A heavy sigh escaped his lips as he pressed the cool green glass bottle against his temple. Hell, he was a warrior and had survived seven centuries of hard-fought battles. But this diminutive beauty had truly brought him to his knees. Closing his eyes, he envisioned himself in that exact position; his arms cradling his goddess, laving the soft skin between her thighs, feeling her fingers grasp his hair and hearing her moan his name.

Damn, the wait wasn't going to be easy. He slowly raised his head, opting to find a more comfortable place to indulge his wayward thoughts. With the flick of his hand, the bottle skidded along the slick counter before landing deftly in the trash bin. He grabbed the remote as he passed through the living room. A press of a button later and the blinds closed and the room plunged in blessed darkness.

He mounted the curving stairs two at a time, ascending to the privacy of his study. The flat screen computer illuminated the room in ghostly blue as flashes of brilliant colors echoed the cascading fireworks of the system's screensaver. He paused briefly and considered using his remaining energy to answer what would no doubt be dozens of unread e-mails.

Later.

He knew his mind would wander to her, so why not just let his thoughts have a field day? He left the room and continued down the hall, turning at the last door on the left. The monstrous four-poster bed dominated the open space, its deep mahogany wood a stark contrast to the pale ivory walls. He stripped quickly as he crossed into the room, tossing his clothes haphazardly on the floor. He'd pick them up later. Yeah, like after reading e-mails and all the other things he was postponing until he got his emotions back in check.

Three more long strides and he was in the massive bathroom. Kai knew he would need a very cold shower if he were to have any hope of sleep. He stepped into the ornate glass box and turned the multiple jets on high. Icy blasts pounded and frozen fingers massaged. He stood under the frigid onslaught until sleep seemed to be a possibility.

He groggily turned off the jets, toweled off, and finally crawled into bed. Closing his eyes, he knew, in every fiber of his being, she would haunt his dreams with her sad eyes, her flippant smile, and her soulful beauty. The mere thought of his impending reveries caused his groin to harden again. Great, he thought as he began to drift off to an uncomfortable sleep, this was not going to be easy.

SIX

Voices, distant and faint, whispered in the darkness. As Voni turned in search of their source, faces appeared from the void. First, eyes became visible; large and misshapen, they bored into hers. Then came gaping mouths forming pitiful wails.

Voni tried to run, but, as had happened each time before in this place, she was rooted to the spot, unable to escape the horrific images as they shambled closer. She twisted and spun, straining to keep her eyes shut.

"Voni, help me!"

She knew the voice, was able to pick out James' screams from the formless masses. Her eyes pried open of their own accord, her brain no longer in control of her responses. She knew what she would see before her, but the knowledge did nothing to temper her visceral response. Her gut tightened as the face she once loved loomed large in her field of vision, his deep-brown eyes wide and fearful.

Then the blood came. Drops at first, spattering his cheeks with crimson freckles. But soon enough, the downpour of gore began. It flowed in rivers down his face, filling his mouth as he continued to cry out for her. "Why won't you help me? Please, help me."

"I'm sorry," she screamed soundlessly as she willed herself to awaken. "Oh God, please. Make it stop." She struggled to raise her leaden arms to cover her ears, desperate for any reprieve from the shrieks.

A strong pair of hands gently clamped down over her ears, bringing blessed silence into her nightmare for the first time. Warm breath washed over her face, calming and soothing her tortured spirit. Focusing her gaze on the source of her newfound comfort, her eyes found the face of her Good Samaritan.

"Look at me, Siobhan," Kai's whispered voiced pierced through the ongoing wails. "This isn't real, *dragoste meu*. It's just a dream."

"I'm sorry, I can't help. I can't. I can't." The words Voni uttered every night, a litany of repentance for a crime she'd never committed, poured from her lips and her heart, in hopes they would assuage the garish vision of her once-perfect lover. Yet, tonight, their meaning seemed different, the tone shifting from apology to explanation.

Her gaze drifted away from the blood and gore, focusing on the man whose hands still fought to shield her from the cacophony surrounding them. His eyes, pale green fire amid the darkness, radiated with a passionate intensity, burning away the haze of doubt and grief.

"I promised that I would keep you safe." The words, spoken softer than a whisper, cut like a knife through the yowls and wails around her. "And I intend to keep my promise."

The figure that was James melted, and something else stood in its place. Blond-haired and black-eyed. Evil rolled off it in waves, slamming into her like a freight train.

"*You can't have her!*"

Voni's eyes flew open as the voice echoed in her ears. Expelling the breath she'd been unconsciously holding, she flopped onto her back, dragging her arm across her eyes. *Damn. That's a new one.* Her dream had not varied in as many months as she could remember. Now, everything was different.

Kai, she understood. From the moment she closed her eyes, she hoped to see him in her dreams. But, the other one, the blonde that appeared as James melted away? A brief shudder coursed down her spine. The feeling was similar to the one she'd had in the restaurant. The same sense of dread, the same foreboding. It wanted her; it had even said as much. But why?

She shook her head to clear away the last remnants of her latest nightmare. A trace of it would remain with her, as it had every day. However, today she would choose what part to remember, which piece to hold on to. A smile tugged at her lips as she brought his face into focus, those piercing ice-green eyes promising passion beyond measure and a body to guarantee it.

Arching her back, Voni gingerly flexed her limbs, stretching and reaching out to begin a new day. A muffled mew of protest sounded from middle of the bed. Glancing down, a small and rather vocal black ball of fur unfolded itself from its curled position, tail raising toward the ceiling before the cat traipsed the length of the bed. The tongue-lashing continued through his soft-footed journey, stopping only once he'd perched upon her pillow. A little flash of pink darted out, and he greeted her with a sandpaper kiss on her nose.

"Good morning to you too, little fuzzball." Stroking the soft, jet-black fur of her constant companion, Voni tried to piece all the events of the past day into some perspective. She had been placed on leave with the dance company, tried to kill herself, been saved by the hottest man on the planet—not just once, but three times in one night if her count was correct—practically jumped his bones in full view of any passersby, and discovered, and survived, another twist to her normal nightly horrors.

If this wasn't a sign to start something completely new, she didn't know what was. She looked around her Spartan bedroom's beige walls, tan furniture, and beige floor. Heck, even her sheets were beige! When had her world lost all color?

Sunlight filtered in through the white wooden-slat blinds, telling her the day still had many hours of potential left. She suddenly felt an inexplicable urge to set fire to the whole place, torch all vestiges of the past, and start anew. Everything was different today, and it was time for her to live again.

She hazarded a glance toward the digital clock on the nightstand. 1:07 p.m.

Holy crap! What day was it? Had she truly slept that long?

No, not possible. The more she thought about it, Voni had never been able to sleep more than five hours a night. Even after several grueling hours of rehearsal and two shows, her body would only rest for a few hours. That meant it was still Friday. Right? Yeah, it had to be Friday. More importantly, it was time to change everything.

Throwing off the blanket, she sprung out of bed with a giggle. She realized she hadn't jumped out of bed for a very long time. Time was, she would greet each day with a sense of possibility as she bounded out of bed, ready to conquer the world. When she'd first moved in with James, he'd scoffed at her daily morning greeting, calling it "silly and too perky for this ungodly hour."

he had been taken aback at his comment. Perky? She had never been accused of being perky in her entire life. She couldn't see the sense in getting up in a pissy mood every day. Waking up cheerful and energized made the day better from the get-go. But his response had caused her to alter her wakeup ritual, causing her to tone down her enthusiasm. Jazz, on the other hand, seemed to care very little about her burst of energy. He simply yawned, circled around himself three times, and curled back up on her vacant pillow.

The dancer in her knew what needed to be done first. Arms intertwined, she reached her crossed fists toward the ceiling, groaning and shimmying away the last remnants of sleep. Starting at the top of her body, she circled her head, then her shoulders, allowing her arms to drop back at her sides. One deep breath and she rippled her body down, her cheek resting comfortably against her knees, while her chest pressed down on her thighs, and arms wrapped loosely around her legs.

Years of training, plus a nice degree of natural flexibility, kept her body lithe and supple. She bent her knees, her body hanging heavy as she sunk toward the floor. With an exhale, she straightened her legs, the muscles stretching along the back of her legs. Two more deep plies and she switched focus. She reached one leg toward the ceiling, her foot flexing and pointing as her knee bent and straightened. Satisfied, she brought her leg earthbound only to do the same with the other.

After taking a couple deep, relaxing breaths, she unfolded herself, flipping her tank top back into place. Standing tall, she pulled her knee into her chest and exhaled, unfolding her leg so her thigh pressed against her rib cage. She wrapped her arm around her extended leg, moving it to rest behind her shoulder, circling her ankle as she took in deep breaths. After a moment, she repeated the same procedure with the other leg. One full, arching backbend later and her morning stretching was done.

With her feet planted firmly on the floor, and the day full of promise, Voni decided to take charge of her own happiness. And she was going to start by brightening up her living space. But first, shower time. She crossed single-mindedly to the closet and shoved aside the plain veneer door. Digging through the myriad of cascading fabrics, she settled on a dark red, long-sleeved two-button Henley and a pair of black leggings, tossing each over her shoulder before heading down the hall.

"Ugh," she sighed as she passed the threshold into the bland bathroom. Even this was beige! How the hell had she even remained sane for this long? She remembered James's words as she talked about repainting their old apartment. *"Why would you want to do that? I like the color. It's calming."*

Calming? More like catatonic. As she reached into the shower and twisted the single knob to start the blessed flow of hot water, a little voice began its guilty berating. She'd had had two less-than-pleasant thoughts about James in the space it took to cover a few feet. What was wrong with her?

She allowed her fingers to dance in the warming stream as she toyed with her own feelings. What had made her remember these moments, especially right now? Sitting along the edge of the midget-sized bathtub—even she couldn't have both knees and knockers submerged—more long-buried sentiments bubbled up to the surface.

"Voni, you have to grow up sometime. Adults don't have posters on their walls." The first disagreement she could remember was over how to decorate their one-bedroom studio apartment. She had had her heart set on a beautifully framed artist's rendering of her favorite movie, *Casablanca*. Bogey's eyes peered deep into Ingrid's while Peter Lorre and Sydney Greenstreet schemed in the corners. Even now, through the lens of time, the image made her smile.

She had given in, without a word. Acquiesced with only a grin and a nod. The longer she thought on it, the more she recalled similar situations. Times when she hadn't spoken up for herself, occasions when she allowed others to determine what was best for her.

She peeled off her garments, kicking them away angrily as she pushed aside the plastic barrier and stepped into the steam. When had she become so weak? She realized it must have happened gradually, cloaked in the guise of grief. *James had been the strong one*, people had whispered. *Voni's going to need a lot of support*, they would say.

"And I let them," she mused aloud, letting the water pound against her skin. Sighing, she washed her thick tresses, the aroma of her lavender-and-vanilla shampoo mixing with the steam and infusing the air. The rich foam trailed down her back and spiraled down the drain, taking with it her muddied thoughts. Once sure her hair was soap free, she grabbed her net sponge and her favorite shower gel, cucumber melon. No. She hesitated mid-lather. Not her favorite, James's favorite. She had preferred the deeper, spicier fragrances.

Much like the dark, sensuous, and exotic scent of her rescuer, her own personal knight in shining armor. Half-hoping, Voni ducked her head, nuzzling her shoulder. She was rewarded with the lingering hint of musk and cashmere, and absolutely 100 percent male. Her lips tingled, as she remembered the sure pressure of his passionate kiss. Closing her eyes, she let her hand roam over her curves. She gently massaged her breasts, trying to imagine his hands caressing her. When she dipped her hands between her thighs, she abruptly stopped.

"Geez, it really has been a long time." She had never been a woman who believed in self-gratification. Besides, she knew her imagination wouldn't hold a candle to the real thing.

In fact, come to think of it, she couldn't even remember the last time she'd even enjoyed sex. James hadn't been much for romance. He was practical. Everything had its purpose, and nothing was done without one. *Spontaneity* and *whimsy* were awesome words used in Scrabble and crossword puzzles, but not truly in his vocabulary as action words.

She set those thoughts aside as she quickly wrapped up her shower. After stopping the flow of the cooled water, she dried off with her threadbare tan towel. *For the last time*, she mused, whipping her hair into a twisting knot and securing it with a heavy plastic clip. The thin towel made a weak toga as she padded back to her bedroom. After slipping into the faded blue cotton panties, she paused and looked at the white spandex slingshot in her hands. With a mischievous grin, she dug deep into the far corners of her underwear drawer. She rummaged and grasped through the bits of cotton undies and sports socks.

C'mon, it had to be here.

Finally, her fingers brushed against the elusive scraps of fabric. Success! She smiled as she emerged with the only sexy lingerie she owned. The black lace push-up bra and matching boy-cut panties looked perfectly naughty, even at rest. A few months ago, Daphne had tried to convince her that what made a woman sexy was lacy lingerie.

"But why, Daph? No one's going to see your underwear."

"Are you sure about that?" was her devilish response.

She slithered out of the blue briefs and pulled on the dark bits.

Crossing over to the full-length mirror attached to the closet door, she surveyed her newest fashion statement. Wow. The underwear fit differently than her normal briefs, riding lower on her hips and barely covering her ass. This would take some getting used to. As for the bra, that would also take a breaking-in period. The front latch added to the uplifting padded cups, giving her an actual hint of cleavage. Not too bad. She swiveled this way and that, examining her pale, svelte figure, taking in the stark contrast of her skin emerging from the tiny black coverings.

"Well, Jazzy, what do you think?" Turning one final time to end facing full front, she gave herself one last glance, this time with open and unflattering eyes. Upon her final viewing, she saw her hair tucked into a haphazard twist, her shoulders and hips suddenly looking too wide and her legs too short. The extreme padding still couldn't create enough cleavage worth anyone's notice, making her remember all those cruel jokes about her needing to borrow socks to fill out her dresses and the amount of makeup she'd need to even make a remarkable shadow between her breasts. The lethargic mewling response was all the answer she needed.

"You're right, this is ridiculous." As quick as a thought, she yanked the offending fabric off, only to replace them with the original cornflower-blue panties and the sports bra. Who was she trying to fool? As if she was ever going to see Kai again.

He was just being polite and making sure she didn't try to finish what she had started. He had probably already forgotten her name. She wouldn't think of him, wouldn't picture his disarming smile, and she definitely would not imagine those eerily piercing sea-green eyes. In fact, as of right now, she was going to stop thinking about him entirely.

Stiffening her spine with steady resolve, she strode back into the bathroom, intent on gathering up her discarded clothes. As she pulled them close to her chest, she was floored as a wave of a scent that was distinctly his assaulted her senses. She buried her nose deep within the pile, inhaling the memories of the previous night. Closing her eyes, she hoped—make that, prayed—he hadn't forgotten her.

The idea of putting the same outfit on again blinked through her mind, but personal hygiene won out over hormonal impulses, and into the wash basket they went. A slight chuckle escaped her lips as she donned her previously chosen ensemble. Had she really contemplated putting on clothes she'd sweated in and slept in, just because they smelled like him?

Yes, yes she had. Rolling her eyes at her own errant thoughts, she looked around her room, determining where to start. Her house, and in some ways, her life, was a blank slate, waiting for the right splash of color.

First of all, it was too quiet. As a dancer, music had always been such an important part of her life. It brought her the entire range of emotions without ever having to leave her home. And right now, she wanted it to be loud. Her mood was playful, energetic, and passionate. She had to have something to match that.

A couple quick bounds and she was in the living room, searching through boxes housing stacks of CDs. She'd been living here for almost a year and a half and still had things stored in their moving boxes. An odd feeling tugged at her, halting her hand. She opted to give her gut a try. Closing her eyes, she took a deep breath and reached into the box. Plastic cases clicked and clacked together as she sought the perfect music.

It was a game Voni used to play when she was bored. She would focus on her mood, or sometimes the mood she wanted to be in, and the right music would just find its way into her hand. She could even find things in other peoples' music collections. For some reason, it only worked with actual music. She tried her friend's iPod once and failed miserably. Her mood, as well as her focus, was dark and internal, and somehow when she stopped the scroll and hit Play, "Hooker with a Penis" by Tool screamed out of the speakers.

Like a penny arcade claw, she clamped down on what would be the exact album to get things started. Disc now in hand, she snapped open the jewel case without looking and deftly popped the shimmering silver disc into the small stereo unit. She pressed Play, listening as the disc whirled faster than her eye could track, and waited. In the back of her mind, she hoped she hadn't lost that rather unique skill.

Yes! Still got it! She mentally congratulated herself as the pulse-pounding electronic beats of DJ Tiësto's "Parade of the Athletes" filled the dead silence. Music was her bastion of energy, and the driving, synthesized melodies blasted away any lingering melancholy. Knowing that most of her neighbors would be at work, she slowly dialed the volume up, stopping once the windows rattled. She felt giddy, excited that her outlook on life wasn't doom and gloom for the first time in far too long. She sent a silent wave of gratitude to Kai, for if he hadn't been walking by... in the park at an ungodly hour.

Voni paused as her mind did quick calculations, reviewing the events. She was alone. She'd made sure. She remembered checking up and down the road, ensuring no one would have to witness her demise. No one was visible for blocks. So...what? He just flew? Appeared out of thin air? Beamed down to her?

Chiding herself for having an overactive imagination, she stood in the middle of the monochromatic nightmare than was her apartment. Where to start? Opting to put her creative mind to better use, she scanned the room and began to dream. In the empty corner, she pictured a black-lacquered corner curio, glass cubicles encasing colorful knickknacks. The walls were peppered with Art Deco prints. Ertés stood alongside her longed-for Bogey.

Her excitement grew as her gaze created a stylish, red-and-black Oriental-patterned couch to take the place of the current futon, its earthy Navajo knockoff design long faded and lost to time. Imaginary and intricate candle sconces brightened the hallway, and bookcases lined many of the walls.

It was time she lived, and she was actually looking forward to the experience.

An impatient meow near her knees gained her attention.

"Oh, I'm sorry, sweetie. Breakfast for you first." Stepping as quickly as possible while avoiding the cat winding between her legs, she poured kibble into the empty bowl near the fridge. A few strokes and a scratch on the head later, Jazz was content, and Voni returned to the living room.

"Time to get started."

Her first project was the box of CDs. After spilling the contents at her feet, she set about categorizing the discs. Two distinct piles formed; the keepers and the why-the-hell-do-I-still-have-this-crap?. She glanced around the room, in search of other things that fell into the second group. Beige throw pillows, tan and brown blankets, and ecru curtains found a new home in the discard heap.

The hypnotic, rhythmic pulse added a bounce to her step as she danced and spun through the small space, clearing away the drab and making space for the new. Room by room, she gathered together more fodder for the good-riddance stack. Clothes, sheets, even the shower curtain fell to the scythe of change.

Time blazed past in her flurry of activity. Jazz supervised for a while, finally letting himself out his pet door, leaving Voni to work uninterrupted. Each time the apartment became quiet, she headed over to the keepers pile, grabbed a new disc, popped it into place, and continued working. Electronica gave way to the alternative sounds of AFI, which melted into the pop melodies of Gwen Stefani, followed by New Wave '80s. Each new sound boosted her spirits, and soon, the daylight faded, leaving the apartment in the deepening colors of dusk.

Voni paused as she crawled over to turn on a lamp beside her bed. She brushed aside a few stray hairs as she spied the clock still remaining on the wall, shocked to see its white face revealed 7:45. A low grumbling sound echoed in the open space. What the hell? It took her a moment to discover the source of the noise. It was her stomach. Almost six straight hours of work and no break for food.

Okay, that's enough for now. Catlike, she stretched her body, easing out the kinks and knots that had surfaced in the wake her sudden burst of energy. The tightening in her gut, however, only seemed to increase the more she moved. Standing, she crossed into the kitchen to grab a water bottle off the counter. After finishing half the contents in one long gulp, she decided on her next course of action. A couple blocks away was a CD trade shop, which happened to be right next door to one of her favorite sushi restaurants.

Two birds with one stone. She walked into the bedroom closet and opted not to change. Her outfit was a little dusty, but she had plans to return to the trenches after her break, so why bother? She quickly brushed any lingering cat hairs and cobwebs off her shirt and pants before unclipping her hair. It fell in a thick, wavy mass, still slightly damp. She combed her fingers through, attempting to detangle it, then, quickly opting to return it to its earlier confinement, grabbed a pair of flat black suede boots. She liked her slightly trendy appearance and wondered if he would like how she looked. Smiling, she shook her head, amused at her own wishful thinking. She had chosen the boots in the hopes of running into him again.

Laughing, she yanked on the finishing touch to her fashion statement and pulled a plastic grocery bag out of the hanging sleeve of other plastic grocery bags After gathering up the bulk of the discarded discs and shoving them into the sack, she picked up her small backpack-style purse and headed for the door. With her keys in hand, bag slung over her shoulder, and the door all locked up, she started her short trek with a bounce in her stride.

SEVEN

Kai awoke with a start. Their connection was real. He had walked through her mind and was then forcibly yanked out of Voni's dream. He saw her still, plagued by demons of guilt and suffering, frozen in terror, held captive by images of unspeakable horror. Remembering the vivacious young beauty sitting across from him, he thought of no reason why she should warrant such nightly punishment. And, judging by her responses, it wasn't the first time she had endured those specters.

He concentrated on the last voice, the one he knew all too well. Konstantin. What the hell was he doing there? The strength and power of his foe's presence told Kai his enemy was deeply entrenched, wreaking havoc on the dreams of his spiritmate. But why?

And how did Konstantin know about her? Did he know something about the death of her fiancé? Jealousy kicked him hard in the gut as he thought of another man holding Voni. The longer he tried to sleep, the more his unanswered questions grew in number. What could she have done, his quiet, diminutive doll? What horrible crime had she committed to deserve such torment?

Sleep would not return, not until she was there, wrapped around his body, her smooth, soft skin gliding over the sweat-slicked sheets, back arched in ecstasy, lips slightly parted as he drove himself deeper inside her. Over and over, he claimed her in his mind. Again and again, he made love to her. But his dreams did not bring him the satisfaction he so desperately needed.

Groaning, he rolled over, only to stab his swollen cock against the mattress.

"Ah, fuck me."

"Not on your best day, boyo," came the melodic, lilting reply. "Wrong plumbing."

An articulate and eloquent flow of curses in Kai's native tongue spilled out as he struggled to focus my half-opened eyes on the whereabouts of his unwelcome visitor. Poised on the edge of the mahogany dresser, Eamon rested lazily, his spiky, short-cropped copper-and-auburn hair in fashionable disarray, piercing blue eyes framed by thick lashes. He perched one arm wrapped in black silk effortlessly on one bent, denim-encased knee, the long sleeves of the button-down shirt folded twice, and only twice.

"Ooh," he murmured, his easy smile twisting into a sharp smirk. "That didn't sound very nice."

"It wasn't," Kai growled, crawling begrudgingly out of his comfortable cocoon. "Not unless you're a fucking contortionist and into S&M." With his feet planted firmly on the floor, he rose with a fighter's grace, exposing his naked backside to Eamon as he crossed to the bathroom.

"What the fuck are you doing here?" he threw over his shoulder before slamming the bathroom door shut.

"Wow. Three fucks in less than two minutes, four if ya count the one I didn't understand," Eamon said, using humor as a tool against his out-of-character expletives. "And here I thought ya didn't care," he added, yelling through the dense wood.

Kai relieved himself, brushed his teeth, and splashed ice-cold water on his face. A second frigid blast helped to clear his mind but did nothing to release the tightness plaguing his groin. Deciding for a soak on a grander scale, he filled the sink to the brim and dunked his whole head this time, still to no avail. Toweling off his head, he combed back his unruly hair and grabbed the pair of black lounge pants from their hook behind the door.

"I just stopped by to make sure ya survived after disappearin' on me," his friend called out, the voice closer to the door than before. "So...how was your night?"

A lengthy sigh seeped through the door, speaking volumes to one who knew how to listen. Something told Eamon things were both good and bad and knowing Kai, it wouldn't be easy to find the whole story. They had been friends for centuries, and still there were many things Eamon did not know about him. Kai lived his life on a need-to-know basis. Eamon knew it was nothing personal; he simply did not open up. It was just his way.

When the door to his right swung open, Eamon waited for a renewed verbal attack. Instead, Kai stepped out, propped his arm against the doorframe, and dejectedly dropped his head onto his arm.

"I found her."

Shock widened Eamon's eyes as he replayed the words in his head. "Come again?"

Kai only shook his head, barking out a laugh. "I know. Hard to believe."

Eamon slowly peeled away from his perch, whistling low as he turned to stand face-to-face with his tortured friend. "You're serious? Just like that?"

"Just like that," he echoed. "But—" he paused, locking his friend's gaze "—that is not the bad news."

Eamon eased back a breath. "Didn't figure it was. So?"

"Konstantin."

"Fuck."

Kai barked a humorless laugh. "See my point?"

Eamon leaned back against the sturdy mahogany dresser. Yeah, he did. That bastard had been responsible for countless deaths and conflicts beyond number, his hands stained red with the blood of innocents around the world.

Whereas the Guardian Warriors fought to preserve life and to give freedom, the Rogue Warriors thrived on chaos and upheaval. Their influence, or push, shaped practically every major sociopolitical, and especially violent, movement throughout history. Kai recalled handed down tales of Rogues standing in the Senate as Caeser was slain and even murmurs that Hitler had been courted by the agents of chaos.

"So, what? Is there some connection between her and Konstantin? Do ya think he's marked her?"

Rage and jealousy oozed from his friend, his eyes darkening into pools of pale emerald fire as he curled his hands into tight fists, as if preparing for battle. Slowly, he blew out a hissed breath. Eamon watched as the muscles at the base of his neck uncoiled, the tension seeping out in a controlled stream.

"Truth is, I don't know," Kai answered, his voice belying his inner turmoil. He crossed to the dresser, yanked a black T-shirt on, and headed back toward the closet. "I felt her call last night, and somehow Konstantin is mixed up in it. He's stalking her, but I don't know why."

"And?"

Stilted silence was the only response Eamon would get. Close to the vest as ever. He would have to wait to find out more details about the events of last night. He gave Kai the distance he needed.

"My heart goes out to ya, boyo. What can I do to help?"

Stepping out of his silk pants before slipping into a pair of black jeans gave Kai time to ponder his response. What could his friend do? Research reasons why his arch nemesis had targeted his spiritmate? Find out who she really was? His mind whirled in circles as he snagged his black motorcycle boots and finally emerged fully clothed with his only logical reply.

"Not too sure about that one." He offered a tentative smile to his longtime friend. "But as soon as I think of something, you'll be the first to know." He grabbed his black leather jacket before heading down the hallway.

"What are ya plannin' on doin'?" he asked, following him down the stairs to end in the kitchen.

That Kai did know. "I'm planning on not letting her out of my sight."

Eamon whistled low. "Ya sure about this?" Kai responded with a raised eyebrow. "It might work better if ya had another someone followin' her, ya know. To keep her even safer, so to speak."

Kai let out a sharp laugh. "Not friggin' likely." He reached into the fridge, drew out two beers, and tossed one to Eamon without a backward glance. He'd catch it.

Eamon hadn't spilled a drop of alcohol in all the years he had known him. "One of the most heinous of all the deadly sins," he had called it once—alcohol abuse. The telltale *shhk* behind him confirmed his friend's adept coordination. Popping off the top of his own bottle, Kai downed it easily before slamming the empty container on the counter top—"dead soldiers" as they called them—echoing Eamon's hollow ring.

The small, sudden silence seeped into his body, eased along by the flow of Heineken. The wait only made him edgier. His desire to make sure she was safe grew stronger by the second. He'd made her a promise, and he had never once broken his word.

"I'm guessin' ya want be findin' her, then," Eamon interjected into the lingering quiet, apparently sensing Kai's agitation. Pushing away from the marbled counter, Eamon headed toward the front door. He paused as he reached the knob.

"Give a shout if ya be needin' anythin', Kai," he tossed over his shoulder, twisting the door open. "Ya don't have to be doin' everythin' by yourself, ya know." Eamon stepped into the cool evening air, glad it was Kai and not him in this fix.

"Good luck, boyo. I think you're gonna need it." His friend's final words whispered in his mind.

Kai nodded as he watched Eamon head out, wishing there was something his friend could do to aid him. Part of him wanted to call him back, offer some half-assed words of thanks. But the truth was he wouldn't be handling it alone. A crooked smile tilted his lips and gave him the shove he was looking for.

He delved inside himself, searching for the connective thread reaching out to her. His center, his soul. There she was, her dark hair tumbling about her porcelain face. She wandered through a small shop, walls adorned with racks and stacks of disc cases. Music store, most likely second hand, by the condition of many of the CDs. As Kai pulled back to gain perspective, the corner strip mall took shape and became more discernable. Street signs appeared, giving him the final puzzle piece. He had never been there, but he gleaned that it was a favorite place for her. She liked the sushi, especially the California rolls.

With his internal bearings homed in on the unique pattern of her thoughts, he grabbed the keys to the Mustang and headed to the garage. His instincts would lead the way tonight, and hopefully they would lead down a softer path.

The streetlights burned a hazy trail through the growing dark, and the temperate day gradually gave way to a cool evening. Traffic on Sixth Avenue led down toward the cozy Hillcrest coffee shops or away to trendy downtown bars. The blocks melted easily under her feet, and in short order she was standing in front of the counter at CD Merchant. Harsh, guttural thrash metal pounded throughout the cramped space. The heavily pierced and tattooed emo boy behind the cluttered service counter, Hank according to his nametag, tallied up her returns.

"Cash or store credit?" he asked, lisping slightly over the tongue stud.

"Um…" She hesitated. "Store credit, I guess." She did a quick mental count of her cash on hand and decided better safe than sorry. "No, wait. Cash, please."

Forty-seven dollars and eighty-six cents passed over the counter, and Voni turned toward the beckoning store. Tables and racks housed well-organized displays, music separated by genre then alphabetically within each style. She stood rooted for a moment, wondering where to begin. Alternative, with the As? Or World? Maybe somewhere in the middle?

Following some internal compulsion, she strolled down the first aisle, scanning the plastic cases, waiting for inspiration. A purple sleeve with silver lettering caught her attention. She reached for it, admiring its powerful simplicity. The cover was adorned with a winged skull intertwined with some string instrument, proclaiming *Apocalyptica* and *Worlds Collide*. Keeping it, she continued through the store, snatching up covers that caught her attention, many from bands she'd never heard of.

Soon, she had a modest amount of possibilities, ranging from Madonna's latest to the single sunflower-adorned cover of *Comalies* by a group called Lacuna Coil. Satisfied with her selections, she moved over to the listening station. The main reason she loved buying used CDs was getting the chance to give them a test drive before making the final decision.

After unfolding the case, Voni gently inserted the dark purple disc into the player and put on the headphones. Apocalyptica. Interesting name.

An idle thought crept through her mind—what kind of music did he like? Would he like this? She was surprised to discover the same little voice answer yes. She prepared herself, adjusted the volume, and pressed Play.

She thought she was ready, but the soul-wrenching symphony that poured out from the small speakers took her by surprise. Deep chords reverberated on large stringed instruments, creating haunting melodies and beautiful airs. She closed her eyes, allowing the music to seep into her spirit. It was soothing and energizing at the same time, calming and bold.

That was a definite keeper.

She listened a few minutes more, hoping this was not their only CD. The booklet inside gave the release date as 2007. Maybe it was their debut album. She would take another look, after one more song. She soaked in the harmonies, closing her eyes to take in note after note of each new phrase.

"Find something you like?"

The deep voice behind her caught her completely by surprise. She scrambled to pull the headphones off, catching her hair in her haste. Twisting around, she found herself facing his broad chest. She raised her eyes to come face-to-face with her late-night Samaritan.

Black fabric stretched taut against his sculpted chest, and one bronze arm braced on the wasll well above her head. The black T-shirt melted into black jeans, finishing in black boots. His hair, though partially slicked back, fell to tantalize her senses, enveloping her in his amber-and-musk scent, pure male and pure sex. His crooked smile brought out a devilish gleam in his ice-green eyes.

My own personal dark angel of mercy. Her tongue and her brain seemed to have a difference of opinion. While her mind fought to make some intelligent response, her tongue seemed only interested in resuming its unfinished battle with his and stumbled over the simplest sounds.

"Oh, wow. Um, hi. I mean," she stammered, fumbling with the bulky plastic headphones and the cord currently tangled in her hair. The more she tugged, the stronger the snare became. *Shit. Great, Voni. Just great! Can't you for once not make him think you're a complete clod?*

Her words rang through Kai's mind, filling his heart with emotions unfamiliar to him, compassion and sympathy. He smiled warmly as he slid His fingers into the thick curtain of dark chestnut softness, sifting through the silken strands to help loosen the offending cable. The scent of jasmine and lavender, laced with vanilla and spices, assaulted his senses, dizzying, intoxicating. He fought to keep his distance, to maintain his cool, when every fiber of his being screamed at him to kiss her. It would be so easy to dip his head, close the final distance, and claim her lips.

"Sorry, I did not mean to startle you," he said smoothly, his hand still buried in her tresses. The cord fell free, and he begrudgingly released the softness but not before he trailed his fingertips gently against her cheek. Not wanting to leave her, but knowing she needed a little space, he pulled back to his original resting place. "So, what are you listening to?"

"It's, ah, Apoca—a, something," she flustered, searching for the now-invisible case. "Where did that go? It was just—hang on." She turned abruptly to face him, stopping mid-search. "How did you know where to find me?"

He opened his mouth to respond, but a quick wave of her hand stopped him cold.

"Wait, never mind." she paused, looking up at him. "I guess last night really wasn't just a dream," she muttered. "Now, the real question is, why did you even want to find me?"

"I would think that would be the easier question," he replied, a devious smile curling his lips.

A sudden blush colored her cheeks. "Omigod, please, do not tell me I actually said that out loud?"

He smiled in reply. "You mean, did you ask why I wanted to find you?"

A frustrated groan escaped Voni's lips. "You know? I give up. I am cursed to say the wrong things whenever you're around. My mouth just won't listen to my brain, so I guess you'll just have to either deal with a blithering idiot, or you can cut your losses now and head for the door." She haphazardly shuffled the stacks of plastic, choosing the next selection. "I'd pick the latter, if I were you."

He tipped her chin up, pulling her attention away from the colorful squares to meet his gaze. He waited only a moment until her amber orbs found his, a reassuring smile growing as the seconds ticked by.

"Then I suppose we are both lucky that I am not you."

He stared deep into those warm, honey eyes, wishing he could drown there. She was exquisite, her ivory skin shimmering in contrast to her wavy, sable hair and brick-red casual shirt. The dark rings around her eyes had faded some since he'd last seen her. Her complexion, still fair and pale, shone from within, the once-veiled light now more apparent. Her appetizing lips, lush and full, parted ever so slightly, invited him, dared him, to take a satisfying sip. His self-control shivered, a tense bowstring stretched to its breaking point. Slow down. So much more was there, just beneath the surface. He had to take it slow, had to take time to discover how much more there was to his beautiful enigma.

"And," he added, "you still did not answer my question."

Her brows knit in a curiously puzzled expression.

"What are you listening to?" He released his tender hold, leaning back against the nearby shelves.

She relaxed a bit, a timid smile playing at the corners of her mouth as she rummaged for the hidden purple container. The elusive case peeked out, obscured by a bright-green flyer for Cane's previous month's concert list. She deftly snatched it and passed it to him.

"Apocalyptica." He gave an appreciative nod. She had excellent taste.

"Have you heard of them?" she asked, replacing the disc before popping open Madonna's *Hard Candy*. He chuckled inwardly. Maybe not that excellent.

"As a matter of fact, I caught their show a few years back. They are quite good."

"Really? Where did you see them?" Her eyes widened, excitement raising the pitch of her voice. "Wow! I just pulled the disc off the shelf on a whim. I mean, the color actually caught my eye first. Wait, you said years, right? So, they have more albums than this?" She turned to glance around the store, her gaze scanning the room before she bounded off on her search. "Now where did I find this?" she muttered half to herself.

There she was. The curious, animated woman he'd discovered in the café last night. The one brimming with life, and with passion. He was glad to see her again, and so shortly into their second meeting.

He followed her with rapt fascination as she flitted around the shelves, retracing her steps in hopes of discovering more music. The brick-red shirt hung loose on her slight frame, but he was more interested in the formfitting black leggings tucked in to a retro-chic pair of calf-high black boots. As she reached over a table, grabbing a top-shelf disc and perching up on her toes, the bottom edge of her shirt rode up, giving him a perfect view of her shapely legs leading to her equally shapely ass. It had that nice heart-shaped curve, the muscular dimples just begged to be touched and licked—curves he could imagine tracing with his hands, followed closely by his tongue.

A sharp twinge tightened his crotch, making him painfully aware of the price of his daydreaming. He tried to readjust, but his all-too-tight jeans made the problem worse. Well, at least he wasn't sporting a pup tent. Yet, even as physically uncomfortable as it was to watch her, the notion of not watching her tore at his soul. He had endured centuries of battle and warfare. He could wait as long as necessary to earn her trust and claim his prize. To alleviate some discomfort, he perused the scattered discs she had laid down earlier.

Voni moved from shelf to shelf, genre to genre, searching the spines. Apocalyptica. She found Apoptygma Berzerk—close, so she grabbed it—an album from AFI she didn't have, and a live recording of Evanescence. Reaching up for a bright-blue case that caught her eye, she snuck a sidelong glance at Kai. His hungry gaze slid over her, trailing heat down the length of her body. She stifled an urge to tug the hem of her shirt, suddenly wishing she had chosen to wear something different. Something…what? Sexier? No way. Not ready to go down that road. Plainer? Not too sure how to get much plainer than an oversized man's shirt and black leggings.

The more she thought about it, the more she realized her current attire was exactly the right thing to wear. Sad. Another look back, and he was flipping through her selections still needing to pass their audition. His midnight-black hair obscured his face as he studied an orange-jacketed Kitaro CD.

Even at rest, she sensed a wildness about him, a lethal current thrumming, barely contained by the form-hugging black materials. He was strong, powerful, and possibly even dangerous. Yet all she had seen was tenderness and affection.

She thought back at his reactions last night, during both her tirade and her episode. In her mind, he had an endless list of possible responses, ranging from boredom to anger to apathy. Instead, he was patient, kind, and understanding. But why? Who was he? And why was he so interested in her? New selections in hand, she returned to the magnificent mystery, determined to have some answers herself.

"Well," Voni started, adding the latest choices to the pile, "I couldn't find any others from them. Have you heard of these guys? Is it kinda similar?" She presented him with the blue-and-white disc marked *Apoptygma Berzerk*. "I mean, are they any good? If you know, that is. I grabbed it since the name was kinda the same, and I couldn't really remember the other group so—"

He laughed, the deep and sensual sound bubbled up and set her blood afire. A sudden blush colored her cheek. As if sensing her apprehension, he spoke quickly, his smile gentle.

"Are they similar? Ah no, not really. Whereas Apocalyptica falls more into the category of classical or even metal, this group"—he reached out to take the disc from her fingers, lightly trailing his touch against her hand—"is most definitely Goth or industrial. It depends on who you ask and which album you are talking about."

Her hand lingered on the disc, her skin still slightly tingling from his tender, electric touch. "Wow," she managed to croak out of her arid throat. "You sure know your music," she noted, carefully retracting her hand.

A Gallic shrug was his first response, one shoulder lifting lazily. "It is a way to pass the time."

"I see. So"—she fidgeted with the stacks of CDs—"are any of these any good? Well, you know, do you think that these—I mean, would you— Shit!" The last she whispered furiously, nearly spat out in frustration. She turned her gaze to meet him, locking him with a confused stare.

"What is it about you? I mean, ah…hell, I don't even know what I mean anymore." She dropped her gaze, pinching the bridge of her nose in a feeble attempt to clear her scattering thoughts. "I just feel like, like…"

"Siobhan, look at me." his whispered, his voice a silken compulsion she could not deny. When she opened her eyes, she hoped she hid the waves of uncertainty that churned in the dark corners of her mind. "Why do you war with yourself? You second-guess your own thoughts at every turn. Why?"

She hesitated. Her breath stilled in her lungs, waiting for its next order. Unable to find the right words, she meekly looked away from the unyielding force of his gaze.

"Voni, please." He stepped closer, sheltering her within the shadow of his body. His urge to touch, to taste, to wrap himself around her, was staggering. His arms shook as he fought to resist the temptation to stretch the distance between his body and hers.

"You can trust me." He remembered the softness of her skin, the way her lithe shape fit into his. The ache in his groin brought his current dilemma into sharp, if not painful, focus.

"I…I think I really could, and that scares me a little," she stammered quietly, her voice timid and unsure. With a huff, her words continued once again. "I don't know. I've never really felt like I'm good at communicating, and if I let my mouth alone, things start going badly. And…well, I don't really know you, but I feel that no matter what I say to you, no matter how crazy it may sound to me or anyone else, I feel like you won't…judge me."

She raised her eyes, her amber orbs pleading with him. "Sounds silly, huh? I mean, I just met you, what, a few hours ago? So," she paused, peering deep into his eyes. "Am I nuts or what?"

"Certifiable." His crooked half-smile was intended to completely disarm any further conflict in her.

"Thanks for the vote of confidence," she grumbled. Sarcasm colored her words, yet she was unable to keep the corners of her lips from forming a deliciously impish grin. Light laughter bubbled up in its wake, and he knew he had achieved some measure of success. The smirk still warmed her face as she turned her attention back to the music spread out in front of them.

"You did ask," he purred in her ear, his breath fanning her soft hair, the tendrils brushing against his lips.

Reaching out into her thoughts, he tuned in to her inner conflict, discerning her current battle. Her body had begun to relax, becoming more comfortable and confident with each new movement, yet he could sense her uncertainty. He would honor her desire to move more leisurely, or as much as his body, and hers, would let him.

"Yeah, yeah, yeah. All right then, Dr. Freud," she piped in, the hint of a smile continuing to skirt her words, drawing him back into the moment. "Which of these would you recommend?" She leaned back slightly, giving him a better view of discs from every genre. Resting a hand on her hip, she studied her selections intently, her brow furrowed in concentration.

Her arm brushed against his chest, her touch feather-light, but powerful and undeniable to Kai. Leaning in close, he inhaled her scent, pulling her as deep into him as was possible—while still being clothed, he thought, grimly aware of his need for the confining denim. He pictured her splayed beneath him, her alabaster skin silhouetted against his black silk sheets, her head thrown back in ecstasy, his hands caressing her glistening breasts as he plunged himself deep...

He ground his teeth, as he struggled to derail his pleasant train of thought and concentrate on even the simplest of tasks. The voice of his former teacher whispered in his memories. *The pull of your spiritmate will seem unbearable until you possess her. And once you have, you will find another as I found you. For the balance must always be maintained.*

The idea of finding another to take his place must now become his top priority. San Diego was a military town, so there would be an ample supply of soldiers. But he needed to find a warrior, one who stood for honor and fought to protect, not for a paycheck. That might take some serious looking. But, first things first. He gave himself a mental shake and made the best choice.

"I recommend we take the whole lot," he said, quickly scooping up the entire selection, then heading toward the checkout counter.

Voni jumped at his sudden haste and watched as he deftly swept up the scattered cases. She had been enjoying his closeness, the purely masculine aura that enveloped her. It made her feel alive. The fact she was feeling anything was a welcome experience. Her life had been a blur until last night.

"Whoa, wait!" she clamored, grasping frantically at his retreating form as he turned toward the cashier's counter. "I've only got enough cash to pick, like, four of them."

Kai flashed a disarming smile at her, his wallet already in his hands. "Then consider the rest my gift to you." Gently, he added, "Please, I insist."

"God, no. I can't let...I mean. You don't need... I don't suppose you'd take no for an answer, would you?" she asked, groaning heavily.

Even though they had just met, she already knew his response. She watched as the bills slipped from his strong hands to the waiting clerk. Smiling, she followed the nimble movement of his fingers as they danced atop the flecked black-painted counter, tapping out a staccato rhythm. Her mind wandered, filed with vivid images of those fingers dancing across her skin. Fire flushed her cheeks as her daydreaming took on more erotic tones. In her imagination, fingers became hands, and hands became limbs.

She hastily cleared her throat, hoping to disperse her errant thoughts. Attempting to distract herself, she glanced away from the counter. However, her gaze traveled to an even more dangerous destination. His eyes. She found herself falling into the pale green depths and actually wanted to drown there. Her mouth turned arid as heat rise to her cheeks and pool in her gut simultaneously.

"You'd say no to a gift?" he inquired, one brow arching gracefully.

"Well, no, but, I mean, if you put it that way," she murmured. A timid smile crept hesitantly across her features as she gnawed on her lower lip. "I suppose that would be rude."

"And we can't have that now, can we?" Kai's voice registered as barely more than a whisper. He reached out and brushed his rough knuckles against her jaw. "Society, as we know it, might collapse," he breathed, inching closer to her slightly parted lips.

Any witty response Voni might have made died on her lips the moment he kissed her. Lightning arched down the entire length of her body, trailing heat in her blood. Her legs buckled, threatening to drop her quite unceremoniously, before a band of corded muscle wrapped tight around her waist. The tender brush built to a delicious pressure, and her mouth opened, eager for more.

Kai growled deeply, his tongue dueling with hers, meeting passion for passion. His arm tightened protectively. Her petite form fit perfectly against his, proving to him she was indeed his mate, the missing piece of his broken soul. Heat poured off her in waves, threatening to ignite every scrap of his resolve, much less every fiber of his clothing. Grinding his hips possessively, he fought desperately not to obey the driving urge to lift the hem of her shirt over her head.

A noise over his shoulder caught his attention, a distant buzz at first, unintelligible and unremarkable. Moments passed, and the sound grew louder, clearer and more distinct. More customers had entered the store and were watching their not-so-private encounter with great interest.

"It seems we have an audience," Kai muttered, begrudgingly releasing her. He watched her reactions closely, wondering about the myriad of emotions that would play across her features.

"Hmm, what?" Voni tried to concentrate on the words. At first, she only realized their kiss had ended. As her gaze became more focused, and she remembered her surroundings, her earlier blush returned to her cheeks like fireworks on the Fourth of July.

"Omigod!" Her hands flew up to her cover her mouth, her cheeks, even her ears. She scrambled to conceal everything at once, trying to find a way to hide from her embarrassment. In her haste to retreat, she backed into banks of stereos and headphones. She quickly surveyed the store and found that many eyes still watched, some with admonishment, and some, especially those of the females, with a kind of catty jealousy.

She glared at him, meeting his Cheshire Cat grin. "What is it about you, Kai? Dammit." Her voice had risen in pitch but dropped in volume. She tried to step away, but found herself pinned between his rock-solid body and the listening counter. Leaning back, she steadied herself on the protruding shelf, not trusting her still-rubbery legs. "You've got me acting like a horny teenager. And I was never horny! Even when I was a teenager!"

Kai couldn't help but laugh. His pixie was full of such a wide range of emotions, and when all of them fired at once, it was quite a display. Her eyes flashed, their honey depths haloed by sparks of emerald. The radiant blush of her cheeks and the rich fullness of her kiss-swollen lips stood in bright contrast to her ivory complexion. And her hair; the waves of darkest chestnut tossed and bounced as if caught in a wind tunnel of her own making. She was truly the most beautiful woman he had ever seen. Her spirit, her fire, all of it combined with her exquisite features would never be rivaled by anyone in his eyes until the last breath left his dying body.

That realization struck a chord loud and clear for him, the sound so real he half turned to see if anyone else heard. She was his spiritmate. Now, he must convince her.

As her rant wound down, his couldn't stop the smile that pulled at the corners of his mouth, nor could he stop the warmth that fired his blood.

A telltale rumbling interrupted his musings. Glancing downward, she gave a sheepish smirk before she shushed her grumbling gut.

He blinked slowly, astonished by her strange response. Did she just try to silence her stomach? Laughter threatened to bubble up, and his halfhearted cough did little to hide his amusement.

"Where are my manners," he stated simply, the lingering smile still playing on his features. Snatching the bag from the clerk's hand, he offered his elbow. "Shall we get some dinner? It is quite obvious that you have yet to eat, and you cannot say that you are not hungry."

He shifted his gaze between the unvoiced refusal in her eyes and her complaining midriff, patiently waiting for her to accept his offer.

"No, I don't suppose I can," she acquiesced, hesitating a moment before looping her arm through his. "Aren't you getting tired of my weirdness yet?"

This time, Kai did not attempt to hide his mirth. "Weirdness? From you? Ah, my dear Siobhan, you are very far from bizarre, I can assure you of that." He ushered her outside, to meet the darkened evening sky. "Now, as the gentlemen you still think me to be, what can I tempt you with?" eyeing her hungrily. "For food, of course."

Voni rolled her eyes, scoffing at his overly obvious sexual innuendo. "Oh, puh-lease. You really think I'm going to buy that? I didn't think you were that desperate. And as for...dinner..." Her words continued to slow as she spied a car straight out of her dreams.

Whistling low, she unhooked herself and, as if possessed, wandered directly toward the velvety blue/black muscle car. Her hand moved of its own accord, stopping a breath away from the steel beast. The owner might not appreciate her drooling all over his baby.

Lacing her fingers behind her back, she circled the vehicle, admiring it from every possible angle and fighting every urge not to touch the shimmering midnight metal. "Wow," she breathed, the word laden with awe and admiration as she paused to peer through the driver's-side window to soak in the pristine interior.

"What?"

Voni never took her eyes of the beautiful piece of American automotive engineering. "I've dreamed about this car for as long as I can remember," she said, her voice barely more than a whisper. Taking a deep breath, she started her holy litany of the car currently within arm's reach of her. "1967 Ford GT350, otherwise known as the Shelby Cobra. High performance 289, V-8 engine, 715 Holley carburetor." She sighed, shielding her eyes to get a better view of the center console. "Four speed manual transmission with a Paxton supercharger." The building desire to stroke the vehicle became nearly overwhelming. The closest she had ever come to this car was a neighbor's beat-to-shit '68 soft top. But he had never taken any pride in it, so it sat, racing green becoming rusted orange, and the engine never purred.

Closing her eyes, she tried to imagine the throaty roar of the vehicle lying patiently before her. "The owner must take good care of her. But the paint job's new. The only color choices were racing green, mustang red, sapphire blue, black, or the standard white." She took a deep breath and opened her eyes to find Kai watching her with nothing short of astonished rapture.

"You know your cars, Voni."

"Nah, not really." Heat warmed her cheeks as she straightened up. Feeling suddenly very self-conscious, she smoothed a hand down her rather sloppy ensemble, giving the hem of her shirt a finishing tug. "I've just always liked muscle cars, especially this one. That's all."

"There you go, making light of yourself again." Kai closed the distance between them. "You can rattle off engine specs and give perfect details of a car you have never owned yourself. I know many car owners who don't know as much about their own vehicles. Perhaps the car's owner would let you take an inside look?"

Voni scoffed in disbelief. "Yeah, right. And maybe monkeys will fly out of my butt." She continued admiring the car when she caught him staring at her backside. "What are you doing?" she asked, looking behind her guiltily, thinking the owner was approaching them.

"Just checking for monkey tails."

A moment passed until realization poured over Voni like a bucket of ice water. "Yours? This is your car?" Her voice was both incredulous and exasperated. She gaped like a fish out of water as she scrambled for something intelligent to say.

"Yes," he answered calmly, resting a hip against the hood, arms folded casually across the broad expanse of his chest.

Imagine that. The car of her dreams belonged to the man of her fantasies. "So…do you just drive around in gorgeous cars rescuing damsels in distress, or do you have a regular day job?"

His smile tilted slightly. "Actually, you are my first, but I hear the pay is quite good."

Voni couldn't help but roll her eyes at the double entendre. "I won't bet the farm on that, killer." Another deep belly-grumbling interrupted her. "Um…sorry about that."

"Come, let's get you some dinner. Do you have any preferences?"

"Actually, I was just going to grab some sushi and head back home." Money had always been tight, so she had learned to indulge in little ways, switching between sushi and the occasional caramel macchiato. As she tallied her new cash balance, she figured she could even splurge and get an order of gyoza to accompany her usual vegetable tempura and California roll.

"Then sushi it is." He gestured toward a small storefront at the end of the strip mall announcing *sushi* in bright white letters. "I take it this would have been your first choice. Shall we, then?" Without a second thought, he unlocked the dark beast in front of her, placed the black plastic bag behind his seat, and resecured the door. He eased his massive frame up, extending her a gentlemanly arm.

Voni was beginning to enjoy this old world charm. It made her feel all warm and fuzzy inside, and more importantly, it made her feel special, unique, and important. As part of her continued to war against his kindness, another part, one whose timid whispers were gaining in strength, held a glimmer of hope that his was genuine.

EIGHT

They walked in silence toward the restaurant a few doors down from the music shop. She felt the piercing gaze of passing women. Their jealous eyes stripped her down to her bare self-esteem. Both her conscious and subconscious were in total agreement this time, and the decision was…hide. Since running behind a trashcan was quite out of the question, she opted to try to make herself invisible. He snaked an arm around her shoulders and tugged her in to the refuge of his body.

"Is something on your mind?" His smooth voice pulled her out of her brooding.

Her eyes drifted on their own accord, narrowing in the general direction of a cluster of giggling girls pointing and smiling directly at him. "No," she muttered. "Not really. Sorry." The warmth of his presence could not penetrate the shell of her self-doubt. She was making a mistake. She should just head home now. But somehow, she couldn't bring herself to pull out of his embrace. Turning around briskly, she half hoped he would release her and she could make her escape back to the solitude of her beige life.

She miscalculated. Her wriggling only managed to bury her deeper into the shelter of his powerful body. The solid, broad chest met her hands, her gaze locked onto the black wall of fabric before her. Bands of muscles wrapped her in a loose, yet unbreakable cage.

She pulled her eyes up to meet his penetrating gaze. Heat washed her features, but her overwhelming insecurity quickly extinguished any hope for intimacy. Unbidden tears pooled, threatening to overflow if she continued to gaze into his gorgeous face much longer.

"You know," he whispered, his breath creating soft ripples against her hair, "you're really not a very convincing liar."

She laughed in spite of herself. He was right. She knew it. Lying had never been one of her strong suits. She always believed anyone worth talking to was worthy of hearing the truth. She relaxed ever so slightly, melting into his embrace. "Yeah, well. Sorry." She sighed.

Kai had sensed a shift in the beauty standing next to him. Her response to his car left him speechless. Most of the women he entertained in the past had as much about cars as he did about *General Hospital*. Yet now, tension poured off her in waves, and her touch on his arm became hesitant and uncertain. Puzzled, he glanced down and found a different person by his side. The spontaneous car-enthusiast had been replaced by the frightened, timid child he had first discovered standing on that ledge.

His heart tightened while emotions long since buried flooded back as he watched the silent battle rage within the eyes of the beauty in his arms. He wound his arms around her, fitting her into him, and locking her firmly in place. He nestled his hands into the silken mass of her thick tresses, both taking and giving comfort. She was still so fragile, so unsure. It was going to take some time and lots of patience.

With a sigh, he gently brushed his lips against her hair, inhaling her exotic fragrance. Jasmine and spice assaulted his senses, driving him to the brink of self-control. The urge to claim her, then and there, threatened to consume him. Finally, the rational voice in his head broke through the haze, recalling him to his current situation and her skittish nature. He opted for temporary satisfaction, placing another chaste kiss atop her head before gently tilting her chin, his knuckles brushing along her jawline.

"There is nothing you have done for which you need to apologize." He spoke with undeniable conviction, his heart warming with an emotion he was still hesitant to name.

Voni gazed deeply into his piercing gray-green eyes. Something strong, something powerful and scary, dwelled there. A cautious voice told her she should run, should go back to her safe, albeit boring life. But the part that held on to hope knew he posed no physical threat to her. Emotional threat? Hell yes! That was a given, and it was now official. The longer she stared into his eyes, the more she truly believed there was no going back to her boring life. She had turned a corner into a new world, and things would never be the same again.

"You obviously don't know me very well." Her voice cracked the thick shell of silence surrounding them. "I'm sure I've done something wrong…or will do something soon."

"I hope to remedy the first," he said, a wicked, knowing grin lighting up his eyes. "And as for the second, I guess I'll just have to stick around you to witness this evil deed."

Voni dropped her forehead into his chest, lightly laughing. "You're incorrigible," she mumbled into his T-shirt. She took a deep breath, inhaling his purely masculine scent. It was heady and dark, whispering of danger and sensual promise. She could easily become intoxicated just being this near to him. She struggled to keep her arms under her own control, stopping them from doing a bit of possibly dangerous tactile wandering. A smile tugged on her lips as she considered the possibilities of exploring the taut muscles that waited just beneath the thin film of fabric.

Her pulse quickened, her breaths becoming shallower and more urgent as his hand found her chin and guided her eyes upward. Dipping his head down, he captured her lips, devouring her mouth as though she were the main course. He flicked his tongue across her lips, eager to sample the sweetness beyond. Her supple curves melted into his body, molding in perfect harmony with his massive frame.

"Incorrigible? Yes, I am." His lethal voice purred against her lips, raising goose bumps despite the heat of her skin. "And you are still hungry, if my memory serves me."

Voni realized her thoughts had been on everything but food just now. It took a few moments for her to regain her senses and take into account her current surroundings. She pinned him with a fierce glare as she disentangled herself from his hold.

With a smile, he tucked her under his arm as they took the final few steps toward the restaurant's front door. He pushed open the door and ushered her inside. Before she crossed the threshold, he laid the lightest touch on her shoulder. "Voni, do not be so hard on yourself. You have much to offer."

The slightest hint of a smile threatened to creep across her lips. "I just don't really get you. I mean, seriously. You've known me for, what? Not even a day? And you just look…" Shaking her head, she entered the brightly lit sushi bar. The counter was scattered with patrons, and several tables were populated with animated faces enjoying an early evening meal. A friendly waiter at the door greeted them, ushering them to a small open booth. Kai smiled easily as she sat, her legs folding under her, and still managing not to bump them against the bottom of the table. The waiter popped open their menus and they were left to their own devices.

Voni glanced at the menu, barely registering the words and images on the pages. She tried to remember the last time she'd eaten a meal with anyone, much less an escaped supermodel. She ventured a peek over the top of her menu to find him eying her with a hunger that had nothing to do with food. She dropped her gaze almost as quickly as the blush rose, painting her cheeks with a now-familiar heat.

Kai watched in silence, intrigued by her pendulum-like mood swings. One moment, her passion threatened to ignite them both, and the next, hesitation and timidity oozed from her entire core. Her most recently censored train of thought had him completely puzzled. Each time she edited her words, he tried to tap in to her thoughts, eager to know what she feared to say. Yet, in each instance, the remainder simply vanished. He would have to use a more direct approach to find out the mysterious ending.

"I have to ask," he started out innocently enough.

"Hmm?" She scanned the menu, overly intent, as if avoiding meeting his questioning gaze.

"Several times, you have begun a sentence but never quite finish your thought."

The laminated fold-up menu rose higher, and her face disappeared behind it.

Kai easily leaned across the table and toppled her flimsy barrier. "Voni?"

"Do I really need to spell it out?"

Silence was her only response. With a heavy sigh, she spoke clearly, though her eyes never reached his. "Kai, you are the most gorgeous man I have ever seen in my entire life, and I have no bloody idea why someone who looks like you would be even remotely interested in someone like me." Retrieving her menu, she kept her gaze downward. "There. Happy?"

88

The table shook gently, becoming more pronounced as the seconds ticked by. Curiosity got the better of her, and up her eyes traveled. The source of the tremors was Kai. His shoulders bounced as he struggled to contain his laughter.

"So glad I could amuse you," she voiced, sarcasm dripping from her words and pooling onto the black-lacquered tabletop.

"Siobhan Brigit Whelan," he said, as he reached out to caress her cheek. "To begin, every moment I spend with you makes me happy." He paused, measuring her initial reaction before continuing. "And if no one before me proved to you why you deserve the best of everything, then I truly apologize for that."

He traced the curve of her cheek with the pad of his thumb before traveling across the softness of her full lips. He held her gaze with the true conviction of his heart. "You are amazing, Voni. I hope to someday help you to see that."

"Are you ready to order?"

Without breaking eye contact, Kai rattled off a lengthy order, including miso soup, gyoza dumplings, and several different and delicious-sounding rolls, finishing off with both cold sake and hot tea. Menus disappeared and so did the unknown server. Time stilled as he studied the enigmatic beauty before him. Eyes like aged whiskey, sprinkled with emerald flecks in contrast to the brick red in her shirt. Skin like ivory, soft and smooth under his fingers. Strands of deep chestnut tumbled in barely confined waves, framing her delicate features. The loose-fitting garment belied the supple athletic build underneath.

And her scent. Pure heaven to him. An intoxicating blend of jasmine and spice, its heady aroma a rich perfume in which he wanted to lose himself forever. His mind spun images of his hands exploring the soft planes and curves of her body, his mouth trailing feather light kisses along the same path. In this latest fantasy, he heard her voice, breathy and strained, words indecipherable, but their meaning was clear. Her skin would be slick, beads of passion-induced sweat trailing down her back, between her small breasts and pooling in the hollow of her flat, toned stomach.

Voni watched raptly, her eyes not once leaving his. Behind those intriguingly gorgeous orbs of pale green, images flickered. She sensed bodies entangled, even heard the moans and sighs. Her breath caught, and her skin warmed at the visions swimming around in her mind.

"You're bound and determined to get me in trouble." Her voice was too airy, shaky, and thin. "Aren't you?"

"If by trouble, you mean wanting to hear you scream out my name in the throes of ecstasy? Then, yes."

She felt heat explode on her cheeks at lightning speed. "I can't believe...I mean..." Words tumbled out in bits and pieces. "We're in the middle of a public place, for heaven's sake!" Her urgent whisper hissed out between her clenched teeth.

"Okay, okay." He laughed lightly, hands thrown up in mock surrender. "I promise to play nice."

"Doubtful." She tried her best menacing stare, but he only smiled more. "But I guess it's a start."

A comfortable silence descended as their drinks and soups appeared.

"Why do you doubt yourself so much?"

His question hung in the air, a tangible presence between them. She had already spilled a lot of secrets to him. Why not add this little tidbit too? Shrugging, she studied her soup intently, analyzing the shape of each tofu square before it slid onto the spoon.

"I don't know. I guess it's because...ah hell. I don't really know. I just find myself second-guessing every decision I make, all the time. Do you want to hear something really lame?" She continued without waiting for his response. "It actually took me about fifteen minutes to pick out this lovely ensemble. Yup, this outfit was actually the act of a conscious effort. And even then, I still feel like I look like a total dork."

"Voni." His gentle voice broke into her babbling. "You look lovely as always." A quick gesture stopped her mid-fashion report. "You look comfortable, relaxed."

"Yeah, well. I've always kinda dressed to unimpress."

"So, let me make sure I have this." He leaned forward, filling both her teacup and the small thimble of sake. "You feel quite secure enough to wear whatever you like and then attack yourself for this...security?"

"Not exactly. I just..." She hesitated, opting for a sip of liquid courage before finishing her next statement. The coldness of the drink did nothing to quench the fire in her blood. If anything, it spurred it to greater heights. A few more cups might be dangerous.

She stared at her empty cup as the soup bowls vanished and were replaced by deliciously displayed trenchers of edible art. Shapes spun into spirals and snakes, punctuated with bright sauces and light pink and green blobs. She was fascinated by the presentation of most Asian cuisine, but sushi would always be her favorite. It almost seemed a shame to eat it and ruin the art created. The tantalizing blend of flavors, however, won over her need to maintain the pretty pictures.

"Yes?" His voice edged gently into her musings. "You just…"

"Have you ever just been okay at something? Wait. Don't answer that. I know the answer is no. I can see it in everything about you. Well, I used to think I was pretty good at things. Not spectacular, but good enough to get by. You know, I wasn't too bad at dancing. I mean, I was in a good company. No lead roles or anything, but I had a steady job. I even thought I didn't look half-bad. Not model looks, but pretty enough, I guess. I had James and he, well… Anyway, afterward, I mean, once he…" She sighed heavily, digging deep to find the strength to finish this line of thought. "Let's just say that more died that night than just my fiancé."

Voni raised her gaze to meet his, the edges of her smile drooped as she prepared to meet the pity she knew would be there.

She did not get what she was expecting.

Kai listened intently, absorbing the words spoken and unspoken. She was courageous and full of love. One moment, she had all the happiness she thought possible in. The next, all her life lay scattered like so many pieces of a broken dream, shards too small to ever make whole again. He knew Konstantin had some hand in this. He had told him as much with his sudden appearance and innate knowledge of her life. The Rogue Warrior fed on her nightmares and bred self-doubt, hoping to fuel her grief and push her into suicide. He had almost succeeded.

No more. No more would she be under his sick control.

"You asked me what I saw in you that would make me want to save you. Voni, you do have strength, the likes of which I've never truly seen. You are more beautiful than any supermodel, for your beauty is natural. It is a part of who you are, not something fabricated in a doctor's office. You have undergone one of the most devastating events imaginable, and yet you keep going."

"That wasn't the case last night."

"So you allowed yourself to give in to despair. That only proves that you're human." Her chin began to quiver, and his heart felt as if it were breaking. "I'm sorry, Voni. I didn't mean to push. Please, don't cry."

"N-now, I've got you apologizing," she choked out, caught halfway between a giggle and a sob. "It must be contagious."

"What say we find a topic that will stop both of us from apologizing?" The sincerity of his smile set her at ease. He gently brushed her cheek, chasing away any lingering unshed tears.

"That sounds like a plan to me," she agreed. "Plus, we don't want dinner to get...cold? Hot? Oh whatever. Let's just eat." One deep breath to help rein in her still-raw emotions and she was ready to take on the enormous spread before her.

"So, what are we eating, anyway?" She scanned the array of plates, only able to recognize a couple of items. "Not that I'm complaining. It all looks really good, but names would be nice." She deftly unwrapped the prepackaged chopsticks before rubbing them together to clean away any stray splinters.

He studied her every movement. Even the simple act of preparing chopsticks was splendidly choreographed, her fingers graceful and expressive as the thin wooden shafts danced between her palms. His mind strayed to how well she might handle other shafts as well. The heavy denim covering his cock sent an unnecessary and painful reminder. Shifting his weight did nothing to ease the discomfort, so he fought to keep his mind on dinner.

"Oh, a bit of this, a bit of that." He opened his chopsticks and plucked a plump dumpling off one of the many plates. With a wicked smile, he offered it to her. "Do you trust me?"

"That's a loaded question, Kai." She leaned in ever so slightly, her lips parting as she nibbled at the tender morsel. She flicked out her tongue over her bottom lip to catch a stray drop of sauce. "Mmm. Tasty."

She was going to be the death of him. He fixated on the glistening mouth and the enticing way her lips engulfed the lucky dumpling. He decided to let her feed herself; otherwise he'd castrate himself with his own jeans.

"Glad you approve," he murmured before turning his attention to serving up a selection to bite-sized rounds, some wrapped in green, others surrounded by white rice, and a few deep fried, tempura style.

Secretly, Voni had wished to try every roll on the menu, even the more bizarre-sounding ones. But, in the end, her budget only allowed the occasional treat, so she never indulged in more than one roll. This feast laid out before her was truly magnificent. And probably pretty expensive too.

Her thoughts drifted to his attire of last night, his car, and the ease with which he scooped up the large pile of music. Granted, it was a secondhand music store, but still. Everything about him screamed money. Hell, even his jeans didn't look as though they had even been worn, and his T-shirt probably hadn't seen the inside of a washing machine.

You already know how this ends, Voni. He is so out of your league. Her dark thoughts continued to bob to the surface, causing ripples of insecurity to dampen her mood.

"You spoke about your dancing," he remarked, his voice redirecting her wayward thoughts. "Exactly what kind of dancing do you prefer?"

Snatched a sizeable dab of wasabi, she shrugged as she set the green blob into the small white dish, added a few drops of soy sauce, and stirred the concoction. "Well, I do ballet, primarily classical *corps de ballet*, but we do a bit of contemporary ballet too."

Once the consistency was right, one step up from avocado-colored wallpaper paste, she daubed the roll, generously coating the small bite and popped it whole into her mouth. Without missing a beat, she grabbed another bite and repeated the process only to stop, wasabi-slathered roll inches away from her open mouth, when she felt his perplexed stare boring into her. "What?"

"Nothing. Isn't that hot?" His voice was a mixture of fascination and astonishment.

Voni laughed, an easy smile covering her face. "A bit. But that's what makes it so good. The spicier, the better."

"If that is the case, then why do you dance ballet?" Her quizzical expression spurred him on. "I would have pegged that kind of fire for something a bit more, more…sensual."

"Yeah. Well, I took a couple jazz classes years ago, but my ballet teacher at the time told me that jazz would only weaken my already imperfect technique. But"—her expression shifted smoothly, this one more whimsical than its predecessor—"I did have a lot of fun in those few classes."

"Have you ever considered a change in venue? Perhaps you have not been given lead dance roles because you're not in the right company?"

A breathy giggle snuck out between her lips. "Sorry, but you're beginning to sound like my neighbors. Daniel and Robert are always trying to get me to do some other kind of dancing, but their suggestions usually involve feathered boas and ass-breaking stiletto heels."

"Now that does paint a rather enticing picture." A devilish grin cracked across his face. "Perhaps I know someone who could help—"

"Just stop right there, bub. I sure as hell do not have the boobs, or the bod, for stripping, and if you even think—"

"I assure you," he interjected, laughing with hands raised, "that was not quite what I had in mind. I do know of someone who runs a studio not specializing in ballet." He paused, his gaze open and honest. "I could introduce you, if you'd like."

Voni pondered his offer, more seriously than she had thought she would. Something besides ballet? The possibility of not being in the background was tempting. Because of her physique, more sturdy than willowy, she was guaranteed minor roles only. She was good as a lift partner, had strong jumps, and her *petit allegro* work was always spot on. But Elspeth, the current prima in her company, had about three inches on Voni, and she had about ten pounds on Elspeth. Still, a new start…

The conversation reached a comfortable stopping point as they ate. Her companion stole sidelong glances at her as she sat lost in contemplation. He had planted the seed, and her musing continued to feed it. She did need to remember why she loved to dance, and maybe he had the right idea.

"You've grown rather quiet, Voni."

"Sorry. I just…I apologized again, didn't I?" She sheepishly looked up from her last bite of pickled ginger slathered in the leftover wasabi.

"It's all right. I forgive you for that one. I did catch you unaware."

"I couldn't eat another bite," she declared, setting down her chopsticks. "I can't remember the last time I ate so good."

"My pleasure." His gaze pinned her with the force of his desire. "At least, for now."

"God, is everything about sex with you?" Voni rolled her eyes at his blatant innuendo. His impish grin was answer enough. "I give up."

"I'd prefer if you gave in—"

"Anyway," she interjected as she glanced at her watch. "Wow, that day just flew by. I hope I didn't keep you from anything." She tried to hide her apprehension, as well as contain her excitement. The prospects of spending another evening with the most mysteriously sexy man on the planet definitely could be fun. Or life-threatening...again.

There were times when she hated the voices in her head. The efficiently silent waiter picked up their empty plates from the table and left the bill and two chocolates in their place.

"Keep me from something?" He arched an eyebrow as he contemplated his evening plans. Truth was, yesterday, he was sure Eamon would have dragged him off to the next nightclub, which would seem identical to the club from the previous night. Today, he couldn't imagine being anywhere else. Well, he could. The venue would be different, but the company would be the same.

"There was a society fundraiser I was supposed to attend."

"Oh," The edges of her smile drooped slightly. "'Kay, then. Well, I guess I should let you—"

"Would you like to come with me?"

"Me?" she squeaked. "In high society? Dressed like this?"

"I'll be dressed as I am," he countered, his tone straightforward and unapologetic.

"Yeah, but you make that look good." She held up a hand, stopping him mid-thought. "Besides, I don't think I'd do that good in that...setting."

"Voni," he said, sliding out of the booth as he reached for his wallet. He glanced down and dropped several bills on the table, leaving many more still available. He extended his hand in the now-familiar gesture. "I would be honored if you would accompany me to the Crown Point Benefit Gala this evening."

He studied her guarded expression, the disappearance of her lower lip a testament to her inner sparing match.

Wanting to make the decision fall in his favor, Kai added what he knew would clinch the deal. He leaned in close, breathed in deeply, inhaling her sweet fragrance, and whispered temptingly. "We'll have to take my car to get there, you know."

Voni's eyes narrowed as she arched her eyebrow. "You're evil, you know that, right?"

He feigned innocence, eyes wide and hand covering his heart, retreating slightly. "Me?"

Voni scooted out the booth, rising to stare menacingly into his chest. "Okay," she capitulated. "But only on one condition." She lifted her eyes to his. "I really don't do that well with highbrow people and—"

"The moment you feel uncomfortable, we'll leave." He trailed his hands lightly down the length of her arms before pulling her in close. "I promise," he added before placing a light kiss on the top of her head.

She pulled out of his enveloping embrace. "I must be out of my mind," she mumbled. She headed toward the door, sure he would be seconds behind her. "All right, we better do this thing now, before I come to my senses and run screaming from the building."

He chuckled at her false bravado, his deep, rumbling laugh following in her wake.

"What are you afraid of?" The mirth in his voice made her irrational fears seem even more ridiculous.

"Oh come on!" She twirled to face him, continuing her journey to the car backward. "Are you serious? Look what I am wearing! And you want to parade me around a bunch of tight ass society people? Who are going to be wearing…what? Something designed in Paris or Milan that cost more than I will ever make in my entire life? Wait a minute…what am I saying? Why am I even considering this? I mean, seriously…" Voni continued her rant, gesturing wildly as she paced the sidewalk, alternating closing and increasing the distance between her and the waiting chariot.

He stood in amazement at the explosive performance. Calmly, he folded his hands across the broad expanse of his chest, his smile growing in warmth. He listened to the ever-lengthening list of reasons not to attend ,and the laughter began to pour out of him, wave after wave.

"…And you want to put me—*me!*—in the middle of that…that, feeding frenzy! Nope, sorry. That's it." Voni slapped her hands together as her pacing wound down to stop directly in front of him. "I have reached my decision. You have a great time." She patted his chest before gripping his large biceps firmly. "I'm outta here." She turned on her heel and headed toward the street.

"Voni?"

One soft word stopped her in her tracks. Shoulders drooping, she spun to face him again, a sheepish grin creeping into being. "A little much?"

Two strides brought him into her personal space. Voni looked up to meet his heartfelt smile.

"Voni, *dragoste meu*, you worry needlessly." He trailed his fingers down her arm and brought her hand to his lips. "You will impress them as effortlessly as you have me." While holding her gaze, he brushed his lips across her knuckles before he flicked his hands and kissed the racing pulse at her wrist.

Heat met his lips, the blush of passion warming the smooth skin. "I, uh, I mean—"

"Are you ready?" he asked, stopping Voni mid-mumble.

She shrugged, trying to appear nonchalant. "Not really. Ah, hell. Why not."

Chuckling, Kai escorted her the final distance toward his car. "You stood without fear on the edge of the abyss, but you tremble at the thought of a social gathering."

"Yeah, well, that was different." Her voice thinned and she shrugged, embarrassed over the memory. "You were there to save me."

He opened her door with a gentlemanly flourish as he ushered her into the pristine interior. "And I will be with you tonight to save you again, if need be." *And tomorrow and after, until the end of days.* The words of the claiming ritual flooded into his mind, providing the final piece of evidence to him. She was his spiritmate, without a doubt.

Voni sank into the sleek, black leather seat, taking in the splendor of the metal beast. She clicked her seat belt into place as she sensed a hesitation in her companion and looked up at him. His face was still, his eyes unfocused, as if he had suddenly remembered a forgotten task. Then his features melted, the smile warm and passionate, and his eyes glowed as if from an unseen fire.

"Wow," air whooshed out of her lungs. "I'd love to know what you were thinking about just then."

Kai held the door a moment longer before securing it behind her. He rounded the back of the car and settled into the driver's seat wordlessly, his smile never faltering.

Voni watched, her eyes narrowing to suspicious slits, a slight smirk crossing her face. "Should I be afraid?"

"I have no idea what you're talking about," he said innocently, fastening his safety belt with one hand. Their gazes connected and he turned the key with a wink, unleashing the throaty V8 purr. His smile deepened as Voni's eyes widened in childlike excitement. The car rumbled as he smoothly shifted into gear, and soon, the strip mall was a distant speck in the rearview mirror.□

NINE

The drive sped by in a flurry of inquiries from Voni. Her working knowledge of the vehicle was impressive, but her desire to find out every tiny detail about this particular model was unquenchable. She fired questions at him at light speed. Her hands explored every reachable surface, with awed reverence.

Kai reached over to turn down the radio, quieting the vocals of Gavin Rossdale, while he marveled at the intricacies of her curiosity. No other woman had ever shown much interest in any of his vehicles, except perhaps the roominess of the backseat. Until now, he had found that particular position rather juvenile and always uncomfortable. Most carmakers did not take into account fitting a six-foot-six man lengthwise in the back. With her, however, he might be willing to make an exception. His imagination strayed, picturing her straddling his lap, her small, ripe breasts bared before him. Her hips grinding, driving him deeper into her welcoming warmth.

"Hey, you okay?"

Her voice broke into his dangerous daydream. He knew he was already slightly lightheaded due to the fact that most of his blood was trapped below the equator. But the last thing he needed to do was cause an accident while indulging in an erotic fantasy.

"Hmmm?" He tried to clear his head and focus on not smashing them into oncoming traffic. These continued lapses could prove fatal if he wasn't more careful.

"The previous owner must have really taken great care of this car. You sure lucked out on that one. How many miles did it have on it when you bought it?"

He chuckled at the thought. Previous owner. He was the car's only owner. He'd bought it straight from the factory, made to his specifications, down to the nonstandard paint job. He wanted a one-of-a-kind and since he had donated a healthy sum to support Carroll Shelby's dream, he was granted his wish.

"Yes. Very lucky indeed. Ah," he deftly changed subjects, "here we are."

Voni had been so entranced by the reality of her dream car she hadn't paid any attention to the car's destination. Now, as she looked beyond the chrome-and-leather interior, she gaped at the expansive mansion coming into view. Stark white stucco curved for miles, illuminated by massive floodlights and decorated by impeccably trimmed giant palms. The flagstone drive looked more like a showroom floor. She spied Jaguars, a couple Rolls Royces, a Maybach or two peppered in among the limousines, Beamers, and Porsches.

Her jaw dropped as women clad in gowns straight from the Paris runway sauntered by, jewels dripping from necks, ears, fingers, wrists, and even the occasional ankle. Tall. Elegant. And blonde, she thought begrudgingly. Another peek and she did spy other hair colors, all of them showroom-spangling and perfectly coiffed. Shrinking back into the seat, she hoped the car would sense her fear and swallow her whole. "I must be outta my mind..."

As he pulled around to the front of the house, he gently touched her thoughts and found a sea of turmoil and apprehension. He choked down an incriminating chuckle as she prayed for solace from the enveloping leather. He traced his fingers along her jaw, turning her downcast eyes to meet his.

"You have nothing to fear in there, Voni. If you would like to leave now—"

"No." A firm response and a deep breath. "No, I'm tired of living my life being afraid. I can't even remember much of the last year because I was afraid of, damn, everything, I guess." She squared her shoulders, as if preparing for battle. "I can do this."

He couldn't have wished for a more amazing woman with whom to spend the rest of his life. A warm smile, fueled by a feeling much stronger, spilled across his face, and he leaned in to place a tender kiss on her soft lips.

"Yes," he whispered, his breath warm against her lips. "I believe you can."

Voni watched as he closed the distance between them, his lips strong yet undemanding. The kiss was brief, designed to assure rather than allure. She felt empowered, ready to face what lay beyond the security of the vehicle.

He moved away from her as a valet in a bright green polo shirt jogged to his door. A man in a matching shirt was visible on the passenger side as well, and both doors opened simultaneously. He disengaged both seat belts before gracefully unfolding himself from the dark confines of the car. He shot the young valet a scathing glare as he tried to assist Voni from the car. The frightened boy stumbled away from the door, rushing a bit too eagerly toward the next luxury sedan in line.

Once she had contained her giggle fit after witnessing his possessive display, she carefully dusted off her wardrobe, trying to magically alter her outfit to something more suitable to the occasion. After three passes, she gave up and stepped out, only to run smack into a sea of black fabric.

"Geez! Would you stop doing that?" she sputtered.

"Doing what?"

"Being so damned polite," she replied. "I can get out of a car all by myself, you know."

Her response baffled him completely. "You're offended?"

That took the wind out of her sails in a heartbeat. "No, it's not that. It's just that, well, to be honest, no one's ever been this formal with me before," she confided timidly. "It's all kinda new to me, I guess."

"Then you had best prepare yourself for the be-all and end-all of formalities." He took her arm, guiding her toward the entry. Leaning down, he whispered hotly, "Siobhan, I present to you the Silver Spoon Set."

"Are you sure you don't mean the Lifestyles of the Rich and Shameless?" she mumbled uncomfortably. The air around her grew unseasonably and impossibly cold. Tugging at her collar, she again seriously questioned her sanity.

With a warm laugh, he tipped his head in agreement. "Touché."

The looks they garnered ranged from snide disregard to blatant hostility. Among the ocean of silks and spangles, they stood out like a beacon in the dark. The hushed whispers grew in waves in their wake. Needing some strength, she glanced up at the mountain beside her.

Kai seemed perfectly content, even at home in this unfriendly environment. Of course, he was relaxed. He was gorgeous, no matter what he wore. Not wanting to give in to her dark mood, she took her lead from him, sighing as she raised her chin a fraction of an inch and walked silently next to him up the steps.

The short incline gave way to a sizeable foyer, scattered with more of the beautiful people she had seen outside. After a brief survey, she began to realize that, although the dresses were varied and chic, the women ran together. They were unremarkable in their attempt to stand out. But they were all still what the world considered to be the definition of beautiful.

The theory intrigued her, so she studied the men as well, wanting to test her hypothesis. Again, she found cookie-cutter, *haute couture* looks on the young men as well as the older set.

"Is this real?" Kai's puzzled expression gave her the courage to finish her thought. "I mean, seriously. All the people look like carbon copies from every high-fashion magazine I've ever seen."

"I am sorry." He truly looked ashamed. "If you would like to leave—"

"No," She shook her head slowly as her gaze pivoted around. "Are you kidding me? I have to see if it's the same inside as it is out here."

"You mean, you wish to stay?" The clear hesitation at this unexpected one hundred eighty degree turnabout had him cautious. "You are certain?"

"Heck, yeah!" She faced him, an open smile warm across her face . "I have a little theory I need to check out."

"Well, anything to satisfy scientific curiosity, I suppose."

They continued until they were stopped by the doorman who looked like an escapee from the latest WWE tournament. Voni stifled an improper giggle as the no-necked wall of a tuxedo-clad barbarian raised a hand to stop them, his bald pate gleaming in the incandescence.

"Name?"

As he raised his head, she spied the expected moustache and goatee, not to mention the attempted evil eye. Oh, puh-lease. Her cat looked fiercer than he ever would. She peeked around the man, eager to see more.

"Vadim. Malakai Gregori—"

"Malakai, you made it!"

Voni turned to see a modestly dressed woman approaching with long strides, her stiletto heels clacking along the flagstones. Her high-waist, black palazzo pants added to her long, lean legs, making Voni feel like a stump. The flowing white blouse and short black suspenders reminded her of some golden-age starlet, like a young Katherine Hepburn. Her ash-blonde hair was even coiffed into stylish finger waves, complimenting her retro-chic attire.

"Allison." Kai released her arm to greet who she assumed was the hostess, or at least the house's owner. She stood by as Allison pulled him in for an all-too-familiar embrace, before she placed two kisses on his cheeks.

"It's good to see you."

The slight spark of jealousy surprised her. She surely had no reason to be possessive of him. But the level of intimacy assumed by the other woman was starting to get on her nerves.

"Allison, I would like you to meet Siobhan Whelan." His formal introduction snapped her back to reality, as did his hand on the small of her back. She stood, dumbfounded. He had said her full name. No one, not even James, had ever introduced her by Siobhan. She enjoyed her nickname, but since it was hers, she preferred to choose who had the right to use it.

"Hi, Siobhan." She flashed a practiced smile before drawing her into a sophisticated example of a hug, barely more than a shoulder tap in close proximity. "I'm Allison Hardinbrook."

"Hey. This place is pretty amazing. Is it yours?" Voni cringed inwardly. Great, Von. Real smooth. Way to sound like a complete moron.

Allison gave her a smile most people reserved for small children or blithering idiots. "Hardinbrook Hall has been in the family for years." Introductions and socially acceptable small talk over, she was dismissed as Allison returned her attentions to Kai.

Clinging to his arm, Allison escorted them past the bouncer, who was still attempting to glare daggers at them. "We were all hoping you'd make an appearance. Your presence does tend to shed a bit of excitement onto these ghastly affairs." Her cultured voice spoke of an expensive education and summers in Europe. Voni was familiar with that tone. Many of her fellow dancers had that affectation in their voices as well. It implied that somehow, because of monetary circumstance, they were better than she was.

"We?" Voni spoke up, hoping her voice didn't sound as nauseated as she was beginning to feel.

Together they languidly ambled into the heart of the event. Voni kept a step behind the two, wanting to both disappear into the landscape and tear Allison's arm off at the same time. Geez, get a grip. They obviously knew each other, and it wasn't as if she owned him or anything. But the nagging, green-eyed monster still gnawed at her gut.

Allison laughed, the sound forced and unnatural. Voni rolled her eyes, shaking her head in disbelief. Looking away from the embarrassing show, she set her mind to admiring the house's architecture, open curved archways, and breezy sheltered walkways.

Since she hadn't seen the road they'd taken, she could only assume something this opulent would be in La Jolla. The drive time felt right. They weren't in the car long enough to be in Rancho Bernardo. Unless… Nah. Well…maybe. She was pretty sure the car could to 100 mph plus and not feel as though it was going to rattle apart. Unlike her little 1962 Fiat, which began to thrash about at 60 mph. She really missed that bucket of bolts.

"Why, all of us, of course. Eamon arrived about an hour ago, and I must admit…" she leaned in, too close for Voni's taste. She pawed at his arms and his chest. "…I was on pins and needles when he said he didn't know where you were."

Wow. Voni was surprised the hostess with the mostest didn't just drop down on her knees right here. The uncharacteristic catty thought sprung up fast, stunning her into silence.

"Let's just say I had something better to do with my time today." His words drew her gaze away from the shimmering, treble-clef ice structure. Voni's eyes flickered between Kai's fathomless ice-green depths and Allison's annoyed blue orbs. His warm smile slid easily in place, and he reached for her, pulling her closer to his side.

Woohoo! Point for Voni! Her inner child had begun keeping a tally since she had first entered and was pleased to finally have a number in her column.

Kai felt her tense and relax several times during their short stroll. While Allison prattled on, his attention had been on Voni. Her thoughts flowed in highs and lows, ebbing like the tide. One moment she was completely captivated by the stylish room design; the next, she was fighting a wave of jealousy aimed directly at Allison. The mere thought that she felt possessive of him was almost enough to send him over the edge.

Allison's expression soured as she spied the gleam in Kai's eyes that was not centered on her. "Well," she piped in, "I do have other guests to attend to, darling." She took a half step away, reluctant to release her hold on his arm. Leaning in a final time, she whispered breathily into his ear, brushing her full and very expensive breasts, against his arm. "Call me later. I'm sure I can help if you don't have anything better to do." She flashed a flat smirk to Voni and made her exit.

Kai shook his head with a weary sigh, unruffled by the overt sexual attack. "Some things never change," he muttered, half aloud and half to himself. He returned his attention to a more suitable candidate for his sensual energy, and found her staring inquisitively up at him.

"So, what you're saying is that she's always been all over you like white on rice? Wow, that was, um…sorry."

Her unclouded and uncensored observation was a breath of fresh air.

"Don't be. You are quite astute, *dragoste meu*. Men aren't the only ones who cannot take no for an answer at times."

"I guess you're right." That was the second time tonight he'd used that weird phrase. At least it sounded kinda nice. "So, what is this all for anyway?"

"This is the annual fundraiser for the La Jolla Chamber Orchestra."

As they continued to walk through the opulent breezeway, making their way to the open bar, Kai was greeted by several more guests, all clad in the latest fineries. As he introduced her to the flowing sea of perfect faces, she realized this would never be her world.

Most of the responses to their odd pairing fit into two categories. The well-dressed men tried to impress Kai with their various bits of investment information. They spoke of health clubs and team sports, all of them commenting on his physique the way men could.

The bejeweled women…well, that was a bit more tedious. All felt the need to touch him somehow. A light brush on the arm here, a peck on the cheek there. Most ignored her completely, while the rest regarded her with mild amusement or open disdain, with only the older set speaking to her as a person and not an object. One woman even had the gall to ask why he'd brought his little sister along. A gentle directional nudge saved all of them from an even more embarrassing encounter. Wave after wave of fake friends approached them, eager to bask in the glow of the ones who didn't fit in.

After the most recent scoop-backed dress sashayed away, Voni believed her membership as a card-carrying female was in serious jeopardy of being revoked. Each new socialite took a chunk out of her rapidly diminishing self-confidence as they passed. She had, however, gathered quite enough data to prove her hypothesis. They were for real, and they would never welcome her into their club. Luckily, that knowledge reached her the same time she and Kai reached the bar.

"I need a drink." Grumbling, she climbed onto the open high stool as Kai leaned his back against the solid counter to contemplate the open night sky. She plopped her arm onto the wooden bar top and sank her head into the pillowed confines of her sleeve.

"Was it truly that painful?"

"No, it was great." The sarcasm dripped heavily, filtering through the thin fabric. "I'll be sure to put this on my calendar for next year, in case my ego needs another reality check." Dejected, she slumped down even farther.

"You were wonderful, and I believe you have definitely earned a couple drinks after running that gauntlet." Kai's voice sounded a bit strained, the event having taking an unexpected toll on him. Normally, he didn't find these functions tiresome. But the longer he listened to the inane babblings, the more he wished to be completely alone with the unique beauty by his side. Never would she dote on the latest designers or compare Jimmy Choos to Pradas.

During the entire ordeal, she smiled and spoke simply and directly, her words fresh and intriguing. She was more than polite to the women, except for the one who thought her to be his sister. Although, to be honest, he would have liked to see her take Claire down a peg or two. Most of the ladies here were nothing more than trophies, pretty baubles for the men to hang on their arms at just these kinds of events. He could never imagine having a decent conversation with any of them.

He shifted his gaze back at the petite pixie seated next to him. Her chocolate tresses fell in scattered disarray against the ashen wood and the deep red of her top, shining like forbidden velvet, eager for his touch. As he turned back to face the bar, he recognized the bartender from one of a dozen similar functions and signaled for two drinks, hoping the man remembered his preferences. Unable, or unwilling, to stop, he reached out to capture a lock of her smooth hair and twirled it idly between his fingers, allowing its softness to penetrate, to soothe his soul.

"So tell me," she mumbled into the crook of her arm. "Are these things always this bad?" Tilting her head to rest her chin on her elbow, she pinned him with an innocently pleading look.

Kai mulled the question over and over in his mind. He recalled when he'd looked forward to the annual galas. There was a time when he fed on the "pomp and circumstance," as Eamon called it on several occasions. The formality, the established order.

He thrived on these canons, reminding him of days long past when people did stand on ceremony. A time when the chivalrous acts so foreign to Voni would have been the expected norm. He knew his lines, acting his part impeccably. His suits were pressed, his hair flawless, both his car and his shoes were polished to a gleam, and his smile stayed firmly locked in place as he rubbed elbows with all the well-to-dos.

Tonight, however, was different, and now, these pageants would never be the same.

For the first time, he stood on the outside of the establishment, his attire unadorned. Even his hair was quite shabby at present. For the first time, he listened, truly listened, to the babbled conversations. He found himself cringing at the superficial language that passed as dialogue. The fake smiles, the forced camaraderie. It was all a façade. Nothing was real.

Nothing, except the exquisite female at his side. In her demure outfit, she outshone every besparkled and bespangled woman this evening. Her gentle grace and natural, unassuming beauty humbled him and brought the evening's festivities into a different perspective. He thought the gala would be a way to end the night on a high note. Only then did he realize the secondhand music store and dinner had been much more fulfilling.

Voni watched as volumes of unspoken thoughts played across his face and behind his mesmerizing eyes. She couldn't read most of them, and she chalked it up to mental overload. Far too many people to have met in such a short amount of time. Just for fun, she tried to calculate the amount of money in dresses, jewelry, and shoes. But after the first few women walked past wearing what had to be enough to finance a small country for the next ten years, she gave up.

"Bad? You mean these black-tie affairs? I would like to answer honestly," he started warmly, clinking two glasses down between them. "But I fear it would only scare you."

"You mean," she stammered, misinterpreting his cryptic words, "they're usually worse?"

An easy, reassuring smile played across his face. "Before tonight, can you believe I actually enjoyed these things?"

She rested her chin in her open palm. "What changed?"

His smile deepened, sparkling his gray-green eyes as he leaned in, shortening the distance between them to a mere whisper. "I met someone who showed me what is really important in life."

Voni sat speechless, her heart lodged in her throat. His breath warmed her lips in sweet promise. Her eyelid fluttered, half open. Their lips were a fraction apart.

"I'm not interrupting anythin', am I?"

A low growl slipped between Kai's clenched teeth.

Voni smiled slyly. "Friend of yours?"

Kai squeezed his eyes shut as he gave a slow shake of his head. "At times, I do wonder," he muttered, his words hot against her lips. He took a deep breath. "Your timing is for shit, you know that, Eamon?" He gave her a mischievous wink, accompanied by a crooked grin meant just for her before he turned to greet his compatriot.

Eamon was dressed in his normal regalia, a crisp all-black mandarin-collared. Ferragamo tuxedo, spit-shined Bruno Magli oxfords, and his hair smartly slicked back. In the past, the two would have appeared to be brothers, fitting nicely within the world of the paparazzi puzzle. Even now, the cameras snapped and flashed, hoping to catch a candid of the dashing pair worth a few bucks from *Esquire* or the like. Despite his earlier displeasure, Kai embraced the man in open friendship.

"Heard that ya'd finally arrived, so I went looking for ya." Kai shook his head as Eamon flashed an easy smile at him. "And it's nice to see that ya dressed up for the occasion."

Voni smiled at the easy interplay between the two men as she settled back into the tall stool. Both men stood eye-to-eye with each other, each a mouth-watering specimen of masculinity. Yet, while this newcomer's bright blue eyes seemed to radiate humor and lightheartedness, Kai's moody green orbs pulsed with a predatory aura, lethal and ready to strike. They were opposite sides of the same coin; alike in their appearance, yet their temperaments polarized the pair.

Watching their banter reminded her of her big brothers and their friends after one of her performances. She would drag Eric and Calvin to every one of her recitals, and they would feel the need to bring their own personal entourage to keep them company while she performed. As they all left, she would watch as they created their own version of the evening's choreography. Their interpretations never ceased to make her smile.

When it was clear to that dance was her passion, her parents sent her to live with her aunt in to continue her training, as well as her education from fourteen on, while the rest of her family moved away, choosing a lucrative ranch in Montana over an overpriced condo in Pacific Beach. She had only seen them three times since then, all the visits squeezed in between hectic rehearsal and performance schedules.

"And who is this?" The lilting brogue took on a sensual tone as the playful blue eyes settled on her.

"Back off, *fratele*." The smile in Kai's lips belied the steel in his voice. A fierce protective streak had been growing and expanding during the course of the evening. While Voni had been preoccupied with the pencil-thin dolls in their expensive dresses, she was unaware of the heated looks from every man in the room. Their sly, sidelong glances caused the hair on his neck to stand on end. And that did not include the jealous stares from the women who had long begged for his affections.

Eamon's light laugh set his mind at ease. "*Reilig, bráthair.* I rather like my head attached to the rest of me, if it's all the same to ya." He slapped Kai cordially on the back.

"Keep your eyes in their sockets and your hands in your pockets," Kai added, grinning evilly. "And I'll see what I can do. This," he said, turning to place his back against the bar and one arm possessively over her shoulder, "is Siobhan. Siobhan, I'd like to introduce—"

"Éamon Alasdair Pádraig McClearon," his lilting voice tumbled out his full name with practiced precision. "At your service," he added, inclining his head toward her.

"Wow. That's quite a mouthful, and no comments from the peanut gallery about 'that's what she said.'" She extended her hand to him amid their rolling laughter. "And you can call me Voni."

"Voni it is," he replied, taking her hand and brushing his lips across her knuckles. The mischievous smile crinkled the corners of his eyes as his friend growled a warning. "And, if ya don't mind, I need to be borrowin' Kai for a couple minutes."

Kai looked quizzically at Eamon then back at Voni with the same hesitation. "What about?"

"Sure, no problem," she said. "I'll just hang here, finish my drink." He looked reluctant, so Voni reached out to touch his arm gently. "I'm a big kid. Really, I'll be fine."

She swung her legs around so she could better gaze at the room as Eamon led Kai to a more secluded corner of the wide open space. As she reached for the slender glass, she took a cautious sniff before taking touching her lips to the contents. Hints of lime and mint made her mouth water, and she decided to take a chance.

It was cooling, quenching and sweet on her tongue. The ice tinkled against the glass. Swallowing deeply, she felt the warming aftereffects of the liberal dose of what reminded her of rum.

"Do you like the *caipirinha*?"

She glanced behind her to see a darkly tanned barkeep patiently awaiting her review.

"This is great. What did you say it was again?"

"It's a *caipirinha*. Think of it as a Brazilian *mojito*." With a happy smile, he went back to cleaning the glasswear. "Let me know if you need a refill, *mija*."

Relaxing a bit, she continued to sip at her drink, enjoying the exotic cocktail. As she turned back to watch the sea of satins and silks, an unexpected, yet recognizable sound made her cringe.

"Oh. My. God."

With a heavy sigh, Voni rounded to find Elspeth Courrington in all her slender glory striding up to the bar, her designer blue-sequined dress draping her tanned, willowy limbs, off-setting her clear, blue eyes and perfectly coifed blonde hair. In her wake was the house's owner, Allison. Their long legs ate up the distance toward the bar and her only place of solace.

Fan-fucking-tastic. She steeled herself for combat. She knew Elspeth, knew her dislike of most of the corps dancers, but she especially knew of Elspeth's intense hatred of her personally.

"Elspeth," she said, hoping to keep the tone light and praying, borderline screaming, for someone to save her. Where was Kai when she needed him?

"Well, well, well. What brings you here, Voni?" The venom that dripped from her perfectly tinted lips threatened to burn through the fine cherry wood floors.

Allison chimed in, feigned innocence glossing across her face. "You two know each other?"

"She dances in the ensemble of my company. Well, if you could call it dancing." Her mouth twisted into a cruel sneer as she laughed through the barbs.

Her company? Egotistical bitch. Voni's gaze drifted to the alcove caught in deep shadow. It looked as though she would have to handle this confrontation alone. The mindless tittering of forced laughter dragged her attention back to the pair of cruel beauties before her.

"I'm here with a friend, Ellie." She smiled pleasantly, using the nickname she knew grated on her nerves. *Tit for tat, you cow.* Voni chose who could use her nickname, and she never considered Elspeth that much of a friend.

Bingo! She watched Elspeth's face curl in disdain.

"A friend? You have a friend who would run in these circles?" She placed a well-manicured hand against her chest, laughing openly. "I find that hard to believe."

"She's the one who arrived with Malakai," Allison said, her voice thick with knowing accusation. Heads turned their direction, and in a blink, the bar became a popular destination for several socialites.

It just kept getting better.

Kai followed his friend, not wishing to leave Voni. She put up a good façade, but he knew that was exactly what it was. For the past hour, he'd sensed the turbulence of her emotions, most of which tended to slip into rather dark territory. Little did she realize that, in his eyes, her modest attire made her look more beautiful than any of the scantily clad toothpicks present.

Once away from prying ears, Eamon pulled Kai into a rough hold.

"My God, man, but she's amazin'. Does she have a sister?"

Kai pushed him away, annoyed. "Do you mean to tell me you dragged me away to just—"

Eamon's laughing demeanor vanished as if an iron door had slammed shut. "No. There is some serious shit coming down the pike. Ya been noticin' the increase in random violence. Well, word is the Rogues have somethin' planned, but no one seems to have any more information than that."

"You sure? I mean, is it isolated here, or is this happening everywhere else?" Kai's thoughts tumbled as he mulled over the horrific possibilities of another Rogue infiltration.

Every major conflict in recorded, and unrecorded, history was the work of one or more of the Guardians' antitheses. Kai could still recall hunting down the true perpetrators of 9/11. A pair of Rogues befriended a young, idealistic freedom fighter who would become the most wanted man in the world. A whisper here, a suggestion or two, and one man's dreams become the world's nightmares. Kai and Eamon had managed to destroy their enemies, but sometimes they were too late to stop the events already in motion.

Never again, they had vowed, as long as they still drew breath.

It seemed history is not without a sense of irony.

"Reports are scattered, but most of the attacks are centered here. This is a military town, ya know. No big stretch there."

Kai craned his neck, trying to see the bar without much success. He picked up on a unfocused sense of agitation. He was unsure if it was his, hers, or Eamon's concern about the shitstorm was just on the horizon. Since the attacks on 9/11, the Guardians had implemented a network of contacts within military, police and emergency response units to alert if another imminent threat of such magnitude reared its ugly head. Plus, the most powerful warriors had placed wards to protect places that were deemed key assault points. He could only pray that not only would the warning system work better, but that their fail safes would never need to be used.

"Yeah, I guess that isn't a huge surprise. There is a huge target painted on the bay."

A silent plea for help sounded in his mind. Voni.

"Eamon." He moved away from the shadows, heading back toward the liveliness. "Keep me posted on any new developments. Gotta run."

He tossed his final words over his shoulder as he rounded the corner leading back into the open-air walkway. A small crowd had gathered by the bar, but his stomach dropped as he noticed that none of them seemed to be drinking. Rather, they were encroaching on the interplay between three females. Two were well dressed, stately, and blonde. And the third...

Oh, crap.□

TEN

C'mon, Voni. Be the bigger person. Yeah, like that's gonna happen. The bitchy Bobbsey twins were laying it on so thick, and so loud, the room seemed to grow hushed, as if waiting to hear more.

"Malakai? Are you certain? I mean, the man must have better taste than that."

"And can you believe she arrived dressed in that?"

"It's quite unseemly for a young lady."

The comments seeped in from the crowd, battering her already bruised ego. Murmurs and whispered admonishments pushed against her fragile walls as if the gathered socialites were eager to see the awaiting waterworks. But she refused to break down in front of Elspeth, much less a gawking group of strangers.

Allison's arrogant tone cut through the turmoil of her thoughts. "I can't imagine what he sees in her."

"I know," Elspeth concurred, her gaze moving between the two women, careful to watch and drink in every reaction. "Oh, our Malakai is always so willing to help out any charity."

Voni's heart stuttered. Charity. That was exactly how she thought of his actions of last night. She was just another lost soul, just like any other lost soul. She looked up in time to see Kai step into the light. He was too far away for her to see his eyes, but there he was. He belonged in this picture, gorgeous, even in a T-shirt and jeans. This would never be her world.

Seeing the response she must have been aiming for, her companion added, "Yes, our Malakai is always out to make the less than fortunate feel a little ray of happiness."

Something snapped inside Voni, and a cruel smirk crossed her lips even as her brain scrambled to censor her sharp tongue.

"Well, obviously, he isn't *your* Malakai since you wouldn't know a little ray of happiness if it bit you on the ass."

She slid off the barstool with as much dignity as she could muster before hurriedly forcing her way through the onlookers. She muttered apologies while she headed straight for the front door. The people she passed huffed at her, their wide eyes appalled at her apparent lack of manners.

Freedom was mere inches away when a strong hand found her shoulder. His touch was gentle but stood in stark contrast to her reaction. She turned jerkily, pulling her arm into the safety of her own body. She was too wound up and she knew it. It had been so long since she'd experienced any severe emotions that each one now fought to have its moment in the sun. First to take the spotlight: rage and embarrassment. Self-loathing also seemed to be making a command performance, having already stolen the show many times tonight.

"Look, I'm sorry. This was a huge mistake." She tried valiantly to keep her tone light, tried to keep her voice under control. "I knew better and I said yes anyway. So, I'm just gonna go and… It's been real, have a nice life—"

"Voni, wait, please."

Determined, she continued toward the awaiting blackness beyond. She angrily brushed away the threatening tears, working patiently to take deeper breaths. The I-told-you-so part of her brain screamed at her as she moved toward any available exit, while the now-smaller part, the part that housed the hope that Kai was different and thought her special, begged her to stop.

The night had gained tangible form and stopped directly in front of her. *Please, I can't do this.*

"Look," she spoke into his chest, unwilling to meet his eyes. "I don't belong in that world. You do. You can't make a silk purse out of a sow's ear, my mom used to say. And it wasn't until right now that I truly understand what she meant."

"Please, Voni, let me—"

She backed up, stumbling away from the jeweled fabric and false laughter. "No, really," her voice strained, no louder than a whisper. "I'll be fine. You should just—"

"—drive you home." He edged around her, using his body as a shield between her and the vicious jet set hiding in the light. "I made you a promise that if you felt uncomfortable, we would leave." They descended the stairs and he gave a brief nod to the valet. "And, using my amazing powers of deduction"—he flashed a quick smile—"I have determined you wish to depart."

"I can take a cab, really I can. You don't need to leave because…because of me." Turning away sharply, she concentrated on keeping her fraying calm.

The dark beast roared into view. Escape was only a few footfalls away. "Siobhan." He pulled her to a halt as the green-shirted youth stepped out of the driver's seat. "I will always keep my promises to you."

The pure honesty in his voice brought her defenses crumbling down. "D-d-dammit. Can't you let me stay mad?"

The corners of his lips lifted at her simple request. "Not if it is in my power to see you smile again."

Voni tossed her head back and released an aggravated sob toward the heavens before seeking the dash-lit solace of her dream car. The war inside her head was moments away from spilling out into the real world. She struggled to hold it together until the white-stucco hell was a distant blip in the rearview mirror. Her vision blurred as tears trickled down her cheeks, darkness once again enveloping the car.

"I suppose it is now my turn to apologize," Kai said, his rich voice breaking the heavy silence as the road rushed beneath them. "I never meant for the night to end up quite like this."

Silence swam up around them again, cocooning them in a blanket of unease.

"Voni?" He waited, glancing over to see if she had fallen asleep. A soft, stifled sob echoed in the quiet. He caught the reflection of her eyes in the passenger window, frantically searching the darkness. For what, he could only guess. Reaching out, he faltered with his hand a breath away from stroking her leg, her turbulent emotions radiating out in physical waves. "Please, baby. Talk to me." He lowered his hand the final distance, hoping to anchor her, to give her some stability.

116

"And say what? I really don't know what to say. I mean, right now, in my head…" Another exasperated cry escaped; the sound broke his heart. "I can't believe I let that bitch get the better of me. And all those people watching…" She paused, dragging in a stuttering breath. "I'm so sorry. I've embarrassed you in front of—"

"Embarrassed me? I believe you think too highly of me." He hoped the lightness of his tone would draw her attention from the darkness. "I have done much worse at several of these events and without as much provocation as you had. I only caught the tail end of the conversation…"

She groaned, turning her eyes briefly his direction, giving him a glimpse of a single tear's trail against her pale skin. He gripped the steering wheel with enough pressure to warp the metal rim.

"You heard that? Oh God. I feel like such an idiot." Voni sank farther into the leather seat, her gaze focused on the window crank. "I should have just kept my mouth shut."

"No." The sharpness of his tone snapped her head around to face him. His eyes were fixed on the road, but his body vibrated with barely contained rage. "You did what was right. You defended yourself against a two-on-one assault." He turned to lock eyes with hers, surprise mirrored in her hazel orbs. "They are the ones who should have kept their mouths shut. You were a guest and all guests should be treated with respect."

She cocked her head as a perplexed frown cut a deep furrow across her forehead. "But I could've walked away and—"

"Voni." He forced down the anger still lingering in his voice. He had to assure her his ire was not directed toward her. "What happened back there was not your fault."

"Yeah, but—"

"No."

"But I—"

A crooked smile tilted his stern mouth. "No buts."

She huffed, her shoulders drooping as she rested her chin on her chest. "But I was a catty bitch back there."

Kai couldn't help but broaden his smile. "And they both deserved it."

"Still, that doesn't make it right. Ugh!" She flopped back against the seat. "I just felt so—"

"Voni," his voice felt like velvet against her skin. "You are allowed to feel. And you are far too petite to continually shoulder the blame in every situation." Kai lifted his fingers to brush away the last remnants of tears from her cheek. "Even the strongest oak will break in the harshest storm."

"So, you're telling me I just survived Hurricane Allison?" Her weak smile buoyed his spirit and he laughed deeply.

"You took it head-on and came through with flying colors. In fact, my dear—" he paused to lift her hand to his lips. "—you were brilliant."

His reward was a stronger smile, her eyes glistening with the sheen of unshed tears. "Now, please, *dragoste*, no more tears."

She nodded before turning her face away from him. The lights of downtown glowed in the distance. Her home would be creeping up soon, yet he was unwilling to end the night on such a sour note.

"You're getting all dark again." He gave her fingers a tender squeeze before his thumb swirled soothing circles on the back of her hand.

She kept her gaze at the lights flashing by. If she turned toward him, she'd start babbling and say something really stupid. Not that she hadn't done that in spades already. If she caught his eyes, she'd be lost. Hell, she felt as though she was already far down that path.

The entire car reeked of him and his raw and demanding power. It was aggressive, hungry and hotter than hell. She stroked the leather, imagining she was caressing his perfectly chiseled body.

She forced her thoughts back to a more harmless subject, but her mind was focused on other things. And her body was going along for the ride. If he didn't get her home soon, she might just crawl over the center console and ride him the rest of the way.

Her cheeks burst into flame, and she was immensely grateful she was daydreaming out the window. Although, after that thought, she was pretty sure the interior was a little bit brighter, and definitely warmer.

"I'm sorry. I just, um, got... Aw hell."

Kai didn't need to be a mind reader to know what had just crossed her mind. Even through her shirt and leggings, he felt her temperature rise slightly, which did nothing to help his own situation. His jeans were in serious jeopardy of castrating him from sheer pressure. No position eased his swollen cock. Well, none that wouldn't get him arrested for indecent exposure, if he didn't kill them in the process. Sex in a car, no biggie. Sex in a moving vehicle, doable with a big enough backseat. Sex while driving? Potentially deadly.

But the confined space seemed to have them feeding off each other's desires. If there were a way to simply flash them both into his bedroom, he would have done it the moment they stepped into the car. However, a driverless vehicle speeding along Interstate 5 might cause a few problems.

"You know," his voice was gravelly and rough, "completing a sentence is not truly that difficult."

"It is when you're mouth moves faster than your mind," was her mumbled response.

Kai chuckled and gave a crooked grin and a shake of his head in response. "I actually believe it's your mind that is stopping your mouth."

"And that's a good thing, trust me on this one."

"Why would it be a good thing not to speak what's on your mind?" The more she spoke, the more relaxed she became. But his motives were much more personal. He wanted... No, he needed to hear her voice. It was soft and sultry, deeper and richer than wine. He'd never realized how thin and airy other women sounded. Their tinny and nasally tones grated on his senses.

But her, he could listen to all day. He could only imagine the way she'd sound while he buried his cock deep inside her, her head thrown back, her fingers digging into his shoulders as she begged him never to stop.

This time, his seat belt as well as his jeans brought him out of his latest fantasy. *Damn, this sucked.*

"Because, when I speak my mind, I tend to get myself in trouble." She turned to glance at his profile. "For as long as I can remember, I've always tried to say what people expect to hear, or what I think they want me to say. Trying to be the good little girl around mixed company. Appropriate. Shy. Demure. Even." She ticked off the laundry list of accepted behaviors and her volume decreased the long she went on. "Maybe that's why I never really healed from, from...well, you know what."

Kai listened, gaining a glimpse inside the mind of the beauty beside him. The delayed strobe of passing streetlights turned her hair from chestnut to midnight black, her skin glowing in the bright pulses. He glanced at her sidelong, sensing her slip further into the depths of her overwhelming emotions.

"You censor yourself because you might say something...what? Unexpected?"

She hesitated, a whisper of a frown wrinkling her brow before she replied. "Well, no. I just say things a little, um, direct. I've been known to be less than, well, tactful at times. So, yeah," she said, smiling sheepishly. "I guess you could say that. Because when I don't, well... You saw the aftermath of that experience."

"Oh, that." His devilish grin returned in full force.

"Yes, that." She giggled lightly without much encouragement.

Kai joined her mirth, until the car was filled with the sounds of their unchecked laughter. She had a great laugh. It was full and rolling, coming from her entire being. Her eyes danced with mischief while, her hands wrapped around her waist as she attempted to stop her sides from aching.

Voni couldn't remember the last time she'd laughed so hard. And over nothing too. One minute, she was brooding over her inability to speak her mind, and the next, she was giggling uncontrollably.

And he wasn't helping at all. Kai had even started it, as far as she was concerned. With his gentle words and impish smile, he managed to bring light to her otherwise dark world. His laughter was deep and sensual. It suited him. She tried to focus on the sound of his voice, but her own cackling drowned out his velvet tone.

All too soon, she recognized the buildings near her home. They had arrived at their final destination. And so ended another day. Yet, as she fought to bring her breathing back to normal, she couldn't be as upset as she first imagined she should be.

It's amazing what a good laugh attack did to raise your spirits.

She wiped away the tears that had escaped during her bout of happiness, as the last of the giggles snuck through in sporadic bursts. "Wow. Now that, I haven't done in a long time."

Kai pulled the car to a halt in front of her little complex. "You should. Laughter suits you quite well."

She ducked her chin into her chest to hide her blush. "Yeah, well, I suppose I haven't had much to laugh about lately." She paused, turning to lock eyes with him. "I guess I have you to thank for giving me a reason to laugh."

He leaned over, reaching out his hand to cup her cheek. His palm felt cool against her warm skin. She watched mesmerized as he drew closer, her lips tasted his with the tiniest sip.

"The pleasure's all mine." He breathed against her skin before dipping down once again.

She deepened the kiss, fumbling with her seat belt while trying to crawl into his lap. Their tongues dueled entwined in their dance for supremacy. With a slight click, she wriggled out of the confining strap.

She dug her fingers through his thick, black hair, holding him firmly in place. Decency took second place to her demands, her desire to feel the press of his body against hers. She'd lived so long without pleasure, without joy or brightness.

And then he came into her life. Though he had an air of danger and power, she was not afraid. She needed to feel. Needed it with all her heart and soul.

Kai groaned, pulling back just enough to give her time to breathe, nibbling along her jawline. He let his hands roam along her sides until, he gripped tight to her waist. With one smooth maneuver, he lifted her across the steering column and placed her astride his lap. Her body fit like a glove against his, lithe legs straddled his hips. Her gaze lowered, her eyes dark with passion and desire.

"Not all yours. Not this time." Her voice was clear and strong. No doubts, no hesitation.

"Mmmm. I like the sound of that," Kai growled, his hands splayed against her narrow hips as he pressed his denim-covered hardness into her soft core.

A soft moan escaped from her lips, and she rolled her head lazily across her shoulders in anticipation. The bulge currently nestled between her thighs was massive and rock-hard. Her body moved on pure instinct, grinding against him and riding the delicious friction between them. "And I like the feel of that." Her brazen words tumbled out as a strangled sigh.

"That's it, baby. That's it." His voice purred into her ear, his tongue flicking her tender lobe. "Show me what you want."

Voni tried to form words, but only inarticulate sounds of pleasure crept from her lips. Her hips undulated, pressing her harder into his ready erection. Tremors shimmered along her spine, and her knees and thighs tightened against his legs as she strove to pull him through her clothes. Arching her back, she began a slow, seductive rocking, pleasure rippling out in delicious waves. She gripped his broad shoulders, clinging to his strength as the storm continued to build.

Kai struggled to play it calm, warring against the demanding desire to strip her bare, thrusting his engorged cock into her welcoming, wet heat. He had to let her set the pace, allowing her to make all the first moves. His tenuous control strained with each rock of her hips and every breathy moan. Voni was pure passion, erotic without effort and intoxicating beyond imagination.

Unable to contain his ardor any longer, he tugged free the hem of her shirt and yanked the offending material over her head. Beneath, he discovered her small breasts confined in a torturous binding. The slender straps held the solid elastic band in place and curved in a crisscross over her back. His teeth gnashed at the frustrating removal procedure. His mouth watered to taste her and she was cocooned in a web of hateful, unyielding spandex. With his strength, he could easily shred the barrier. But he knew that might spoil the mood a bit, since she would most likely run screaming from the car.

An animalistic growl rumbled in his throat, fueling the fire in her and heating her blood to a fever pitch. She glanced down, and spied her poor choice of undergarments. She should've stuck with the sexy black number. Doubt began to cool her mood a degree or two. Attempting to make a graceful retreat, she rose as far as the narrow confines allowed, pushing down on his shoulders. Immoveable steel coils wrapped around her waist, pulling her exposed skin to meet his hungry mouth.

He kissed and licked her satiny stomach, his tongue swirling sensual patterns around her taut muscles. He slipped his fingers under one of the narrow straps, pulling it along her shoulder, partially exposing one breast. She was helpless to stop the needy whimpers as the cool air kissed her sensitive skin. A wicked smile pulled across his lips and he playfully nipped her tender flesh.

"Were you going somewhere?"

His rough voice caressed her quivering midsection; his breath tantalized her bared flesh. Voni buried her face in midnight waves, her ragged breathing and racing pulse driving her blood to pool slightly south of his lips.

"Yeah," she whispered into his silken strands. "But whether it's to heaven or to hell, I'm not entirely sure."

He dragged his tongue up the length of her body, until stopping to lave the newly revealed mound. A hungry growl poured over her skin while he teased the veiled nub poking against his palm. The stronger his mouth tugged at her yielding flesh, the deeper and more demanding her moans.

Voni gave her fingers free rein, stroking his arms and his chest, desperate to reach the elusive flesh underneath. She scooped beneath the black silk T-shirt, gasping as her hands met with rippling, defined muscles coated by a thin sheen of sweat. She traced her fingers lightly up toward his chest.

Her gentle touch nearly caused Kai to shoot his load. He yanked his mouth away from her breast and kissed her hungrily, thrusting his tongue deep as he rocked his hips against her soft, feminine core. The cage of his arms pinned her to his demanding frame while he gave his hands free reign, one delving into her wild sable locks and the other kept her hips firm against his primed cock.

Electronic musical tones cut through the space, the sounds at first unclear. The longer it drilled into his head, the angrier Kai became. Recognizing that particular song, he knew he couldn't just let it go to voice mail. He let out a string of obscenities in every language he could imagine before digging into his front pocket to retrieve the disrupting device.

"This had better be life or death," Kai growled fiercely into the phone, his breathing labored. He listened intently as he traced light swirling circles on her trembling back, each slow, ragged breath she took cooling the heated skin beneath his palm. He placed a soft kiss on her bare shoulder, a smile curling his lips as he flicked out his tongue to catch a bead of sweat just forming along her collarbone. Savoring the taste of her, he shifted his gaze as his brain deciphered the words pouring into his ear.

"You have got to be shitting me," he spat out, dragging a hand roughly through his disheveled hair. "Where?"

"Found two bodies down by the shipyards. Or I figure it was at least two from the number of body parts and the amount of blood. Could almost buy it as gang related, especially in that neighborhood, but the eyes were burned out and no heart was in the final tally."

"What does that make the count now?"

"That makes six separate attacks in the past two days. They are gearing up something massive..." Kai nodded, aware of the importance of the grave news, but he had a tough time focusing on Eamon's words with the half-clad minx wriggling against his rock-hard cock. Even now, as she bent to retrieve her discarded top, the slight movement almost sent him over the edge. Leaning with her movements lest he lose what little self-control he had left, he wrapped his free arm about her waist, hoping to still her motion.

She looked at him, lips swollen and cheeks flushed, her eyes full of questions. Words perched on his tongue, a heartbeat away from spilling.

"Kai, boyo, did ya hear what I said?"

"Yeah, yeah. I heard you, Eamon." He groaned sharply, looking into her honey-brown orbs. He mouthed, *I'm sorry* as Eamon gave him the final details. Nodding, but only half-attentive, he kept one hand on the small of her back as the loose shirt slid down her arms. He frowned and quickly shook his head, hopefully communicating that she should cease her redressing attempt.

"All right," he sighed into the receiver. "Give me twenty minutes." He closed the phone and returned his attentions to the now fully dressed beauty in his lap. "And just where do you think you're going?"

"I know that's my cue to leave," She continued tugging the material back into some semblance of its original placement, her gaze focused on everything but him. "No worries. Look, I had a really great time. So, I'll just be going." During her ramblings, she attempted to extricate herself from his entwining limbs. He coiled one arm tight around her back, as he cradled her head in his other hand.

"If you think we're done here, you are quite mistaken." He captured her lips again, branding her taste into his blood. He broke the kiss, giving her time to breathe. "I have every intention of completing what we started."

His voice was hot and demanding, his words full of passion and promise. He desperately wanted her to believe him and prayed that she trusted him to keep his word.

He waited as her emotions played tag behind her eyes, hope overriding doubt, desire taking an upper hand to despair. A slight victory, but a victory nonetheless.

"This is only a delay. A small hiccup." He placed his knuckles under her chin and raised her gaze to meet his. "But I'm afraid duty calls." She nodded, her gaze pensive as she studied his face. He wondered how long he was going to be able to keep hidden the true nature of his duties.

Kai opened his door, watching in rapt awe as she climbed over him to make a graceful exit. His cock twitched in appreciation of her lithe movements, not to mention the breasts that he found at eye level as she crawled out of the car. He swallowed back a strangled groan. His skills were needed elsewhere tonight.

"I'll walk you to your—"

"That's ok." She leaned against the open door, her hand poised to close it. "I think I can manage it the rest of the way myself."

This time, the hesitation was his. It appeared he would try to overrule her, so she spoke quickly. "Look, you said you'd meet Eamon in a few minutes, and I'm sure you need to, well, drive to wherever he is. So, um…" Truth be told, she only wanted to pick up right where they'd left off, and she would do whatever she had to, to make it so.

Exhaling, he gave a slow nod in agreement. "Very true, indeed." He settled in behind the steering wheel. As soon as he had pulled the door shut, he rolled down the hand-cranked window.

"Voni." His voice called her back to the open window and to the object in his hand. With a light sigh, she retrieved the purse she would have left behind.

Oh, yeah. Keys would be nice.

She stood in silence, unsure of the correct thing to say. "Thanks for the almost-sex" somehow didn't sound right. So she just went with her gut. "Good night." Her voice was soft, yet clear, the smile across her face ringing through the two simple words.

"*Somn sunet, dragoste meu.*" A gentle brush of his fingers against her cheek and in an engine roar, he was gone.

Voni sighed, watching the taillights disappear before she turned to face her quiet complex. He said duty called. Until that moment, she hadn't given any thought to exactly what that could mean. She knew he was rich, but she didn't know how he earned his keep.

Was it dangerous? Was it illegal? Somehow, she knew it would be yes to dangerous, but no to illegal. Though she could sense he was a predator through and through, he didn't seem the type to cause undo harm.

She touched her fingertips to her kiss-swollen lips and smiled slyly. Meandering toward the front gate, she reveled in the memory of his passion and prayed they could finish their interrupted activities soon.

ELEVEN

Kai was still muttering obscenities in a wide variety of languages, his phrases becoming more and more creative, when he pulled the car to a stop at Eamon's location. Her scent clung to the very metal of his car. Spicy and flowery, a walking dichotomy. Just like her. Fragile and strong, timidly powerful. He craved her, even more after the glimpse of the passion lurking beneath the surface of her ivory skin.

The strings of colorful language grew in volume as he stepped out the car and crossed the open lot toward his friend's bright red BMW M5, where said friend rested against the hood. "I swear to Christ, if you weren't always so god dammed right every fucking time, I'd rip your balls off and make you eat them."

"Did I miss somethin'?" Eamon's mischievous grin belied his innocent question.

"No," Kai snarled. "But once you find your mate, I will make it my personal mission to call you every fucking five minutes to ensure that you never get your rocks off."

"Easy now, boyo. Ya know I wouldn't disturb ya completely on purpose now, right?" He paused. "Right?" he repeated, leaning in slightly.

Kai huffed out an exasperated breath. "Yes, yes. I know." Running a hand through his disheveled hair, he shook his head to clear the cobwebs. "So, what's the plan?"

Eamon pushed off the car, the movement fluid and calculated. "Tracked 'em down and, big surprise, they've gone into the Black to hide."

"How many?" The Black, the In-Between. He hadn't traveled through

126

the Void for a long time. The last trip had proven useful—painful and scar inducing, but useful nonetheless. Besides, what were a few more scars compared to the numerous lives saved? That was the mantra he mentally repeated each time they ventured into hostile territory.

"At last report, they're only about six. But—"

"I know," he added tiredly. "Konstantin is there."

Eamon paused, his hand reaching through the car's open top. "And ya knew this because…?"

Kai pulled the collapsed staff from his inner pocket. "Because I sent him there last night."

Eamon arched an eyebrow suspiciously as he fished out his own staff. "Plan on elaboratin', now do ya?"

Kai shrugged out of the coat and tossed it into Eamon's vehicle. "Not really," he answered flatly.

Removing his coat as well, Eamon stood by his stoic friend. "Fair enough." He turned to face Kai. "Ready?"

Kai snorted. "Does it matter?"

"No."

Eamon nodded sharply, twirling his staff above his hand and slamming in forcefully into the ground. Power sparked out, encircling the pair in blue light before snapping the lot into darkness.

Kai let his eyes, as well as his stomach, adjust to the confining air of the In-Between. The journey in was always unsettling, but after a few hundred years of practice, at least he didn't toss his cookies anymore.

Unlike someone else. He smiled smugly as Eamon righted himself after losing the last of his very expensive dinner. "I can't believe you still hurl."

"Sod off," Eamon mumbled, wiping the back of his hand against his mouth. "Gawd, I hate this shit."

"Same here." He looked around, searching for an artificial light source. "Let's get this over with quickly and get the fuck out of here."

"Damn, boyo. I don't think I've heard ya swear so much in the past two hundred years as I have in the past twenty-four hours." The impish grin from earlier returned full strength. "If this is what I get to look forward to, then I hope I never met Ms. Right."

"Yeah, well," he answered, still peering into the penetrating blackness. "Don't forget the nonstop, raging hard-on."

"Wow," Eamon breathed. "That was just not what I needed to be hearin'. And thank ya for paintin' that TMFI image in my mind." Daring a glance at Kai, he added, punctuating his statement, "Prick."

Kai hazarded a triumphant smirk before a distant spark caught his attention. "Ten o'clock." A flick of the wrist and the staff snapped to its full length, nine feet from blade tip to steel-covered butt. Eamon responded in kind, his blade augmented with a vicious curved hook.

The deep black around them began to solidify; ground and walls appeared from the vast nothingness. Bracing for battle, they calmly strolled a few steps, closing the distance between them and the oncoming storm.

"Did I mention that I really hate this shit?" Eamon remarked, his gaze flicking across the faces of the eight Rogue Warriors.

Kai spun the *naginata* idly, the shaft finally slamming to rest under his arm. "Yes, I think you did. So, do you want the four on the left or on the right?" The opponents stood before them, ready for whoever made the first move.

"Oh, actually, since I took ya away from your delightful lady friend," Eamon said, keeping his tone light and pleasant, "I'll let ya make the choice."

"How very kind of you. But if my memory serves me, I believe I made the decision last time." Their conversation seemed to confuse the gathered attackers, who exchanged puzzled glances. "Then, that would make it your turn, my friend."

"But, truly, I stole ya away from a much gentler way to spend the evenin'. I insist." The longer their seemingly cordial banter went on, the more hesitant their assembled foes became.

Kai sensed the lapse in his opponents' guard, and he struck without pause. He arced the long weapon, easily slicing through two stunned enemies who simply evaporated in a crimson fog.

Eamon quickly dispatched another pair as the remaining warriors launched their attacks.

Along with reinforcements, more weapons materialized to aid the battling Rogues. Four became twelve in a flash, each armed to the teeth. Kai's weapon, though great at keeping his opponents at a distance, proved cumbersome as the walls narrowed, creating a closer-quartered battlefield. Thrusting out, he caught one of the warriors just below the rib cage before driving the tip home, smiling as the man burst into a hail of red mist.

"Behind you!" Eamon's voice cried out an instant before pain exploded along Kai's exposed back. Rolling quickly with the direction of the blow, he grabbed the nearest discarded weapon and flung it toward the backstabbing bastard. The blade landed with a sickening thud, burying hilt-deep in the hollow of the man's throat. Blood gurgled up before he too vanished. "I hate people who won't face me in battle," he grumbled, wincing against the searing ache.

Kai turned to find Eamon ass-deep in Rogues, their numbers multiplying with each round. Goddamned Void mathematics. On their home turf, they played by a rather different, and quite biased, set of rules. For each who fell, two would rise until the First was found. Kai's sword arched and spiraled in a deadly dance with two more foes. "Dammit all, what I wouldn't give for a machine gun right about now." The air rained shimmering red as two more Rogues howled their last.

"Yeah," Eamon's darkly humored voice chided. "Or maybe a grenade, or twelve. But this is so much more rewardin', don't ya agree?" A quick flick of his wrist and the hook removed the head from another warrior. "Do ya have an eye on him yet? I mean, not to rush or anythin', but if ya could—" Eamon brought the great spear up with both hands, quickly avoiding an all-too-close haircut. He pistoned his leg forward, skill landing his heel in the warrior's groin. As he gasping man dropped to his knees before him, Eamon swept the blade with deadly accuracy. "Hurry the fuck up!"

Kai scanned the area for the hiding First. "What the fuck do you think I'm doing? Looking for a parking spot?" His eyes swept in fast glances as his blade continued to flash and slash. "Gotcha," he whispered, finally discovering the Rogue's shimmering aura behind three well-armed brutes. *Not safe from me.* He spun low, cutting out the legs of two Rogues not quick enough to dive and clear the path for him. Hefting his long weapon's shaft over his shoulder, he threw the blade like a javelin, his aim true. A strangled scream, and the remaining warriors vanished in a puff of scarlet.

"Well, that was fun," Eamon said unenthusiastically as he wiped the blood from his blade. "That should at least keep them off our plane for a bit." He flicked his wrist, and the blade and butt retracted silently, returning to their inert form.

Kai gingerly extricated himself from the receding ground. *That's going to leave a mark*, he thought, feeling the sticky warmth creep down his back. He collapsed his weapon as well, ready to return home.

"You make it too easy, you know." Words echoed in the abyss. Kai spun around, eyes peering into the blackness. A slow, joyless laugh filled the emptiness. "You always were such a gallant knight, Malakai."

"And you were always a deceiving, over theatrical piece of shit, Dmitri. What's your point?" The voice came from everywhere and nowhere. Kai caught Eamon from the corner of his eye, his frenzied search also coming up empty.

"She really is so very lovely, don't you think? So innocent and full of life." The darkness began to change, morphing into a tiny, nondescript room. Shades of ecru and tan blanketed the scene. Yet, tucked between the bland sheets was a familiar cascade of sable locks. A small black tuft of fur guarded her sleeping form, but Kai knew the feline's meager protection would not be enough tonight.

"You leave her out of this," Kai growled, his long, angry stride chewing up the blackness between him and Voni's sleeping form. The strides soon became jogs, finally ending in a full-blown run.

"But she is already in this, so to speak. You see, I've been watching her for quite some time now."

The harder Kai ran, the farther she moved out of his reach. Damn this fucking place! In his haste, Kai forgot the main rule of the In-Between. This was Rogue territory, and it only worked according to their wishes. He struggled to slow his pace, only managing to stop as Eamon tugged hard his sleeve.

"He's fucking with us, boyo. Don't let him control you."

Kai snapped his head to lock eyes with his friend. *"I can't let him hurt her, either. Just be ready to send us out of here."*

"Her sorrow cried out to the In-Between…oh, must have been almost a year ago."

Kai clenched his teeth as he directed his thoughts to entering the space that showed Voni's room. Her head tossed to and fro against the pillow, her mind deep in a dream state. Her lips moved and her eyelids twitched as her sleep grew more restless. He bit back his anger and focused on the destination.

"Her lover dead, she was so lost, so lonely, and so beautiful." Lecherous design dripped through the disembodied voice, raising Kai's hackles.

The tranquil scene before him shimmered, and the grizzly vistas he recognized from his dream walk replaced it. Voni stood rigidly across from a blood-soaked apparition, her soft lilac sleep shirt in sharp contrast to the garish surroundings. A bony limb beckoned her from the yowling darkness.

Kai fought against his urge to rush forward. His slow, steady pace had brought her closer to his grasp. Eamon walked beside him in silence, his channeling staff charged and ready. *Hang on, baby.* Just a few more steps. He silently flooded her with his strength and prayed she would hear.

"She was almost mine, you know. Standing along that ledge, she was ready to give herself to me." The ghostly outline of Dmitri Konstantin hovered in evil harmony with the pleading corpse before Voni. Unable to take complete form, he borrowed the body of his creation, inhabiting the fabricated shell of Voni's former fiancé.

Kai kept his boiling emotions barely contained, watching in horror as the tears fell down her pale cheeks, apologies tumbling from her trembling lips.

Siobhan, he channeled his thoughts, finding the mental line he'd created specifically for her. *"Siobhan, I'm here, dragoste meu. You're safe."*

"Then you had to show up and ruin everything!" Blood fountained in a crimson shower as the force of Konstantin's anger shredded his surrounding shell. Voni shrieked in absolute terror as her face and body were splattered in gore.

Patience prevailed and Kai closed the final inches. grasping tight onto her narrow wrist. *"Now!"* He projected their destination to Eamon the instant his friend slammed the staff down. Konstantin's impotent rage echoed through the Void as three figures flashed out of the dark.□

TWELVE

Voni awoke, her eyes flying wide as her own screams still bounced in the beige silence. Frantically, she clawed at her arms, wiping away the nonexistent blood and carnage. A mewling ball of fluff bounded off the bouncing mattress, hissing in outrage as she continued to flail about.

Her movements slowed, and she drew her legs up under her, winding into a tight ball. The tears fell uncontrollably as she struggled to calm her racing heart and ragged breathing. Her body shook with the force of the worst nightmare she had ever experienced.

"No, no, no, not real. Not real." Covering her ears, her eyes squeezed shut, she repeated the simple words, using them to anchor her to reality.

But everything had seemed so real, so much more visceral than any of the nights before. Tonight, it was different. There were others present, two comforting entities, and one vibe of pure evil. She wanted to believe one of those was Kai, thought she'd heard his voice at one point.

Even now, her body racked with sobs, she swore she could feel his arms surrounding her, smell his scent invading her senses. She curled into a tight ball as she buried her head and wept.

"I can't do this anymore," she whispered unsteadily. "I just can't, I can't, I can't." Her litany continued through her tears, her body rocking as she cried.

The imaginary arms embraced her as her dream hero spoke soothing words in her hair in a language she didn't understand. As time passed, her heart found a calmer rhythm, her breathing deepened and steadied. Her tears even began to slow as her shoulders gradually relaxed.

She remembered this situation, these sensations from before. Kai had held her during the episode and it had passed much quicker than normal. Could he be here with her now? She was too drained to open her eyes, and she wanted to keep this fantasy for a little while longer.

"I wish this were real." Her sleep-laden voice spoke to the emptiness of her room.

"It is as real as you want it to be." Her imagination must have been working overtime. She even thought she heard his voice inside her head, his breath warm as his lips brushed against her hair.

Exhaustion threatened to draw her back into the night. "Don't...want to go back there...please," she mumbled, afraid to sleep again.

"I will stay and keep you safe. Rest, my love." The voice was comforting and hard to resist.

Weariness finally overtook her, and she tucked herself further into the make-believe arms encircling her and drifted into unconsciousness.

Kai remained still, holding her gently as she slipped again into sleep. He continued to stroke her hair, weaving a protection spell around her fragile psyche. The barrier would keep out any wandering Rogues tonight. As gently as possible, he edged out of her mind, giving the lightest push, ensuring she would continue to sleep once he had left.

Reluctant, he slid off her tiny bed, maintaining physical contact to keep her calm. She murmured a small protest as he laid her against the sweat-drenched sheets. He caressed her cheek, wiping away the remnants of her last bout of tears. His heart had ached as he held her through the aftermath of her nightmare.

He tucked her in, tenderly brushing the damp tendrils that surrounded her face. Leaning over her, he took one last breath, dragging her scent deep into him before placing a chaste kiss on her forehead.

"You're safe now, my sweet." He knew he couldn't stay. His presence brought up too many questions he wasn't ready to answer just yet. But he couldn't pull himself away from her. He remembered her, standing before the ghoulish apparition. The horrors she must have endured for so long, tortured and tormented by the likes of Konstantin.

At that moment, he wished his enemy was still in the flesh. It would give him a much greater satisfaction to tear him limb from limb. His hand trembled, his rage barely contained. He unclenched his fist, opting instead to run his fingers through her damp locks spread out against the pale fabric.

"As much as I'm enjoyin' this Hallmark moment," Eamon's hushed voice broke the silence of the night, "I'm thinkin' it's time we left."

Kai sighed heavily, begrudgingly stepping away from her sleeping form. Nodding briefly, he turned and crossed the small space to stand beside his friend. Daring one final look back, he clasped Eamon's shoulder and both disappeared into a crack in space.

Back in his own house, Kai paced the floor, moving from one end of the living room to the other. His mind spun faster than his feet could travel, eager to unravel this new mystery.

Eamon took a sip from his beer, his gaze following Kai's hamster-like circuits around the massive room. "You're gonna wear through your carpet, ya know."

He stopped, glaring at his friend, who sat lazily on his couch with one leg slung haphazardly over the arm. The open beer bottle rested on his knee as he calmly observed his obvious agitation. He had lost track of how many trips he had made since returning. It must have been at least one round ago, judging by the three bottles gracing the top of his coffee table.

Taking a page from his friend's relaxed state, he dropped down in the nearest chair, the air in his lungs escaping with an audible groan. He retrieved his own drink, slick with condensation and tossed back the remainder in one gulp. "I just don't understand the connection between her and him. How the fuck did he find her in the first place?"

Eamon shook his head. It was the umpteenth version of the same question Kai had been asking for the past two hours. Finishing his own bottle, he set it to rest with its empty brethren on the table. "Ya heard what he said, boyo. Her grief called out to him."

"Bullshit," Kai spat. "I don't believe that for a second. Bull-fucking-shit!"

Eamon stared at the ceiling for guidance. He'd heard that too, and around the same number of times. They had gone over the same ground since arriving back at Kai's place, their cars safely parked in the massive open carport. His mind, fogged by lack of sleep and a few beers, begged for reprieve. But his heart knew better. Kai would not give up this quest until he discovered a solution. Single-minded asshole.

He looked out into the stark white chamber, noting the hint of brightness behind the thick shades.

"Give it a rest, Kai. It's nearly dawn and my head can't keep up any more."

Kai raised his head, noting the encroaching light. "You're right, you're right." His voice was laced with fatigue. He stood smoothly, swallowing the last dregs from the bottle. "The guest room is made up and ready to go."

Eamon smiled warmly. "Ya do know how to make a man feel at home."

Kai was nothing if not generous with his home. Eamon waited, his gaze fixed on his host's back, at the shredded and bloodied shirt, the vicious slash still raw and angry. Tension oozed off him in waves, pulsating with a life of its own. He empathized with him. Konstantin was danger personified, and he had set his sights on Kai's woman. He knew Kai wouldn't stop until Konstantin was destroyed, and for good this time.

Kai headed toward the stairs leading to his bedroom. He had ascended two steps before pausing. "Eamon?"

His friend emerged from the kitchen. "Hmm?"

Unspoken words filtered through the silence, words of thanks and camaraderie echoed soundlessly.

"Get some sleep, boyo."

"*Multumesc, meu frate.*"

"*Oíche maith, mo chara.*"

Kai journeyed the final distance to his own awaiting bed. Peeling off the remnants of his shirt, he winced as the fresh wound threatened to reopen. He tossed the shirt in the trash, kicked off his boots, and fell face-first onto the mattress. He would find no more answers now.

"I promised I would keep you safe and I mean to do it." Sleep claimed him moments later, his thoughts still dark and brooding.

**

An incessant tapping bled into Voni's muddled thoughts. Struggling to focus on the source of the irritating sound, she pried her sleep-caked eyes open. She shook her head, trying to clear the fog, only to be met with a sudden and powerful wave of nausea. Scrambling, she clawed her way out the entangled sheets before retching into the small metal trash bin.

"What the fuck?" Voni wiped her mouth with the back of her hand, rolling over to stare at the ceiling. She hadn't felt this hung over in years. But for the life of her, she couldn't remember having had that much to drink. All she had was a few sips of the Brazilian concoction at the fundraiser. She had always been a lightweight when it came to alcohol, but come on. A few sips and she's spewing her guts in the morning? Not likely.

The tapping became a knocking, and the source was her front door.

"What!" Her own voice echoed through her empty space as well as through her aching head. Cringing, she waited, listening for some answer to her shouted question.

Merciful silence greeted her. She sighed, sinking back into the waiting arms of her twisted linens.

The knocking returned, this time as a pounding coupled with frantic, muffled voices.

"All right, all right already." Dragging her hand through her chaotic hair, she gingerly disengaged herself from the coolness of the sheets. She stood carefully, allowing her head and her stomach adequate time to return to their standard resting places.

Voni shuffled her too-heavy feet toward the vibrating door. "What, what, what?" she asked the wooden barrier. She reached down and turned the handle, having a good idea of what stood on the other side.

Overly bright sunlight pierced her half-closed eyes as she squinted at the anxious faces of her doting cottage mates, her hand lifted to shield herself from some of the evil rays. Sans wigs and feathers, they were actually quite handsome. Today, they almost looked like any number of guys she'd met. Okay, maybe guys who wore pink chiffon, eyeliner, and red fingernails.

"*Madre de Dios, mija*. What the hell happened to you?" Robert crossed himself as he leaned against his roomie.

She panicked and her hand thumped at her chest. Grateful to meet cloth, she sighed heavily. She rubbed at her eyes, weary from…hell if she knew. "What are you two doing here? And what time is it, anyway?"

Daniel shooed her back inside her entryway, away from prying eyes. Robert gave one final look over his shoulder before closing the door.

"What are you two—?"

"We heard screaming last night," Robert blurted out.

"Bobby." Daniel swatted his arm delicately. "I said I'd handle this."

Turning back to Voni, he walked her backward to the nearest chair.

Voni plunked herself down, meeting the dramatics with a hint of fear. "Will someone tell me—?"

"Girl, last night, we heard horrible screams coming from here." Voni's eyes bounced from face to face, confused at the hint of tears glistening in both sets of eyes.

"What happened?"

"Are you all right?"

"We've been knocking for an hour now-"

"It's been ten minutes."

"-And if you didn't answer this time, we were gonna call the cops."

"Did someone hurt you?"

She dropped her head into her hands, searching the muddled memories for suitable answers to their rapid-fire questions as well as her own unvoiced concerns. What the hell had happened last night? Screams, loud enough for them to hear a couple doors down?

A gentle hand touched her shoulder, bringing her mind back to the confines of the room. Looking up, she caught Daniel's penetrating stare. "Talk to me, girl."

"I...just don't know what to say." Her eyes flicked from Daniel's deep brown orbs to Robert's impossibly blue ones. "I guess I just had a bad dream."

"Bad dream?" Robert scoffed as Daniel sat back on his heels. "*Chica*, I've heard bad dreams and I've heard people being slaughtered. What we heard last night was definitely more like the second one. Are you sure there isn't something you wanna tell us?" He looked over at his partner, who was busy impersonating one of those annoying bobble-head dolls. Voni thought for a moment Daniel's head might actually come loose.

"No, honest. I've just been sleeping bad lately. Really," she said, starting to rise. "I'm fine." Her head, however, had a different idea. Objects swam before her eyes, and she thrust out an arm to grab the nearest stationary object. Her hand connected with Daniel's shoulder, and she held on tightly to keep on her feet. Solid wood met the back of her legs once again.

"Sorry. I guess Just not feeling too good, I guess," she mumbled, her free hand trying frantically to keep her remaining brain cells inside her skull.

Robert eyed her suspiciously. "I ain't never heard of no one known you to get shit-faced."

A hesitant grin curled the corner of her mouth. "I didn't know you could get blitzed on one drink."

Daniel nodded sharply. "Girl, you could get drunk on cough syrup."

Voni tried to look astonished but only arrived at mildly surprised. "What is that supposed to mean?" She knew what the answer would be though, the same as it always was.

"She means, chica," Robert interjected knowingly, "you need to put some meat on your bones. You're too skinny. You need to have something for that sexy man to hang on to."

And now it would start, Voni thought as the pair began cackling.

"And speaking of Mr. Mm-mm-mm…are we going to see more of him?"

She blushed as she latched on to one extremely vivid image from last night. His lips devouring her skin, the feel of his arms wrapped around her, not to mention the obvious arousal pressed between her thighs.

"God, I hope so," she sighed, her voice deep with need.

Laughter rang though the living room at ear-shattering levels. The blush in her cheeks quickly became a forest fire as she realized what she had said.

"Omigod! Please tell me I didn't really say that out loud?"

"Said? Damn, girl! You practically sang it!"

Voni hid her face as Daniel's words mingled with Robert's tittering. "Voni and Sexy Man…sitting in a tree…F-U-C-K—"

"Robert!" Voni snapped her head up, cutting off this new and improved rendition of that little song.

"What? Am I wrong?" His laughing eyes dared Voni to contradict him.

Voni gaped like a beached fish, struggling to deny the desire. "I— I…I'm not having this conversation." Sure her head was clear, she rose gracefully.

"Aw, now don't be like that," Daniel admonished. "You know we just want to see you happy. You deserve to be happy."

"And mija, if that gorgeous man don't make you happy," Robert chimed in, "we seriously need to talk."

Voni shook her head, a shy smile playing across her lips. If they kept this up, her cheeks would look permanently sunburned. "Okay, you two. I think that's enough prying into my private life for one morning. Besides, I look like hell and don't feel much better."

Her companions were still giggling to each other, but they did get her not-so-subtle hint. They stood and sandwiched her in a bone-cracking hug. Arm in arm, they all walked toward her front door.

Voni took a breath, enjoying the simple pleasure of good friends. Images of the plastic people she'd seen last night filtered through her mind. All their fake smiles and phony physiques amounted to absolutely nothing. At that moment, she appreciated her quirky friends with all her heart.

"Thanks for checking in on me…again. I guess I never realized what a problem child I was."

"Girl," Daniel said, his warm brown eyes playful. "You just need to let go and stop worrying—"

"And apologizing…"

"Yes, Bobby. And apologizing all the time. We like worrying about you," he finished, heading toward the open doorway. "You just don't do anything to get rid of that sexy hunk of manflesh."

Voni shook her head, knowing they would not let up. "Like a dog with a bone," her mother would said. "Good-bye, you two." She gently pushed the door closed.

"Don't forget to call us later on! We still need details!" Robert's voice raised in pitch as their footfalls moved down the stone pathway, the giggles receding in their wake.

Resting her head on the solid doorframe, she slowly surveyed her very vanilla living space. She spied the wall clock, reading the not-so-overly-early hour of 10:16 a.m. Those two were never up this early on a Saturday. A cold chill ran down her spine. She must have been really loud if they had to come over at this hour to check on her.

Her mind spun as she reached for fragments of memory beyond the front-seat make-out session. She smiled shyly, her hand brushing against her lips, which still tingled even then. Heading back to her bedroom, she grabbed the trash can, intent on emptying its contents before making any more grand plans.

Knock, knock, knock.

She left the can in the shower, laughing as she headed back toward the front door. She twisted the handle quickly and threw it open. "Ok. So what did you for—?"

She slammed the door just as quickly. Her heart fought to keep pace with her thoughts.

A second set of knocks, these a bit more hesitant, vibrated through her back. She looked down at her attire, or lack thereof. Did she dare rush back to her bedroom to grab a pair of shorts? Gulping down her heart and her courage, she fumbled with the metal handle one more time, using the paint-stripped wood as shelter.

Beyond the opening door stood Kai, looking incredibly sexy and quite confused. The sunlight sparkled in his slick, black hair, the ends brushing the tops of his white T-shirt-clad shoulders. The thin fabric stretched taut against the chiseled muscle tapering toward the narrow waist of his deep-blue denim jeans she knew lay beneath. A brown leather bomber jacket was hooked lazily over his shoulder, held by one long, strong finger.

With his shoulder resting casually on the doorframe and his pale, ice-green eyes dancing with mischief, she now deeply regretted her earlier rudeness.

"I, uh, umm... Hi there," she finally said, opting against her standard "sorry."

"Good morning. I take it you were expecting someone else?" His smile sent shivers down her limbs, and his voice sent warmth in its wake. Torn between her embarrassment and her desires, she chose neither, choosing instead to simply stare.

"Well," she fumbled, finding her voice at last, "Daph, I mean Dan and Robert just left a couple minutes ago. So I, um, thought it was them...you know, coming back for something else, and so, yeah..." Stupid! Invite him in!

An awkward moment passed.

"You left your CDs in the car last night," he said, producing the small black plastic bag from behind his back.

"Omigod, you didn't have to, um...I mean, I didn't mean to, uh, leave them. Oh, gawd, what am I saying? I am so sorry," she blurted out, stepping aside. "Would...would you like to come in?"

Kai breathed a sigh of relief as she backed away from the doorway. For a moment, he thought her fears, or memories, might keep him out. Even though he had moved quickly through her mind, removing all traces of her trip to the In-Between, he prayed he had been thorough. He tuned his mind to hers, knowing the exact instant she awoke and in what condition. A nagging sense of guilt still gripped him and he wished he had been able to alleviate the standard, gut-wrenching reaction to such a jolting jump.

As he edged past her, his gaze traveled hungrily down the length of her body, her slender limbs emerging gracefully from the hem of her lavender T-shirt. Her hair fell in sleep-tousled waves. His hands itched to weave his fingers through its chaotic softness. The jasmine-and-spice scent slammed into his body, igniting his blood and sending it with lightning speed out of his brain and into his crotch.

Fighting his driving instinct to pull her into his arms, he entered the modestly furnished abode. Shades of beige, ecru, and tan blanketed the space from floor to ceiling. Peppered in were a couple nondescript modern-art prints. He examined the room from corner to corner, searching for something, a keepsake, some personal item that spoke only of her. Yet everywhere he looked, he met with an aching emptiness. The place reminded him more of a mausoleum, a testament to her recent lack of life.

"Um, sorry, the place is a mess, but..."

He turned from his surveillance at the hesitation in her voice. She dropped herself into the nearest chair, cradling her head in her hands.

"Oh, who am I trying to kid? My life is a mess, a dull, bland, beige mess! You know, it wasn't until yesterday that I realized what a shithole I live in. A bleak, monochromatic dump."

Kai knelt beside her and captured her hands with his. She raised her tired eyes, their honey-brown depths ringed with dark circles. A spark of a smile teetered along the edges of her full lips.

"I really hate beige," she admitted plainly.

Kai smiled warmly at her flat declaration. "Tell me what you would rather see."

She hesitated, her lush lips parted.

"Close your eyes," he whispered, reaching up to brush her lids down. "What do you see?"

A devilish grin melted her expression. "The inside of my eyelids."

He groaned, "Sorry. Couldn't resist." Peeking through one eye, she regarded him carefully. "Promise you won't laugh?"

"Unless you say something purposefully amusing, I promise," he said, giving her a reassuring smile.

Taking a deep breath, she closed her eyes again. "All right. Black bookcases…um, one of those glass-door corner curio cabinets. Wrought-iron candle sconces. A black-and-red couch."

"Sounds quite Oriental and in need of a shopping trip." He sensed there was more she was leaving out. Her ivory skin heated with the skittish blush he was beginning to love. The color set off the deep sable of her wild hair and the soft lilac of her loose-fitting shirt. Her small, high breasts rose and fell with her telling. His mouth watered at the remembered feel of those petite mounds and her delicate nipples.

Grinding his palm into his engorged cock in an attempt to relieve some pressure, he was grateful her eyes remained shut. He was fidgeting like a horny schoolboy, trying desperately not to play pocket pool. He cleared his throat to hide an uncomfortable growl.

"I've actually always been partial to IKEA. I like their simple designs. I find it kinda, oh, I don't know, straightforward. No-nonsense. Just straight lines and stable construction. Does that make any sense?"

"I hadn't thought of it in that way, but it does make sense." His mind traveled to his own house. His extravagant furnishings were from years of living. Her Spartan living conditions were from one year of solitude. He suddenly wanted to liven up the space. Her light was beginning to shine, and these bland four walls would need to reflect that glow for it to continue to grow.

"You were going to add something else," he encouraged.

"And…well, I've always been a really big movie fan, especially old movies and I remembered seeing a movie poster for Casablanca years ago and I thought it was just so cool." Her words tumbled out, barely contained by her excitement. Her honey-brown eyes popped open, brightly tinted with flecks of emerald green.

"And then there was that Erté print I found in San Francisco about eight years ago. And I've always kinda liked…" Another stoppage. "Dragons."

Kai blinked in surprise. "Most women would have said fairies, or horses." His mind whirled. The ancient symbol on his family crest was a red dragon, breathing fire and eating its own tail. The image was designed to incite fear and respect. Most humans shied away from the raw power of the dangerous beast. He waited to her to continue.

"Well, I'm not like most women," she stated, calmly shrugging.

"And of that, I am certain." He reached up to caress her soft cheek. With a smile, he traced his thumb along her bottom lip. "And eternally grateful." Leaning in, he was a breath away from letting his tongue follow the same path.

Voni pulled away timidly, ducking her head before standing, distancing herself from his sweet temptation. "Sorry. I've had an, um, strange morning and I, uh, need a couple minutes." She fiddled nervously with the edge of her shirt, dragging it farther down to cover her very exposed legs.

He rose smoothly, his massive form filling the cramped space with his presence. His natural sensuality oozed from every pore, threatening to drown her where she stood. She wanted nothing more than to drag him back to her bedroom and finish what they'd started last night, running her hands along the hardened, flat planes of his stomach and following the dark dusting of fine hairs that flowed below the low-slung waistband.

But she knew she must look a sight, not to mention she'd woken up spewing whatever remained from last night's meal as soon as her eyes peeled open. What to do today? Brush teeth. Shower. Get laid. An incriminating blush touched her cheek as she fought to control her errant thoughts.

"Forgive me," he said, bowing slightly. "I was hoping you would be interested in a day out and about, but I did not realize you had just risen. I could come back—"

"No." She captured his forearm, her hand sizzling as it met his exposed flesh. Desire flooded through her body and pooled deep in her gut. Her rational mind screamed for her to remove her hand, but her heart as well as her fingers refused to comply. "It'll just take me a few minutes to clean up." Her eyes delved deep into his eyes, seeing her own bedraggled reflection. "Okay, maybe you should make that a few hours."

Kai sighed, a soft smile touched his face. "You look beautiful."

She scoffed. "Yeah, right. I look like something the cat's been sucking on. I'm in desperate need of a shower, and I haven't even brushed my teeth yet."

Warm laughter rumbled and spilled out, quickly filling her apartment with mirth and joy. She swore she heard him mutter something that sounded like, "Lucky cat," but she couldn't be sure.

Voni took a deep breath, steeling her nerves, hoping she wasn't making a huge mistake. "Please, don't go. I'd...I'd..." Her eyes searched the room, looking for the right words and the courage to say them.

"I'll stay."

His smile staggered her, pulling her deeper under his spell. She responded with a crooked grin of her own. "How the hell do you keep doing that to me?"

If it were possible, his smile grew larger, deeper, more seductive. "Doing what?" he murmured.

"You make me feel..."

She turned sharply, retreating quickly down the hall toward the security of her bathroom. Door shut, she leaned her forehead against the solid barrier. Her heart beat a frantic rhythm as she gulped down much-needed air. She had to clear her head, get her thoughts straight.

What did he do to her? He made her...feel. And that's what scared her. She felt everything. Every emotion, every color. Even the molecules in the air had tangible meaning with him around. It was as if he'd opened the floodgates inside her soul, pulled aside all her well-constructed barriers, and all that made life, well, life, came cascading down in full force.

She had cocooned herself for so long inside her cottony, beige grief, she had forgotten the colorful beauty that had surrounded her all along.

But he brought everything back into sharp, vivid, and undeniable focus. His intensity terrified her. At times, when he looked at her, she felt as though she was somehow on the menu. He was a predator. His every move screamed danger, from the rippling of his muscles when he walked to the gleam in his eye when his gaze raked her body.

Yet somehow, she couldn't bring herself to be afraid of him. He had stood by her, offering his strength during her lowest moment out on that ledge. And again, when her heart raced out of control, he steadied her pulse. He had even taken away the pain during whatever it was that had happened in the coffee shop. He was danger, but not to her.

She pitied anyone on the receiving end of all that power.

She took the trash can out of the shower as she adjusted the water temperature. As she waited with her fingers dancing in the warming shower, her mind wandered, wondering what today would bring to her and to her gorgeous guest just beyond the thin door.

Kai stood rooted to the spot. Her flight surprised him. One moment, they were discussing furniture; the next, she was sprinting down the hall. His thoughts reran the last words she had said before her hasty retreat. "You make me feel..."

Feel what? Fear? Desire?

She had fled before finishing her statement.

His immediate response was to follow her, pin her against the nearest solid surface, and kiss her into submission. His second choice was to delve into her thoughts and search for her final words.

Yet, he instinctually knew neither of those options would be the best course of action. Especially the latter. Finesse needed to be the order of the day. Now if only he could get his dick to listen to his brain. Every moment that passed without him buried deep into her soft, slick, wetness was agony.

His thoughts sped back to the earliest days of his training. Remembering how long he had kept Tashiharo from his beloved spiritmate, he suddenly gained a great respect for the pain he must have endured. One week he had stayed to train him. Just one week.

Hell, he'd only known her for less than two days and he was going fucking insane.

Shaking his head, he rolled his shoulders to relieve some pent-up tension, but the sharp sting of the still-healing gouge across his back cut short the movement. He hissed at the painful reminder of last night's events. A few more hours of rest and the gash would have been no more than a memory. But his eagerness to see that she was all right refused him that needed time. The wound would heal, just not as quickly as it could. He'd placed a large bandage over the gash, hoping the jacket would cover any seepage.

The sounds of running water cut through the silence. He closed his eyes and pictured her, water dripping in rivers down her pale skin. Soap caressing her slender arms, her shapely legs, and her most amazing ass.

His hands remembered the feel of her against his palms, her supple body pressed tightly to him. Her body was soft in all the places a woman was supposed to be soft, yet just beneath the surface lay strength and power. Dance had gifted her with a strong and lithe body he was eager to explore.

All in due course. He ground his teeth to stifle a growl before unclenching the fist he didn't remember making. Her wishes, and her pace, must be the guiding force here. "A heart freely given is a heart free to take."

More fortune-cookie wisdom from his ancient mentor. Only now did he begin to understand those cryptic words.

In an attempt to distract himself from his nagging problem, he resumed his study of her home. Last night, Eamon had dumped them directly into her bedroom, following her spirit link to its corporeal host. Even in the dark, he had sensed the drabness that surrounded her. She was too vibrant to be lost in a sea of ecru waves. She was bright red and royal purples. He could see her lavished in the colors of Mardi Gras: greens, reds, purples, and gold. She deserved better. And he was certain he was going to make damn sure she got everything.

He would shower her in silks and diamonds. She would enjoy caviar and the finest champagne. The latest fashions, the hottest events, the most exotic locations. She would want for nothing. She would…

The remainder of that thought fled his brain as she emerged from the bedroom, dressed simply in a curve-hugging turquoise T-shirt and black capri leggings. The gentle scoop neckline accentuated her pale flesh and her small, pert breasts; while the black form-fitting cloth drew his eyes to her narrow waist and heart-shaped derriere. Her hair fell loosely in haphazard waves of deep chocolate. A large, lone clip restrained the bulk of it, but several tendrils floated free, framing her pinked, ivory skin. Her amber eyes sparkled, the dark rings faded but still too visible for his taste. The longer he looked at her, drank in her pure and natural beauty, he realized she didn't need any of those material things. She was silks and diamonds, caviar and champagne.

Voni paused, watching his strange response. It seemed as though he was frozen, stopped mid-thought. She wondered what could have distracted him so completely.

Yet, there he stood, pure predator. His stillness a preamble of what, she could only imagine. The stark white V-neck T-shirt strained against the tension of the solid, well-chiseled frame beneath. His muscular legs, encased in blue denim, were silhouetted against the bland surroundings.

An image flashed in her mind of another time and place. Kai stood as he did now, arms resting with barely contained lethal power at his sides, legs planted firmly into the ground. But his body was encased in black armor, an elaborate winged helm covering all but his piercing eyes. The sounds of steel and the cries of the dying echoed in her ears. She shook her head gently to dislodge the cryptic vision. The pictures didn't scare her; she simply wasn't ready to deal with her ridiculous imagination just yet.

She continued down the hallway, unwilling to examine her emotions. Or his reaction. Instead, she walked casually into the living room to retrieve her prized black Converse high tops. She knew they clashed with the current trends, but she believed in function above fashion. They were comfortable, and she always liked the way she felt in them. *I am such a dork.*

The hint of a smile touched Kai's lips as she grabbed a clearly well-loved pair of Chuck Taylors. As he watched her lace the shoes, he decided they were the only choice for her. She belonged in a world of simple pleasures. With all his influence, he could provide her with everything, but in his heart, he knew she would never become like the women at the gala last night, shallow and self-absorbed.

When she looked up at him, her task completed, her unadorned beauty stole his breath. His smile deepened, adding a devilish sparkle to his gray-green eyes. "You are amazing."

"Huh?" Voni met his dazzling smile with a puzzled expression, her hands resting on her hips as she rose from the floor.

"I thought you looked delectable last night. But now I see this is your basic attire."

Scoffing, she dropped her arms as she shook her head incredulously. "You are nuts. Either that, or blind." She bustled around the apartment, looking for something to distract her from his presence. As if that was going to happen. "Or both. Yeah, that's it. You're crazy and blind." A bit under her breath she added, "Not to mention desperate."

"My beautiful Siobhan," he purred, his long strides eating up the distance between them before he stood in her immediate space. "When will you simply accept compliments?"

"When? Are you serious?" She took a small step back, gesturing to her plain clothes. "I haven't bought new clothes in, like, a billion years, my hair always looks like an explosion in a hayloft if I don't pull it back into a friggin' ponytail. All. The. Time. And you..." Her voice faded, becoming a whisper as she continued. "You're like...next month's GQ cover."

Her gaze climbed up his frame to capture his eyes. "Why me? What can you possibly see in me?"

Passion darkened his eyes, making her gasp. When he found his voice, he spoke with an immeasurable weight, a power she couldn't resist.

"What I see is beauty, unaltered and unassuming." His stroked his fingers through her loose hair. "It comes from deep within you, not surgically created or cosmetically enhanced. Your mind, your heart...Your hair, your eyes, your body..." As he spoke, he let his hand follow his described path. "You looked at those women last night and thought you were somehow less than them."

Voni looked away, unable to face her insecurities reflected in his eyes. He caught her chin and gently raised her eyes back to his own, his gaze intense and demanding. "But to me, you were more tempting and more intriguing than all those carbon copies combined."

He silenced her next rebuke, kissing her tenderly. He trailed his hands down her shoulders. He meant it to calm and soothe her. His own response, however, was much more volatile. The overwhelming drive to claim her, here and now, was bordering on unbearable. Blood pounded in his ears, its beat demanding action. Words screamed in his brain, begging for release into the open. His hands itched to shred the flimsy fabric that hid her flesh from him, to explore every inch of her creamy skin and to bury himself deep inside her welcoming wetness.

The gentle pressure on her lips sent bolts of electricity through her, starting at her lips and ending at her toes. Fire blazed along her skin, ignited at the touch of his rough hands against her arms. Instantly, she was back in the front seat of his car, straddling his lap, half-naked and groaning for more.

Her heart stuttered, snapping her back to reality. She placed her hands against his firm chest, her fingers splayed across the soft white shirt. He broke off the kiss, easing away slowly. Another skip. She closed her eyes and concentrated on steadying the staggering rhythm.

Breathe in, hold, breathe out.

"Voni?"

Breathe in, hold, breathe out.

"Voni? What's wrong?" The urgency in Kai's voice threatened to break her focus. Shaking her head, she silenced him with her fingers against his lips. His warm breath tickled the pads of her fingers. The corner of her mouth twitched at the hint of a grin. Still, her eyes stayed shut and her mantra resumed.

Breathe in, hold, breathe out.

A couple more loops and her heart returned to its normal rhythm, her lungs drew in deep and easy breaths. Her eyes fluttered open, her gaze clear and sure. "I'm okay." Her voice was weakened and distant.

His brow furrowed as his eyes hardened.

She smiled, warmed by his genuine concern, not to mention his searing kiss. She let her fingers slip from his lips to return to the safety of his chest. "Really, I'll be fine. If I can catch it fast enough, I can usually bring things back to normal."

"Would you rather not go out?" His eyes softened but still held a dangerous edge.

"No, I guess I just need to get something to eat. It's been a really weird morning. That's all." He held her gaze fast. She squirmed self-consciously under his intent stare. "Gee, for someone who keeps on me about my lack of self-confidence, you think you'd believe in me a bit more."

Kai's face dropped a fraction of an inch, the color draining from his gorgeous complexion. "It was not my intention to—"

Voni caught his gaze, surprised at his sudden change in demeanor. "Oh, God. I'm sorry. I was joking. I didn't mean it like that. I was..." She was babbling and didn't know how to stop. She turned away from him, unwilling to see what her flippant words had changed. "Aw hell. I'm just going to shut up altogether one of these days and life will be so much easier for everyone."

"Voni," his voice whispered, his breath fanning her hair as his mouth brushed the edge of her ear. "I only am concerned about your well-being. I do not mean to doubt you." He circled around to face her. "And I personally would be very saddened if you stopped speaking."

"Why?" Her curiosity won out over her sense of self-preservation. "Wondering what stupid thing I'm going to say next?"

An impish grin tugged at the corners of his tempting mouth. "Actually, I just like to watch your lips move. I don't really pay attention to what they say."

Her eyes shot wide, her mouth gaped.

"Gotcha." His smile reached across his entire face, crinkling the edges of his eyes before breaking into a gentle laugh.

She glared at him through slit eyes, a playful smirk skittering along her lips. "Ha, ha. Very funny." She pushed against the massive wall of fabric before her as he continued to be amused at his own joke. "All right, all right. So, what are the plans for today?"

"Well," he said, between fading chuckles, "I suppose food would be the first order of the day. And after that…" He led the way to her front door only pausing as she grabbed her purse and her keys off the small table near the door.

"After that what?" She set the lock and closed the door behind them. He had descended the single front step and still towered over her.

Kai marveled at her, the lightness of her step, the inner smile that seemed to radiate through her every movement. She was beginning to emerge from the dark cocoon that had blanketed her life for far too long. She was the picture of curiosity. Her eyes twinkled, and a hint of a grin lurked just beneath the surface. The urge to wrap his arms around her lithe figure nearly undid him. He settled his raging hormones as best as he could, stepping back to give himself a bit of breathing room.

"You'll just have to wait and see."

"Sounds…ominous," Voni remarked, arching one brow as she dropped her keys into her bag.

Her voice, deep and throaty, set his blood aflame. Everything she did, every move, every word, was so incredibly erotic. He wondered how every man within a five-mile radius wasn't affected by her. Yet, no sooner had the thought raced through his mind that it was quickly followed by a dangerous level of jealousy. If any other man ever looked at her, he would hand that man his eyes, not to mention another, more precious part of his anatomy.

"Do you trust me?"

He held her gaze, reading the unspoken thoughts swirling in her mind. Did she trust him? Did she even know him enough to trust herself? She'd only met him just two days ago. His breath stayed locked in his chest as he waited for her to speak.

"I don't know why," she started hesitantly, "but I do."

Kai brushed his fingertips along her cheek. "Wow. And no 'I guess' in that sentence. I am honored by your gift." He leaned in to place a chaste kiss on her forehead, careful to keep things light. He was eager to spend an uninterrupted day with her and did not want to have a repeat performance of the earlier episode.

"Come." With a wink and a smile, he lifted her easily off the step and deposited her next to him on the sidewalk. "Time for breakfast."

Voni squeaked in surprise, laughing as her feet once again found solid ground. "Don't you mean lunch?"

Their gaze met, both of them nodded, adding in unison. "Brunch."

"I know the perfect place."

THIRTEEN

Kai led her down the walkway toward his awaiting car. He'd opted for the Mustang again, knowing she loved it so much. And as he opened the complex's security gate, he got the response he was looking for.

The smile blossoming on her face as she approached the gleaming piece of American craftsmanship told him he'd chosen wisely. "Aw, man. That thing looks even better in the light of day."

"I couldn't agree more." His eyes drank in the sight of her toned backside before she glanced over her shoulder. He flashed a hungry grin, earning him yet another delightful blush as she dipped her head, hiding the hint of a smile.

His words tripped easily off his tongue. But as the sunlight struck her dark brown hair, illuminating tones of chestnut, auburn, and pure black within the depths of the waves, she truly stole his breath away. Her honey-gold eyes sparkled like bright topaz beacons in a porcelain sea.

The longer he gazed after her, the further his jeans shrank, threatening to cut off blood flow to his brain. Get a grip. She still needed time. He would wait forever, but his body had other plans. He struggled to walk normally, even in his relaxed-fit denims. Limping to the passenger-side door, he opened her door like a gentleman, motioning her into their conveyance.

As he stepped around the vehicle and slid into the sleek leather cocoon, he hoped the car masked his awkward and stilted movements.

"Are you ok?"

He frowned slightly. "Why do you ask?"

She shrugged. "I dunno. You just seem, a little…oh, never mind."

Kai gnashed his teeth, attempting to alleviate some of his discomfort. He needed to be more careful around her. She was getting more attuned to him as he grew more connected to her. He tamped down his demanding nature, driving it deep inside and away from her still-fragile emotions.

Or he could just tell her if he don't screw her six ways from Sunday in the next five minutes, he would be useless as a man for the rest of his life. Yeah, that would go over great.

"One day, you will finish an entire sentence and I might just faint from shock," he said, opting for lightness. He gunned the engine and the car leaped into action. The quick jolt gained the desired peep of surprise from his passenger. A smile melted his stern expression, and the car's interior breathed a sigh of relief.

Voni's carefree laughter spilled out of her before she could stop it. Not that she wanted to. Why couldn't she just let go of the past and rejoin the real world once again? And this absolute god of a man wanted to spend time with her. Were all the gorgeous ones this crazy?

She snuck stray, sidelong glances at him as the car sped along the streets of the quiet warehouse district. The sunlight warmed his golden skin. His long black hair was held back by a thin leather strap, but a few stray strands refused to stay with the rest. His mouth, lips full and beckoning, tempted her and she remembered those lips roaming across her skin, and heat pooled low in her gut.

And those eyes. No sooner had the thought flown across her one-track mind than those piercing orbs swiveled toward her. Her mouth dried, and electricity licked along the length of her body. Heat rose to her hairline as she fought to tear her gaze away from his.

"Shouldn't your eyes be on the road?" Her voice tumbled out in a raspy whisper.

A slow, seductive smile crept across his luscious lips. "Not when I'd rather have them on you, *dragoste meu*."

Voni tried in vain to curb her responding grin. "Yeah, well. I'd rather arrive in one piece to wherever it is you're driving me." Besides being crazy, the man was pushing her hormonal buttons as if he were a kid with a PlayStation and she was the latest version of Halo. But, to be totally honest, she secretly loved the attention. No one, not even James, had ever looked at her the way he did. She felt beautiful, almost cherished. And the thought terrified her. How could she be worthy of such adoration?

Kai peered at her through half-closed lids, watching the emotions skitter across her face. Every part of her communicated her feelings. From the easy blush on her porcelain cheeks to the graceful arch of her brow over her expressive amber eyes, she spoke volumes without uttering a word. He wondered if she knew how much she told him with the slightest turn of her head or the flick of her hair. Especially that hair. His groin tightened as he imagined threading his fingers into that thick, deep-chestnut mass, dragging her up the length of his body.

He quickly shifted his gaze back to the road before his overactive mind began another dangerous, yet delicious, detour. The buildings thinned out, giving way to the picturesque shoreline. Sailboats and ocean liners sat like glittering jewels on a sea of sapphire blue. People from all walks of life crammed the sidewalks and spilled out onto the street.

"Uhh. Exactly where are we going?"

Her sultry voice didn't mesh with her apprehensive tone. A quick peek into her mind told him of her continuing inner turmoil. She was still a hard sell. Truth be told, he would have been unconvinced about his motives were their places reversed. How did you tell someone they were destined by fate to spend the rest of eternity with you? Oh, yeah, and that you'd been looking for your mate for the past 700 years. Talk about a deal breaker.

"Don't worry. We're almost there." Tourists and locals mingled along the boardwalk, beach cruisers wove treacherous paths between busy pedestrians, and joggers pushing baby strollers. Scantily clad bodies paraded their bronzed flesh before the eyes of all. Miles of well-oiled skin dotted the sandy expanse. Physiques ranging from paunchy to perfectly toned engaged in all manner of activities.

They continued on, passing small, beachfront strip malls and a bevy of surf shops. Spying a vacant spot along the street, he deftly maneuvered the steel beast into the narrow spot. Kai cut the engine before turning his attention toward her. He reached across the distance between them and caressed her warm cheek. "Siobhan, I made you a promise," he whispered, drawing her close. "And I have every intention of keeping it."

He brushed his lips across her forehead, though the tightening in his gut demanded much more. Forcing himself to release her, he pocketed the keys before emerging. The chivalrous gentleman in him refused to give in to her independent streak, so he "forgot" to unlock her door from the inside. He tried not to smile as he watched her fumble with the handle.

"Here, allow me." He smoothly released the door, causing Voni to nearly tumble onto the pavement. A coughed chuckle snuck out of him as he swooped in to catch her. "Are you all right?"

Voni scowled as best she could, mustering her remaining dignity. "Yeah, great," she grumbled. "I know you did that on purpose, so don't even try denying it, buster."

"Did what?" His pale green eyes opened wide while he brought her to her feet. His hands triggered paths of electric friction from the top of her head to the tips of her toes, the lightning congregating low in her belly. She swallowed hard against a blossoming dryness. His eyes promised pleasure and adventure, both things her previous life seriously lacked. Since meeting Kai, however, it had been a nonstop journey into the unknown realm of new sensations.

Constant embarrassment did seem to crop up quite often. The blush returned to her cheeks as she extricated herself from his iron grip, and flashed him a crooked grin. "Yeah, yeah. Act innocent all you want."

"My God, but you're beautiful." He wound his fingers into the stray locks that fluttered in the fragrant ocean breeze. "But still so unsure." He gave a wistful sigh. "I wonder what it will take to convince you."

"The way you keep looking at me is a good start." She cringed as the words fell out of her mouth as ungracefully as she had fallen out of his car. She looked up at him sheepishly. "I really did say that, didn't I? Gawd, I'm so pathetic." Looking around, she spied several eating possibilities and twice as many bathing beauties. "Well, do you have a place in particular or did you just come here for the scenery?"

Kai's gaze scorched a path down the length of her body, threatening to combust her clothes from the inside out. "As a matter of fact, I do have a place in mind, and as for the scenery..." He paused, his voice dropping to a heated whisper. "I am quite happy with the current view."

She rolled her eyes as she blushed so fiercely, she felt heat reach the tips of her ears. "Would you cut that out? I mean, seriously. I'm gonna end up passing out from constant blood loss due to excessive blushing. Do you enjoy watching me squirm?" Her hand flew up quicker than his mouth could move. "Wait. Never mind. Don't answer that."

Kai reached out to capture her raised hand and brushed his lips across her palm. "My dear, I thought you would have figured out by now I enjoy watching you do anything." His eyes darkened as his tongue tasted the racing pulse at her wrist.

"You're making it difficult to stay annoyed at you." Her voice was thick and sultry.

A sinful smile played on his devilishly gorgeous features. "Lucky for me, then." His gaze shifted and found their destination. "Are you hungry?"

Voni arched one graceful brow. "Is that a loaded question, or are you really asking if I want food?" Two could play at this game.

Kai intercepted both her tone and her thought. Play they would, but not before he kept a couple promises to her, and to himself as well. "Yes, to both, of course." He gently led her to a very busy corner café. "But I find that answering a loaded question is easier on a full stomach, don't you agree?"

"Oh, always."

Kai saw her cautious demeanor relax. Their light banter continued as they strolled closer to his favorite weekend breakfast nook. Her warm smile came easier, and confidence returned to her steps. Even her laugh, the sound that sent fire jetting through his body, crept out more frequently. Curious eyes followed their progress, female and male alike, staring at her with unabashed disdain or lascivious lust. His urge to defend his spiritmate rose up like a firewall, sliding his arm possessively across her back and around her narrow shoulders. His eyes narrowed to slits as he projected a clear hands-off-mine message to all humans within a four-block radius.

The painted sign on the rounded white cornered café proclaimed Kono's Surf Club. Red-shuttered windows on the second level offset the green wooden trim and the large street-level windows. Across the cobblestone boardwalk lay a narrow, grassy pathway, and just beyond, the beauty of the Pacific Ocean. As they approached the bright façade, Voni took note of the long line gathered outside the crowded little restaurant. Several groups scattered along the grass and sand, enjoying everything from breakfast burritos to pancakes and omelets, using plastic utensils on foam plates.

Light laughter bubbled out of her. This was the last place she expected to be taken. This cozy little shack was so unlike Kai. He was sophistication and manners, china and fine wine. Styrofoam and paper cups? Who knew?

"How did you find this place?" she asked, scanning the ever-growing line. Customers seemed to be filing in and out in a steady stream, but for each happy eater leaving with their meal, two more joined the end of the line. At that rate, it was going to be more like dinner.

"Are you kidding? This place has the greatest breakfast anywhere. Eamon and I stumbled upon the food here after...well, after a long night." He hesitated, believing it wiser for her to think they had pulled a late night of wine, women, and song. In truth, they had battled a trio of young Rogue Warriors, eager to cut their teeth on a group of unsuspecting late-night revelers. By the time they had sent the Rogues back to the In-Between and wiped the memories of the victims, which, considering their level of inebriation, was not terribly difficult, morning had rolled in and Kono's was just opening. One of the humans caught in the fray was the youngest son of the owners. Since that morning, in a show of their eternal gratitude for their son's life, he and Eamon had a reserved table every weekend morning.

"Long night, huh?" she remarked.

The edges of her easy smile wilted, and he realized the possible implication of his words. Kai saw her eyes lose their earlier sparkle, and she drooped in upon herself. Stopping near the doorway, he hooked his thumb under her chin and tilted her face to meet his gaze. "That did not come out as I had intended. Forgive me. I did not mean to—"

"Hey, no harm." Her flippant gesture and tone indicated nonchalance, but he had already sensed the flicker of self-doubt. "Besides, you're a total god. Like I'd expect you to not grab any woman who'd throw themselves at you." She looked away, as if ashamed by an unaccustomed spike of jealousy. "That sounded pretty catty, didn't it?"

"I'd call it protectively possessive." His voice held a smile that brought her eyes back to his. "And I find it flattering." The light returned to her hazel eyes, and the fire returned to his blood. He wanted to lose himself in her eyes, as well as some of her other assets, for all eternity. Her mouth, for one. And if he didn't lose himself in her tight, hot, welcoming heat and soon, he was going to spend an eternity in excruciating agony.

Dragging his thoughts back to the present situation, he ushered her into the shelter of the café, bypassing the still-growing queue. A few faces looked at them, yet not one person seemed anxious to growl at them. A friendly, grandmotherly blonde woman smiled as he approached the counter, waving him up to come closer.

"Kai! It's so great to see you. Where's Eamon?" She managed an awkward hug over the waist-high barrier, her eyes shining behind her wire-frame glasses.

"It's good to see you too. I'm afraid Eamon is on his own today. Rachel, I'd like you to meet Siobhan."

"Voni," she said as she reached out a hand in greeting. "Nice to meet you."

Rachel pulled her in to an awkward yet still comforting bear hug, her proper Southern upbringing still evident in her voice. "Oh, hun. I am so glad Kai finally met a nice girl. And so pretty too!" She extended her arms, beaming with pride. "Oh, you are just gorgeous. Kai, where have you been hiding her?"

He laughed at the owner's delighted response. Rachel worried like a mother hen about both him and Eamon, constantly trying to set them up with "nice girls." They both knew it was pure luck on their part that she had been blessed with four sons and no daughters. "I could tell you, my dear, but I'm afraid I might embarrass you," he said, wiggling his brows for extra effect.

She swatted playfully at his shoulder. "You are such a bad influence. And I'm sure you've been nothing but a gentleman, as you always are." She turned her motherly grin toward Voni. "He is such a nice young man. Always so polite, standing when a lady enters the room, helping out others—"

"That's quite enough of that," Kai steered Voni closer to the floor-to-ceiling menu. "If you continue on, you might actually have her believe I am a good man. And I would rather convince her of that myself." His rich voice was laden with innuendo.

A warm giggle rose from her, and she tutted. "You can't fool me, young man. Well, now. I guess I'll leave you two lovebirds alone. Voni." Her smile brightened the room. "It was a pleasure to meet you, and I hope to see much more of you. And I suppose it'll be the usual for you, Kai?"

"You are the best, Rach." Grinning, he leaned close, his breath fanning Voni's hair. "And what sounds good to you? For breakfast, of course."

"Maybe an omelet?" It would go well with her scrambled brain. Her voice wavered as she kept her gaze glued to the wall-mounted menu, determined not to lose her cool again. His body heat burned through her thin shirt, his masculine scent flooding her senses. She needed some distance from him to think clearly, but she wanted nothing more than to lean back and press herself against the solid wall of man just inches away from her.

He made the decision for her, closing the distance between them as he snaked an arm around her waist and nuzzled his chin into her hair. Her eyelids drifted down as his chest heaved at her back, a whispered, yet possessive growl fluttering her hair as he placed a kiss atop her head before stepping back.

"A very good choice. Just order whatever you like and I'll grab a table." He turned and crossed to the only open place inside, removing the small Reserved sign.

The air around Voni chilled a fraction at the absence of her walking radiator, but her brain now functioned. She placed her order with the young man behind the counter, concentrating on forming coherent answers to his laundry list of questions. Once she completed it, she picked up the plastic number tag and scanned the room.

Tables were full of tourists and locals alike, laughing and enjoying the start of the day. Kai, however, was quite easy to find in the crowd. The eyes of every woman in the room gravitated toward his sultry presence as he sat casually, his long legs extended.

Straightening herself, she walked directly over the corner table. Kai rose as she drew near, manners well in place, he easily guided her into the seat next to him with a hand.

"So, I guess the question of 'Do you come here often?' would be a bit silly, huh? I mean, a Reserved sign?" Her eyes pierced him with curiosity. "I've lived here practically my whole life and I've never even heard of this place. And the coffee shop the other night? What other little, amazing hidden places do you have tucked away?"

A Gallic shrug and hint of a smile was his response. "I enjoy the finer things in life, and many of those are not found on the well-traveled path."

"Spoken like a true poet. Now I have a question—"

"Just one?" His words brought a warm smile to her face.

"Ok, I've actually got tons of them. But I need to start with this one. What do you do for a living?" She pinned him with a serious stare. "I mean, your clothes cost more than my apartment is worth, you drive the hottest car as far as I'm concerned, and it looks practically new. You get invites to charity events and that obviously wasn't the first...so?"

Time paused as he puzzled out the best way to answer her. Even as their meals arrived, he fumbled for a suitable response. He was unable to lie to her. His promise to his spiritmate made that an impossibility. She would learn the truth eventually, but he preferred it to be in a more private setting. He opted to only tell her part, the more socially accepted answer. "I work in private security," he stated, watching for her reaction.

"You mean like a bodyguard?" Her brows shot up, surprise blazing across her face.

He chuckled at the glint of dangerous excitement in her bright eyes.

"In a sense, but not quite. Usually, it's much more boring than that. I set up contracts for people looking to protect their investments." If he were completely honest with her, she would know her first guess was more accurate.

Her expression dropped as she began to spear her potatoes. "Oh. Well, that sounds, um...great, too."

He snaked a hand out and brushed her soft cheek. "Your enthusiasm knows no bounds." Sarcasm dripped thickly from his voice. He raised his plastic coffee cup in a mock toast. "To the start of an eventful day..."

Voni smiled and returned the gesture, then lifted her orange juice. She added a clinking sound as she tapped their drinks together. "Ditto."

FOURTEEN

"So, you mentioned the start of an eventful day…" Breakfast finished, they started the trek back toward his car. Her curiosity about his enigmatic comment had kept her silent through the majority of the meal. She had some ideas of her own and hoped his might overlap on several points.

"Hmm?" His long, easy strides ate up the distance to the vehicle at a leisurely pace.

"Aw, c'mon! You can't keep teasing me like this." The kid in her reached out and tugged the sleeve of his T-shirt. The woman in her hungered to touch the exposed flesh of his bronzed bicep. Both ended up satisfied.

"Teasing?" She arched a brow arched seductively, matched by an equally dangerous smile. "I have yet to begin to tease," he whispered as he unlocked the passenger door.

The warmth flooded her cheeks as well as low in her gut. "God, do you have to do that all the time? I mean, I look like a friggin' landing beacon. All you have to do is look at me and I light up like a Christmas tree. I'm not a teenager, you know. I'm no virginal, innocent babe…" She dropped her jaw as a devilish grin played upon Kai's handsome face.

"Now that paints an intriguing picture," his voice lowered to a temptation-laden growl. He leaned an arm against the metal frame and pinned her between the door and the shelter of his body, pressing her against his obvious sign of attraction. "And I can be a very imaginative kind of guy."

"Of that, I have no doubt." Voni surprised herself with her strong and seductive tone. She rested her hands against his chest. "After all, you find me attractive, so you must have some vivid sense of—"

"Beauty?" His interrupting voice was velvet-encased steel, uncompromising and unyielding. "Passion? Adventure? Elegance? Since I'm sure that was going to be the correct ending for that statement?" His fiery gray-green eyes locked with hers. "I have some wild senses, but I do know I find you absolutely irresistible. Every timid smile and even every blush. Is it truly so hard for you to believe that you are beautiful?"

Voni found it hard to focus on forming coherent thoughts as he held her tight against his solid, well-muscled body. The large, rock-hard bulge pressing into her hipbone kept her attention diverted south of the border. Her imagination worked overtime as she visualized the flesh just a few layers of fabric away. "I feel like I have to apologize—" She paused when she saw his eyes narrow slightly. "But I just don't know how to get you to realize that, well, this is all kinda new to me. I've spent the last year in a...fog? No, that's not right. Ah hell. Before I met you, the only men I'd hung out with wore more makeup than I wear in a month and weren't interested in my plumbing."

He pulled her tighter into his body, he crushed her to him with his strog arms. "I can assure you I am more than interested in your plumbing." His final words were poured directly into her mouth; his tongue punctuated the sentence.

Voni gasped at the ferocity of his kiss. Her body lit up, fire racing through her veins. She met his attack move for move. She slithered hr arms around his neck before weaving her fingers through his thick, black mane. Every sweep of his tongue sent shockwaves through her. Her knees buckled, threatening to drop her where she stood. On instinct, she collapsed her weight against the car, pressing her body deeper into the massive wall of masculinity mere threads away.

The growl rumbling deep in Kai's throat was purely animalistic. He roamed his hands possessively north and south, one across the slender expanse of her back, one cupping her shapely ass while he ground his swollen shaft into the sweet spot between her legs. He pulled his lips away and trailed urgent kisses along her jawline as he lapped against her racing pulse. He found purchase in the hair still confined by her clip. She arched her back, giving him further access to her throat and exposing the flesh of her neckline.

Voni couldn't think beyond the sensation of his lips against her skin and the press of his body against hers. A hungry groan escaped her lips, and her eyes drifted closed as she reveled in the sensation of his breath, warm and enticing against her skin. She smiled slyly, and a wicked chuckle rose up from her chest.

He slowly dragged his tongue along the flesh edged by her shirt before lifting his head to gaze into her enraptured face. "I take it you are convinced?"

Voni's opened her eyes languidly, blinking slowly as a shy smile tilted her lips. "I guess you could say that. You do make a strong argument."

"You should see my counterpoint," he added, driving his hips into her, unable to resist the obvious innuendo.

"Geez, I can't believe you really went there." Her laugh was light and buoyant, bubbling up from the depths of her soul. It lifted her spirits and drove deeper cracks into the weakening walls of her lingering sadness. She was going to begin living, starting right now.

A tender smile played across his chiseled face. He toyed with a stray lock that fanned her face. "Well, hello there."

Voni shifted her eyes slightly, a coy grin hovering on the edges of her lips. "Hi."

He placed a gentle kiss against her forehead. "This smile suits you, *dragoste meu.*" He pulled her into the shelter of his arms, enjoying the nearness and simplicity of her company.

"I have no idea what that means," she murmured, curling her arms between their bodies. "But I like the way it sounds."

"It is a term of endearment in my native language." She sighed contentedly against his chest. Releasing her, he reached behind her and opened the car door. "Come. We have more things to do today."

Voni slid into the comforting leather seat, the smile still warm on her face. "So, you still haven't told me where we're going," she said, after he had settled into the driver's seat.

Kai turned and faced her. "Siobhan, my dear, we're going to reacquaint you with life."

**

The hours drifted by in a pleasant blur. Their first stop: IKEA. Voni browsed the entire store, leaving no corner explored. At each section, she made new discoveries and found things that would look great in her place. The black-lacquered, corner curio she imagined was only feet away from the gorgeous sleigh bed and the simple red-cushioned sofa. Around each bend, she took mental notes, calculating the costs and determining which she'd buy first.

At Bed Bath & and Beyond, she pictured cobalt-blue and gold replacing the bathroom beige, while royal purple and chrome took out the kitchen cream. She perused the wall art, searching for her Erté and Bogey. No such luck, but she did spy several nice Oriental dragons.

They had a late lunch and then made one final stop at Macy's. Voni giggled as they ate at Ruby's Diner, sipped thick chocolate malts, and devoured their burgers and fries. She had never been a fan of burgers, but the company made the meal much more delicious.

The famous, fiery southern California sunset was painting the skies a brilliant collage of oranges and purples when they emerged from the mall, signature white and red-starred bags in hand. Kai had insisted on purchasing at least one new outfit for her, so she had settled on a calf-length black skirt, a jewel-toned, patterned wrap-tunic blouse and a stylishly elegant pair of black-heeled boots. She had her eye on the entire ensemble, as it decorated the Macy's mannequin. It spoke to a level of sophistication she admired but never saw in herself.

However, today was a new day, and she allowed herself to think beyond her past preconceptions.

"Now, for the piéce de resistance," he said, ushering her back into the vehicle after securing her packages in the trunk. Unbeknownst to her, for each mental note she made, Kai did one better, keying the item number slyly into his BlackBerry. Every detail was cataloged and sent down to the information to an acquaintance of his in customer service, along with Voni's address. The boxes would be delivered during the course of the upcoming week, and he would be sure they were present for their arrivals.

He gunned the engine, heading toward the coast as he drove toward their next destination. With sidelong glances, he caught the subtle changes. Life and light poured from her entire being, and the heavy weight around her heart dissipated into mist. Throughout their day, she had smiled and laughed with barely a trace of her previous sadness.

Exiting the freeway in a rather industrial section of town, he hoped her sense of confidence would remain.

Voni listened carefully, music a dim undercurrent in the enclosed interior. The voice sounded somewhat familiar, but her mind was focused on other things, namely the hunk driving her to the next mysterious destination.

"Who is this?" She moved her hand to the volume control, her curiosity needing to be quelled. "I think I've heard this song before."

"It's Bush's lead singer, Gavin Rossdale." He maneuvered the vehicle easily between the light evening traffic. "He's actually done some acting. He was in the movie Constantine." He glanced at her for some signs of recognition. "Keanu Reeves? Demons in Los Angeles?" She lifted her shoulders apologetically, shaking her head slightly. "I guess we have some movie watching to do. Looks like you need to play catchup."

"Sorry. I haven't been to the movies in a long time. Been kinda busy...or maybe I've been kinda not busy. Well, busy living in a state of depression, I guess."

He reached over and gently brushed her cheek. Her soft skin warmed to his light touch. "Then it is time to see what you have missed during your absence."

A comfortable silence fell between them, broken only by the now-audible music. Voni watched as the car traveled into one of the grittier parts of the city. Skyscrapers cut jagged silhouettes in the fading light and warehouses lined the quiet street. Cars lined the fence separating road from railroad tracks. Her curiosity piqued as he turned into the parking structure beneath the three-story building wedged between the self-storage and the rock-climbing gym.

The engine's rumble echoed through the cement basement before roaring to a stop. Voni waited until the door beside her opened, resigning herself to his sense of old-world chivalry. As she stepped out of the car, a slight shiver tickled her arms.

"Ooh," she exclaimed, briskly rubbing her hands across her chilly skin. "I guess it got cold while we were out, huh?"

"That does tend to happen once the sun goes down, my dear," he murmured, wrapping his body protectively around hers. "Come. It will be warmer once we get inside." Entering the elevator, he pressed 2, and the chamber lumbered upward.

The doors opened to an open-air corridor, rounding toward a glass double door. Beyond the frame, brightly painted images of graffiti-styled dancers covered the wall, the ceiling, and even the floor. Large letters loomed above the front counter, exclaiming Culture Shock Dance Center, along with the words Unity, Diversity, and Respect. Loud, thumping beats vibrated through the walls, intermingled with a deep voice booming out numbers and notes.

The music pulled Voni through the lobby, calling her closer to the expansive studio just beyond the foyer. Inside, the sight that greeted her brought a shimmer of tears to her eyes. Dancers, their faces every color of the world rainbow, moved in perfect synchronicity. Bodies in all shapes and sizes stepped and rolled, snapped and rippled through each well-choreographed sequence.

Calling out directions was a tall, well-built man, his dark-chocolate skin drenched in a glistening sheen of sweat as he gestured at and encouraged the performers. The mirrored wall reflected the enthusiastic expression of each baggy-clothed figure. Smiles, pouts, and playful snarls flowed across the faces as the driving rhythms drummed into her very soul.

That was dancing. It was honest, authentic, and it fired her blood. Dancers in that studio were there for the love of their art. Not one face looked pained, or bland, or noncommittal. More importantly to her was the fact each dancer was different from the person next to them. For so long, she had been surrounded by slender wraiths trying to look like the next slender wraith, all striving for that "perfect dancer body."

"Hey! There you are! Glad you could make it!"

Voni turned to find the source of the welcoming words. Striding confidently toward them was a lean, athletic woman wearing a black-and-purple Jabberwockies T-shirt with the sleeves folded up to the shoulders. Her short-cropped salt-and-pepper hair spiked in all directions and her bare arms were tanned and tattooed, a broad, silver watch her only adornment. Piercing blue eyes danced as a warm smile broke across her features. One leg of her baggy black sweatpants was rolled to the knee and exposed more tattooed muscles. Without breaking stride, she pulled Kai into a solid hug.

"Angie. You look wonderful, as always. It seems things are going well for you."

"Couldn't be better, Kai. Couldn't be better." She instantly liked the older woman. Her exuberance was infectious, and Voni smiled in spite of herself. "And this must be Siobhan," she declared, refocusing her attention.

Kai placed a comforting arm about Voni's narrow shoulders. "You are so right. Voni, I'd like you to meet Angie Bunch, founder of Culture Shock Dance Troupes and co-owner of the Dance Center."

Voni grasped Angie's extended hand before the older woman pulled her into a friendly embrace.

"So Kai tells me you're a dancer?" Her bright eyes sparked with interest. "And that you might be looking for a new place to study?"

Her eyes widened the words slowly sunk in. "Are you serious? You've got to be kidding me! I can't dance like that." Her voice rose at least one full octave as she gestured toward the rehearsing performers. Her gaze bounced between the two looming figures before her and settled on the Kai's mischievous eyes. "Kai, my only real training is in ballet. You know, bal-let?" She drew out the word into two distinct syllables. "Hell, I took one or two jazz classes, like, a billion years ago—"

"And you said you loved it." His voice was sure and solid, his eyes boring into hers. He caressed her unsteady shoulders with strong ands. "You can do this. I know you can."

"I've got an idea," Angie chimed in. "Why not come on in? Watch for a bit and talk to a couple of the troupe dancers and see what you think." Her open, honest expression belied any hidden agenda.

Voni gnawed on her lower lip as her heart fluttered. A new start. A totally different dance company. And never another leotard or pair of tights. The softest voice inside her head ached to be heard. She actually wanted this so much. It was just a look, after all. No harm in looking, was there?

Her timid smile strengthened the longer she considered the possibility. A quick nod and a word of assent finally broke the silence.

"Great!" Angie said, rubbing her hands together in delight. "They'll be taking a break in a few minutes, so let's go on inside and watch until then."

As she entered the spacious studio, Voni felt as if she'd stepped into a whole new world. Gawd, I feel like I should be wearing a harem costume and sitting on a flying carpet with a prince. Her eyes strayed to find Kai intently following her every move beyond the glass. Turning away quickly, lest another blush color her cheeks, she continued on through the room. So many different faces; she hoped she would be able to remember some of them. Hair every color of the rainbow, every length, metal gleaming from earlobes, lips, and eyebrows. Fit, defined muscles covered in ink on both males and females alike. Each person reveled in their individuality, and that made the company stronger.

The short break appeared to be ending, although many of the dancers continued to work on their craft while their two guests mingled. A group of young men used the time to challenge each other to show off their moves in the midst of a ring of onlookers, each new contender attempting to out spin or out twist the previous one.

The two women left Kai to his thoughts as they entered the bustling dance space, closing the door behind them. He made himself comfortable in a chair in the hallway that looked into the main studio. Voni and Angie stood on the steps leading down to the polished wooden dance floor, deep in conversation. A couple minutes later, the rehearsal wound down and they stepped out into the mix of standing and sprawling bodies.

He knew it would take no effort to eavesdrop on the discussion only feet away from him. Yet he chose to remain outside, gaining his information from her reactions and responses instead. Shyly at first, she followed Angie around the room, shaking hands with several of the dancers, including the rehearsal director. With each new meeting, her smile broadened and grew. Laughter and camaraderie flowed easily from artist to artist.

The unabashed joy on Voni's face made his heart skip. The sight of her laughter, the sound hidden by the thick glass, tingled his blood, which fled his head for destinations in a southerly clime. Soon, he told his engorged cock.

Not soon enough, was the imagined response. Great. He was talking to his dick and hearing it talk back. Someone shoot him now.

Kai rose from his post as Voni and Angie waved their farewells. The voices of well-wishers filled the hallway as the door reopened.

"Omigod, Angie. That was amazing. Everyone was so great. You've got a really cool thing here."

Angie beamed from ear to ear. "Yeah. I'd like to think we do. So"—her eyes twinkled as she spoke—"Are we going to be seeing more of you?"

"Oh wow," Voni breathed. "It's just, um…God, I'd really love to. I mean, I just don't know if, well…I don't know if I'd be any good at it." She stammered on nervously, all the while the hint of a smile playing at the corners of her mouth. "But I'd really love to find out."

"Wonderful!" Angie pulled her into another gripping hug. "We have a full schedule of classes, but if you'd like, I can arrange for some private lessons to get you up to speed. The studio's pretty open in the middle of the day, and I'm sure some of the company members would love to help out."

Voni looked quizzically at her. "You'd do that for me?"

"Why not? You're a dancer, we teach dance…seems like a no-brainer to me. Besides," she added, glancing over at Kai, "with all the support we've gotten from Kai over the years, it's going to be nice to feel like I can return the favor."

"I don't want to be an imposition or anything—"

"Nonsense!" Angie laughed easily, maneuvering behind the front counter and pulling out brightly colored schedules and studio contact information. "Here's all the info you'll need. I can be reached at the number on the front or by e-mail. I'd love to have you here, Voni. I think you'd make a great addition to our family."

Voni graciously accepted the papers, handling them as though they were delicate, filigreed glass. The innocuous pieces of parchment held her dreams, possibly her new path.

"Thank you so much."

Angie reached across the desk and grasped her hand. "No problem. Absolutely no problem. We'll see you soon."

Voni followed as Kai led the way to the door, tucking Voni into his side, sheltering her from the chill night air. He looked back toward the still-grinning master of Culture Shock. "Thanks again, Angie. I owe you one."

"Naw," she scoffed at his praise, waving her hand in dismissal. "You've done so much for us. Besides, it'll be fun corrupting a ballerina."

"I couldn't agree more."

Voni couldn't be sure, but she thought she heard his voice rumbling just under his breath. She turned her face up to him. His eyes sparkled in the encroaching dark, and a devilish grin tilted his kiss-worthy lips as they headed back to the elevator.

With a silent prayer sent to whatever love gods might be watching over them, she stepped inside the small cage.

FIFTEEN

Darkness oozed and melted around the small cottage, and a chunk split off from the whole. Limbs morphed from the sliver of shadow, and soon a figure clad in scraps of night stood outside, peering in through the large front window. Its features became solid after a couple of wandering steps around the building. Blond hair spilled over the hunched, broad shoulders, and a pale hand shielded dark eyes from the distant streetlights.

Konstantin could smell Kai's arrogance clinging to this place. He must have missed him by only a few hours. He reached for the flimsy screen but stopped shy of tapping his knuckles against the aluminum frame. His projection would only appear as flesh. He continued to peer inside while a slow, smirking grin tugged up the corners of his mouth. Perfect timing. The silhouettes of two overly curious onlookers emerging from the dwelling just behind his right shoulder crept closer in window's shimmering reflection. He took a moment to practice his most charming and honest smile before he turned to face the men as they fought against their unease with each step.

"Excuse me? I was wondering if the young lady that lives here is currently at home?" Focusing all his will on ensuring they saw a complete man, not a semi-corporeal shade, he made sure to stay out of the bright glare of the security floodlights. The men, if you could truly call them that, whispered to each other, their fear oozing off them. The delicious scent made his mouth water. It was mother's milk and the best sex bundled into the same cocktail, and only the fact he could do nothing more than intimidate them in his current state kept him from licking his lips, just for a small taste.

With a self-indulgent sigh of disappointment, he waited with a patience he did not truly feel as the shorter, Latin boy struggled not to hide behind his Nubian companion. Why was it that artists tended to see more than standard humans? The black man finally gained enough courage to speak.

"Who wants to know?" The voice was forcibly deep and meant to strike fear in the heart of its recipient. He coughed to cover the laugh that snuck out.

"Oh, I'm merely a friend of a friend. Ah, such a pity I missed her. I am sure I will...catch her later." His smile was beginning to fail, and he could feel his essence being drawn back to the void.

He furrowed his brow and glanced over the shoulders of the odd pair before him. As the men turned to see what had caught his attention, he slipped into the shadows, vanishing into the surrounding darkness. He chuckled, watching from the Void, as they spun back to find themselves alone. The large man crossed himself several times in rapid succession before grasping the arm of his companion and they clattered quickly back into the bright safety of their stucco-and-brick abode.

Humans. So easy to manipulate.

**

Voni remained silent as they journeyed back to Kai's car. Her mind spun with the prospect of yet another new start. First, the gorgeous hunk walking next to her, who for some reason found her irresistible. Dangerously rugged looks, a powerful physique and piercing green-gray eyes. Yet he attended charity functions and donated money to local dance companies. Not to mention raced around in the dead of night, rescuing damsels in distress. Well, okay, only one damsel she knew of, but still. Geez, did he volunteer at the soup kitchen too?

And now, a diverse and exciting dance company where it didn't matter if she wasn't eighty-five pounds and five-foot six. As she crawled into the passenger seat, she recalled all the faces she had seen in the studio, the spiky hair, the lip rings, and tattoos, and the biggest smiles she had ever witnessed. Things seemed to be going her way.

Where the hell had he been for the past year? Her thoughts and her eyes strayed to the dark angel sitting behind the wheel. His rugged profile, chiseled out of the hardest marble, all harsh lines and fierce angles, camouflaged a compassionate soul. She realized all of his actions, since their initial meeting, were to make her happy. Each meal, every destination, and even the topics of conversation. He always put her needs and desires first. Just as he promised he would.

"Did you enjoy your day?" His low voice sent shivers down her bare arms, trembling that had little to do with the cold.

"Yes, I did. Sorry...I mean..." She paused, sighing deeply. "Thank you. Again." His gaze slid across the space between them. "This has just been so amazing. I never even knew about that place. And did you see them dance? That was...and the guys. All that twisting and spinning and... Do you really think I learn to do that? I mean, I'd seen that stuff before but, wow. And did you see that all the dancers weren't all skinny people? And a couple of them were even shorter than me! And their hair! Omigod, my director would freak out if I even mentioned trimming my hair, much less dying it purple..."

A hint of a smile tugged at the corner of Kai's firm lips. Her mind projected so loudly into his own he couldn't help but respond. He knew his intentions were not quite so pure. Did he do everything to please her? Yes. But he also wanted to please himself as well. And that pleasuring had better start damn soon, or else he didn't think he'd ever be able to walk normally again.

The slight smile grew into a full-blown grin as she spoke, her words tumbling out faster and faster. Her excitement actually had her bouncing in her seat. And all this time he'd thought that was just a turn of a phrase, he mused as her excitement gained ground the closer they came to her humble home.

"...and Sherman, that was the guy leading the rehearsal, well, he said he'd even be willing to teach me some stuff too." Voni stopped long enough to breathe and to look around. "Did I just ramble on for the entire drive back?"

"If it makes you feel any better, it was not a long drive." He didn't even try to keep the amusement out of his voice. People were still out and about on the well-lit streets, enjoying the cool night air. It was still early enough that weekend partiers would be roaming the streets. That meant necking in the front seat again was completely out of the question. Good thing too. He intended to finish what had been started last night.

Voni collected her thoughts as she waited for her knight to open her door. The night was still early, in the greater scheme of things. But here they were, parked in front of her little cottage complex. However, it was Saturday, and most people would be just getting into the swing of the weekend.

The door clicked open and the cold air flooded the car's interior. She briskly rubbed her arms, sending up a silent prayer that this was not to be the end of her night.

With a gallant ease she was beginning to enjoy, he helped her out of the car and wrapped his jacket around her narrow shoulders. "Come on. Let's get you inside and warmed up." He gave her a wink and a smile as he unlatched the trunk and retrieved her bags.

Bags in hand, they walked the short distance to reach her front door, his arm draped over her shoulders, the heat from his body taking away some of the chill. She restrained herself from running to the door, fumbling with her purse to retrieve her keys. In her haste, the devious metal bits leaped from her purse and clattered loudly against the flagstone walkway. Her hands shook from cold and other feelings as she bent to pick them up.

"Shit. Sorry." The words fell as easily from her lips as the offending keys had slipped from her fingers.

He grasped the keys and her hand as well with his long fingers. Fire licked its way through her entire body in the blink of an eye, his simple touch the catalyst of her inferno.

"No need to apologize." His piercing eyes captured her gaze, boring deep into her soul and bringing heat to her cheeks. Voni froze with his face mere inches away from hers. All she had to do was lean forward. He was so close, his breath fanning the flames growing in her blood. But her body stayed glued to the spot and her legs rooted in the concrete of her front steps, held by something other anticipation.

Apprehension? Her brow furrowed as she studied that reaction. She'd damn near rounded the bases in the front seat of his car last night. So why should finishing the deed be so scary? Did it have anything to do with the fact she hadn't had sex in well over a year, not to mention the fact that, even through his jeans last night, she could tell he was very, very well-endowed?

No, that wasn't it. Something else, something she couldn't put her finger on. She pulled her gaze from his, her eyebrows tugging closer together as she searched for the true source of her edginess.

"What is it?" The sudden shift in emotions across her face sent Kai into overdrive. He quickly dropped the bags and opened his link with her, scanning to discover the reason for her fears.

"I-I'm not sure. Something just seems, I don't know, wrong."

With a roll of his massive shoulders, Kai stood tall and imposing, his movements coiled and primed for action. He scanned the space beyond the door. There. It was faint, but still present.

Konstantin had been here. Not in flesh, but he knew where she lived, and he must have crept in through the dark corners as soon as the sun set. He was gone, but his evil still lingered over the entire apartment, waiting patiently for her return. Waiting to continue his nightly torture.

How the hell had she sensed him before he did? He had to be more on guard. "Wait here." His voice purred with menace, his self-directed frustration rumbling through his words.

Keys in hand, he carefully opened the flimsy screen, his palm pressed against the wood. No sound or movement beyond. Taking a deep breath, he slid the key into place. The tumblers fell noisily as the metal groaned slightly. "So much for stealth," he mumbled.

"Don't go in there!"

Voni squeaked, bolting out of her crouch and knocking her shoulder against the silver screen.

Kai swore as the metal slammed into the back of his knees. Turning, he saw Voni's eccentric neighbors emerging from their apartment, dressed in flowered robes and armed with a baseball bat and a large frying pan. The two huddled together, trying to both hide and protect each other.

He would have found the whole scene much more comical, if not for the telltale signs of the Rogue's visit. Plus, the sharp corner of the screen jabbing his still-healing shoulder was not adding to enjoyment factor.

"Christ Almighty, Daphne," Voni said, her voice a breathless whisper. "You scared the shit out of me. What the hell are you talking about?"

"Ahem." Her head jerked up to see him uncomfortably sandwiched between the two doors. With a muttered apology, she hastily retreated, giving him the space he needed to extricate himself.

"Chica, you had us worried." Roxanne cautiously lowered the bat. "There was this strange guy who stopped by asking about you and where you were and when you'd be home."

Daphne dropped her frying pan and rushed to pull Voni into a rib-cracking embrace. "Girl, you're gonna give me a heart attack by the week's end." Roxi joined in the huddle.

"What did this man look like?" Kai's deep baritone cut through their concern. He needed to get a visual idea of his opponent's temporary form.

"He was incredibly tall…"

"And very well-built…"

"Ooh, and his hair was that kinda dishwater blond …"

"Yeah, except he had the whole nappy grunge look going…"

"And those dead eyes…"

Daphne and Roxanne hurled more details at him, but he heard enough to know this visitor. He raised his hand, silencing both of the storytellers. "Thank you. I think that's enough of a description."

He sighed deeply, shaking his head to dislodge the all-too in-depth visualization of his adversary. At least, his foe had stuck to his normal MO. How the fuck had he gotten out so damned soon? "What was so strange about him?"

"Well," Daphne hesitantly took point on the rest of the details, "after we told him that you would be probably be out for the rest of the day…"

"Yes?" he prompted, already knowing the answer.

Roxi chimed in. "He just hung around, you know, peeking into the windows and stuff. Then he was just gone. One minute he was there. And then, poof. Like magic almost. We looked away for a second. Oh, mija, it was so scary." Broad hands adorned with hot-pink nails fluttered frantically, attempting to brush away the dread clinging to the walls themselves.

"Did he get inside?" Voni pushed away her neighbors, needing some space to think and breathe. She reached for the door handle, only to be stopped by frantic squeals and a strong hand enveloping hers. A dark force pulsed about her once-warm home, the essence familiar but only in her nightmares.

"We don't know, child, but please, just don't go in." Daphne urged, batting feathery lashes.

Voni sighed, unwilling to argue the point. Something was definitely wrong, and her instincts told her to let the matter lie until daylight. Which did leave an interesting question.

"Fine," she conceded, shoulders drooping a fraction. She turned her gaze to her best friends. "Mind if I crash on your floor tonight?"

"Of course—"

"I believe," Kai said, his voice laced with an undeniable power, "it would be best, since this mysterious stranger knows where you live, that you stay further away than next door."

Voni's heart raced at the possible implications of his words. Was he seriously asking her to go home with him? Yeah, right. He was probably going to suggest a nearby hotel. That small fragment of doubt refused to vanish, squashing her newly blossoming confidence.

"I guess, but—"

"But nothing. You will be my guest tonight, should you wish it."

"She does," was the answer in unison from her friends.

Voni's jaw dropped, locking her in stunned silence. True, her response would have been the same. But she wanted to be the one to give it. And it would have been even more enthusiastic.

"Good. It's settled then." Kai swiftly twisted the key, relocking the door and attempting to return the now off-kilter screen to its home.

Voni swiveled her gaze toward him, her mouth still agape. "Now, just wait a darn minute here—"

"Nope. Sorry, darling. Too late." Daphne pressed her hand against the small of Voni's back and pushd her into the shelter of Kai's body.

"That's right, chica. We gotta make sure you're safe," added Roxi, attempting to smooth and style Voni's tangled hair.

Kai chuckled as the two mother hens practically shoved her into his arms. He stood firm, wrapping one arm protectively around her narrow shoulders. Sparks erupted beneath the surface of his skin where her petite form touched his.

She still trembled, her exposed skin covered with goose bumps. Stroking her arms, he sent waves of ease into her mind, dispelling the lingering poison from Konstantin's visit. He would be able to scatter the remnants of the Rogue's tracking spell, but that would have to wait until he was alone. If Voni's neighbors were freaked out by Dmitri's simple disappearing act, they might run screaming once they saw him at work.

He placed his fingers beneath her chin and tilted her gaze to meet his. "Voni, you are about to shake apart out here, and I dare not let you go inside." His eyes bored deep into hers. He considered adding a push in his voice, ensuring her compliance, but it wasn't needed.

A smile tugged at the corner of her mouth, and his own lips answered with a grin of his own. "Are you sure? I mean, I don't want to be a bother or anything…"

Please say yes, please say yes, please say yes.

Kai heard her mental plea, and it broadened his smile wickedly. "My dear, I would not be much of a gentleman if I did not insist on seeing you safe."

"Ladies," he turned his eyes to the two robed figures huddling against the chill night air. "Thank you for being good neighbors." He extended a gracious hand toward them and grasped each hand in turn, still keeping Voni tucked safely into his chest. "And now, I believe I should get her to someplace warmer."

Voni wrapped her arms tighter around herself as she watched, amazed, at the simple gesture. Most guys she knew got freaked out by Daph and Rox, treating them as neither male nor female. Hell, she even saw one who didn't even act as if they were human. But not Kai. "Good night. Oh, wait!" She jumped, remembering someone else who relied on her. "What about Jazz?"

Kai looked down quizzically, one brow raised. "Jazz?"

"Oh girl, don't you be worrying about that stray." Daphne brushed off imagined lint, folding beefy arms across the blue-flowered silk. "He's sure to mooch off someone else while you're not around."

Voni searched their immediate surroundings, hoping to see her furry friend or at least find some clue he was not inside the house. "But he's my cat. Okay, so I'm more his servant…but—"

"Mija, I saw him out behind our place about five minutes before you got here, so he's just fine. Go on, chica." Roxi shimmied rather than shivered. "I'm getting cold just looking at you."

"And hot looking at him…"

The pair giggled as her face went from white to red in record time.

"Omigod! We're leaving." She turned on her heel, dragging Kai along in her wake as she raced for the gate.

"And don't you even think about behaving now..."

"Oh, girl. You better believe they won't, not with those m-m-mmm vibes he's sending out, and she needs—"

Their continued commentary faded into the night, and Voni cringed as the metal grate clattered behind them. "I am so embarrassed."

Laughing, his voice was light and reassuring. "I believe that was their intention." He unlocked her door, ushered her inside, and placed the bags in the trunk. Once tucked in behind the wheel, he gunned the engine and pulled out into the night traffic. She managed half a shudder before the heater kicked in.

A warm rush of air swirled around her legs, the heat a welcome relief. "Yeah, well," she stammered. "That still doesn't make it any better."

"They are only looking out for you," he defended. "And in truth, I find that quality very endearing."

"Whose side are you on, anyway?" She rubbed her hands furiously together, circulation beginning to return to her fingertips. Between the cold air and the eerie chill surrounding her home, she wondered if she'd ever get warm again.

A large, comforting hand wrapped around hers. Heat seeped through the dread, igniting a fuse that fired her blood. She drew her gaze to his chiseled profile. Streetlights added a strobe effect as the car gobbled down the miles to the next, and final, destination of the night.

"The side I'm always on." His eyes snapped her direction, desire blazed in the ice-green depths, threatening to consume her here and now. "Mine."

The word held a lifetime of promise, leaving her mouth suddenly dry and other regions damp. "Oh." The single syllable crept out in a breathless whisper.

The car sped up, racing forward momentarily, only to return to a more socially acceptable speed as he turned his eyes back to the road. He was in a hurry to get somewhere, Voni surmised. Could it be he was just as flustered as she was? She silently prayed that was the case. He slipped his hand away from hers as he worked the gearshift, navigating seamlessly through the few cars heading away from downtown.

Unable to form coherent thoughts or conversations, she stared out her window only to realize the true view was visible from the driver's-side window. That meant staring past his profile. Yeah, like that was going to happen. Not look at him. Sure.

She dropped her gaze to study her hands, feeling warmer, yet cold and vacant without his surrounding them. Soft music drifted through the silent interior, and a small, nagging thought chewed at her.

As attuned to her every feeling as he was, he sensed her tiny shift immediately, as if she screamed it in frustration. "Is something troubling you?"

Voni huffed out a disappointed sigh. "It's going to sound silly…"

That crooked smile flitted on the edges of his kissable lips. "I promise not to laugh, if that helps."

"Yeah, I can tell." Voni countered with a smirk of her own. "It's just that, well…"

He waited for her to continue, his gaze bounced between her and the road.

"I didn't get a chance to listen to the new CDs we bought last night." Way to go! She had a mysterious person staking out her home, and she was whining about music.

"If it makes you feel better, I do own several of them." He snuck a sidelong glance as he rounded the curve of the freeway off-ramp. "Once we arrive at my home, you can listen to your heart's content." Or it could be in the background for all he cared. Mood music might be nice for a change. His most recent one-night stand believed her pornographic encouragements would be music enough. Although he wasn't into erotic asphyxiation or other elements of the bondage world, he'd had serious thoughts about the use of a ball gag with her. He quickly banished the memory, not wanting to sully the moment with past exploits.

"Really? You wouldn't mind?"

"Why would I mind bringing you a small measure of happiness?"

A shy, tender smile spread across her face, making his pants uncomfortably tight. Now, here was one seriously sexy woman, and she didn't even know it. Her actions were natural, easy as breathing, and almost innocent. And they were driving him bug-fucking nuts. The restraining seat belt put his throbbing manhood in jeopardy of permanent damage.

He could blink them straight into his bed. Even divest them of their clothes. But the car…Yeah, that would definitely be a little tough to explain. Not to mention, she might just be a tad bit surprised to find herself naked in a strange bed when she had been a car just a moment ago. And somehow, he didn't think the whole Transformer story would hold water with her.

Refocusing on the road, he concentrated on stilling his wavering hand as he reached for the slim radio remote. A quick scan of the dial and soon the sounds of Amy Lee's haunting voice poured from the perfectly balanced speakers.

"Wow." Her awed tone sent chills and fire racing through his body. One word was the entire response she granted him, the interior filled only by the voice on the radio.

Curious at the cause of her deep silence, he dared a glance and found her eyes glassed over, staring at some distant point, her mind lost in deep contemplation. Daring a peek inside her head, he was overwhelmed by images of bodies in motion, twisting and spiraling in time with the driving sounds of Evanescence. Limbs forming lines and shapes, pirouetting and leaping. Moving with slow grace or quick power.

So that was how a dancer saw the world. The intricately writhing forms in her mind conjured images of bodies tangled in the heat of passion in his. It was possible for two minds to be on the same track but just arrive at the station from different directions.

Smiling at the new information, he began the final few turns, and the cobblestones crunched under the tires. And none too soon.

The pulsing rhythm bled into her soul, feeding her long-starved spirit. Music had always been such a crucial part of her. Her dancing had been driven by her passion for music, deep and haunting, soothing and consuming. It had been so long since she sought the comfort of sound, she only now realized she had forgotten why she danced. The performers she'd met tonight, they knew. Their dancing had fire and conviction, drive and purpose. She wanted to feel that again. She had to.

The road sounds serving as undercurrent to her choreographic daydream shifted, the smooth pavement disappeared, and a rough, gravelly surface now rolled beneath the vehicle. Blinking out of her musically induced stupor, she peered into the darkness surrounding the headlamp's gleam.

The private path wound up, leading to a massive white-stone-and-stucco mansion. Floodlights illuminated the winding driveway, which terminated in a carport bigger than her entire block. Her jaw dropped as the Mustang swung easily in place, sandwiched between a wicked-looking black crotch-rocket and a sleek, silver, low-slung sports car that rivaled those driven by James Bond.

"I am so out of my league here," she muttered. The brisk air jolted her, setting her teeth to chatter.

"There you are wrong, my dear." His voice warmed her, and he gently wrapped his fingers around her hand as he helped her from the confines of the car and brought her knuckles to his lips. "For you are truly in a league of your own."

Grateful for the shadows hiding her deepening blush, she climbed out into the auto museum that was his garage. She tried not to gape, but once she spied the fourth classic car, a powder-blue Ford T-Bird, she could no longer keep silent.

"Oh. My. God." She spun, ogling everything from the gleaming chrome tailpipes to the hand-stitched leather interiors. She even paid homage to the red-and-black standing toolbox, flitting from car to car, leaning in but never touching. She continued to worship at the altars of foreign and domestic alike.

Voni caught his reflection in the polished sheen of the Aston Martin, his eyes hungry and demanding. He stood still, coiled and lethal, his strong arms resting almost casually across his massive chest. Almost, because she could feel the tension rolling off him in waves; the heat of his gaze ignited her blood. His eyes narrowed, focused so sharply on her ass, she thought her clothes would burst into flames.

She rose with a deliberate slowness, not wanting to make any sudden movements. Would he attack? Ravish her right here, out in the open? Press her against one of the many gorgeously solid pieces of machinery and have his wicked way with her? Oh, God, she hoped so.

Folding his arms across his chest, the cold temperature temporarily forgotten by his companion, Kai grinned as she danced through the garage, bounding from car to car. His gaze followed her as she examined each vehicle with an attention that made other parts of his anatomy very jealous. He marveled as she bent forward, twisting her hands uncomfortably behind her back as she attempted to avoid the temptation to stroke the metal inches away. At that angle, he only needed to take three small steps and her perfectly formed ass would be grinding against his rock hard cock.

"It seems you and I have similar appetites." He growled, the blood racing below his belt faster than a holiday shopper to a sale on Black Friday. His restraint was wearing thin. He needed to get her inside the house so he could get inside her. Now.

"So I guess that means they are, right?" She said, her eyes wide and her tone breathless.

He nodded, his movements deliberate, not quite ready to trust his voice. The longer he stared at her, the hungrier his gaze became, focusing on her lush, kissable blue lips.

Blue?

The sight sobered Kai immediately.

"I apologize. You must be freezing out here." He quickly secured the vehicle after grabbing her packages. "Come. I promised to get you someplace warmer."

"Wow. You mean there's more to this?" A thin veil of sarcasm curved the corners of her lips into a sinful smile. "I can't wait."□

SIXTEEN

The door swung silently open as he led her into the pristine recesses of his house. Voni had an overwhelming desire to remove her shoes lest she sully the immaculate pale-oak floors in the hallway or the thick Persian rugs scattered on the arctic-white living room carpet. Everywhere she looked, beauty and luxury met her gaze. Objects d'art and state-of-the-art electronics rested side by side in harmony. A massive screen that rivaled the one in her local movie theater dominated the spacious living room and was offset by a large black-leather sofa that looked able to seat a party of twelve with ease.

Her mouth refused to stay closed as she peered deeper into the huge place he called home. The longer she looked, the lower her jaw dropped. She fought the urge to look for the registration desk. It had to be a hotel. That would explain the numerous expensive cars in the open-air garage. That had to be it.

Bullshit. This is his house, you are way, way out of your league, and you know it. How much longer are you going to keep deluding yourself?

Kai pressed his chest against her back, leaning over her shoulder, his voice a hot whisper in her ear. "Are you planning on going in, or are we going to sleep in the entryway?"

"Sorry, I mean, it's just that..." She was stammering again. "Should I take my shoes off?"

His laughter rumbled through her body, and heat flashed quickly through her blood and pooled between her legs. He rested a strong hand on her shoulder, his voice hot against her ear.

"My dear, this floor has seen much worse than your delicate little high tops."

Timidly, she stepped farther into the room; his pure-masculine presence still clung to her clothes as he ushered her inside. Flames licked her skin at his light contact.

"Somehow I find that hard to believe," she grumbled, carefully eying the mirror-like finish on polished veneer. His exasperated sigh caught her attention, dragging her gaze from the floor over her shoulder to find his hungry ice-green eyes locked on her face.

"Trust me, just this once."

Trust him? Her mind scrambled, grasping for something solid to latch on to. He was talking about knowing his own house, right? He would know about what else had passed over these floors, right? He did live here.

Yet something in his eyes told her he was speaking beyond the literal. Gnawing her lower lip nervously, she offered a shy smile and a subtle nod.

The bags slipped from his hands as he scooped her into his arms. His mouth descended, and hungrily devoured her slightly parted lips, her gasp of surprise swallowed by the force of his hot kiss. He thrust and parried his tongue into her mouth, dueling hers for ultimate supremacy. He wound one hand through her loosely contained hair while using the other to pin her hips firmly against his straining erection. His momentum propelled them into the kitchen, and they stopped only when he set her down on the first available countertop.

She entwined her arms around his shoulders, wanting to touch the corded muscles a thin sheen of fabric away. Backpedaling, she felt the floor disappear. The weightless sensation lasted a heartbeat, until the solid ground under her feet was replaced by a hard, cold surface under her ass. The kiss never faltered, nor did it lose any intensity during the short journey to her destination.

Kai trailed his hands down her slim body, kneading her shapely legs and pulling her hips possessively against his throbbing member. Inching his hands the entire length of her legs, he then hooked her feet securely behind his back before making the slow return trek. He slid his mouth from her lips and nibbled a path across her jaw. A deep groan brushed against her skin as he nuzzled her ear, teasing the tender lobe.

Fire lanced through her veins as Voni gulped in air, her fingers laced through his thick, black hair. She clung to him, his flesh her personal lifejacket. She roamed the vast expanse of his muscular back with her hans, feeling the ripple and roll beneath her fingertips. She had to touch more than that damn T-shirt. She clawed at the blasted material, and her fingers scraped against something not fabric.

His sharp hiss froze her wandering hands as she recognized the feel of medical gauze and reality crashed in.

"Omigod, I'm so sorry. Are you okay? Did I hurt you?" The words tumbled out of Voni's mouth in a frantic stream as she wiggled out of his embrace to study his face. She ran her fingers with tender care over his back, seeking out the edges of the large bandage. She searched his face for answers, her eyes wide and her heartbeat gradually returned to its normal rhythm.

Kai dragged in a raged breath to steady his lungs, exhaling in a slow stream as he inwardly cursed himself. Opening his eyes, he found her, cheeks flushed with kiss-swollen lips, intently focused on his face. He slipped his hands through her silken tresses and traced the line of her jaw and the edge of her pouty lower lip.

"I do not deserve you," he whispered, a smile curving across his lips.

Voni blinked in disbelief. "What?"

"I invite you into my house, practically screw you on the kitchen counter, and you're worried about me?" He let his hands stray back into the chestnut locks begging to be touched as they framed her pleasure-pinked face.

"But you're hurt and I've hurt—"

He pressed his fingers softly against her lips, silencing another bout of what was sure to be self-recrimination. "It is nothing."

"But—" Her hot breath tingled the pads of his fingers, causing his already-primed cock to jump against the confines of his jeans. Clenching his jaw as he growled deeply, he held her gaze, his smile both warm and wicked.

"No buts tonight, baby. No apologizes, no second-guessing." He studied her darkening amber eyes, the flecks of emerald like spring leaves on a sea of honey. "And no distractions."

"That would be nice," she replied, her voice breathy and strained.

"Nice?" Kai dipped his head, his lips inches away from hers. "Personally, I prefer to think of it as delicious." He pressed a gentle kiss on one eyelid. "Enticing." Another kiss on the other lid. "And soon to be oh so much more than nice."

Kai sensed her whirling thoughts, her timid fingers searching along his spine, their feather light touch driving more blood out of his brain. "I thought we agreed no distractions..."

She opened her mouth, a single word ready to tumble out, but he claimed possession of her lips before she could utter any sound.

"And no apologies, either."

He sensed that his whispered words eased her curiosity as her inviting lips curled into a shy smile.

His self-control tenuously back in his hands, Kai breathed deeply, inhaling the intoxicating jasmine-and-spice scent that was uniquely hers. He lingered a few moments, savoring the simple pleasure of her embrace, before releasing her. "Would you like to see the rest of the house?"

Voni nodded at first, opting to keep her mouth shut until her mind could complete a coherent thought not involving another apology. As he stepped away from her, her brain returned to its more normal pattern. Her body, however, whined at the loss of his solid masculine form. An impish thought crossed her mind, followed quickly by an equally impish grin.

"Is each room as, um, exciting as the kitchen?"

The smile she received from her quip could have melted the polar ice caps. If not for the fact she was still perched on the counter, her legs would have dropped her flat on her ass.

"Undeniably so." His smooth voice flowed over her skin like a velvet promise. He gripped her hips in his strong hands and led her back to solid ground. He leaned down to place a gentle and safe kiss on top of her disarrayed tresses. His closeness fogged her thoughts, fired her blood, and eased her soul. How could one man make her feel all those things so quickly? It was as though he was meant for her, like her perfect match.

Perfect match. The realist in her scoffed, while the romantic refused to listen. Why not? Was it so wrong to think, so silly to believe?

You don't even know him. You don't know what he does, or even really know how he feels about you, the realist screamed.

Kai took her slender hand in his as her fingers trembled slightly. Her lingering uncertainty tickled along his skin, her mind still trying to overrule her heart. He understood her conflict but knew she wasn't quite ready to hear the truth. That would go over just great. *Don't worry, hon. You are my perfect match, and I've waited 700 years for you.*

"On to the rest of the place, then, shall we?" Kai tugged her out of the stainless-steel-and-marble kitchen, pulling her toward the opulent living room. He laughed, watching as she cautiously unlaced her dainty black sneakers, opting to place them on the two-year-old hardwood rather than on his fifteen-year-old carpet. "If you want to be more comfortable, please feel free. But do not, for a moment, believe that you are unfit to walk on this very old carpet."

"Old?" Her voice lifted in question as she peered down on the pristine flooring. "You must have one hell of a cleaning lady."

"Actually, I have a service that comes in once a week." More often, if the blood got too thick on the kitchen tile, he finished the statement silently. He led her into the spacious living room, watching as she lightly crossed to peer out to the night, transfixed by the view.

"Oh, wow. This is amazing. I bet you get some gorgeous sunsets here." She edged forward, balanced on her tiptoes to see farther into the inky darkness.

Kai rested his palms against the black leather sofa, admiring her tempting backside. His mouth watered and his cock twitched, desperate to continue his seduction. The urge to pin her body between him and the safety-tempered glass was driving him right to the edge. Needing to keep it in his pants, for the moment, he crossed over to the stereo, remembering her concern about music.

He flicked the Power button, scrolled down to find the perfect choice, and pressed Play. Silently, he crossed the living room, his steps slow and measured.

The haunting and sensual voice rippled through the room as he closed the final distance between them. She lolled her head back, eyelids drooping, as the sultry female singer crooned on.

"Who is this?" the words rasped out, breathless and rushed.

"The group is called Lacuna Coil..." His breath warmed the shell of her ear, his chest pressed into her back. He trailed his fingertips, teasingly light, against her arms before wrapping his arms around her petite body. "...the singer is Cristina Scabbia..." he whispered. As he suckled her earlobe, he snaked an arm around her shoulders and used the other to grind her ass possessively against his groin. "'...and the song is called 'Entwined.'"

Kai growled as she melted against him with a hungry sigh, gripping his arm tightly. Her legs buckled as he trailed his lips down her slender neck. Steadying her, he slid his free hand beneath the hem of her soft turquoise shirt, eager to touch her smooth flesh.

She gasped, and the muscles beneath his seeking hand tightened as he brushed her sensitive skin.

"Oh, G-g-god," the sound of her voice was caught somewhere between a prayer and a plea. "This is really going to happen, isn't it?"

Kai pried open his eyes and gazed deep into their combined reflection. Her skin was both cool and slick, a thin sheen of sweat still lingering from their earlier make-out session. "Only if you want it to, *dragoste meu*. Only if you want."

The intensity and sincerity of his words dragged her heavy lids apart. A myriad of emotions played chase across her face, and he waited until she arrived at her final decision.

"I want it, Malakai." Her words were strong and clear. "I want you."

He tilted her chin up as he claimed her lips in a slow, burning kiss. Burrowing one hand farther beneath her form-hugging pants, he brushed his fingers against a slinky scrap of fabric, all lace and temptation. He trailed kisses along her spine, kneeling and moving down her body to get a better grip on her short, tight pants. Peeling away the offending covering, he then lovingly lifted each delicate leg to divest her of her pants, which created an inky spot against the white carpet when they fell away.

"I approve." He smiled slyly, admiring the wide, hip-hugging lace band and narrow silk strip concealing the tender juncture of her thighs. He placed butterfly kisses along her smooth curves as he worked his way back up her gorgeous backside until he stood once again at her back. A crooked smile tilted his lips as he delved under the tantalizing black barrier, reaching farther until his fingertips met with a small, well-groomed patch of soft curls.

"Mmm. What have we here?" he purred hungrily against her ear. He plunged his hand deeper, seeking her hot, wet folds. She gasped, writhing against his intimate invasion.

"Have to keep it trimmed for costumes," she groaned out, her body eager for more of his touch. She sought out his solid flesh, snaking an arm around his neck to wend her fingers through his thick, black hair. Thrusting her hips back into his hardened cock, she then wound her leg along the length of his calf and hooked his ankle for balance.

"That's it, my little, nimble one," he murmured into her mouth. He slid his fingers between her velvety lips and teased the sensitive fleshy pebble to a fever pitch. "Show me what you want."

Voni sunk her fingers deep into his sinewy muscles, searching for an anchor in the rising storm raging through her blood. The flames licking up from the magic his hand was creating between her legs threatened to incinerate her clothes. Her breath came in urgent gasps, her body undulating with the music that filled the room. "Don't. Stop. That."

Kai groaned, swirling his tongue along the edge of her mouth as he slipped one finger into her wet core, then two. As a throaty moan escaped her lips, her muscles clenched, grasping him and drawing him deeper inside. He held her tight against his body, supporting her trembling legs as he rubbed the sensitive knot of nerves above her hot nether lips.

Unable and unwilling to stop herself, she ground her hips in slow circles against the raging hard-on pressing firmly into her ass. Fed by the friction of his rippling fingers, her thoughts scattered as the sweetest pressure began to build. She arched back, forcing the air into her lungs only to have it escape again in a frenzied moan. The rhythm of his fingers, caressing and teasing her, spiraled her closer to that most delicious breaking point.

Voni screamed as her climax slammed into her, firing her blood as it ripped her apart. Her head flung back as she clung to the strong arms about her shoulders, her legs rubbery and useless underneath her. Wave after sweet wave crashed through her body, robbing her of reasoning skills and intelligible language. Her hips continued to buck as his deft movements wrung out the strongest orgasm she had ever experienced.

"Now that was quite a start to the night," he whispered, his voice thick with desire. Kissing her flushed cheek, he slipped his fingers out, slick with her flowing juices. Her inner muscles had tugged so powerfully on his fingers as she came, he'd almost shot his load just imagining what that tight core would do with his cock buried deep inside it.

"Start?" Voni croaked.

"Oh yes, my sweet. Start." Kai stared at their reflections in the glass, willing her to open her eyes. Her heavy lids fluttered up, passion darkening her hazel depths. With her locked in his gaze, he brought his hand to his lips and licked her nectar from his fingers.

He tightened his arm about her shoulders as her cheeks paled and her eyes flared wide. His tongue savored the liquid heaven coating his fingertips.

With a hold on his arm, she turned to face him. Her gaze held his as she pulled his hand to her lips, tasting her own cream.

He groaned as she slipped his fingers into her hot, wet mouth, and her tongue caressed and teased them. He slid his fingers out of her warmth, pulled her into his arms, and slanted his mouth possessively over hers. He dove his tongue deep, fighting a territorial battle with hers. He guided her arms about his shoulders while he trailed his hands down her back and cupped her perfect ass. Scooping her legs up, yet unwilling to break their kiss, he then maneuvered backward, angling them toward the sprawling couch.

She locked her ankles behind him and dug her heels into his ass as she wound her fingers through his hair. He tilted her head, scrambling to discover every inch of her delectable mouth. He splayed his free hand between her shoulder blades and used the other to knead the toned thighs resting against his palm. Shuffling his feet until soft leather met the backs of his knees, he then carefully sat down still cradling his delectable cargo.

He unhooked her feet and settled back into the overstuffed cushions. Her legs folded daintily as she straddled his lap. Breaking away from her lips, he dragged her clingy shirt over her head, eager to finally glimpse the creamy flesh beneath. Inch after gorgeous inch of unmarred ivory met his eye, culminating in a matching sexy black lace bra, supporting the mouth-filling mounds he desired. He slipped the cloth completely off and tossed it somewhere out of reach.

"Ooh. A matched set," he purred, his gaze dragging away from the midnight scraps to the face of his angel. "I definitely approve." He thought he spied another tempting blush on her cheeks. It was difficult to tell with the pleasured flush still warm upon her skin.

He savored her with his eyes, drinking in the sight of her firm muscles, her narrow rib cage, and her soft breasts still hidden from view. But what a disguise. Her bare legs straddled his lap; his already ramrod-stiff cock strained painfully against his jeans, yearning to find the tight sheath a whisper away.

"My God, woman, but you're beautiful," he murmured, his gaze roaming her exposed and unexposed flesh. "And I have wanted to do this since I first saw you."

"Do what?" she asked, the simple words more like a sigh as his eyes returned to hers.

Kai reached up and searched with his fingers for the clip that bound her thick tresses. Finding the offending piece of plastic, he pulled it free and tossed it aside, releasing the soft waves to flow about her face and halfway down her back. He ran his fingers through the tangled mass, wrapping it around his hands before burying his face in it, inhaling the pure scent of her. It was October heat and autumn leaves, sweetness and spice. It calmed his spirit and fired his blood. He knew it now. Now, he was certain. She was his spiritmate.

And he intended to claim her.

Tonight.

Something in his eyes, a slight shift, set electricity through her veins. Somehow, Voni knew this was turning into something more than just sex. The thought frightened and excited her at the same time. As he nuzzled her neck, she wrapped her arms around him while he held her as if she were something precious. She began to tremble, his hot breath against her skin raising the fine hairs along the length of her entire body.

A throaty growl escaped between his lips, the hum driving her excitement further. Ever so lightly, he trailed his fingertips along her back, and a breathy moan escaped from her slack jaws as she dug here nails into his shoulders.

His strong, sinewy arms became her anchor to reality. His feather light tickling sent spasms of pleasure through her entire body, flooding her core with moist heat. She ground her hips into his lap, her body desperate for more than the friction of fabric between them. She ran her hands down his chest, seeking the edge of the thin tee.

Kai covered her grasping hands with his, halting her actions. Taking handfuls of material, he yanked the shirt off in one swift movement and threw it behind her, his gaze never leaving her face.

She struggled to hold his gaze, but her curiosity was too great. Voni gaped as she saw a body truly chiseled out of the strongest stone, made all of solid, smooth planes with a light dusting of black curls that trailed enticingly beneath the top of his jeans. She explored each ripple and ridge with her hands, finding a barrage of crisscrossing scars in many places.

"Did they—"

"Shhh. Later," he whispered, his eyes searching her face. "I promise. But for right now," he leaned in, his mouth soft against her shoulder. "I plan on driving my cock deep inside you." He flicked his tongue out and tasted her tender skin. "Or licking every inch of your body until you scream." His desire-darkened eyes met hers. "I haven't quite decided yet."

His explicit words should have offended her. Instead, they only heightened her passion. "Either one sounds amazing." But in her mind, the picture of him buried to the hilt inside her almost sent her over the edge.

Kai smiled devilishly, picking up on her loudly projected desire. "Mmmm, I agree." Holding her gaze, he led her hand down to the waistband of his jeans. She moved her fingers smoothly and without hesitation, unfastening the top button and sliding the zipper open, all the while her eyes never wavered from his. The metal teeth gaped open, and she slid her hand down to release his cock from its denim prison.

She slid her fingers around his throbbing cock, the light pressure a velvety torture, eliciting a possessive groan as he thrust the slippery head against her palm. Another stroke and her curiosity finally got the better of her. Turning her gaze downward, her jaw dropped as she took in the sight of his massive cock, the head of his shaft reaching well above the top of his jeans. A slight groan escaped her lips.

"Ah…crap."

Kai saw awe and fear flash across her face, followed by an air of defeat. She was afraid of not being able to fit his sizeable erection. He knew from their earlier foreplay that she was tight and he would need to move with tender care as not to hurt her. He eased the taut fabric apart and wriggled his jeans down lower until the entire package was unbound. He caressed her cheek, wending his fingers through her hair, opting for lightness to alleviate her fears.

"What? Not enough for you?" His flashing eyes mirrored his devilish grin.

She snuggled into his hand, her soft skin warm against his palm. Her eyes fluttered closed as she glanced away. "Very funny. No, it's just that—"

Kai silenced her, pulling her into a slow, sensual kiss, tenderly plundering every inch of her mouth with his tongue. He traced the edges of her lacy ensemble with his free hand, sliding his fingers beneath the hem to tease the flesh underneath. He swallowed her sigh as he deepened the kiss, pouring his desire for her and her alone into every lick. To drive home his intentions, he rubbed his throbbing cock against the thin fabric barrier.

"No second-guessing." He whispered against her lips. A barely audible gasp echoed in his ears as Kai moved to taste the tops of her breasts. He slid his fingers down her neck and dragged her bra strap over her shoulder and watched silently as the soft mound of flesh slipped free, exposing a pert nipple. Leaning in, he breathed hotly against the hardened nub as she bucked and writhed on his lap. He smiled wickedly before flicking his tongue against the responsive button. She tasted of salt and spice, of passion and promise. He laved her breast while making short work of the front bra clasp. Tugging the garment off her arms, he directed his attentions to the other mound.

She dug her hands into his hair, rooting him to the spot, and her breath came in frantic pants while her hips swayed of their own accord. He sucked and teased her sensitive orb, then pulled back anguishingly slow. When his teeth grazed her nipple, she screamed out, arching her back as she came again, digging her fingers into his shoulders, as her body writhed against his.

Kai continued to suckle as he milked her second orgasm. He knew she would need to be good and wet before he could think about claiming her. She rippled and shuddered, her knees gripping his thighs to the point of pain. Damn, he thought, smiling wickedly. She might actually leave some nice bruises.

"Can you give me one more, baby?" He rumbled against her flushed skin. A little voice in his head told him to listen to her heart rather than her words. With his ear pressed close, he found the beat fast but steady. He could control the rhythm if the situation arose, but he wanted this to be on her own terms.

"W-w-why one m-m-more?" she asked as her forehead rested against his head. Sweat dripped in tantalizing trails between her breasts, and he was entranced by the droplet.

Kai nudged the final barrier aside and pressed the head of his cock against her wet opening. Her legs tensed up, her natural reaction to his impending conquest. He guided his shaft up and down the length of her hot slit, only teasing the nether lips.

He continued to tempt with slow, sure strokes, never actually penetrating as her legs opened wider, her hips rolled in invitation. His own self-control balanced on a knife edge, the innate knowledge of the impending sweetness the only thing holding him in check. He sought her pebble-hard clit and rubbed his thumb against the sensitive, fleshy knot. He was rewarded with breathy moans and an erotic lap dance.

"Come on, baby," his words spurned her on. "Come for me one more time."

Voni arched and writhed under his skillful attentions. The muscles in her belly and low in her gut twitched, her breathing shallow and gasped. She had no way to deny him his request, nor did she want to deny him. The fire rose between her legs for a third time, and she could only cry out as the flood rocked her all over again.

At the moment of her climax, he slid the head of his cock between her spasming folds. Her orgasmic screams melted into a new set of moans, deeper and more urgent, her eyes flying open at this sweet intrusion.

"Oh...G-God," her voice caught in her throat, lodged somewhere around her heart. Lightning lanced through her veins as she watched in rapt fascination as his hard shaft disappeared between her legs.

Her wetness helped guide him along, but his massive girth stopped mere inches in. Placing his hands on her hips, he carefully eased out before dipping back in, gaining another sweet inch.

"So...tight." He breathed the words against her neck as he nibbled her tender skin. He repeated the process patiently and lovingly, drawing himself out then plunging back in, his guttural growls in perfect harmony with her breathy moans. Each time, her body ground and bucked, keeping her passageway damp and slick.

"Am I hurting you?"

Voni lost count of the orgasms once he slipped between her soft folds. Every time he plunged, pulled back, and drove in again, she lit up like a Roman candle. Again and again, he plumbed her, each drive ripping a breathy moan from her air-starved lungs. She held on to his strong shoulders, his skin slick with sweat. Her damp hair clung to her back and tickled her hypersensitive breasts. Her hips swayed and undulated, her body rippling with the music filling the silence between their sighs.

His voice blew hot against her ear, but her brain had trouble putting meaning to the sounds.

Kai paused and pulled away slightly to capture her gaze, encircling her shoulders with his arms. "Baby, am I hurting you?" His voice was laden with pleading concern, his breathing ragged.

She slid her hands down and let them come to rest on his chest as she held his gaze. "Only by stopping now."

He devoured her mouth in a furious kiss as he drove his cock the final inch home, her strangled cry lost in the midst of his primal growl. He cradled her body close to his, her heartbeat pounding against his chest. He broke away from her lips to drag his tongue along her sweat-laced skin, tasting her spice and desire. Her inner muscles grasped him in a viselike grip, her orgasms drawing him closer to his own release.

"*Eu te sustin, organism si spirit. Eu te sustin, inima si sufletul.*" *I claim you, body and spirit. I claim your, heart and soul.*

His voice cracked as the ancient words flowed unbidden from his lips, his native language a heated prayer against her damp skin. I claim you, body and spirit. I claim you, heart and soul. Once begun, he had seven days to complete the ritual or risk losing his immortal soul for all eternity, becoming a Rogue Warrior himself.

He dismissed the errant thought, focusing instead on the vixen whose legs of satiny steel clinched his thighs, pulling him deeper into her hot, wet core. He bowed his back and dipped his head as he gently quickened the pace.

"So beautiful," he hissed between clenched teeth.

Sweat poured from his body as he strained against his own impending release. He struggled to keep control, but her sweet, damp channel pulled and milked his shaft to the point of pleasurable agony. He sensed her climax near and continued to drive her until she reached her peak.

Gradually, his thrusts gained speed, increasing the sweet friction between her legs, sending a wave of molten heat to flood her tight channel. Her hips rolled and bucked, her heartbeat raced ever onward, her breaths shallow but strong. The mother of all orgasms grew and continued to build, his velvet voice only stoking the flames to greater heights. She trembled as he trailed his hands across her back, holding her delicately yet firmly against his slick, solid skin. Her fingers flexed and clawed, searching for a stable hold.

Faster and faster his thrusts came, pushing her closer and closer to the edge. Her keening cries scaled higher, her eyes squeezed shut as she tried to make the moment last. She lowered her chin and rested her head atop his deliciously scented hair. His purely male fragrance seeped into her being, calming and igniting her all at once.

"I-I-I," she moaned, her trembling lips not cooperating with her desire to speak. "Oh God."

"Come for me, Voni," he urged, his cock pistoning faster and faster inside her, and she knew she was helpless to resist.

"Let me feel you come."

Time froze, her breath held in her chest for the tiniest measure, and then everything exploded. Her body shattered, and a deep scream shot skyward from her ragged throat, his name pouring from her lips. She clung tightly to his shoulders as he thrust one final time before she felt him join her in ecstasy, his hot seed spilling deep into her.

Voni trembled and shivered, her body slowly coming back down to earth. She shuddered as she gulped shallow breaths, her pulse beating out a speedy, but steady tattoo. Her cheek rested against the wide expanse of his chest, her arms folded into her own chest, tucked in close. With his hard body pressed so close to her, she felt cherished. She felt safe.

More than that, she felt as though she had just performed Swan Lake in its entirety, all the parts, herself. Every muscle in her body ached, some she never even knew existed. But what a delightful workout. A satisfied smile played on the edges of her lips, fighting to take hold if only they'd stop twitching long enough to hold the shape.

"So," she croaked, her voice weak and thready. Coughing, she attempted to clear her abused throat.

"Hmmm?" His chest rumbled beneath her palms. "Would you like to try that one more time?" She didn't need to see his smirk; she heard it in his carefully chosen words.

"The speaking or the sex?" Obviously, her quick tongue hadn't been slowed by her earth-shattering orgasms.

Laughter rolled easily from his lips, pouring down her back and teasing her responsive skin. "Is that an invitation?" Sensually, he ground his slick hips against her, his cock still buried deep inside.

She gasped, her own giggle spiraling into a groan. "Omigod, you've got to be kidding." Her body rippled as he drew long, lazy circles across her back with his rough fingertips.

Kai trailed his hand to her face to take a gentle hold of her chin. He tilted her head and pressed kisses against her eyelids, tender and soft. Another kiss fell on the tip of her pert nose. Two more graced each cheek before his lips met hers. "And what if I'm not?"

Damp warmth flooded between her legs instantly. The immediacy and intensity of her response stunned her into an embarrassed, muted silence. A flush heated her skin from her naked breasts to her sweat-slicked hairline.

"You were saying?" he murmured against her delightfully pink cheek.

"Well," she began once more, her voice a bit more sturdy. Her thoughts were not so sturdy, though, especially with his shaft still hard and nestled in her fleshy pocket. "I was wondering if there was more to the house than this."□

SEVENTEEN

Kai had the noblest of intentions when he drove out of his garage that morning. Well, perhaps not entirely noble, but he had at least hoped he would be able to curb his ravenous desire until he got her to the bedroom. Instead, the couch was a far as he was able to hold out.

If given the choice, would he change anything?

Not one second of it.

Even after what they had just shared, he found it charming that she still blushed. In his soul, he knew she would never cease to amaze him. And even after what they had just shared, he still hungered for more. Was he serious? By all the gods in the heavens, yes.

He gazed into her bright eyes, shining pools of emerald-flecked amber peering out from the curtain of disheveled sable locks. The pink flush on her cheeks poured down her throat and covered the thin skin over her heart.

Her heart! His own skipped a beat as his thoughts returned to the fragile state of the beauty still cradled in his arms. He trailed his fingers down the column of her throat to splay them between her breasts. The beat beneath the pads of his fingertips was quickened, but the rapid pattern belied any undue stress. Closing his eyes, he dipped his head down and rested it against her crown of wavy silk.

He feared he had pushed her too far, demanded too much too soon. Her sweet, tight, and lithe body drove him to a fever pitch and beyond. Even now, with her straddling his lap on the sweat-slicked leather, he wanted her again. He would never be completely sated as long as she breathed. Once the claiming ritual was finished, every moment, every action until the end of his days would be to ensure her happiness, her pleasure, and her love.

His silence caught Voni off guard. She was prepared for more wordplay, ready to match wits again. Instead, he simply held her close, his breath tickling her heated skin. As if he wanted to burn this moment into his physical memory. As if he were unwilling to release her.

"Kai?" Her tone was quizzical. "Are you ok?"

A deep, masculine rumbling shook his chest beneath her hands. "My dear, what in the world could possibly be not okay?"

"No, you just got all quiet and I thought, maybe—"

"No second-guessing." Kai kissed her head gently. "But, to answer your question." He paused, leaning back to rest on the supple, butter-soft couch. "Yes, there is more to the house than this. Ready?"

Voni knew this question had many more than one possible interpretation. Her answer, to all the variations, was the same. "Why not?"

A wicked smile curved his full and kissable lips. "Why not, indeed." He gripped her hips with both hands and regained his feet in one smooth movement, still keeping her firmly impaled on his thick shaft. A surprised gasp hid in the giggle that slipped between her lips. With one arm wrapped beneath her ass, he wriggled the remainder of the denim from his legs, each twitch and kick causing her legs to wind tighter around his waist.

"Damn, woman," he growled between clenched teeth. "At this rate, you'll be getting round two right where we stand."

"Standing up like this," she groaned, "was your idea, genius. God d-d-dammit." Her hands shot out, and she dug her fingers into his firm shoulders as her body writhed in response. Hair whipped out in every direction, and damp tendrils still clung to her face as her head snapped skyward. Her thighs quivered, her hips bucking as he took ground-swallowing strides toward the stairway.

With his lips, he teased and tasted the salty, heated skin that flashed before him. Dragging his tongue across the hollow of her throat, he reached the first step. Her tight, wet channel clenched around his stiffening cock, holding him soundly in place.

He managed three more steps, gaining the first landing, before his need overrode nicety.

"Ah, hell," he hissed. He turned quickly and pressed her back against the solid wall. He slid his hand up her body and claimed her mouth in a fiery kiss, raking her sides with his fingertips as he worked his way toward her hands. With sleek strokes, he drove his shaft deeper and deeper into her hot, slick core. His tongue twisted and danced with hers as she swiveled her head from side to side to allow him greater access. He reached her wrists and ever so gently raised her arms over her head.

The solid purchase behind her back grounded her for a moment, and she extended one leg in search of the wooden surface below. Her toes drifted far above the floor, their rather large height difference making contact with the floor a pipe dream for her. Opting for Plan B, she wound her calf along the back of his thigh, her hips pulsing in harmony with his and the music droning idly in the background.

Kai held her hands in place with one hand. The other was free to travel the ins and outs of her body, from the soft mounds of her breasts to the handhold dimple on her ass. He continued to devour her mouth, their breath mingling as one. His body lunged forward, hips undulating as he pounded her with a primal need. Her muscles fisted around his throbbing cock, her own orgasm building.

She broke the kiss, gasping for air as his teeth grazing her jaw and her earlobe. Rasped sighs escaped from her lips as he swirled his tongue along the curvy path, stopping only to plunge into the sensitive opening. She pushed gently against his hand, eager to touch him, only to meet with an unbreakable resistance. She pried her eyes open, lids like lead weights, until she found his passion-darkened eyes.

"Do you trust me?" His voice, like warm velvet along her skin, thrummed along her veins, the music calling to her soul.

"Do you still need to ask?" The words caught in her throat, the power of his gaze shaking her to the core. This was more than a harmless roll in the sack. She saw it in his eyes, heard it in his voice, and felt it in his every touch. It did frighten her, but not nearly enough to make her want to stop.

A crooked grin tempted his lips as he drove himself deep into her, one hand easily pinning her arms securely against the smooth wall, allowing his other hand to roam. Her back arched, her small, firm breasts thrust upward as an offering to him, her nipples hardened beads. Not wanting to refuse her gift, he rubbed his flattened palm across her sensitive nibs. Her eyes rolled back in ecstasy, her soft keening sounds dancing along his spine.

His strokes gained in speed and in intensity, his frantic pace testing the limits of his self-control. His desire to lose himself so deep in her soft, wet sheath, and to stay lost within her, both calmed and drove him. Inhaling her sweet perfume, a musky jasmine-and-spice scent that intoxicated his senses, he forced himself to slow, to savor her, to ensure her ultimate pleasure.

He pressed his forehead against hers, his body attentive to her every movement as she shifted her legs higher. One found purchase around his waist as the other seemed to have another pathway in mind, lifting and raising until her knee reached into his armpit.

"Oh, what do we have here?" He purred across her lips, as he slid his free hand down from her nipple to caress her thigh. Gripping her hip, he dipped his mouth to claim hers, only to pause as she extended her leg straight. Her foot touched the wall near her trapped hands before she lowered it to rest across his shoulder.

The remaining blood in his body charged into his pistoning cock. Words of wonder and adoration flowed from his lips, his native tongue tripping against her heated skin. Nuzzling her neck, he licked, nipped, and teased the sensitive flesh there, trailing his tongue up the column of her throat, nibbling her tender lobes. Her body bucked and rocked, breathy mutterings the only sounds echoing in his ears.

The delicious friction built, her deep inner muscles tightened and tightened further. Her breaths came in ragged gulps and blew hot against his face, spurring him on to one final plunge that pushed her over that sweet precipice. His name flew from her lips, serving as both a prayer and an anchor.

His head arched back as a guttural shout ripped from his lips and he came a second time. Holding her with unbreakable tenderness, he kept her pinned, his powerful body continuing to shudder until he was spent. He forced air into his burning lungs, each fragrant breath feeding his blood and his soul.

Since the claiming ritual was unfinished, no child would come from this coupling, or any others, one safeguard for keeping Guardians in line.

An uneven pounding against his chest brought him jarringly back to the present. His eyes flew open, searching her too-flushed cheeks.

"Voni? Voni? Talk to me, baby." With a delicate urgency, he untangled their limbs, clutching her shaking body. "C'mon, love. Breathe for me."

She blinked rapidly, tears slipping down her cheeks as she struggled to pull in air. Her arms fell lifeless against his sweat-dampened shoulders. He delved quickly into her mind, catching the pinpoints of light dotting her blurred and fading vision. *No, please.* Her mental words were a silent prayer. *Not...not...*

"Shit." The word hissed out between his clenched teeth. He blinked them into his bedroom and laid her down on the large four-poster bed. He flattened his palm against her stuttering heart, channeling his own energy directly into her, signaling both heart and lungs to work. "Stay with me, baby." His rough voice was barely a whisper against her skin. "Stay with me. Breathe with me."

Her powerful orgasm had clamped a vise around her chest, and neither heart nor lungs seemed interested in cooperating anymore. Panic began to put a serious damper on her post-sex high as she forced gulps of air into her aching lungs, darkness threatening to drag her under.

An electric jolt shot through her body. Her first breath was a painful gasp as her eyelids flew open and slammed shut just as quick. Fiery pain rocketed through her blood as air filled her starved cells. Time crawled by as the tightening in her chest gradually eased; the pain ebbed away.

She returned to her body, noting that the once-solid wall behind her was mysteriously gone. Something soft and cushy had replaced the hard surface. Peeling her eyes open, she was greeted by the relieved smile of a reclining angel.

"Hey, beautiful." His gravelly voice warmed her skin, his breath tickling her cheek. Propped up on his elbow, he trailed his fingertips lightly against the line of her jaw, his knuckles caressing her cool, slick skin. "I knew I was good, but I've never had a woman practically die in my arms." His whispered words, their playful tone aside, were heavy with apprehension, bordering on outright fear. He captured a stray lock of her hair and entwined his fingers around its damp softness before pulling it into his lips, as if savoring the texture.

"Well, they're not called *la petit mort* for nothing, I guess." He'd saved her life yet again. Voni was beginning to lose track of the number of times his actions had altered her life's path. Her latest episode had come too dangerously close to rendering her unconscious, if not worse.

Images of white walls and pinging machinery blurred into her vision, and the acrid stench of antiseptic and lingering death stung her nose, but she quickly brushed them aside. That had been years ago, before she'd learned the trigger signals, as well as some simple breathing techniques and mediations to halt an oncoming attack.

"Sorry," she said, smiling weakly at him as she pulled air into her lungs, his strong, masculine scent of raw amber and smoky musk permeating her body. A warming fire began to smolder in the pit of her core, licking flames to life deep within her. Despite the recent near-death experience, she wanted him again.

"I must be nuts," she mumbled, dragging her arm across her eyes in a feeble attempt to hide from her building desire and his tempting lips. "Um, not to sound ungrateful, but how did I get here?"

Kai drank in the sight as she lay spread before him like a banquet, her arm draped over her eyes, exposing her soft ivory breasts to his hungry gaze. Her well-toned stomach rose gently with each slow breath. Her lush hips, her firm legs, and the small thatch of deep chocolate curls above her sweet junction painted sheer perfection before his eyes.

A devilish grin tugged the edges of his mouth as he recalled the image of her leg reaching straight toward the sky before landing on his shoulder. In all his years, never once had he taken a dancer to his bed. Most of the women he slept with were simple, beautiful creatures. The most recent distractions had had their bodies surgically engineered to meet the current superficial standard of perfection. They played their parts without fault, moaned at the right time, screamed at the appropriate volume, and knew their lines impeccably.

But here, now, he had truly found the living, breathing definition of feminine sensuality. His heart was happily lost. His spirit buoyed by her sharp wit and open honesty.

"By magic, of course." His voice was a deep rolling rumble that thrummed along her sensitive skin. It was the truth. For the most part. He lowered his head, coming to rest on her forearm. "I am sorry for causing you pain, Siobhan," he said, his words laced with anguish and compassion.

Voni removed her arm to gaze into his eyes. She reached up and took his face between her hands. "I thought we agreed no apologies."

Her gentle words crumbled any walls Kai still possessed. He cradled her against his body, cherishing the way she fit perfectly against him as once again the words of his native tongue fell from his lips, reverent as a prayer.

"*Viata ta am cravata mea sa.*" He paused, stroking smooth circles on her back. *Your life I tie to mine.*

"*Voastra si buciria jalea.*" Briefly tightening his embrace, he pulled back, tracing his hand along the soft curve of her cheek before continuing. *Your joy and your sorrow.*

"*Eu va dau toate ca eu sint, si toate ca nu va fi.*" He placed a small, tender kiss on her forehead before pulling her back into the shelter of his arms. *I give you all that I am, and all that I will be.*

Kai held her, drawing languid lines along the length of her spine with his fingers. Her breathing had eased into a relaxed rhythm, her body melting deeper against his chest. He sighed. This must be what heaven felt like. He closed his eyes, covering their bodies with a thought, and allowed sleep to claim him.

Again, the beautifully mysterious and sensuous language spilled like warm honey along her skin. He had slipped into that otherworldly language so easily. She knew it must be his native tongue, his accent giving life to each uttered syllable. She would have to ask him what the words meant, but the thought of moving any part of her body for any reason just didn't seem like the right thing to do.

Right now, tucked against his solid frame, she didn't want to do much of anything, and her eyelids seemed to be more than willing to oblige. Truthfully, she wanted to stay like this forever, feeling safe and more loved than she'd ever thought possible.□

EIGHTEEN

The yowling darkness was beginning to become boring. Purely evil beings tended to be rather dull conversationalists, Konstantin thought. As time ceased to flow in a constant forward direction in the In-Between, the days had passed like weeks. Moment followed monotonous moment, his every whim materializing and dematerializing as quick as a thought.

It felt like forever since that braggart Vadim and his over-sexed boy-blunder Eamon had robbed him of his prize. That small sparring session only managed to whet his appetite for mayhem. His little toy. Malakai had called her "Voni," and she was starting to slip through his fingers. Each day with the do-gooder was bolstering her confidence. He needed her to break down again. He yearned to feast on her beautiful sorrow. And in order to do that, he had to get the hell out of Hell, to put it plainly.

Waiting for enough strength to once again call corporal form, he occupied his time training his fighting skills. Weapons from all corners of the world lay strewn against the black marble floor. Staves and swords, dirks and daggers, and all manner of machinery designed to strip flesh from bone sat in mute display. A wooden sparring dummy and punching bag occupied the farthest corner.

A table appeared against the wall, his midday meal glistening like melted amethysts in its multifaceted pitcher. He manifested a small towel and wiped his brow as he filled the rock tumbler with the lifeblood of his kind. In an effort to speed his fleshy recovery, he had amped up his daily meals, adding the emotions he craved: anguish, despair, grief, and for flavor, sexual brutality. This concoction gave him a heady rush, the sweetness licking through his spirit at lightning speed.

As he drained the last drops from the glass, an ornate, gilded chair materialized off to his left. Ah, shit. Just what he didn't need.

He replaced the glass on the table, his attention glued to the crisscross pattern of the lead-crystal decanter and not on the figure stalking into his little corner of the Void.

"I see you have been keeping yourself quite busy, Dmitri." Cabal's singsong voice filled the openness with ease. "And all this after only two days and a bit in the human realm. You must truly be..." He paused, placing a deceivingly delicate hand softly against his chin, brows furrowed in concentration. "Oh, what is the phrase I'm looking for?" His long legs ate up the ebony slate beneath his feet, then he stopped suddenly before his throne. "Ah yes, I remember now. You must have a real hard-on for this girl." His oddly accented voice gave an ugly and lecherous tone to the words.

"Just trying to keep my skills sharp during my..." His what? Sentence? Vacation? Time-out?

"During your stay, you mean to say, yes?" The radiantly beautiful man settled into the ornate seat, pinning Konstantin with languid red eyes.

Konstantin bowed his head, respect and fear guiding his movements. "Yes, of course, my Master."

Richly evil laughter floated in the space between them. "Oh, Dmitri, you never cease to amuse me." Konstantin drew his gaze up from the floor as the white-clad figure leaned forward to lock his eyes with him. "Your continued desire to possess both this elusive female and Vadim's soul has driven you to gather enough essence to regain your physical body sooner than any Rogue."

Konstantin's eyes widened, and he quickly shut down his elated response. Their leader could just as easily find some other task for him to accomplish prior to going back. "Now, before I grant you your wish to return to the human realm, I have one simple question."

He waited, the seconds lengthening. Cabal eased back into the chair, steepling his long fingers under his noble chin. "Why her? What is so special about this female?"

The question caught Konstantin off guard. Why, indeed? He had asked himself for months. He had first heard her sorrowful wails across the Void less than one year ago. The darkness had swallowed her screams, converted them into a delicious essence he had savored for days. Intoxicated by her grief, he had tracked her into her nightmares; the gory sight of her lost love brought a smile to his face. With the intensity of her pain, coupled with her teetering self-confidence, he gorged himself on her sweet misery.

"Ah."

The single sound cut into his meandering thoughts, tearing him away from his memories and dropping him unceremoniously into the reality of the present. Raising his eyes, he thought carefully before speaking. "Master, her spirit is strong even though it is beleaguered by sadness. I wish only to consume her wholly before she is given to the Void."

A cruel smile twisted the lush lips of the seated man. "Very well said. And to discover that your opposition chose her as his own only adds sweetness to the deal, doesn't it?" Cabal rose smoothly, the gaudy throne disappearing as quickly as a thought, his flowing white silk slacks swirling like an angry cloud about his legs. "If you are so determined to see this through, then I do wish you luck."

A flick of his wrist and pain exploded in Konstantin's chest. Cells split and multiplied, painfully knitting together to create organs and tissues. Bones solidified and snapped into place as they gave his body shape. Flesh coalesced with excruciating sloth, and the moments stretched out in a flurry of enticing agony as his body settled into a solid form.

As his body became his own again, he found his newly created cheeks wet with tears, his throat raw from his own screams. The ground beneath his hands surprised him. He didn't remember falling, but the return of the flesh was always a jarring experience. Cabal insisted the purpose of the pain was to give meaning to the task.

But Konstantin knew the truth. The fucker got off on pain. But, since he did as well, he couldn't really hate the bastard. He slowly extricated himself from the floor, rising at his master's feet.

Quick as lightening, one of the bare feet before his eyes disappeared, landing firmly between his shoulder blades, forcing him to remain in his groveling posture. "I am allowing you to finish your little task, this...distraction." The hissed words fell closer to his ear, dripping with promised menace as the sickly scent of scorched flesh assaulted him. "Suck the little bitch dry for all I care, but your first job is to dispose of that fucking Guardian."

Cabal swore so rarely, his genteel veneer cracked under the force of his ire. The man was walking, talking evil, and every so often he gave these reminders to his minions. The timing was not lost on Konstantin. Whenever he was sent back to the earthly realm, he was given the same pep talk. Basically, "Fuck me over and I swallow your soul."

As if Cabal hadn't done that already. As a human, Konstantin was a thinker and philosopher, a dogmatic idealist whose eye was on the politics of the day and the struggles of man As a Rogue Warrior, he gave up his soul freely for the chance to cause chaos in the human world and once he had forfeited his promise of heaven, his worldview became more pragmatic.

He choked past the knot in his chest that was once his pride. The words burned like acid on his tongue as he spit them out. "Yes, my Master."

"Good." The simple word poured from Cabal's cruel mouth, long and lethal. The weight lifted off his back and breath came easier. Crawling unceremoniously off the floor, Konstantin kept his eyes downcast as he stood before the powerful creature wrapped in angelic white. Savageness rolled off Cabal in waves, threatening to drown his newly formed lungs in liquid evil.

"Now that that's settled, I think I'll leave you to your endeavors." Cabal casually plucked invisible lint off his impeccably clean attire. Konstantin watched as his strangely graceful body strode into the darkness beyond the confines of the partially visible room. Shaking his head, he reached down to finally grasp the weapons before him with his own flesh.

"Happy hunting." The words were whispered like a lover's caress into his ear. His skin still tingled from the heat of Cabal's breath. Spinning around, he found himself unnervingly alone. He rubbed his hand along the raised flesh of his arms, willing warmth back into his shuddering body. Cabal had taken him off his leash and would not be pleased with failure.

He stuffed the remaining toys back into their neat homes and returned them to his stash. First order of business: to savor the delightful suffering of his beautiful, tragic heroine. He sighed, imagining his hands caressing her cheek, tickling her breasts, and wrapping around her pretty throat while watching the life fade from her eyes. Ah, such sweet torment.

A vicious smile slashed his face and he melted out of the In-Between.

**

Voni awoke to a strange sensation. Well, several strange sensations if she was being honest with herself. First off, she had actually slept. No nightmares. No visions of blood and terror, just quiet slumber. She couldn't recall the last night of uninterrupted sleep she'd had in past eight or nine months.

Heaving a deep, contented sigh, she soon discovered another abnormal sensation. A distinctive and warm presence against her back, strong limbs across her middle and between her thighs pinning her to the feather-soft bed. She inhaled a heady aroma that was pure male mixed with the lingering scent of their lovemaking.

Nestling into his looming frame brought to attention the final odd sensation. A very hard, very thick, and very interested piece of his anatomy pressed along her backside. Her nipples hardened into diamond peaks as she remembered the feel of his engorged shaft thrust deep within her. Heat pooled at the apex of her legs. Her mouth went desert-dry, all the water in her body on a decidedly southerly course.

Her body ached deliciously from their hours of passion, yet it craved more. Her mind screamed for her to keep still, but her hips had other ideas. They rolled hungrily against the solid length inches away from the entrance of her heated core.

She gasped. Her spine rippled as her hips rose to meet his encroaching hand and backed into his crotch. Breathless moans tripped from her lips as she fought to create words, her brain powerless against the flood of hormones. She reached out, grasping for something solid, fingers clawing to find purchase in the sheets.

She dragged her lower lip between her teeth and bit down, struggling to ground herself in reality. She needed to talk to him, needed to speak of important things. Damned if she could remember any of them now, but she knew she had to push Pause on this sexual ride for just a moment.

Kai stirred, the erotic movements of his entangled partner drawing him out of his protective trance. The wards around his house were strong, but since Konstantin had infiltrated her dreams, he wasn't sure how well they would keep him out should the bastard decide to use her as a backdoor. Guarding her dream state took a bit of effort, her mind being fragmented from too many months of envisioned horrors. He struggled but

209

was finally able to calm her troubled thoughts and give her a dreamless night. Although he wished to give her a pleasant vision, he opted for silence.

But now, she seemed awake, and so was his cock. Nuzzling his lips into her tangled waves of hair, he purred softly, undulating against her writhing form.

"Mmmmm," he rumbled. "Now this is my definition of a good morning." He moved his hand downward from its resting place along her ribs and held her tight against his throbbing shaft.

"W-w-wait," she managed to push a word out of her lungs. "Pl-please...I-I-I." Her voice vanished in a sigh.

Kai heard the stress in her thready voice, and his instinct to protect went into overdrive. Quickly, albeit painfully, he shut down his libido, guiding her shoulders back against the bed so he could read her eyes. "What is it, *dragoste meu?*"

His gentle words disarmed her, making her irrational fears seem even more ridiculous. The intensity of his gaze threatened to make her lose her newfound resolve. Lowering her lids, she mustered the strength to say what was first and foremost on her mind.

"I'm not really sure how this is going to sound...ah hell." Squeezing her eyes shut, she spoke plainly, the words tumbling from her tongue in a rush. "All my life, I've wanted what we had last night. The passion, the energy, the fire. It was like a dream." She paused, a tightness starting in her chest, compressing her heart like a vise. "But now, it's morning. And I think it's time I woke up."

A feather light touch brushed the line of her cheek, following its curved path to the edge of her lips.

"Look at me, Siobhan."

For as long as she lived, she knew she would never be able to deny his voice.

"Please."

Her lids fluttered briefly and then opened to gaze up into heaven. Raised up on an elbow, the muscles in his arm bunched as he held himself away from her, giving her some breathing room. Warm gray-green eyes peered straight into her soul. Falling farther into the depths, she found only honesty, passion tempered by something she wasn't willing to name. He slid his fingers against her jawline and captured a stray lock of her hair.

"Hear me now. Since the moment I first saw you standing alone on the very edge of life, I have been entranced by you. Your hesitant smile, your razor-sharp wit, your intoxicating scent..." He paused, a wistful grin curling his perfect mouth. "...the blush that warms your skin when you come, the strength of your body as it holds me, buried so deep inside you that I never want to leave." His gaze roamed over her face. "I am glad that it is now morning, and I wake to find this has not just been a dream. I made a promise to you, that first night we met. I will honor that promise until the last breath leaves my body." He lowered his lips down to hers and claimed her mouth gently, thoroughly, and lovingly.

The kiss deepened sweetly as Voni heard a strange sound. Muffled sobs met her ears, coupled with a dampness on her cheek. Listening carefully, she was surprised to discover that she was the source. His full lips left hers, trailing butterfly kisses across her face, holding her close, murmuring soft words against her skin and into the deep brown waves.

"Let it go."

As she didn't remember starting to cry, she was unable to make it stop. The floodgates had opened, the waterworks undeniable this time. Within the safety of his arms, she gave in, and let the tears fall unhindered. Moments blurred one into the next until she began to calm. Her shoulders shuddered, her breath akin to gulped hiccups. Focusing on taking deep breaths, Voni slowly returned to herself. She expected to feel exhaustion from her catharsis, and yet she was oddly reenergized.

She edged carefully out of his iron embrace, her back finding the cool silk sheets. Silk? Real silk sheets. And black to boot. Didn't those only exist in romance novels? She nestled her back into the slick surface, reveling in the feel of fabric.

A sly grin played across his face as he picked her musing out of the space between them. He pulled her in tighter the moment he felt her relinquish her wavering control. Words of comfort fell from his lips, spoken in every language he knew. He cradled her in his arms as emotions bottled far too long seeped out in each sob. He hummed half-remembered melodies softly as she clung to his chest, her fingers digging into his very soul. He traced the length her spine with his hands, keeping a watchful ear on her already taxed heart and lungs.

"Feeling a little better?" The question was safe since he knew exactly how she felt. Since he had begun the claiming ritual, his connection to her was now unbreakable. It had been a living hell to hear her sobs, so strong was the urge to remove all her sorrows. Yet he knew that was not his call. He only kept her heartbeat calm and her breathing even. He brushed her chin with his knuckles, drawing her eyes to meet his.

A reassuring smile warmed his lips as he gently wiped away the last few drops still clinging to her lashes with the pad of this thumb. She huffed out a heavy and measured breath before she gave him a timid smile, the curve of her lips somehow both tempting and tender.

Her brows furrowed, and she locked his eyes with a pensive stare. "How do you do that?"

"Do what?"

"You know..." She sighed.

Deep laughter rumbled through his chest, vibrating the entire bed. "If I knew, I would not be asking, now would I?"

Voni dragged a hand through her hair, stopping after meeting a massive knot. "God, this just sounds so crazy."

With a patient smile, his fingers replaced hers in an effort to comb through the tangled tresses. "You seem to be convinced most of what you say is crazy already, and therefore, I too must be crazy for wishing to be with you. So what's a little more crazy?"

Voni lowered her eyelids, a curious smile melting on her lips, her head shaking gently. "That."

"I'm afraid you've lost me on this one, baby."

"You see me and..." She opened her eyes, the warm pools of amber flashing with clarity, "...and you just see, well, me, and you know what I'm thinking. What I need to hear, but not in the 'I'm saying this because it's what I'm supposed to say' way. Not like it's dialogue from a movie or something. Ah, hell. I'm not making any sense, am I?"

He chuckled as he allowed her thick hair to continue to slide between his fingers. "Just keep talking. I'm sure you'll find your sense."

"See? Like that. Most people in this situation would just laugh, pat me on the head, and say, 'Oh, Voni. You're just being silly.' Not that I've been in this exact situation with anyone. But you know what I mean." She punctuated her thoughts with her arms, cutting through the air and slapping them back down on the dangerously exotic sheets. "Silk sheets...fancy cars...a house more ginormous than my entire block..." She paused, her gaze returning to his, a wistful smile touching her lips. "You literally walked out of my dreams."

"And into your arms?"

Laughing, she reached up to caress his strong face, tracing the line of his strong mouth. "Actually, I think it was me who practically fell into your arms. But I feel like you are my own personal angel. You continue to save me."

"That is because you are worth saving."

That ever so tempting blush fired her cheeks, and his blood shot like lightning through his veins, racing below the beltline. He gripped her hip with both hands, angling her underneath his massive frame. Trailing his fingers toward the juncture of her legs, he groaned, finding her wet and welcoming. The warm amber receded as desire darkened her eyes and her trembling lips parted in anticipation.

Kai froze an instant before driving himself into her. Then the hair on the back of his neck raised in a flash as he realized they were not alone.☐

NINETEEN

Eamon stopped at the threshold of Kai's bedroom. His friend had not met him, nor returned his phone calls. He hoped he was busy with, well, what he was busy with right now. But prudence still demanded he check in on Kai. E-mails, voice mails, texts. Hell, he was one step away from semaphore flags and smoke signals. Kai never turned off his phone or left e-mails unchecked for more than an hour. He had to make sure he was all right.

However, as he looked at his friend's scarred back undulating, shoulders straining, hips a cat's whisker away from consummating the glorious deed, and the lean, pale leg wrapped high on his ass, he began to regret his decision. He couldn't leave; Kai had sensed his presence. Moment ruined, so he might as well just make the coitus interruptus complete.

"I'd be givin' ya pointers on your technique there, boyo, but ya don't seem to be needin' any."

The wisp of white flesh vanished in a blink, and waves of ire slammed into him so hard, he nearly lost his footing.

"Get. Out. Now."

Each word pushed him farther out of the room. Once he was beyond the doorway, the wooden barrier crashed home with a resounding click of the lock to seal the deal.

"Okay, I'll just be waitin' out here for ya, then, all right?" Eamon swore he felt even the floorboards vibrate in the wake of his friend's anger. "Ya know, on second thought, I'll be headin' downstairs, then."

Guess he's a little possessive of her.

The grin remained glued to his face as he headed back downstairs to the kitchen. Making himself at home, he pawed through the fridge, grabbing two beers in anticipation of Kai's inevitable appearance.

His wait was not long. Three swallows in, a dark fury stormed down the stairs, a whole lot of pissed-off warrior wrapped in black silk. "Have I ever told you that your timing is for shit, *dearthár*. Why the fuck are you here this early in the goddamn morning?"

Eamon lazily smirked over his beer bottle and tossed one to Kai. "And good morning to ya too, sunshine."

The heat of Kai's stare threatened to wilt the flowers on the table, but its effect was lost on Eamon. The shit-eating grin was firmly plastered in place and growing by the second. "C'mon, boyo. I'm happy for ya. Truly I am. Now if ya'd only returned a message or two…"

"I've been a little busy."

"Just a little?" Eamon raised a brow in question. "Must—"

"If you want to see the next sunrise," Kai growled, "you'll stop that thought right there." Leaning against the counter, he cracked open the bottle and took a long, slow draught. "Now, tell me again why I shouldn't throttle you where you stand?"

"I'd say it's because of my wit, my charm, and the fact I keep ya so entertained, but it seems like someone else has taken over that job for me." Eamon tried to sound upset, but his voice couldn't hide the happiness he felt for his brother. Kai had always walked alone, choosing to remain a solitary figure passing through history, while he had opted for as much female companionship as possible, as often as possible and as varied as possible. As he thought about his innumerable partners during the long years since he'd accepted the mantel of Guardian, he couldn't remembered a single name.

Kai's bland look spoke silent volumes.

Eamon laughed easily, breaking the tension. "All right, all right. Ya didn't check in or answer any calls all day. Or could ya be forgettin' we have a right proper job to be doin'. Now, while you were enjoyin' your newfound sex drive—oh, and congrats on that, by the way—things in the outside world have gone sideways." Eamon's voice grew more serious the longer he went on.

Pinning Kai with harsh blue eyes, he spilled the news of Konstantin's reappearance, as well as a rash of separate and, according to the police, unrelated random acts of violence. All the events had one key element in common: the Guardians. Each place hit, and every person affected had been a trusted helper or a safe haven. Moments blurred into the next as Eamon continued his report.

Kai studied the marbled countertop as his mind furiously scrambled to untangle this sudden influx of Rogue activity. Deep in his gut, he knew the reason but refused to accept it.

Voni.

She had been marked by Konstantin, somehow, in some way, and now he sought to claim her.

The tinkling sounds of glass shards raining down on the tiled surface brought him back to reality. Looking down, he saw hat his hand clasped nothingness. The green, long-necked bottle was no match for his rage. His eyes leveled, locking with the clear blue eyes across from him.

"Yeah. That was my thoughts as well." Eamon's voice was tinged with understanding and sympathy.

She was the target, and now the real battle would be on—for both of their souls.

"When we returned to her place last night, I felt his aura, but…" Kai paused, expelling air in an angry huff. "But how the fuck was he able to regenerate this fast? He should be out of commission for at least two more days and only if he's been on his best behavior. Hell, I just blasted the bastard three damn days ago. This is not good."

Both men stewed in visceral silence, brooding on the ramifications of this newly unearthed knowledge. Rogues thrived on hate, chaos, and unfortunately, actually fed on the living essence of souls given freely or taken in acts of violence. The world had taken a few bad turns of late with more political conflicts and territorial aggressions, which presented their enemy with a virtual smorgasbord of dining opportunities.

Eamon gave voice to the thought racing around Kai's mind. "Ya gotta tell her."

"Tell me what?"

***

Voni waited until her heart rate returned to normal before moving.

The disembodied voice had put the brakes on their most recent session—which, in hindsight, was probably a good thing. Her body was in need of some serious recuperating. It has been more than a year since her last sexual encounter, and James most definitely did not measure up to the passionate angel who loved her so tenderly and so completely.

A wistful smile curved her lips, and after a few languid stretches, she hopped off the bed and headed into the bathroom. If you could call it just that. Hell, she could have fit her living room into the bathtub.

After freshening up a little bit, she wandered through his immense walk-in closet in search of something to cover her nakedness. The clothes were perfectly organized, silk shirts neatly pressed, pants impeccably folded on padded hangers. Damn, even his shoes were all matched and lined up like little soldiers. She trailed her hands along the rows and rows of attire, tuxedos, casual T-shirts and denims, and...

Was that leather? She peered closer, her hand meeting the butter-soft black pants. It was. He actually owned leather pants. Several pairs of them, in fact. Her knees wobbled as she pictured him striding toward her, his legs wrapped in the formfitting leather sheath. And nothing else.

An evil smile warmed her lips. "Maybe I can con him into a fashion show for me," she muttered.

With a light laugh, she reached for a cornflower-blue silk oxford. After slipping her arms into the massive sleeves, she nimbly worked the buttons, humming to herself. As she began to roll up the sleeves to a more manageable length, she caught sight of herself in his ceiling-to-floor mirror. The tails of his shirt reached to her knees, her hair was in tangled disarray, but it was her eyes that caught her attention. Gone were the dark circles, replaced by an inner glow, a brightness she almost did not remember.

Happiness.

She was happy. For the first time in far too long.

Not wanting to wait before sharing the revelation with Kai, she opened the bedroom door to the sounds of glass shattering downstairs. She remained fixed for a moment, building her courage to continue her journey.

Step by cautious step, she descended to find the two boys in rapt silence in the kitchen, Kai leaning over the countertop, wrapped in the silk robe he'd grabbed off the door hook as he'd muttered what had to be cursewords, though she did not know the exact language.

Eamon was dressed casually, his bronze-and-golden hair spiked into that fashionable "just-crawled-out-of-bed" look only supermodels could pull off. His shoulder rested against the silver refrigerator. Both of them seemed lost in their own thoughts, and none of it looked good.

Eamon's lilting voice caught her as she reached the final step, prompting her initial inquiry.

Both heads snapped her direction, startling her to take a step backward. Self-preservation strengthened her resolve, and she crossed the threshold, her voice gaining volume as she repeated, "Tell me what?"

Eamon fled the question by nonchalantly diving into the fridge to retrieve another beer, leaving his friend to fend for himself. Kai narrowed his eyes toward his wingman, glaring daggers at his exposed back.

Kai stood for a heartbeat, his eyes drinking in the sight of her, his dress shirt looking more like a dress on her petite frame, her graceful limbs extended beyond the fabric's edge. His legs ate the distance between them in one stride, and he wrapped his arms around her silk-shrouded figure. Pulling her close to his chest, he inhaled deeply, taking solace in her spice-laced jasmine scent. He nuzzled her hair, kissing the tousled locks, a throaty growl escaped from his lips. He would move all the elements from here to the Void and back to keep her safe.

"I don't believe that shirt ever looked that good on me," his rumbling voice hummed along her skin. Tilting her chin up, he leaned down to sip from her lush lips.

And a sip was all Voni allowed him, pushing him away gently but firmly. "Nice try, bub," her voice mumbled against his mouth. "But don't think you're gonna kiss your way out of this one."

The challenge was issued, and Kai more than eagerly accepted the gauntlet. He slid his mouth along her jawline, nipping the sensitive skin along the bone, moving his way to her delicate earlobe, his warm breath raising gooseflesh. "Are you sure about that?" He pressed her hips possessively against his hardening shaft. He gripped her shapely ass with one hand while threading the other through her hair, anchoring her head in place.

Bottles clinked behind him, ruining the moment. Again.

Voni stifled a breathy moan as she heard the telltale whoosh of the refrigerator door closing. The fact they had an audience cooled her flushed skin and returned her sense of reason and rationality.

She sensed Kai's frustrated response to the unwelcomed background noise and smiled weakly, peering up into his strained face. "You present a very convincing argument." Her whispered words wrung the hint of a grin from his stoic expression. "Maybe you can plead your case later."

His eyelids drifted shut, the long lashes hiding the troubled pools of green as he pulled her close to him once again.

Something was very wrong. He didn't seem like himself. His grip was more protective than passionate, not loving as it had been just moments ago. She struggled out of his iron grasp; her gaze roamed his face for answers.

"Okay, Kai. You're freaking me out here. Tell me what's going on?" Her gaze flitted back and forth between the two silent towers, Eamon's bright-blue orbs hooded as he contemplated his beer and Kai's gray-green eyes clouded and sad. One thought pierced through her mind.

Married.

Self-doubt took a step to the forefront of her emotional onslaught but was quickly overtaken by anger. She yanked herself out of his arms, her frustration giving her power.

"You know...whatever. I just thought...ah, screw this." She turned on her heel and headed back for the stairs only to run smack into a black silk wall.

"Voni, wait."

"Wait? For what? Why?" When her question met more silence, she tried to sidestep the moving blockade.

Kai struggled for the right words. She was getting more agitated, her heart rate rising steadily. This situation was going from bad to totally fucked in 0.2 seconds flat. He reached out to steady her shoulders only to meet with more physical resistance. Damn, she was strong. Her body pitched and spun, gracefully breaking his grip.

"Voni, please. Let me explain." He ducked his head, bobbing with hers as he struggled to catch her gaze. Their avoidance duet ranged around the kitchen, moving through the dining room and the living room, his combat skills tested by the only opponent to whom he would gladly surrender.

"Needin' some help there, boyo?" He didn't need to see Eamon's face to know he was thoroughly entertained by the impromptu tango. He heard it in the simple words. Unwilling to take his eyes off his ultimate prize, he growled as he gave him a one-fingered salute.

"No, I do not need any help, thank you very much."

Each time he thought he had her cornered, she vanished, her lithe body slipping out of his reach with an admirable show of her own skills. Short of pinning her against the wall, he could only hope that she would tire of this terpsichorean tirade. Too bad she showed no signs of stopping or of even slowing down.

With an exasperated groan, he managed to grip her elbow as she rounded the corner of the table, and he quickly sidled around the wooden obstacle and captured her other arm before she got away again. Her wild hair whipped him in the face as she tossed her head, seeming intent on keeping her eyes from him. The scattered and desperate waves of conflicting emotions poured from her, the intensity and range nearly breaking his heart.

"Voni. Stop, please."

With her safely in his arms, he held her tight, praying for the strength to tell her what he knew would terrify her. And rightly so. She had been chosen as a target of an enemy she couldn't begin to understand. His fears for her threatened to turn him into a quivering ball of flesh before her.

Tears pooled in her eyes, these born of impotent rage and betrayal. "If you don't trust me enough to say it to my face, then I'm outta here." Her struggles gained force, but she was still unable to completely break his hold. "Let me go." She willed her voice to be harsh, but it ended up as more of a weak plea.

Kai held each wrist in a gentle and unyielding grasp. He spun her back to him and wrapped his arms about her body. "I'm sorry. I never meant to hurt you."

"And that's supposed to make it all right?" Her trembling voice popped in and out in volume, tears flowing freely down her cheeks. With a slinky struggle, she twisted in his embrace to glare into his eyes. "God d-d-dammit all. I knew it. Knew you were too good to be true. None of this was real, was it? Was it just a game to you? Just something to do to pass the time? Why couldn't you just tell me you were married?"

The world stopped turning for the briefest of moments as she stared into his stunned and frozen gaze.

"Married?"

His eyebrows drew deep furrows across his forehead as his frowning countenance turned toward Eamon. The answering expression on his friend's face was equally confused, and Kai's gaze returned to lock with hers. "Baby, I'm not married."

She fought to gulp down air as his measured words washed over her like a warm summer rain. The arms encircling her softened, and she clung to them for dear life. "You're not?"

Her body shook as Kai chuckled. "My dearest, I can assure you there is no one else in my heart, nor will there ever be, save you." He whispered his oath into her blush-tinged ear, kissing it before tucking a lock of hair behind the peaked shell. Her mottled cheeks threatened to bring tears to his own eyes.

"Then why did you say you hurt me?" Her voice, still small, was masked by tiny sniffles.

He sought to allay her irrational fear, only to be replacing it with a very rational one. "I'm afraid I've put you in danger, my love."

"But you're not married?"

He shook his head slowly, smiling. "No."

"And you're not leaving me, right?" She blinked up at him, tears still clinging to her lashes.

Smiling, he leaned down and rested his forehead on hers. "Never."

"Okay."

He opened his eyes to regard her, pulling back to see in through her eyes, straight to her heart. "Okay? I tell you I've just put your life in danger and you say okay?"

She met his gaze with an unshakeable calm. "Yeah. I mean, I survived my own fear of you being married. I think I can handle a little danger, as long as you're with me."

"Will you ever cease to amaze me?" His face beamed with love and admiration. She was strong, beautiful, witty, mercurial, and, most importantly, she was his.

She smiled crookedly, sniffing her last tear away. "Well, I hope not, because I'd hate to break someone else in."

Laughter filled the room from two very different sources, joined meekly by a third.□

TWENTY

Voni sat quietly sipping her cooling coffee as Kai and Eamon discussed strategies just out of earshot. Her day had taken a very unexpected turn that morning, and she mulled over the latest information as she toyed with the scattered toast crumbs on her empty plate. Her inner realist began ticking off facts. Gorgeous man: check. Beautiful house: check. Phenomenal cars: check. Oh-my-fucking-god amazing sex: double check. Oh and a crazed psychopath out to kill her for no apparent reason: check.

Memories of watching Sesame Street came flooding back as one skit's song about something not being like the others around it bled into her musings. The childhood tune rang through her ears as she finished her cinnamon-hazelnut caffeinated heaven. An hour ago, she stood in a massive closet, admiring her reflection as she stood in her lover's shirt. Her only worry was when he would return to finish their interrupted adventure.

Now the story had changed drastically, this new tale sounding more like the plot of Hollywood's next summer blockbuster. But when it came right down to it, although she was still quite fuzzy on all the details, someone seemed to wish her dead.

Her. Dead.

Those two words still did not compute. What had she ever done? She was nobody, a minor dancer in a tiny company. Her entire life had passed unnoticed by the world, but now, a few days after she'd found a reason to live, she realized she'd also found a reason to die. Her mind swam with dwindling possible scenarios for such a violent response to her wish to continue breathing.

Kai mentioned that the fault was his own and that he had somehow dragged her into harm by his affections for her. She shook her head, doubting his explanation. His words, meant only to soothe her, caused her mind to churn faster, spinning wilder and wilder yarns the longer she waited in silence. Yet each new story, every new wrinkle, circled back to one simple question: why her?

Trailing her finger along with bone-white ceramic plate, lost deep in her own imagination, she closed her eyes for the smallest measure, hoping to find answers in the dark of her mind. But the sinister laugh behind her told her that she was no longer in a safe, or even familiar, place.

As she struggled to calm her nerves, voices bled into her mind, as if she were underwater wrapped in a thick blanket. Her body moved of its own volition, seeking solace in the voices she felt she recognized, heading away from the cackling behind her. The darkness around her had weight and depth, and it sank into her soul, threatening to trap her for all time. Her limbs began to twitch more violently now, breaking through the grip of the deepening silence.

Icy breath chilled her neck as lips as cold as death brushed against her ear. "Soon, my pet. Soon."

Opening her mouth, Voni screamed.

***

Kai continued to shake Voni's shoulders, trying to wake her. "C'mon, baby. Wake up, please? Voni! C'mon. Follow the sound of my voice. Come back to me." Looking around, he glared impotent daggers at Eamon, his angry stare wasted on Eamon's shut eyes . "How the fuck did he get past my barriers?"

Eamon shook his head, his eyes pressed closed and mouth murmuring the words that Kai knew would act as both wall and tunnel. Kai forced his body to remain still as his friend chanted feverishly, struggling to find her spirit in the vast nothingness of the In-Between, a wisp of silvery joy among the sorrow and misery. Time was against them since neither of them knew when she had been taken.

Kai swore softly in numerous languages, the words flowing into elaborate descriptions of painfully eloquent yet physically impossible acts as he tried to rouse her from her unnatural slumber. After Kai had allayed her fears about his marital status, Eamon sought to make an apology by fixing a gourmet brunch.

Omelets and quiches, eggs benedict and crepes, every sweet and savory imaginable were bubbling in the massive kitchen. Right down to the champagne and strawberries. Both he and Eamon had ensured that Voni was happy and sated.

They had only stepped away for a few moments, wanting to discuss the more grisly details farther away from her. Kai was in the process of outlining the warding of her cottage when he heard a crash from the dining room. He'd rushed in to find his beautiful spiritmate face down in a halo of broken china; blood smeared the blond wood from several small cuts the damaged plate had given her. Her eyes fluttered behind heavy lids as her body thrashed violently.

Kai gathered her up into his arms, steadying her in his lap as he wiped away the blood and healed the cuts with a pass of his hand. He yelled, he shook, he begged, and he kissed, all efforts unable to break her from her trance. In one final act, he placed his fingers on her temples and, taking a deep breath, pressed his forehead against hers, eyes closed in concentration. "Come back to me, baby," he pleaded heatedly. "Please, love. Come back to me."

Voni's eyes flew open as a scream tore from her lips. Control returning to her limbs, she lashed out in all directions, shoving away an unseen evil. Her panicked cries filled the room, ringing in her own ears. Time returned to a normal directional flow as she slowly came back to her surroundings. Her arms were pinned to her sides, wrapped in a sinewy cage of muscle and black silk. As she breathed in, her senses filled with the purely male scent of the man who now meant everything to her.

"Kai?" Her heart knew the answer, but her brain needed more verification.

"Oh, thank the gods." Kai held her close, stroking her hair and kissing its tangled waves. Cradling her to his chest, he rocked her gently, whispering against her skin. "I am so sorry, baby. I should have never left you." He pulled back, stroking her cheek and pressed his lips reverently against both lids, taking away her terror and her confusion.

Voni sniffled in stuttered breaths, fighting to keep a grip on her teetering emotions. She laced her fingers through the slippery smoothness of his robe and buried her face against his chest, drawing strength from the very scent of him. Inhaling deeply, she forced down her apprehension, contained her insecurities, and calmed her racing heart.

He was real, her Malakai. He had called to her from the darkness. He hadn't left her.

"Well, I guess that'll teach me for falling asleep at the dinner table." She tried to keep her tone light, but her voice seemed to come out thin and airy. "Always heard it was bad manners, but I didn't think it was inferno-worthy."

"My dear Siobhan, you will truly never cease to amaze me," he said with a rumbling laugh and a shake of his head. He wound his fingers through her hair, and she leaned closer until she captured his lips with her own. "I promised that I would keep you safe, and I seem to be falling down on that job."

Voni melted under the weight of his sincerity. "Yeah, well. I was gonna talk to you about that little factoid."

Drawing a deep and shaky breath, she looked up into the tormented sea-green eyes peering down at her. "Sorry. When I can't deal with things, I tend to get a little sarcastic. Okay, maybe a lot sarcastic. I just need some time to try and wrap my mind around all this, you know? I mean, just the other day, I was at the lowest point in my whole life, and now…"

An uneasy silence followed her unvoiced thought. Tension seeped back into Voni's shoulders as her brain raced, following the very convoluted path of her past few days. Bridge. Coffee shop. Record shop. Restaurant. Black-tie gala. Hell. So much in such a short amount of time.

Would you trade one second of it? the voice in her head whispered, egging her on to respond. But the voice in her heart knew the answer without hesitation. Not a one. Even at the peril of her soul, she felt more alive at that moment than in her whole life. She would face this new obstacle.

Steeling her resolve, she pulled out of the comfort of Kai's embrace. Two steps later, she raised her head and met his gaze. "I need some time to think." She lifted her hand to stop the protest on his lips. "I know there is a lot I don't know yet and a lot you still have to tell me. I know this. But, right now, I need to attempt to process all…all this," she stated, waving her hand dismissively.

She pinched the bridge of her nose, mentally willing away the burgeoning headache while fighting to keep down the glorious breakfast. But where could she go? Home was, well, just plain weird. Here? Here is... The piercing pain between her eyes refused to diminish. Instead, the dagger's point drove deeper and deeper, forcing the tears closer and closer to breaking the dam of her sealed eyes. *I'm not going to cry. I'm not going to cry.* The mantra repeated over and over in her head as she tightened her shoulders to stem the impending flood.

Kai stood by helpless as Voni fought to be strong. He imaged Konstantin's throat between his hands as they curled into dangerous fists, taking the daydream to its end as life drained from his foe's imaginary onyx eyes. Rage burned under his skin as his hands continued to squeeze, boiling his blood and straining his muscles until they shook. A hand settled on his shoulder, bringing him instantly out of his maniacal reverie. He turned his head to find Eamon, the lingering stress from his rescue apparent on his ashen face.

"She's got a point, ya know." He leaned in, his voice barely above a whisper. "She's been through a lot and hasn't had but one second to try to make heads'r tails of it all. I know ya swore to protect her an' all, but what she's got goin' on her head? Unless ya plan on crawlin' in there an' make yourself to home, she gotta do this herself."

Glaring angrily into Eamon's eyes didn't stop the bastard from being right. His body sagged under the weight of his friend's words as the push of Eamon's Channeler skills flowed into his rigid and tense shoulders. He'd shielded her fiercely as she'd slept by his side, relied on the strength of his own wards to keep her safe when the sun came up.

Still it was not enough. Still his enemy, and now hers, had slunk in from the dark recesses of the shadows and tried to take what was Kai's. Again. Images flashed before his eyes. The flash of a blade, the splatter of gore, the gurgled cries, then silence. Each time, the faces were different, the time, the clothing, even the location. But each one, be they friend, companion, or lover, suffered greatly before paying the ultimate price to Konstantin's lust for destruction and mayhem.

"She is stronger than you think, brother."

A frown tugged his brows together as he held Eamon's pensive stare.

"I've seen that look too many times before, brother, but she is different from the

others. She is your match. I know that just as well as you do. We will not let her slip away."

Unable to stand by a moment longer, he moved toward her, his long strides eating the distance separating him from his heart. He knew full well the price he would pay if anything were to happen to her. Without their mate, a Guardian's soul would eventually be swallowed by the In-Between, their life purpose to protect sapped from years of endless battles. And if a Guardian's spiritmate was taken before the claiming ritual was completed, well, that was the endgame. Go directly to hell. Do not pass go, and all that.

He wrapped his arms around her body and held her back firmly against his chest. Burying his chin amid her silken hair, he stroked her arms and spoke the hardest words he had ever voiced. "Take all the time you need, baby. I'm not going anywhere."

"Except maybe crazy."

Kai lifted one graceful brow at Eamon for his wayward thought. Eamon shrugged noncommittally and went back to sipping his beer.

Voni tensed as strong arms wrapped around her shoulders, but his presence soothed her frantic mind. Words rang in her head and she scoffed, mumbling almost to herself, "I agree. And I'm on that crazy train too. Ah, who the hell am I kidding? The moment I close my eyes, no matter where I am, the nightmares start, and now I fall asleep for two seconds and it's worse than ever. I mean, seriously. That one felt real. I could almost smell the sulfur and that...that smell hospitals try to cover up with all the antiseptics but don't quite completely get rid of."

Her voice climbed in pitch as she stepped out of Kai's arms. "And now I'm rambling again. Well, I don't care if I'm being a hysterical female. And you two..." Her arms scattered her frustrated energy toward Kai and Eamon. Both stood-stock still, mouths slightly agape. "Yeah, you two. With all your secrets and...and...and...I give up!" Flustered beyond reason, she turned on her heel and made a hasty retreat back upstairs, hoping to retain a tiny shred of her dignity as well as her sanity.

As if by magic, she walked straight into Kai's chest before reaching the first step.

"What did you say?"

Oh, fantabulous. You go on a phenomenal rant and he wasn't even paying attention. And you're surprised by this, how? He's a man, he's already gotten his rocks off...a few times. You thought he'd really care enough to listen?

Kai shook his head, clearing her enraged and scattered thoughts screaming through his psyche as he met her perturbed frown. He swore the words that started her rant were more directed toward Eamon's mental link, not his offer of space. How was this possible? Was that the reason Konstantin sought after her? If her grief called to him, as he claimed it did, then she might be in more danger than she could imagine.

"I didn't mean it that way, baby. I was listening. I was, really. But you said something about..."

"What he's meanin' t'ask," Eamon's clear lilt cut through his sputterings, "is ya said ya agreed when ya began." His deep blue eyes met her troubled hazel ones. "What did ya agree with?"

Voni wrinkled her brow at his question, her gaze flitting between Kai and Eamon. "You said that you weren't going anywhere, and you said, 'Except maybe crazy.' Was I the only one paying attention to the conversation?" Speaking with her entire body, she punctuated her tirade with her hands firmly on her hips.

"Ea e o circuitul, fratele meu." The words spilled in a stunned stream from Kai's lips. She's a Conduit. No wonder the fucking bastard had such a hard-on for her. If he were able to turn a Conduit, either living or dead, he could channel his influence from a distance, even across the globe if the Conduit proved strong enough.

She was unaware of her abilities. He blinked slowly as he struggled to let this newfound tidbit mull about in his brain. Had the old ways been so lost that families no longer maintained the Mystical skills? The Conduits, the Channelers, and the Marshals were born into the world, and their skills used to be revered and cultivated, with many of them sought out and recruited by Guardians to keep them safe.

Over the years, the stories of those pure, guiding souls being hunted and exploited by Rogues and their agents had come to the attention of all Guardians. Tales of mental torture and assisted suicide chilled his blood. A groan escaped as the pieces slipped into place. Her nightmares. The incident in the café. The puzzle became clear, each new clue bringing the picture into sharper focus.

"Have you ever had problems with headaches?"

Voni stared at the solemn look on Kai's face; Eamon's expression was a perfect mirror image. "Yeah," she answered slowly, drawing the word out as she took a retreating step toward a solid handhold. "I mean, doesn't everyone?"

Kai gently took her elbow and led her back toward the couch, where he sank down next to her on the creaking leather. "I'm talking about more than just your normal, standard ones. You have, haven't you?"

He took her silence as an affirmation and continued in his subtle search, holding her hands to steady her. "Maybe you believed it to be a migraine, but the pain was unbearable. Like a steel spike being driven through your mind. Colors faded into a wash of grays, while other colors shone brighter than the sun. Normal sounds disappeared, and new sounds, from somewhere else seemed to take over. And you could hear voices of people not in the room with you."

She sat rigid, eyes distant, but he knew she still heard his words. Hating to hurt her, but needing her to understand, he pressed on. "Sometimes, the feeling only lasted for a moment, and others seemed never ending. And other times, you'd awake on a floor or somewhere you don't remember going to."

"And the eyes of something"—her voice was small and fragile—"wrong seemed to follow me for a while after each one. I've never told anyone about these. I just chalked them up to stress, migraines, too much rehearsal, not enough food or sleep. My aunt wanted to have me tested when they became so bad I had to miss school at times. But I refused. I knew that no one would be able to make them go away."

Her gaze locked with his, fear shining in her amber eyes. "How do you know? How could you know? What is wrong with me?"

He caught Eamon's movement, giving a relieved sigh as his friend's light touch calmed her frantic thoughts. Kai met his friend's gaze, nodding an almost imperceptible thanks. As a Channeler, Eamon settled her racing emotions so Kai's explanation wouldn't cause her to freak out too much.

"She's a Conduit. Good luck with that one, bro."

"Thanks for the vote of confidence."

Her gaze ping-ponged sloppily between them. "I can hear you both. Just thought you'd like to know that. And what's a conduit? And why do I feel a little drunk?"

"I think that last trip into the Black mighta opened her up there, boyo. This could

help us. If she can Link, then she can—"

"No." The word erupted from Kai's mouth in a solid breath, and his head snapped up hard to find Eamon's eyes. "I'll not have an untrained Conduit, much less my mate, traipsing in that hellhole, fighting a battle that is mine. Konstantin is my problem, not hers."

"Do ya really believe that? Can ya look me dead in the eye and convince me of that?" Eamon's eyes bored a tunnel straight to his soul.

They both knew the answer, and Kai had to face facts. This was just as much her battle as it was his. But where he was fighting for the power of right, she was fighting for the right to exist. Unable to hold the truth of Eamon's stare, he dropped his gaze, finding Voni's open, upturned face before him. Unvoiced questions fluttered behind her amber eyes, cries for explanations left silent on her lush lips. Cupping her face reverently in his hands, he sipped at her lips, needing a taste to give him strength.

Pulling away before his body had a chance to demand more, he took a deep breath, motioning for Eamon to take his hand away. If she was going to hear the truth, she might as well be allowed to react as she saw fit.

The thick curtain of peace that cocooned Voni vanished in a flash and dread quickly took its spot. "Okay, the weird-shit-o-meter needs to start getting dialed down around you two. Do you guys like watching me freak out or what? Now, will one of you please tell me what the hell is going on?" She swiveled her head between Kai's cloudy ice-greens and Eamon's baby blues. Another moment passed. "Like now would be nice."

Kai's voice, soft and barely audible, broke the silence like a shot. "We are not what you think we are."

Voni's sharp laugh, tinged with both fear and relief, bounded around the room. "Gee, and here I thought you two were just a couple of big-time drug dealers with a flair for Gucci."

Eamon threw his head back, and his hearty laughter was joined by Kai's deep rumble in short order. *"Tá súil agam go bhfaighidh mé mar ádh le mo maité.* She's a right good one, she is."

Voni lifted a shaking hand to wipe at her leaky eyes. "I sure hope that was a compliment, that…whatever you said." Sliding farther down the couch, she found her eyes focusing on the beautifully polished ceiling beams. The wooden pattern was beautifully orchestrated with the straight grain lines, swirling in perfect harmony. She wished life was as simple as those beams above her head were.

A gentle touch, hand touching hand, roused her from her musings.

"It was, my love. That it was. But no, we do not do anything like that. Nothing that would cause harm to any innocents." With her hand in his, he placed her palm flat against his chest; his heartbeat was strong against her cool skin. Meeting her eyes, his words began to tumble out.

"Siobhan Brigit Whelan, I am one of a chosen brotherhood, a Guardian Warrior. I was born in the year of our Lord 1310, recruited in 1342, trained by my Master, Tashiharo Makamuro, and have fought our sworn enemies, agents who live on chaos and mayhem known as Rogue Warriors. I have—"

"Stop." One whispered word and silence dropped like an anvil. She sat woodenly as he gathered her into his arms and simply held her against his chest, allowing the first chunk of information to sink it. The words banged around Voni's empty brain, thumping against each other. She hoped static would hold them together and give them sense and meaning. Too bad the dryer was her mind and she had run out of quarters.

What had he said? Oh yeah, the whole born in 1300 something. Which made him...uh, yeah, a much, much, much older man. She tried to make sense of the sounds, but the strung-together letters were still gibberish to her ears. But that couldn't be possible. This is the real world, right?

From nowhere in particular, and for reasons unfathomable, she had a flash from Star Wars. Darth Vader standing on that rickety expanse, his black-gloved hand reaching out toward Luke.

James Earl Jones' voice rang through the cotton candy fog in her head, telling her to search her feelings to find the truth. Only Vader wasn't her father, but the search did arrive at the same conclusion as Luke's did.

That's not possible. But, in her heart, in her bones, she knew from the moment she'd laid eyes on Kai that something was different about him. She'd felt that connection on the bridge and it had scared her then. And now that she knew a little more, it downright terrified her.

The strong hand that ran up and down her back was real. The heart that beat beneath her ear too. The midnight silk she'd threaded through her fingers, the golden skin she had caressed and tasted only hours ago, all of it was real. So which senses did she trust? Her five given ones or the sixth, imaginary one?

Holding her close, her breath tickling his chest, he felt like the world's biggest asshole. Here she was, the one person he'd searched the entire planet to find, and she had to have a crash course in the fucked-up-ville that was his life.

With his lips pressed against her hair, he inhaled the sweet perfume that was exclusively hers. The spicy jasmine clung to his skin, bathing his senses and awakening his unending need for her. A growl, dark and hungry, rolled deep in his throat. His hands became more demanding and possessive as he clutched at the silk shirt separating them from her softness beneath.

Words seemed meaningless as they swam in circles in his mind. But the one that seemed to be ahead of the others was probably not the one she wanted to hear. Somehow, I'm sorry just didn't seem to do it. I love you? Again, not right. That would diminish their meaning. The blood was trekking south of his beltline the longer he pressed her against him. He needed to say something, if only to ease his conscience, so he chose the simplest words.

"Please. Stay with me." He poured everything, body and mind, spirit and soul, into those few words, praying it would be enough. "I promised you I would do all in my power to make you happy and to keep you safe. If you will still have me—"

Voni rested fingertips against his lips; the attached limb trembled like twig in a tornado. She dragged her gaze up to reach the summit of the man—no, the warrior—standing before her. Pieces slid into place in her mind: his confident stance, his keen eye, and his chiseled form. The scars. They were honest-to-God battle scars. From people trying to kill him with swords and knives and every other kind of weapon there was in the past 700 years.

Oh God, how many women had he slept with? Where the hell did that thought come from? Oh come on now. You can't be seriously thinking your feeble attempts at sex were gonna tempt a tasty morsel like this to stay?

But that was what he'd asked. His words, in fact. Stay. With. Me. She would have to be an absolute idiot to seriously consider this. He was either delusional and should be sporting a white, extra-long-sleeved jacket, or worse, he was telling the truth, in which case, she was truly out of her league.

As she gazed up, falling into the icy depths of his eyes, his soul stripped bare in those crystal, green pools, her mouth formed the only possible answer she could.

"I'll stay." □

TWENTY-ONE

Voni stood under the pounding jets of the multiple showerheads, her scattered thoughts mirroring the water's splatter patterns. She half expected to see words circling the drain the longer she remained in the spray storm of luxurious heat. Kai was still conversing with Eamon, discussing strategies and tactics. Excusing herself once their words no longer held any meaning, she'd fled to the solace of the shower in the hope that the focused waters would drive them into her brain.

No such luck.

They spoke in a code almost. She remembered words like guardians, conduit, and the void. Which she assumed was a bad thing, the way they spoke of it. Other concepts fought for time on the dimly lit stage of her psyche. But one shot forward, leaving all the others in the dust.

Spiritmate.

The word ran on an endless loop, bouncing around between her ears. The one person who was destined to ground the Guardian back into the real world. Someone who would be able to give him a mortal life. This person would call to him through the ages, guiding him to her side when the time was right.

But that couldn't be her. That just wasn't possible. She didn't guide anyone, or anything. Up until a week ago, she was a walking shell, going through the motions of normal life. She woke and ate and danced and slept. Nope, nothing about calling or steering anyone near anything, much less the Adonis downstairs with the most amazing bedroom eyes and hottest ass she could have possibly imagined. And the things he did with his hands.

And his mouth, much less his...

Her lids drifted closed as she lost herself in the memories of last night, the tastes, the touches, and the scents. The dark, intoxicating spice that cried out "male" surrounded her as if it poured out of the pipes, flooding her senses and firing her body, which was eager to continue their interrupted session from earlier.

Familiar hands slid down her sides, and a deep, rumbling voice filed the glass chamber. "Now that..." A kiss fell against her shoulder. "...sounds like..." Another graced the column of her throat. "...a very, very, very good idea to me." Each very earned her a nibble, a lick, and a growl. By the time he reached her ear, she was wound so tight, her orgasm so close, his breath on her skin had her spilling her juices.

Kai had sensed her need for release as soon as she'd headed up the stairs. The past two hours had passed better than he had expected. She quietly took in the information and voiced her questions with a calm, almost disconnected, ease. Her sponge-like behavior rattled both him and Eamon, and once he realized she was at the breaking point, he'd turned the conversation toward Eamon and given her a chance to escape.

That had been two minutes ago.

"Boyo, get the fuck outta here. I'm gonna let myself out and you're gonna take your ass upstairs." The grin splitting his friend's face was devilish but sincere. "Ya just be rememberin' to eat and call me later." They exchanged man hugs and silence stole into the living room.

Until the gentle rain from the upstairs shower whispered in the empty space. Blinking himself into the bathroom, not wanting to startle her with his sudden appearance under the streaming water, he was bombarded, her mind spilling vivid Technicolor images of last night's activities as well as the desire to pick up where they had left off.

He couldn't agree more, nor could his cock, which was currently tenting his robe with a vengeance. With a quick tug, the fabric slid to the tile below, and he stepped into the cascading water.

Voni, his woman, his spiritmate, his prime reason to draw breath, stood under the jets, her skin pink from either the pressure or the heat, her sable tresses snaking down her back, their ends stretching eagerly toward the soft dimples of her ass. Gods, just looking at her made his already-solid shaft hammer-worthy.

He reached around her body and found the soap bar, which he worked into a thick white froth. He pressed his lips gently against her shoulder as he lathered her body, his hands slipping across the soft, strong planes of her skin. Using one hand, he massaged her breasts, tugging at her nipples as his other hand headed south, pinning her sweet ass against his raging hard-on. His tongue laved the racing pulse at her neck. He growled deep, as her body writhed and contorted, eager to find release.

Voni raised her arms, pushing her palms against the wall, needing to feel the cool tiles beneath her quickly heating skin. Steam filled the box, the scents of the sandalwood and lust creating a heady and intoxicating mixture. Her eyes drifted closed, and she lost herself in the pure sensation of his hands sliding possessively over her body as he licked and nipped his way around her shoulders. She arched her back, driving her hips back so his shaft nestled tantalizingly close to her moist nether lips. A needful sigh escaped her as he dipped his fingers between her legs, stroking her slowly and with tender care.

Her head drooped forward to rest weakly on her damp forearm as inner voices began the next shouting match. One voice gained a face, her oh-so-proper and ever-condescending aunt, Sondra, whom she had never pleased in the years she'd spent under her roof after the passing of her parents. The nasally tone still grated on her nerves, even though the woman had long since left her life.

You never could do anything right, could you? Now look at you. All hot and sweaty for a man you don't deserve and will never be able to please. He's had lovers the likes of which you will never rival, and soon he'll tire of you and be eager to move on. Maybe he'll throw himself in front of a bullet like James did. Anything to be rid of you...

"No." The word snuck past her lips as she squeezed her eyes shut, blocking out that horrid voice and its unfounded accusations.

Kai paused, her weak protest catching him off guard. Had he somehow hurt her? Was she still too sore from their long session the previous night? He softly pressed his lips against her ear as he delved into her mind, only to find utter chaos. A spindly wraith of a woman berated Voni with swirling words full of self-loathing and hatred. The harpy heaped blame upon her shoulders for her fiancé's untimely demise, and most importantly, she gave a continual litany of reasons why Kai would never stay with Voni. This was no angel on her shoulder, cautioning her to think carefully. This was a demon, darker than any he had ever faced.

He found her huddled in the dark corner of her mind, hands clasped over her ears, desperate to escape the flood of disappointment from her guardian.

Guardian. That would be his job from now on.

He was her true Guardian and he was here. With her. Now. Even in the dark recesses of her mind, he stood watch, armed to the teeth in full battle armor, its crimson dragon, twisting upon itself, emblazoned upon his chest, his sword drawn in preparation.

Her eyes lifted, capturing his soul, and the spinster faded into mist. Extending his hand to bring her to her feet, he wrapped his arms around her and pulled her back tight against his chest, his caress giving her the strength to face any imagined opponent.

"I would be there for you. Always."

With a touch of his hand, he guided her back to reality; her body cozied up against Kai's chest, and he stoked the fire building deep within her core. He let his lips linger on the shell of her ear, soft words of adoration spilling from his tongue as he held her.

"Come for me."

The orgasm that hit her shook through Kai's bones stronger than any cannon blast. The keening cries wrought from her soul drove away the doubts and insecurities of her past, leaving her liberated and breathless.

"Now, Kai," her words tripped out in a strangled whisper. "Please. I need you inside me. Now."

Kai responded quickly, plunging himself within her quivering channel with one swift stroke. The primal growl escaping his lips formed one single word. "Mine."

Faster and faster he drove, his breath fanning the flames that threatened to consume them both. He ran his hands frantically over her skin, a caress here, a tease there. He kneaded the weight of her small, firm breasts and gripped her narrow hips. All the while, she met his onslaught with equal fervor. She held one hand stiff-armed against the wall while she reached the other reached behind her and grasped at his ass, using her fingers to ply his flesh and urging him to increase his speed.

Gods, he had well and truly found heaven. He buried his face into her hair, nuzzling his nose into its exotic aroma. Her scent was forever branded upon his soul. He kissed his way down to her neck and laved it. He found her quickened pulse with his tongue and grinned as it jumped and danced just beneath his lips.

His deft strokes pushed them both higher and higher, her tight body rippling in sweet pleasure as a wordless, impassioned plea filled the silence around them.

"Oh, sweet God, yes." The words slipped from Kai's mouth the instant before he devoured her lips, her release spurring him on to find his own. Growling possessively and holding her tight against his body, he gave one final thrust, and his seed spilled deep inside her.

He held her tightly, one hand rested on her hip while keeping careful watch over her heart with the other. The fast, pounding beat was strong and steady against his palm as he placed butterfly kisses along her collarbone.

"Guess I don't have to ask if that was good for you too?"

His brain, still pleasure drunk, let his native language fall from his tongue, his answer warm against her skin. "Um, I'm not sure if I should be excited, offended, or check for the pizza delivery guy."

Kai threw his head back, his laughter bouncing off the white porcelain box. "You have the most interesting mind I have ever known." With tender care, he eased himself out of her slick core. As he turned her to face him, he cupped her flushed cheeks with his palms and placed a chaste kiss on her lips. "Not to mention the sweetest ass I've ever seen," he added, wagging his eyebrows.

Smiling against his mouth, Voni wrapped her arms about his waist, rising up onto her toes to meet his kiss. "Uh-huh, Yeah, right. You either need to get out more or pay more attention, seeing as you've met a lot of minds…and seen a lot of asses, I'm sure." Her words, though she attempted to stay light, smacked to the truth deep in her heart—her fear of truly being enough to keep someone as well-versed, worldly, not to mention traffic-stoppingly gorgeous, interested for a long period of time.

"As sure as I stand before you now, all the thinkers I have met, all the lovers I have had…" He paused, lifting her chin with his thumb to hold her gaze before continuing. His eyes bored deep into hers, burning straight through to her soul. "Not one of them has moved me as you have.

Through all adversities, you maintain a beautiful grace and a disarming charm that has me utterly captivated. I have never loved anyone as much as I love you." He stood completely still, watching her face intently as the words moved past her mind's cautious filter.

She froze. "You...You love me?" The words squeaked out, hesitant and fragile. His face grew blurry before her, the mist of tears just on the edge of spilling. Her chin trembled against the firm and rough knuckles supporting it.

Kai's smile grew until the radiance rivaled the sun. "How could I not?" His voice, rich and deep, slipped over her skin like warm chocolate. "You are truly my spiritmate. I could have never dreamed nor wished for a more amazing companion." Giving her a rakish grin, he added, "And I've been known to have some very wild fantasies."

"But," she stammered, "I mean—"

Kai quieted her doubts with a searing kiss, his passion lacing her blood with the surest fire and the strongest desire. His hand held her firmly against his lips and she reveled in the intoxicating dichotomy of his hard physical planes and his tender touch. As he broke the kiss to gaze into her eyes, she heard the words she never dreamed she would hear again.

"I love you."

Cupping his face with her hands, Voni rained tiny kisses over his face, standing on tiptoe to cover as much of it as she could reach. Tears streaked down her cheeks even as she laughed and smiled.

"Omigod...omigod...omigod..." The litany halted only as long as her lips met his skin during the onslaught of kisses.

"I take it you approve."

Deep, rolling laughter pinged off the glass and showered the room with warmth. He pulled her into his arms. A broad and open smile was affixed to her face.

"Are you sure? I mean, yeah, of course I approve. But, I mean, I... Ooooh. I am so going to remind you of this moment." Words and tears leaked from her. She dropped her face into her hands before tucking herself under his shoulder, her tear-filled laughter muffling her remaining words. Which was probably for the best. Any more blathering and he might take back those wonderful words.

Rubbing her narrow back in soothing circles, Kai drank in the flood of emotions pouring out from her very skin, marveling at her resilience yet again. How could someone run such an emotional gamut? Shutting the water off with no more than a thought, he stepped out of the humid confines with his bundle still held close. He snaked his arm out to retrieve two large, fluffy towels, then cocooned her in them and briskly dried her cooling skin. He rubbed her down in movements both tender and teasing. Her giggles encouraged him to join in with laughter of his own.

"All right, all right, all right. I think I'm pretty well dried or peeled...or whatever it is you're doing. Hey!"

Kai's rapid actions and her squirming escape attempts soon had both of them in an impromptu wrestling match, squeaks and peals of laughter spilling from the bathroom into the bedroom. Deciding they needed a more level playing field for the continuation of this bout, Kai dipped down and easily hefted the giggling bundle over his shoulder and covered the few steps toward the still-chaotic sheets. The mummified parcel struggled and bounced against his back, fingers gripping his waist through the thick terry cloth shroud.

"Kai? What...where? Put me down, you big..." The rest of the statement whooshed out in a futile race to catch up with the air leaving her lungs. Bouncing once on the feather-soft mattress, she scrambled to emerge from her fluffy prison. As she laughed, tossing aside the towel, the eyes she met were not the ones she was expecting.

Black orbs ringed in red started out from a beautifully cruel face. The harsh lines and sharp planes told of gleeful torments and pain, loving dispensed over millennia. Lips peeled back, a snarl more than a grin greeting her shocked gaze.

"I told you we'd see each other soon." Her skin crawled as a voice like razors on glass cut through to her soul. "Oh, and you came dressed for the occasion. I'm flattered." He pawed at her with hands cold as the grave, and their touch promised of a lifetime of agony. "Now, you will give in to my embrace and be my mate!"

Bony fingers wrapped around her arms as the visage lowered toward hers, and its thin lips angrily attacked her own. Ghastly pressure tried to pry her mouth open, and a sickly force attempted to wedge between her locked jaws.

Desperate to escape from the crushing weight pressing against her chest, Voni kicked and shoved, clutching at the earlier discarded scrap of fabric. Eyes slammed shut, she continued to scratch and claw at the looming figure, the stench of decay and slaughtered innocence choking her. High-pitched, hyena-like sounds rang in her head, driving all rational thought from her mind.

Voni covered her ears.

"Get away from me!" The words exploded out of her, the force of her fears and frustration becoming tangible. Waves of crackling energy pulsed through her body and pushed against the confines of the room, shaking picture frames off the wall and rattling the furnishings.

The weight holding her down vanished only to be quickly replaced by another one. Yet this one she knew. This one she welcomed. This one dragged her from the darkness and held her gently, filling her with warmth and love.

Kai shook his head, willing his brain to get back into its proper place in his skull and not sloshing out his ears. He had done it again. Somehow, Konstantin had pulled her into his realm. He had just plopped her on the bed, still tucked in her towel, when she froze and began to seize.

Just like before.

But this time, he was alone. Eamon was a Channeler as well as a Guardian. And the two of them had barely pulled her out. Half-tempted to grab his phone, but afraid to leave her side, he simply held her, softly calling her back. Her body convulsed and sweat beaded on her brow. Seconds ticked by until she screamed out and he was thrown clear across the room.

What. The. Fuck?

She had tapped into her Spirit Force.

She truly was a Conduit. The blast brought Konstantin into focus for the briefest of moments, his black eyes wide with shock as he was cast back into the In-Between to find another pathway to his enemy. He vanished, but not before smiling smugly toward Kai, licking his lips and giving a quick wink.

Fucking bastard.

A menacing growl rumbled deep in his chest as he crawled across the floor to scoop his quivering beauty into his arms. "Baby? Baby, talk to me. Talk to me, Voni."

He lifted shaky hands to tunnel through her disheveled locks. Cautious breaths escaped her trembling lips, and her voice still failed her. "I...I..."

Kai pulled her close, crushing her against his chest. "I'm sorry, I'm so sorry." Unspoken emotions thickened his voice, choking off his words as he swallowed past the lump of tears in his throat. "I never wanted to see you hurt."

"I have to face him..." The words, mumbled into his chest, filled the empty silence with the weight of ages. She lifted her head, meeting his eyes, and he knew the truth written in the sad lines of her expression. "Don't I? It's the only way he'll ever stop. The only way I can ever have any peace."

"No." Shaking his head vigorously, Kai's voice was sure and steady. "I'll not let you face him. Not alone, you won't. We will. Together, *dragoste meu*. Together, always."

***

The blackness filled with peals of dark laughter as Konstantin coalesced, flopping into the newly created chair. He threw his head back as he continued to howl until tears of glee leaked from his eyes.

He had done it. He'd triggered her unique Conduit skill. And now, he thought, now you're mine. The cat-with-the-canary grin remained as he reached for the glass. The deep amethyst liquid quickly filled it, poured from an unseen hand. He had drawn her one step closer to joining him. Soon enough, she would come to him, thinking to stop him.

As he took a sip of the smooth and heady brew, his smile grew. And that would bring her and that pompous fucker Kai right to him. His day was getting better and better.

With the glass's contents absorbed, Konstantin stood with the ease of a predator, and his weapons and armaments materialized at will. Knowing his foe as he did, he needed to be ready for a full-frontal assault. That bastard was nothing if not predictable. He and his annoying sidekick, Eamon, would come in guns blazing, and his real target would be left in a safe place, far from his reach.

Or so they believed. He was sure he could find her anywhere in this world or any other. His earlier forays had proved the fact. And it had been so easy. Her natural, untapped abilities had greased his transition, seamlessly allowing him to pass directly through the In-Between and to wherever he wished. In her mind, behind her shoulder, or directly above her naked body.

His groin twitched as he remembered the feel of her beneath him, so soft and pliant. Her skin had paled once she'd seen him. Obviously, she was expecting that prick Vadim. A smirk curled his lips as he slid his eyes shut, recalling the helpless expression on Malakai's smug puss just before he'd winked out.

It was going to be so satisfying. Finally, after all the long years of waiting, he would put a permanent damper on the Guardians. Malakai had been a thorn in his side for far too long. Soon enough, he thought. Soon enough.□

TWENTY-TWO

"No, no, no, no. No."

Voni sighed, the exasperation weighed down her already-fatigued voice. She pulled her fingers through her wild mane as she eyed Kai. His head was swiveling so madly, she feared he would shake it right off his neck.

They had been over the same ground, going back and forth in a never-ending battle of wills. He was not going to agree to her plan, but it was the only viable option. It just plain sucked in so many ways.

"Kai, you've been saying that for the past two hours." With her feet tucked underneath her, her gaze followed Kai as he paced the wooden floor, his jean-clad legs eating up the space. She remembered a trip to the zoo once, watching the panthers in their old enclosure. At first, their beauty and grace had awed her. But after a few moments, sadness began to creep into her, seeing all that lethal power confined in an all-too-small space. She'd left soon after, but the sorrow remained.

She felt the same now, his long strides reminding her of the caged predators, both eager to escape their surroundings, but helpless all the same. She hated knowing her plan was the right one, despised the fact. But just as in the case of the cats, no amount of laps around the cage was going to change their situation.

"And would you please stop all that pacing? I'm getting exhausted just watching you...not to mention seasick." She extended her hand and waited, her pale arm peeking out of his roomy black T-shirt. "Please, Kai. Believe me. I'm not trying to be brave. Hell, I wouldn't even know how to do that.

But if this…Konstantin knows you as well as you've said, then he'd be expecting you and Eamon, and anyone else you know, guns blazing. And I'd be somewhere far away and safe."

On his next pass, she nabbed his arm, fighting to catch his roaming gaze. Hand over hand, she pulled him to the bed. His body strained against her gentle yet forceful touch. Finally, he sat with a resigned thud next to her, his head drooping forward. She reached out and tilted it toward her as she sought to catch his eyes. A hesitant smile warmed her lips, hoping to instill a sense of resolve in him that she barely felt.

Kai watched as his beautiful pixie put on a strong front for him, trying to ease his mind. A wave of honor and love flooded him, humbling and powerful. He gazed deep into her entrancing eyes and saw the promise of a future he'd only once dreamed about.

She was right. It was their only plan.

And he hated every part of it.

Cradling her face in his palms, he kissed her, thrusting his tongue forcefully into the soft recesses of her mouth. He poured his love and his fears, his apprehension, and his desires into one perfect moment. He then paused the fury of his plundering, giving her time to catch her breath as his eyes locked with hers, the amber depths reflecting the same emotional turmoil. He closed his eyes, taking a calming breath and rested his forehead against hers.

"I just found you. I cannot lose you." He trailed his fingers down her jawline, lightly skimming the soft fabric covering her chest before bringing them to rest over her heart. "And the thought of you…in that…that place." The words dried up, the lump in his throat blocking anything more. In the space of a second, he had her in his lap, holding her tightly.

Groaning in frustration, he held her closer ,tightening his arms around her narrow shoulders. She was so small, yet she managed to drive him to his knees with nothing more than a smile. If she could accomplish that feat, he prayed it would be enough to face his enemy.

Voni wrapped her arms around him, taking comfort from the powerful beat of his heart as it thrummed in her ears. She was still reeling from the sound of those three little words, followed by the surprise grope fest with her mental invader. At least now she had a name to attach to the phantom who had made her life a living hell for almost an entire year. Dmitrius Konstantin. Hell, even his name sounded creepy. A chill raced down her spine as she remembered the blood-red lips and his onyx eyes, her body shivering at the unabashed evil reflected in those black pools.

He had worn James' features like a costume for months, preying on her grief and self-doubt, hoping to push her over the edge and into his realm. If not for Kai, he would have succeeded. Kai had pulled her from that precipice. Now it was up to her to take back the reins of her life. Closing her eyes, she sent up a silent prayer to whoever was listening. Please don't let me be wrong and screw this up.

"Kai?"

"Hmmm?"

She looked up at him, her eyes shadowed with worry. She gnawed nervously on her bottom lip before she found the strength to get her voice to work. "If I don't...I mean, if things go—"

The shimmer of ice forming beneath his hands had nothing to do with the weather. He drew in close and brushed his lips along her thick hair, trailing his fingers in long strokes down her back. The fear had begun to grow within her. He couldn't let her do this. There had to be another way to put that fucker in his place, way more than the standard six feet under. With a heavy sigh, he settled back against the headboard, cradling the precious cargo on his lap.

Anger blazed in his eyes, the heat of his ire licked along his skin, tingling her fingertips. "You are not to even think like that." His voice growled in possessive menace, startling her. "Not ever. Do you hear me? Siobhan? Look at me." He shook with barely contained rage as he waited until he held her gaze. "You are going straight into the very mouth of Hell, where every fear and doubt you have will be amplified and used as a weapon against you. And I'm not speaking metaphorically, either. Each little self-recrimination, every 'I don't know' will become a blade in his very capable hands, and he will use it. Cut you to the bone and shred your spirit without a moment's hesitation."

He searched her face, praying that he wasn't terrifying her as much as he knew he was, but hating to do all the same. "Konstantin wants you to fall, needs you to fail to possess you, heart and soul." His voice dropped as he pinned her with his stare once more. "And he needs to know that those are not his to claim."

Heat flushed Voni's cheeks at his fiercely protective timbre. Her chin trembled as she fought to make any words come out. Since her fish-out-of-water routine only succeeded in frustrating her, she sighed and lowered his eyes, taking solace in the warmth of his arms. Her thoughts churned and swirled, spinning a wild dance timed to the pounding of her heart. The more Kai protested, the shakier her resolve became. Was she strong enough to really face him?

Voni spent the rest of the day, and the better part of the next, listening to Kai and Eamon talk tactics and strategies. The boys plotted and planned, discussing points of entry and how best to configure the In-Between to give them an advantage when the battle occurred. She spent the night learning to protect herself, to shield her mind from the weapons of Konstantin and his fellow Rogue Warriors, not to mention tangled in Kai's loving arms, his passion boundless and intoxicating.

In the daylight hours, Kai instructed her how to use her gifts. A Conduit, he had called her; one who could conduct thoughts and focus mental energies into the minds of another. Her headaches, he explained, were the result of missed communications.

"So, I'm what? Like some Ghost Whisperer-type person?" she asked, incredulous. A crooked smile flitted across her lips as she sipped on her third cup of coffee. Her legs were folded beneath her as she sat in the kitchen wearing one of his T-shirts, which served as more of a dress on her. The night had been another dreamless one and the day had been long. Kai had stood guard over her, sheltering her mind from any possible intrusion. The lack of dreams was a nice change, but the stress-induced fatigue still lingered even after the caffeine infusion.

Kai shook his head, raking a hand through his hair. At every turn, at each new detail, Voni's quirky sense of humor continued to amaze him. Her resilience, along with her ability to look for the silver lining of every situation, filled him with pride and hope. If only she would believe in herself as much as he did.

"Uh, no." His lips curved into a smirk as he leaned lazily against the countertop, wearing only a pair of faded jeans, the pale blue fabric hung low on his hips. "She hears the voices of people who are dead. You, my dear, hear the voices of those still living. But, think more along the lines of mental voice mail, messages from those seeking to be heard."

***

Swallowing the last of her coffee, she fixed her gaze on his. "Okay, but why me? I mean, I'm nothing special. I'm just...well, I'm just me." She shrugged, seeking for some divine answers among the dregs swirling at the bottom of the white mug. She was just being honest; she was just a standard, boring person. She wasn't overly smart or gifted in any way. Why would such comic-book-worthy powers be given to someone so...normal?

Gentle fingers tilted her chin, forcing her gaze away from the interesting dance of the coffee grinds to scale the chiseled abs before her. When she finished her visual assent, she found Kai's deep icy-green eyes peering into her heart.

"You're overthinking this, baby. No one truly knows why some people are given these gifts and others are not. It has nothing to do with genetics or intelligence or...hell, or anything. It's one of those random events, something that just is." He kneeled so she didn't have to crane her neck and trailed his fingertips along her jaw, wending them into her hair.

"And for the record, I think you are so very much more than special. You are the most honest and real person I have ever met. You take things as they are, without blinking an eye." He grinned impishly before adding, "For the most part. I know that many others would have run screaming from the building when things really started to go weird."

Voni exhaled slowly, her shoulders drooping. "Yeah, I guess I'm kinda stubborn that way. Not to mention certifiable, since...well, aside from the near-death experiences..." She hesitated, gathering her thoughts and her courage before continuing. "I wouldn't trade one minute of it. Well, I mean except 'I'm being sucked into the pit of Hell' painful ones, those I'd trade in a heartbeat. Don't get me wrong, I'm crazy, not stupid. And let's not mention the fact that there's some psycho demon thing that wants my soul for some strange reason. Oh, and you know him, and he hates you. And don't forget my stupid heart that keeps thinking it wants to take a permanent time-out whenever it feels like it... Oh, forget it." The words tumbled out in a mish-mashed pile of emotions, many of which she wasn't ready to really analyze just yet.

Quick as a thought, she stood, needing to make a hasty retreat. She slipped out of the chair, and she quickly maneuvered her way to the sink. The splash of cool water and the furious swishing of the dishtowel covered the sounds of Kai's footfalls behind her, but she knew he was there. She sensed his concern, a palpable heat pouring from his skin at his approach. Channeling her frustrations, she scrubbed the innocent coffee mug until the finish began to lose its luster and her fingers glowed red.

"Voni? Look at me, baby." Her shoulders remained solid, her body strung too tight to respond to his gentle attempt to steer her away from her compulsive cleaning. "Siobhan, please—"

"Please, what?" Tears of confusion tinged with exhaustion began to slip from her eyes. She sought answers in the flowing water. "Kai, I won't lie. I'm terrified beyond all rational thought. My stupid brain and my dumb mouth don't know how to say it right, so it comes out all strong and witty. But, I'm not that. Hell, I'm not any of that. I don't know why I was chosen for any of this. What short straw I drew in life."

A ragged inhale and more words poured from her, like the water under her watchful gaze. "I've heard voices in my head for most of my life. I never thought they were real, I just figured they were my imagination, kinda like characters in a story. But the thoughts didn't come from me. They weren't mine at all. Situations I had never experienced, places I'd never even heard of. People, stories, things I'd never dreamed of, and they just seemed to live in my mind. But, the funny part is, it didn't freak me out. Not ever. I don't know why. I guess it just...well, didn't."

She stared at the swirling water circling the sink and studied the disappearing bubbles for another moment before shutting off the stream. Kai's hand remained in place, warmth seeping through the thin fabric barrier. She finally mustered the courage to lift her eyes to his clear gaze.

"I've been one of these...these things..."

"A Conduit." His voice provided the word stuck in her throat.

She scoffed at the title. "Yeah, what you said, for a long time, haven't I?"

He met her troubled gaze, his eyes mirroring her own mixed emotions. "It does sound like it. Honestly, I do not have much knowledge about Conduits. Eamon is what's called a Channeler. He can focus the emotions of himself as well as control the feelings of those around him. Conduits focus thoughts, and Marshals can focus physical skills and strengths. Heart, mind, and body."

Voni narrowed her eyes, brows furrowing in concentration. "So do all people with these, these…whatevers. Do they end up as, well, one of you, one of the good guys?"

With a light laugh and an easy smile, Kai brushed the growing creases from her forehead. "No, my love. That would be nice, but sadly no. Free will allows each person to follow any path, even the ones shadowed in darkness."

"Yeah, I guess so."

Silence filtered in, blanketing the kitchen within moments. The thickening presence of all the things left unsaid fortified Voni in a way she had never imagined. She could do it. She had to. Squaring her shoulders, her thoughts were unclouded as her voice rose clear and strong.

"Kai? Take me home. I'm ready."□

TWENTY-THREE

The Aston Martin's engine hummed down the road as the miles disappeared in a flurry. The soft, charcoal-gray interior buffered any outside noises, allowing the confines to become a haven for the sounds of yet another musical maestro. Voni allowed her gaze to flit out the window, catching her reflection in the dimming daylight, one of his button-down, crisp, white oxfords covering the turquoise T-shirt she had worn the last time she recalled wearing clothes that were her size. The sleeves were rolled past her elbows and still she swam in it, but knowing what she was about to face, she wanted to have something bearing his scent, something to keep her heart grounded in why she could not fail.

Violins and guitars threaded together pulsing harmonies and sweet melodies. Bond, he had said was the name of the group. The cover image of four beautiful women had her intrigued. Smiling, she returned the case to its home in the dividing console.

"Nice to see that beautiful people can be kinda nerdy at the same time."

"Hmmm?" He gracefully arched his brow at her random comment. Dressed simply in a black tee and black jeans, he fought to keep his eyes on the road ahead. Already, he could feel her receding from him, shoring herself once again behind her high walls. Yet she still was able to make him smile with her lightning-fast mind. He wondered at the sheer speed of her thoughts. Perhaps it was one of the gifts of a Conduit, the ability to follow several trains of thought, keeping up with their various stories and pathways.

"Well, I mean, they're just so pretty, and I keep thinking about all years they must have spent studying to become really good. And at such an amazing art, like playing the violin—"

"Well, I happen to know of a very gorgeous dancer," he interjected, a hint of a smile curving his lips as they raced toward their destination, "who, I am sure, spent many years studying to perfect her craft. Who, even now, manages to steal my breath each time I see her."

"Really? Anyone I might have heard of?" Her teasing words lacked the lightness she had clearly hoped to imbue them with. A nervous tremble laced the simple question. Kai reached across the seat and laced his fingers through hers. He lifting her hand to his lips and brushed her knuckles with a gentle kiss, hoping to steady her unease.

A melody she recognized filled the silence. She sighed deeply as Barber's "Adagio for Strings," one of her favorites, began to play. The urge to close her eyes and fall into the music's trance tapped at the front of her thoughts. But the fear of chance encounter with her nightmarish opponent kept her eyelids firmly open, garnering another heavy sigh from her.

The remains of the day slipped silently into the bosom of the night as the building she had called home for so long edged into view. Six small cottages nestled in two neat rows, with hers at the back, the gated path leading straight to her front door. Directing him to the alley behind the complex, she focused her thoughts as she fumbled for her keys. Even tucked into the safety of his silver chariot, she sensed a heaviness in the space surrounding her tiny house, an oppressive shroud blanketing the walls.

She clutched clumsily at the belt release, her hands shaking and sweaty. Once again, Kai's sun-kissed hand enveloped her pale skin, the rough pads of his fingertips sending chills through her blood. A weak smile lifted a corner of her mouth, a mirthless action that did little to calm or inspire her.

"We could—"

She shook her head, stopping him mid-thought. Their combined efforts finally triggered the button. The resounding click startled her. "No, this has to be the way. If I don't do this..."

This time, it was his action that stopped her midsentence. He devoured her lips in a kiss, thrusting his tongue possessively into every warm corner of her mouth. He tunneled his fingers through her tightly braided hair, holding her firmly in place. Breaking off the kiss as suddenly as he started it, she held still as his gaze roamed across her face before his stormy eyes locked with hers.

"Be safe and remember what I told you." He quickly pressed his lips against her forehead. "I will only be whole when you are again at my side."

Swallowing hard, she nodded almost imperceptibly. Her heart hammered a strong and steady beat as she clamped her emotions down as far as she could and reached for the door latch. A sharp pull on the handle, and the cold slithered in, stealing the warmed air and returning only sickening dread. Before she lost her nerve, she stepped out and crossed to her back gate.

Cold sweat beaded on her skin with each step she took closer to the gated opening. "C'mon, you dork. If he's in there, he already knows you're here, so what the use in waiting?" Her mumblings did nothing to hasten her movements, her hand unwilling to quicken its snail's pace toward the twine hook. Finally, blowing out all the air stored in her lungs, she yanked on the threaded string. The creaky wood swung toward her, and she stepped inside.

The small backyard appeared inky in the flickering streetlight. She white-knuckled the bits of metal in her hand, hoping the tight grip would stop her arm from trembling as she slipped the key into its slot and turned. The tumblers clanked in the silence. Swallowing hard, she pulled open the door.

Voni hardly recognized her own home. The thick, clingy air fouled every room and practically dripped down the beige walls. She was sure that, if she were to reach out, her fingers would find a sticky sludge on the solid surfaces. The despair was physical, and it was choking her as tendrils of sadness snaked around her throat. Fighting the overwhelming desire to run back to the security of Kai's car, and his arms, she placed one foot in front of the other and crossed the tiled kitchen.

As she passed through to the living room, she rubbed vigorously at her arms. Its normally buff blandness was now masked by the veil of cold and lingering dark. Shaking to dispel the growing chill, she walked farther into the abyss. The pulsing core of dread centered down the narrow hallway and terminated at her bedroom door. It all seemed to have started there, the first of the vividly real nightmares, so it would make sense that the final meeting would be there as well.

She hovered her hand over the doorknob, and her mind reeled as she fought to recall all the tips and tricks both Kai and Eamon had so diligently described. There were so many rules that governed the place Konstantin called home, and none of them worked in her favor. Once she opened the door, once she entered his world, she would be at his mercy.

Not friggin' likely. As she leaned in farther toward the handle, she took a deep breath to settle her nerves. She was rewarded with the fragrant scent that was purely male and purely Kai. With renewed strength, she closed her fingers around the cold metal knob and turned.

***

Kai sat in the shadowed confines of the luxury sedan, rapping a staccato tattoo against the dash with his fingertips. His breath escaped in angry huffs as the seconds crawled on. Another check of his watch confirmed it again. Peering into the darkness surrounding his car, he waited one more moment before finally grabbing his cell. He flicked his fingers across the screen and the waiting began again as it rang.

"Kai? Kai, please tell me ya aren't sittin' in front of her house right now?" By the gravel in his friend's voice, he must have just been waking up.

A growling sigh was all the answer he could muster. Eamon matched the sound before replying. "All right, boyo. I'll be there in two."

"Thanks, man. I…"

"Don't thank me yet. Wait 'til I do something heroic…and there's a beauty nearby."

Shaking his head as he ended the call, Kai took a calming breath. He'd promised he'd let her handle it her way, but there was no way he wasn't going to stand guard. Just in case. With a click, the door swung open, and he headed for the trunk, opting to change into more appropriate fighting gear.

Please, love. Hang in there, help is coming. I promise.

Voni felt a strange pull, as if someone yanked on her belly button and then threw her down an elevator shaft. The bottom dropped from beneath her feet, and her stomach settled somewhere north of her rib cage. All the while the darkness remained. Toes, knees, and then hands met with a solid surface, and the movement stopped. She blinked to prove that her eyes were indeed open, though she could see no ambient light could from anywhere.

Kai had said the In-Between, or the Void, could be a little unnerving. Unnerving? Fuck, it was like being inside a cow. She remembered them telling her that thoughts held substance here, but only for the bad guys. She would only have what she'd brought. Oh great, fabu. So she was gonna be fighting evil with...what? She didn't even have a nail file.

Giving an exasperated sigh, she rose to her feet, sure her presence wouldn't go undetected for long. Might as well get this started. Both Kai and Eamon had tried to explain the weapons she would be facing, the foes she would meet. Her hands started to shake, rational fear beginning to take root in her blood.

"I must be outta my mind."

In the blink of an eye, her surroundings changed. Paper-like walls coalesced and solid furnishings appeared from the nothingness around her. Her breath swirled as the temperature dropped like a curtain, and shapes squirmed, various body parts pressing against the malleable barrier. Her heart pounded and her lungs burned as the acrid smell of rotten eggs and burned burgers filled the space. Her stomach lurched. Bile rose to combat the stench of death. She fought to swallow hard, keeping the urge to vomit at bay.

Rubbing away her tears and coughing to cover her gags, she struggled to keep her feet when she sensed an evilly familiar chill.

"Well, well, well. What do we have here? I thought Vadim cared for you. Obviously, I was mistaken."

The voice brought forth images of jagged nails across a black slate board. Voni fought another wave of nausea, blinking fast to clear her tear-fogged eyes. One final, deep swallow and she sought the source of her revulsion. Her gaze trailed up the tall, lean figure, dressed simply in loose, dark slacks, his feet bare, as was his chest. Dirty blond hair fell emo-like over his right eye, his jet-black left eye pinning her with a gaze darker than pitch.

His looks could have caught the eye of anyone. But to her, something about him was just...off. A coldness surrounded him, bleak and joyless. His features were hard and unyielding, his thin lips curving into a cruel sneer as his onyx eyes flashed in anticipation as he stalked her.

"Because I didn't think he'd risk his precious spiritmate without some kind of half-baked backup plan. Let me guess." He paused, stepping behind his fear-frozen prey. "He sends you in to…soften me up." She yelped as his tongue flicked snakelike against her earlobe. "Then what? He and his bosom buddy would swoop in and save the day?" His mocking sarcasm singsonged down her spine, battering her weakening resolve.

"But no… This, this was your idea. Somehow, you believed if you faced me, if you faced your fears, then all of this…" He paused again. Leaning over her shoulder, he motioned to the encroaching dark. "Would just, what? Go away?"

Oh God. Please tell me this is still going to work. Voni snapped her eyes shut, tucking her head against her shoulder. She was rewarded with a whiff of Kai's scent, still clinging to the fabric sheltering her. The thought of returning to his arms gave her a needed boost of courage.

Mocking laughter bled into her ears, spoiling her stolen moment. "Oh gawd. You really do have it bad, don't you? And I'm sure he told you about what happened to the other girls, didn't he?"

She lifted one eyebrow in curiosity and peeked at him suspiciously. Knowing he was baiting her did nothing to stop her from wanting to hear more.

"Oh, I see he neglected to mention that little bit." Clicking his tongue, he shook his head sadly and circled her, a shark scenting blood in the waters. "You're not the first, you know. He had a mate before. Ah, she was stunning. Tall, beautiful, with soft blonde hair, and clear blue eyes. Much more of what was considered the standard of femininity of the times. This would have been a century ago, another lifetime."

"Shut up." Her voice was little more than a whisper.

He turned away from her, crossing over the table, where he poured a glass of thick, bluish liquid that looked like no alcohol she had ever seen. She watched as he sipped languidly, as he enjoyed both his drink and her torment. "She also thought as you, that somehow she was the one. And she died calling his name, just as you will. So strange how our hearts won't let us believe what our heads know to be true."

"You don't know—"

He raised an eyebrow quizzically, dragging a corner of his lip into a sardonic sneer as he peered over his shoulder at her. "Really? And why would that be? 'Because he loves me.' Am I right? Let me guess, you shared something…passionate? Something special, something deep and meaningful?" He tossed a hand in the air with lazy arrogance. "Some amazing fucking, that's all it was. All sweaty with him balls-deep and whispering sweet nothings in your ears. Sounded like a dream come true, didn't it? But there was trouble in paradise, wasn't there? Tell me, exactly when did he tell you about me, about his 'foe'?" He leveled a condescending leer of pure disdain at her, making air quotes with his hands. Turning his back to her, he continued to poke at her thin wall of confidence.

"Or even what he is. Bet that was a bit of a surprise. Oh, a fighter on the side of good, battling all things dark and evil. The whole 'pure good versus pure evil' storyline, straight out of the movies. But did he really tell you everything? Did he tell you this love of yours has a time limit? Guess he left that part out too. The whole claiming ritual? In a few short days, this 'love' of yours will only be a memory to him." Oily laughter bubbled up from him, as he slunk toward her, the sounds mirthless and depraved.

Tears of impotent frustration hovered a blink away as he pushed further against her fragile resolve. As he rounded to face her, the evil glint in his eye chilled her blood. "You are very close to the expiration date on this fuckfest. And then, you'll be all alone. Again. Forgotten. Consigned to an eternity of nothingness and sorrow, just like James."

Her heart sank as the mention of that name. She wanted to be filled with righteous indignation but too many other, more dangerous emotions were fighting for supremacy. "You don't get the right—"

"What? I can't say he knew you'd forget him? That soon he wouldn't matter at all in your life? Knew you were just going to move on, feeling like he could never really make you happy?" Voni gawked as the features before her melted. One moment they were solid and scary, the next her fiancé stood before her, his short brown hair and gentle brown eyes just like the last time she'd seen him. "A little bit of time, and then you'd act like I never ever was there."

Her brain screamed at her to turn away, to stop looking, and not believe. He wasn't James. James was gone. "No. This…this can't be possible." Her voice was weak and incredulous.

"I am, Voni. I am dead, but my heart, my very soul, has stayed with you. I can't move on without you." Voni had almost forgotten how soft his voice was. That was what had attracted her first.

"No! It's not him! Don't listen!" Voices screamed inside her head, argued and debated.

She reached out a trembling hand, shaking her head in disbelief. "J-J-James? No, this…this can't. It's not…" Her voice trailed off as her fingers neared the figure before her.

A sad expression graced his ghostly lips. "I've called to you. Every night, I pleaded for your help. For weeks, months, I waited for you. I need you. Please, come with me. It will be just like it was before. I've missed you so much."

Tears slid down her cheeks as she listened to the apparition confirm her darkest suspicions. Her dreams were more than ramblings of her idle mind. They were messages from her dead lover. "James, I'm so sorry. I didn't know…"

"No. You mean you didn't want to know. Everything I ever did was for you, to make you happy. To let you follow your dreams, I sacrificed everything I wanted. I gave up everything, including my life, to see that you never wanted for anything." His voice, his face as well, began to twist as his condemning words flowed across the short distance between them. The longer he spoke, the deeper she felt her heart sink as her own guilt and self-doubt rose. The voices in her head started pounding against her skull, yelling for her to run away, to stop listening and to remember where she was and why she was there.

"No. That's not what I wanted. That was never what I wanted." She shook her head violently in protest. "I just wanted us to be happy."

"Then take my hand." He reached a pale hand out to her, beckoning her. Slowly, her gaze trailed from the outstretched hand and the chocolate-brown eyes before her. A glimmer caught her eye, a spark within the hidden depths of his eyes. He wasn't James.

Her gaze slipped down to the white shirt hanging loosely off her arm. She was happy, as she could never have been with James. James had always done what he wanted, claiming it was all to make her happy, and for a time, she'd believed she was. But not until she met Kai did she realize that true happiness came from acceptance, from understanding, and from trust.

Do you trust me? The words Kai has asked her so many days before rang in her head, clearing away the illusion before her. The face she had once known shimmered and was replaced by Konstantin's cruel sneer.

"Go fuck yourself."

Pain exploded as his hand flew across her cheek, sending her spinning into the table. "Well, that wasn't quite the response I was looking for. I guess we're going to do this the hard way, eh? So be it." Flicking some unseen annoyance from his fingers, he turned back toward Voni as she staggered to regain her feet.

Little flashpoints of light danced on the edges of her vision, and blinking didn't seem to send them away. She tasted copper mingled with the salt of her tears. A sharp kick connected with her ribs, throwing her back onto the floor. Coughing to gain her stolen breath, she scrambled once again to a standing position. Fingers closed around her throat, an unbreakable vise constricting fast. Instinct kicked in, and so did self-preservation. She snapped her leg out, connecting her knee with the meaty part of his inner thigh. Dammit. Too short to reach the sweet spot.

"Little bitch," he growled, gritting his teeth as he stumbled backward.

Free from his grip, Voni pushed away from the table, sucking in a deep breath as she regained her feet. Her head swiveled as she searched for an exit. A rectangular glow off to her right caught her eye, and she ran toward what she hoped was a doorway only to feel a sharp tug on the collar of Kai's shirt. Her feet appeared before her face, and she knew the ground would meet her soon enough. Taking a page from a Jet Li movie she'd seen, she twisted her body, spinning in a tight spiral mid-fall. The world spun and the ground became real under her knees, but her opponent was left holding her tangled baggy top, a rather bland expression on his brutal features.

"I am curious what you thought that was going to accomplish."

Shrugging, she answered with a sheepish smile. "Well, couldn't hurt to try." Yanking hard on the shirt, she pulled him off-balance, swung her leg around, and planted the side of her foot solidly against his face. "Hey, I'm pretty good at this." She grabbed the shirt from his hands and thrust her arms back into the roomy sleeves.

Konstantin wiped the trickle of blood from his lip, his pitch-black eyes narrow and glowing. "I need you to choose to stay to keep your powers, but if you choose to leave, then your death will at least drive Malakai out of his fucking mind."

His right hand shot out, sending her hurling into the wall and holding her suspended high off the ground. The back of her skull bounced like a rubber ball, a sickening crack echoing in her ears. Again, the force around her throat grew and her breath came in short, shallow gasps. Her eyes rolled back into her head. She clutched and clawed at the invisible tendrils wrapped around her neck, her heels digging into the whitewashed concrete pressing into her back.

"Let her go! Now!"

Voni's eyes popped open and scanned the expanding room. The space seemed to anticipate a brawl. Two shapes strode in from the darkness, their long, steady steps making short work of the distance between them. Kai held his head high, dressed in those leather pants she had ogled in his closet a few short nights ago, his upper body clothed in a fine silk-like shirt similar to the one she currently wore. Eamon was sporting what looked like club wear, as if Kai had pulled him away from a night of carousing. Both were armed with short, unassuming staves. No other weapons were visible to her.

Great, that asshole had phenomenal cosmic power, and they brought sticks. She coughed weakly, hoping to draw in a few more gulps of life-giving air. Time was beginning to work against her, and her fears were starting to return in force. The wicked words of Konstantin's jeers started to creep around her mind as she watched Kai move closer.

"You're not the first, you know."

He did tell her that he'd had other lovers. Hell, after as long as he'd been alive, she wouldn't be surprised if he had generations of kids floating around the planet. But another spiritmate? From what she'd gleaned from Kai and Eamon's talks, each Guardian only had one spiritmate, one perfect partner for their soul. That had to be real.

She gasped a shallow breath as Kai's icy-green eyes hardened into narrow slits, his ire focused on Konstantin's smug smirk. The air crackled between them, tingling the exposed skin on Voni's arms. Her vision dimmed, the last gulp of air vanishing quickly. As her eyelids dropped, she regretted that she would not be seeing the impending brawl.

"I. Said. Let. Her. Go."

Air whooshed into her lungs and solid ground appeared beneath her feet, then her knees and finally her hands. Gasping and eyes watering, she sucked down the blessed air greedily and opted to stay ground-bound for a little bit longer. She reached a shaky hand to her chest, making a quick double-check of her heart rate. The beat was off, but not dangerously so. Not yet, at least. If she was going to be of any use in this final confrontation, she'd need to keep her wits about her, or fake it as best she could.

Kai found his breath again once Voni no longer hung like a twitching painting, her pale skin growing more ashen by the second. The primal urge to run to her, to scoop her into his arms, had to be shoved deep into his gut. From the instant he and Eamon had appeared in the Black, his heart lurched, attuned to her every emotion. She was hurting, and all he could do was slowly make his way toward the glow of his enemy, all the while trying to maintain a calm demeanor. He grumbled colorful obscenities as they traveled, his heavy steps muffled by the dark around them as Kai kept his thoughts focused on one image: Konstantin's throat under his fingers.

As soon as the room became tangible, only Eamon's strong hand on his shoulder kept him from lunging at the bastard. Voni's cheek was beginning to swell. A nasty purplish bruise arose around her left eye, and her lip was split, the slow trickle of blood showing signs of stopping. Rage narrowed his vision, and power sparked the length of the staff in his hand. Morphing fluidly, the harmless stick became an impressive weapon, a wicked blade on one end and a heavy metal cap covering the other.

The grin on Konstantin's face grew broader the more aggravated Kai became. So it was true after all—she was his spiritmate. It was even better than expected. This was the edge he needed. Kai would be so off-balance from his emotions, he would be easy prey. Sensing victory, Konstantin laughed, softly at first then growing in volume as Kai took his final step across the threshold.

He wrapped his arms around his gut as his opponents strode closer acting as if they owned the fucking place. The grin remained plastered on his face as the walls breathed out, expanding the room to allow for a serious ass-kicking. This time, that smug Vadim was going to get his due. Large speakers materialized in the high corners of the walls, and he folded his arms across his chest in confident readiness.

"Careful, boyo. I'm not likin' the sound of that hyena's laugh right now." Eamon stalked cautiously around the room, the tinge of evil and deception oozing from everywhere. He headed straight toward Voni, making sure she was not injured worse than was visible. If anything permanent happened to her, Eamon knew his friend would never recover, and losing his temper here could be deadly for way too many people. Dropping to his knees, he made short work of his examination, finding most of the damage to be superficial.

"Come here often?" He earned a nervous smile as he trailed his fingers along the nasty bruise on her cheek. He hissed softly when she cringed. "Och, I'm sorry there, darlin'. Just stay here, right?"

She was projecting her terrified emotions so loudly he had to fight the urge to cover his ears. "Voni? Ya have to be strong here. Remember what we told ya? Cuz if that beag cac gets wind of it, he's gonna cut our boy there to the bone." He held her gaze as best as he could, nodding as he called on his skills to help her get centered. One shared deep breath and she calmed enough for him to return his attention to the show just about to ramp up.

Kai kept his eyes focused on Konstantin as his heart thundered, struggling to keep his thoughts calm and controlled. "You fucking bastard. This ends here. Tonight." He sharply struck the ground with his staff, punctuating the last word. The sound echoed through the open silence.

Konstantin swept his arms theatrically, his maniacal laughter ringing against the walls. "And just what do you think you can end here? This is my world, you arrogant prick. Here, I'm a fucking god!" Energy shot out of his entire body, filling the air with the stench of sulfur as it blasted Kai off his feet.

Kai sailed back, landed on his back, and rolled nimbly and swiftly to a low crouch, his weapon held away from his body in a menacing guard. "You're no god, Dmitri. You're just some punk who hides in the shadows and preys on the innocent. And you've been a thorn in my side for far too long." Kai rushed toward the other man, arcing the blade behind him as he closed the distance.

"Kai! No!" Voni cried out in terror and sprang up, only to be dragged back down just as quickly.

"Girl, ya get between those two right now, and it'll be doin' more harm than good. Now, please. Just stay put." Eamon's frantic whispers only agitated her further but, in her heart, she knew he was right. She spun her head back to the action as Kai's long blade swept wide, narrowly missing the man who had tormented her dreams for so long.

Eamon stood and snapped his outstretched arm, and his staff transformed into an equally vicious-looking weapon. As soon as he gained his feet, the rules changed. Two against one became five against two in a heartbeat. Voni's jaw dropped, stunned as four more men appeared out of thin air, walking out of the walls into the conflict in progress. Eamon sighed, rolling his shoulders as he faced off against the four newcomers.

Weapons blinked into being. Most of them sported curved blades and razor edges that seemed to cut the very air. Each man paced the room, their movements a deadly dance of give and take, a step forward here, a sneered growl there. The testosterone began to flood the chamber, thickening the air and making breathing nearly impossible for Voni. Her heart started a slow ascent to lodge in her throat. Swallowing hard in an attempt to send it back to its rightful place, she sat frozen with her back against the wall.

Konstantin ducked Kai's wide-sweeping blade as pulsating electronic beats filled the air, a pair of sais manifesting into his empty hands.

Kai cocked his head a fraction, a hint of a scowl marking his brow. "Techno? Dude, are you serious?" He launched a blinding flurry of powerful and calculated attacks at Konstantin.

The ringing clang of metal on metal blended into a strange, symbiotic symphony, rising and falling in time with the blaring music. Voni watched the fluid grace of Kai as he fought, each movement a stunning display of predatory skills well-practiced through the centuries. Her gaze flickered over to see Eamon in a deadly dance with four opponents, keeping them at bay and away from her.

Time crawled on as the sparks rained down, the blades glinting as they glided, cutting through air and flesh. A yelp caught her ears, and her head snapped in the direction to find one of the Rogues crumpling to the floor, his head strangely absent from the rest of his body. The weapon in his lifeless fingers slid to a stop at her feet, its silent message not lost on her. Her hand shook as she reached toward the discarded blade, its long sharpened edge disappearing into a leather-wrapped wooden grip. She picked it up, taking only a moment to admire the lightness of it, before gaining her feet and stepping away from the wall.

Eamon slashed and dodged, his feet shuffling against the blood-slick ground. A warrior plowed into him, wrapping an arm around his midsection, taking them both to the ground. Eamon slammed his elbow into the man's back, loosening his grip. Scrambling to his knees, he cold-cocked him with a right cross, bringing the number of targets down by one. "Kai? Is it just me or do ya feel like we stepped into Sabbat on a bad night?"

Kai blocked a glancing blow with his sword, driving his knee up into Konstantin's gut. "Nah, more like amateur night at Soma."

Eamon's opponent groaned slightly before countering with an elbow into the side of his head. "Ow, fucker."

"Do you two ever shut up?" Konstantin growled as the banter continued. "You're drowning out Prodigy." He flicked his wrists and the sais spun, their points slicing through the air inches away from Kai's retreating face. He pressed forward, his arms punching in combinations, forcing Kai to backpedal to retain his footing. An evil grin cracked his somber lips as a quick feint drew blood, the sai now dripping in crimson.

Kai hissed, clasping at the oozing gash across his ribs. "That was one of my favorite shirts. Now I have another reason to kick your ass." He twirled the long weapon with ease, the steel whistling as if hungry for some liquid nourishment of its own. Rushing in, he whipped the blade against the paired points, catching one of the cross guards. He gave a twisting yank, and the weapon skittered across the floor. Konstantin used the winding spin to attack, his now-vacant hand sailed lightning fast, the punch narrowly missed Kai's exposed throat. The trailing hand, however, did not miss its target, and the force snapped Kai's head back. Kai allowed the momentum to carry him back, flipping over and landing in a kneeling crouch. A flash of white caught the corner of his eye, and his blood froze. Voni had moved from her safe place, a sword held tightly in her trembling hands.

No!

Voni took a deep breath as she stepped away from the sheltering wall. She scanned the scene frantically, looking for some way to help. Eamon was battling five men while Kai was locked in an all-out brawl with Konstantin. She had to be out of her mind. No, come on, Von. You can do this. She'd seen enough Jackie Chan movies to pull it off. Shaking herself, she ventured silently forward, hoping her knocking knees weren't making as much noise as she heard in her own ears.

"Eamon! On your six!" Kai sprung, sword raised above his head as he lunged at Konstantin. He had to keep him occupied and unaware of Voni's movements. Blow after blow rained down, his attacks ruthless and undaunted. Dammit. Why couldn't she stay put?

He strained to keep his eyes on the battle at hand, fought to maintain focus as his heart screamed for him to rush to her side. As the seconds ticked by, he had to trust in his friend, and in the strength of his beautiful pixie. Eamon would protect her.

Eamon swiveled his head to find Voni slinking up, the weapon looking far too big for her tiny frame. "Aw, fuck." The words slipped out in a frustrated whisper. Quickly palming a dagger, he flung out his arm. The blade flipped end over end to land with a sickening thud, imbedded deep into the chest of the Rogue closest to Voni. "Girl, are ya tryin' to get yourself killed?" he screamed over the din of the synthesized beats and clashing steel.

"Don't yell at me! I just want to help!" Voni stepped over the still-twitching body to stand eye-to-chest with Eamon, the sword in her hand dangling by her side.

Eamon growled a curse before spinning her behind his back and thrusting his arm out, catching a passing Rogue with a crippling blow to the gut. His mutterings grew more angry as he lashed out again and again, striving to keep the ever-growing number of foes away from his best friend's spiritmate.

The presence at his back trembled before moving farther away. He clamped his teeth down, shuffling back to keep her nearby.

"Okay. Shouldn't be that hard, right?" her soft voice mumbled at his back, and he caught the quick gleam of steel as she raised the sword before her and swung at the nearest target. She bumped against his back as the blade slid through her opponent, stopping as it met bone. Blood sprayed in a scarlet mist, thickening the already-heavy air and splashing onto his back. Eamon spiraled to find her frozen in mute terror as the warrior crumbled in a heap, shuddered once, then stilled.

A sharp cry caught Kai's ear, drawing his focus away from his opponent. There, with her back pressed against Eamon's, Voni stood still, her eyes wide in horror as the warrior before her breathed his last. The bloodied weapon slipped from her fingers, and she looked dangerously close to passing out. "Voni? I know you can hear me. Please, baby, listen to me. This is not real. The thing you just killed was not human. He never was. It's just a trick of the In-Between. He only existed here because Konstantin willed him to be."

Pain exploded along his side as Konstantin took advantage of his lapse in concentration, the stab of a driving elbow bringing him back to the battle at hand. Baring his teeth, Kai grabbed Konstantin's wrist to keep his weapon hand still before slamming his forearm into the side of his adversary's head.

"Damn, man. You hit like my grandmother. I thought you were supposed to be the big and bad fucker around here."

He slid his gaze lightning-fast to his spiritmate. His heart shattered as she remained immobile, her trembling so violent he could see it from across the room. His arm gained strength, his muscles adding more power to each new attack as he split his attention between his attacker and his love, battling fiercely as he yelled her name over his shoulder.

A soft, soothing voice filled her panicking mind, the words awash with love and compassion. Yet, as her gaze traveled down toward the figure at her feet, the face once again melted into that of her former lover. Her eyes widened, and she whipped her head around to see each attacking warrior clad in his skin, carbon copies of James armed with swords and daggers, bent on the destruction of Kai and Eamon.

"No, no, no, no, no...not real, not real..." She shook her head violently, pressing her hands against her ears and clenching her eyes shut. Every muscle in her body tightened, straining to keep her tenuous grasp on reality from slipping through her fingers. Behind her closed eyes, the cries of the battle bled through her hands, the slash of steel, groans from the lips of the many Jameses, and one voice above the rest.

Kai.

He was screaming her name.

"No!"

The word exploded from her and with it, a wave of emotional energy. Her frustration and fear coalesced into a ripple of power, thrusting out from her soul and flooding the room. The James clones vanished in a blink and hurled the real warriors about like rag dolls in a young child's tantrum, leaving them to lie scattered amid the splintered space. Peeling open her fluttering eyelids, she fought to remain standing. Her knees, however, had other plans, buckling beneath her and tumbling her to the ground. Her heart stuttered and blood leaked from her nose as her eyes rolled back into her head and the black swallowed her.

Kai clamored to his feet, rapid blinks bringing his vision back into focus. The blast from Voni had taken all of them by surprise and landed him clear on the other side of the room. He watched as she toppled over, collapsing onto the cold ground. His heart dropped and his vision narrowed as he sprang to his feet and took off in a dead run in her direction. Yet, each step only brought her farther and farther away.

Goddamn this fucking place!

"Eamon! Eamon!"

He forced his steps to slow, while his voice cracked and strained as he continued to yell for her. His mind spun in dizzying circles. She's all right. She'll be fine. She's strong. She's okay.

"Kai? What the bloody hell just happened?"

He jerked his head up and spied Eamon staggering to his feet, blood leaking from his ears.

A slight hint of a smile curled one corner of his mouth. "Remind me not to piss her off anytime, boyo."

As Kai shook his head to clear the fog, he searched the room for any Rogues still standing and came up short. Whatever she did had somehow managed to tip the scales, decimating their enemy and greatly leveling the playing field. Not even Konstantin remained visible.

With each terrifying inch he gained toward her, the sweat poured down his body, coating his clammy hands. Twice during the journey, he had to switch his weapon from hand to hand to wipe the dampness from his palm. After an agonizingly long crawl, he reached his destination and landed hard on his ass next to her. He scooped her into his arms and cradled her still form, listening to her slowing heart.

"Voni?" He fought to keep his voice calm, to hide his deep fear. "Baby, wake up. Voni? Voni? Please, baby, I need you to wake up so we can all go home." He prayed his soft words would tunnel into her loving heart. Gently, he stroked her hair, caressed her cheek, and watched as her skin grew pale. "Come on, baby. Show me those beautiful eyes."

Trapped in the darkness, Voni saw rivers of blood. Their tides rose and fell like the breath of a great beast. And everywhere she looked, James' gory face screamed out at her, pleading, accusing, unvoiced words breaking her heart and tormenting her spirit. As she cowered deeper into the shadows of her mind, tears stung her eyes as more voices added to the litany of her failures. Apologies fell thick from her lips, her voice weak, and her pulse skipped. "No, please...I c-c-can't... Don't, I...James, please...I'm sorry..."

"Eamon!" Panic laced his friend's voice as Eamon looked up from his search for Konstantin. The bastard couldn't just disappear into thin air. Then, with a dangerous growl, he realized that in the Black, that's exactly what he could've done.

"Shit! I can't find that prig anywhere."

"It's... She won't..." The rest of the words caught in his throat, trapped behind the tears falling from his eyes as her heart beat out of time.

"Dammit, babe. Don't you give in. Don't listen to them. Listen to me. You are my only love. I've seen the beauty of your soul and the passion of your spirit. I've seen the future in your eyes. Our future, together. From the moment I first saw you, standing on that ledge, you have held my heart." His hand shook as he wound his fingers through her knotted hair and pulled her close. "I've never gone back on a promise, and I don't intend to start now. Please, wake up, Voni. I love you."

Eamon eavesdropped on his friend's loving litany, each word threatening to break his own heart. It had gone on long enough. He slapped the ground until his fingers latched around his discarded staff. Teeth clenched in ire as he struggled to regain his feet, he spun the wooden shaft and slammed the butt against the ground, cracking the very foundation of the In-Between as he stepped out of time.

"Cabal!"

He twirled his staff to rest under his armpit, the metal end cap coming to rest behind his shoulder, the more dangerous point held toward the ground. He had only waited for a moment when he was greeted by the sounds of approaching footsteps.

"Eamon, my brother. Why do you insist on such flair?" A pale, almost ethereal man emerged from the shadows with a toss of his head, his long bright-blonde hair falling over his shoulder. A hint of a smile touched his lips, his red eyes dancing with devious pleasure. "I was rather enjoying the play, weren't you?"

Pinching the bridge of his nose, Eamon took a slow, calming breath. Why couldn't he have been an only child? "No, you bastard. I wasn't enjoying the play." His normal lilt disappeared, hidden by his outrage. "Her soul is innocent and should never have been brought into this. Leave her be."

Cabal sighed dramatically, studying the buffed sheen on his perfectly manicured fingernails. "As you well know, brother—"

"And stop calling me that," Eamon growled, hating the nagging reminder of their shared parentage. He was just grateful they looked different enough that neither Rogues nor Guardians had ever made the connection.

"Fine," Cabal huffed. "As I was saying, she came of her own free will. She must again use free will to leave." He lazily lifted a shoulder as he folded his arms across his chest. "And since this isn't exactly neutral territory, you might want to keep all eyes open. Hmmmm?"

Eamon shifted his gaze toward Kai and Voni. Their stolen moment would have been Kodak-worthy if not for the shadow appearing over Kai's shoulder. His heart lodged somewhere near yesterday's lunch.

"Aw crap."

TWENTY-FOUR

From out of the blanketing darkness, Voni heard the voice of an angel. No, not any angel. Her angel. Kai. He was...crying? She reached to touch her cheek and found it wet, but not with her tears. He was near. She could feel his arms around her. She touched her arm, closed her hand around...nothing. Was she dreaming? Wait a minute...

Dreaming... Her mind hit the Rewind button, playing all her recent nightmares on super-high speed. Everyone was the same. For months, they'd been the same. But then, he'd showed up and everything changed. The images were more frantic, more graphic, more...desperate.

Locked in her dream world, Voni opened her eyes and saw the floating image of James, scarlet rivers surrounding him on all sides. His mouth fell open, a blood-gurgling shriek echoing off the empty space. "No." She uttered one single word, taking strength from its power.

Silence crashed, all movement frozen.

Voni lifted her eyes and stared into the face of her adversary. Not the mask he wore, not the shroud of James. She looked deep into the eyes of Konstantin, saw him clearly and knew the truth in her heart.

"I let you play upon my fears and doubts long enough. I know now that what I had with James has gone. I'll not let my life end because fate chose a different path than the one I was on. And now, I found someone worth living for. Me."

Her eyes flew open, and air rushed into her starved lungs. Tightening her grip on the strong arms around her, Voni coughed and gasped, life returning in a painful burst. She leaned back to gaze into the eyes of her Good Samaritan. The man whose voice had called to her in the deepest dark and never allowed her to give up. Her Malakai. Her Guardian and her spiritmate.

"I'll not lose my prize!" Konstantin shouted, materializing behind Kai and thrusting his blade into his exposed back.

Voni screamed as Kai's head jerked backward, a jagged bit of steel piercing the smooth silk fabric. A crimson rose spread quickly, dampening his chest. The tip vanished with a sickening slurp.

Eamon's mouth gaped, a cry of warning died on his lips the instant the tip of Konstantin's blade emerged from Kai's chest. He lunged toward his friend only to find a linen-draped barrier. He snapped his head back to lock eyes with Cabal, rage contorted his features into a snarl. The eerie red eyes of his brother were serious, and his unwavering gaze reminded Eamon of the rules of engagement, the only rules that held sway in the ranks of both their armies.

"Have patience, brother. And remember, it will be her choice that decides the outcome."

Damn bastard was right, and his righteous indignation would not help his friends.

"You cannot keep stacking the deck and expect me to just stand by, Cabal. This is your fucking home and I'm calling bullshit."

The canary-eating-cat smile he got in response made him want to shove the smug asshat's teeth down his throat. Too bad another rule was that neither of them could harm the other, nor could they remain near the other for more than one hour. Eamon cast his eyes down at the face of his Roman Gauthier Platinum Prestige, the dials telling him that time was truly running out.

With an angered growl, he turned heavy eyes back to the horrific scene unfolding before him.

Kai's momentary sigh of relief was replaced by bone-sheering agony. He'd turned all his focus on Voni and her struggle and the lapse might have very well cost him his life. He felt the metal drag along his rib cage on its retreat. Konstantin had missed the sweet spot. Damn bastard must be getting rusty on quick kills. The lights dimmed and sounds faded in a slow retreat. His arms jellied and wobbled, threatening to spill his precious cargo onto the cold ground. The irony did not escape him, even though he could only watch as his blood escaped in staggering volumes, its seeping warmth filling the cool space.

"N-n-n-no. Kai? Kai!" Voni looked on, her voice too high and panicked to her ears. Scrambling to gain some kind of seated position, she caught Kai as he pitched forward, twisting with him to bring him to rest. She pressed her palms against the gushing tide. "Please, don't you dare leave me like this!" Sobs racked her body and her tears rained down, adding to the growing damp spreading across his chest. Voni remembered the smoothness of his massive chest as it rose above her, remembered the silk-wrapped steel beneath her fingertips when he cradled her so close she felt each beat of his heart.

"Kai? I can't do this…not without you. You…you've made me believe in everything. Even myself. Please, Kai. Don't leave me alone." Leaning in, she pressed her trembling lips against his. "I…I…"

He reached up to touch her damp cheek, his eyes losing focus. "I'm sorry."

Voni dipped her face and nuzzled into his palm, cupping his cool hand with hers. "No, no apologies." Her voice cracked, and words crept through the tears still streaming unchecked. "Oh God, Kai. I want to spend the rest of my life with you. I love you."

* * *

"Nooooooooooooooo!"

The space became fluid, flowing all around them. Voni grabbed on to Kai, clutching him close while the world became an E ticket ride. She kept her attention focused on stemming the blood still leaking from the gaping wound. She'd only worried about the one in the front, the entrance, not the exit wound. Her sobs gained in force and she held him tighter, terror taking root in her blood and winding through her whole body.

"Please, Kai. I'm so sorry it took me so long to face my feelings. I…I need you to help… Oh God…" She choked back the rest of the thought, burying her face in his wavy black hair, every ounce of her being screaming for him to stay.

Spinning, swirling out of control, only Kai as her rock, she tumbled in formless darkness that seemed both endless and brief. Then solid ground once again appeared beneath her, and the familiar scents of her home surrounded her.

As did a pair of strong, and very much alive, arms.

She pulled back with a jerk and landed unceremoniously on her ass, looking slack-jawed at Kai as he lay sprawled across her tiny bed. He inhaled deeply, his blood-soaked shirt lifting and stretching as his chest expanded fully. Gingerly, she crawled along the wooden floor of her bedroom and reached shaking fingers toward him, her own breath frozen in her lungs.

"Ow."

She peeked over the edge of the bed, watching in disbelief as he forced his eyelids to open. He blinked rapidly and shielded his eyes. His tilted his head at an awkward angle, searching to find her eyes as a tempting grin touched his lips.

"Well, hello there."

Voni tried to laugh through her tears, the emerging sound more like a dog choking on a squeak toy. "Hi." Her voice was too breathy, her emotions too raw. He was here. He was alive. Her damn chin wouldn't stop quivering, and the frigging waterworks didn't look to be stopping anytime soon. Now her whole body was not getting with the game plan, either, every muscle locked in a state of unbreakable tension.

Just under her fingertips, beyond the damp fabric, was the heart she feared would never beat again. The heart that had taught her to trust herself and to believe in love. The longer she watched him breathe, the more the tears fell.

As he drew a deep breath, he felt a slight catch, a lingering trace of his brush with Konstantin's blade. Add another scar to the collection. With a rumbling growl, he lowered his hand to rub away the ache in the center of his chest only to find a trembling set of fingers already on the job. Clasping her hand, trapping it against his heart, he looked up and fell into the most beautiful set of honey-brown eyes, the sprinkling flecks of green brightening the room with more power than the sun.

He gave one gentle tug on her hand, and she fell into his arms, her lips raining kisses in time with her continued tears. Calming her frantic actions, he stroked her hair and rubbed quieting circles against her back, while hushed words poured from his lips. His heart beat strong and true, and it was because of her. She had saved him. She had chosen him, her choice the key that had pulled them both from the Void and back into the world of the living.

"But, how? I mean…what? How did—?"

Kai kissed her tenderly, ending her question session. He caressed her face, the pads of his fingers tracing the trails of her tears. Pulling back, he watched her eyes flutter open, the light of his life reflected back in the shining pools of honey leveled at him.

"You, my love. The answer is you."

Her brow furrowed, confusion clouding her thoughts. "Me? I…I don't understand."

"The In-Between truly exists somewhere between Life and Death. You stood at the brink of everything…" He paused to brush away a tear still tangled in her lashes before continuing. "And you chose life. And love."

Voni turned away, color flaring to her pale cheeks as her mind churned. The vile words uttered in that dark place clawed their way back into the forefront of her thoughts. *"You're not the first, you know. In a few short days, this 'love' of yours will only be a memory to him."*

Kai picked the fear-laced words out of the air. Konstantin sure did know how to run a mind fuck. Well, the asshat was quite high up in the gutter-slime ranks; it would make sense. Gently tilting her face to meet his, he placed a tender kiss on her forehead.

"I love you, Siobhan Brigit Whelan, as I have never loved another. And if you would have me, I vow to make good on the promise I made the night we first met. And about the claiming ritual…" A mischievous grin tugged at the corner of his mouth. "I, um, already started it."

Voni listened to the words she'd never hoped to hear, his eyes boring straight through to her soul and shattering the remnants of her doubts. The last part, though…

"You what? Wait…those words in that other language? But, but…" Her brain fired rapidly, the logical conclusion slamming into her with more force than a brick wall. "You wanted…wanted me even then?"

Kai's smile melted her confusion and shook her to her bones.

"How could I not? You are my spiritmate. Just as Konstantin claimed your grief called out to him"—he pulled her close as a whisper of cold raised the hairs along her arms and chilled the room at the mention of his name—"your love called out to me, drawing me to your side. When I first felt you, felt you beneath me..." He lingered over the vivid image of that first night in his mind, smiling as the temperature of her skin ratcheted up a notch or two. "The words started and wouldn't stop. Not that I would have wanted them to."

"But, but..." Sniffing, her breathing still ragged, she continued to process his words. "Why did it take so long?"

Laughing lightly, he wrapped her further into his arms. "You waited only one year, *dragoste meu*. I have waited almost seven hundred years for you. And the wait has made the reward that much sweeter." He captured her lips in a fiery kiss, burning away any lingering doubts.

Ending their embrace, she cocked a devilish eyebrow his direction. "Now, about finishing this ritual thing..."

Eamon lit a cigarette and watched the smoke spiral and disappear into the evening sky. Inhaling deep, he listened for another moment, certain his friend and his spiritmate were safe. When the words became more urgent and hushed, he stepped away, a slow smile growing on his ageless face.

"Enjoy the peace, my brother. I'm sure it won't last long."

"Now why would you ever think that?"

Eamon sighed, turning his narrowed eyes toward the white-clad apparition emerging from the shadows. He approached silently, his bare feet peeking out from flowing linen pants. Cabal's long white-blond hair flared out, caught by an errant spring breeze, feathering tendrils against his tanned skin. He pushed a finger against the bridge of his Bulgari sunglasses, casually sliding the tinted lenses to cover his eerie red eyes.

"Cabal. Damn, guess they'll let anyone on this plane." He continued to head back to the bright lights of downtown San Diego, brushing his hands down his modest black Henley. Black jeans and motorcycle boots completed his midnight ensemble, the dark of his outfit hiding the light in his heart. "And I know that this is far from over. I know you too well."

Giving a Gallic shrug, Cabal joined Eamon's sauntering path. "I had nothing to do with any of this. It was her choice. It has always been her choice."

"So I guess we have another Conduit on our team." Puffing out a cloud of smoke, Eamon grinned contentedly, enjoying the weighted silence between them.

"So it seems," Cabal ground out, a sour sneer across his lips. "But this is only a minor setback. I have several pieces still in play in this little game of ours. Nothing is ever over, you know that."

Eamon shrugged this time, his slight movement speaking volumes. "This isn't my game by choice. And as soon as Mom and Dad see eye-to-eye, we can end this stupid contest." Glancing back over his shoulder, his gaze lingered on the simple cottage where within, two hearts were becoming one.

As it should be.

Checking his watch, he then smiled at Cabal. "And I believe that about does it for our little chat."

Cabal nodded, one eyebrow raised. "Until next time, brother." With a graceful bow, he phased into a mist and vanished with a breath of Eamon's smoke-filled air.

Eamon's blue eyes stared out at the peaks of the city's sky scrapers barely visible in the distance. "Yeah. Next time."

Crushing the last of the embers under his booted heel, he stepped out into the night.

ABOUT THE AUTHOR

Tessa McFionn is a very native Californian and has called Southern California home for most of her life, growing up in San Diego and attending college in Northern California and Orange County, only to return to San Diego to work as a teacher. Insatiably curious and imaginative, she loves to learn and discover, making her wicked knowledge of trivial facts an unwelcomed guest at many Trivial Pursuit boards. She also finds her artistic soul fed through her passions for theatre, dance and music, as well as the regular trip to The Happiest Place on Earth with friends and family.

www.tessamcfionn.com

@TessaMcFionn

www.facebook.com/tessa.mcfionn

Made in the USA
Charleston, SC
27 November 2016